A World Between

A World Between

Robert M. Herzog

THE STORY PLANT

Dedication:

I start with Mom; about my future she always said, "and someday he'll..." My brother Richard, who with Barbara supported that faith through times that tested its credibility. To the wonders of Stuart and Steph, Henk, Willem, Nate, Sasha, James and Jack. And to Margot, who has made it all possible and, even more, filled it with meaning.

Studio Digital CT, LLC
P.O. Box 4331
Stamford, CT 06907

Jacket design by Barbara Aronica Buck
Cover photo courtesy of the Town of Atlantic Beach, South Carolina

Story Plant Paperback ISBN-13: 978-1-61188-217-9
Fiction Studio Books E-book ISBN-13: 978-1-943486-77-9

Visit our website at www.TheStoryPlant.com

First Story Plant paperback printing: March 2016

Printed in the United States of America

0 9 8 7 6 5 4 3 2 1

One

Parts of the World

Parts of the world were disappearing; for a while, nobody noticed.

Yes, there were reports. Clear, emphatic. But every observer has a flaw when a bright light shines on them. Three black kids caught in the wrong place, who'd say anything to stay out of trouble. A pilot with a few too many hours staring at the sky. A river rat who told tall tales even when he was sober. An old mountain man who saw paths best from memory. Their reports were greeted with mistrust, bemusement, skepticism – all the ways but one. They weren't asking what was the matter, but rather, where was the matter. There was no box that contained that question.

And, it must be admitted, they were saying the damnedest things.

Chapter One

Nowhere.

That's where we're headed, Susan thought. The rutted, dirt-crusted road which the jeep bounced over in backbreaking intervals was going to lead nowhere, as far as she was concerned. Still, something out there was stirring the local tribes so deeply that they were ignoring the food cartons she'd finally gotten to the Distribution Center. Not that there was enough for all of them, nor would they find all the food edible, but like Susan they had gotten used to what was, not what might be, and usually crowded in when a shipment arrived. Not today. Stuck in a makeshift warehouse where the trapped heat and inactivity were equally oppressive, Susan finally yielded to the impulse to find out what was going on.

That morning she arrived expecting to find a bustling mob lined up at the warehouse door. Instead there was just Ambway, ready to work as always. Ambway was her translator, guide, liaison, and lifeline. When not with her, he worked as a guide for the safaris and hunts that still passed through. Most shots were fired with cameras these days, often by teenagers accompanied by their parents, or couples on honeymoon; only the well-to-do could visit here, drive past the huts, avoiding the notion that inside people were hungry beyond their comprehension, a hunger unto death. But Susan couldn't drive past; she lived to feed them, on mission from the United Nations, here now for sixteen months, her third such tour.

She asked Ambway where everybody was. He shrugged his shoulders. They stood in front of the warehouse, looking onto the barren dirt streets that wound through the quiet huts. Several tribesmen came up the street, riding donkeys or running alongside them. She recognized one of them, a man in his thirties who often helped her. She called out, but he kept riding by. Ambway yelled, and they yelled back to him without breaking stride.

"What did they say?" she asked. "What's going on?"

"Don' know, Ms. Corporell. They just say they going to big junction, like everybody else."

"Gee, a party and we're not invited. What do you think, Ambway?"

"Don't know."

She decided to wait around, convinced that soon people would come for the food. By mid-afternoon nobody had, and no one else had passed by. The junction was a long, tough ride off, but it beat standing around doing nothing; they did that in the offices in the capital, which is why she always opted for the field. They got the Land Rover the UN Mission had bought cheap from one of the diminishing number of hunter guides, and Susan drove into the flat, dry lands that preceded the jungle.

The dust poured through the open windows along with the heat. Her face became a reddish clay mask under her blonde hair. First makeup in over a year, she thought. After several miles she didn't even bother trying to brush it off. Swatches of dense growth closed in on them, around the river beds and mud flats, where the wheels spun resolutely, only to open up again into broad dusty flats.

They kept swigging water from bottles in the back, and after a while stopped talking, trying to adjust their bodies to the bucking and bouncing over routes that were barely roads, occasional long straight expanses that Susan navigated with Ambway's help, for there were no markers and nothing to indicate what was road and what was just the flat land that surrounded them; other times through narrow paths where limbs and brush swept over the car, streaking its dirty sides, enveloping them. Ambway instinctively pulled back as a low branch hit the windshield; Susan didn't flinch. The leaves reached through the open windows and brushed her, as if they were trying to devour anything that passed their way.

The skies turned dark quickly, as they did here; one moment there was sun, the next her vision was obscured by a dense pouring rain. The wind beat against the windows and doors. Susan preferred the Land Rover to the Toyotas they used with the rest of the Mission; they were heavier, steadier in storms, more sure-footed in the mud. It was hard to prepare for the worst, and often unaffordable, but out here the worst came often.

Susan slowed as a stream appeared, normally a trickle swollen wide from the sudden downpour. She downshifted, kept them at a steady pace to maintain a cavity in front of the car to keep the water that was nearly over the top of the hood from flooding the engine. Ambway nodded at her in admiration. She felt good.

The rain didn't let up, and they had to skid to a stop as they came over the crest of a slight hill onto a vast encampment. The local tribes had scattered on it in a large semicircle. Susan recognized some of the tribes and their elders, for she had worked with many in the region. Others even she had never seen before. Ambway muttered that this was most unusual. They hopped out of the car, trying to see in the distance what was going on. All they could see was a ridge in front of them, surrounded by large trees. They started walking past the people, most of them sitting still, ignoring the rain, ignoring them. Small huts dotted the camp, out of which poured the howls of children; other than that there was almost complete silence broken only by the push of the wind and the pounding of the rain. They made their way to the front, where Susan and Ambway stood next to some elders dressed in traditional robes. They all looked east to what would be the center of the semicircle the tribes were arrayed in.

The old men stopped them, indicating they could go no further. Susan and Ambway looked in the same direction as the elders. The low clouds and dark storm limited vision sharply. It seemed to Susan, but she couldn't quite tell, that in the distance was a section within the ridge where the rain didn't seem to be falling, but it was hard to resolve the image. The storm blew from the north; most of the jungle around them swirled as it collided with the massive winds, but to the right of the section the trees simply swayed gently, curling around and towards the spot.

Despite the storm, a sense of quiet pervaded the area. Even the normally talkative Ambway was subdued. She turned to him, stood close, and asked him to ask why they were there. Ambway spoke to the man next to him, the eldest, who wore a small white cap atop his creased brown face, itself a mask of stoic calm, in a dialect she didn't understand, then turned back to her.

"Hard to understand. Very old language. He says maybe, 'Sacred spot, don't go near, take you in, don't see you.'"

"Don't see me?"

"Yes."

"You mean I'd disappear from view, or not come back?"

"Yes." Ambway shook his head.

Susan was used to the limitations of talking with him, but as she looked at the spot she felt a chill run through her, whether of ancient recognition, current fear, or the rain she couldn't be sure. The mists made it hard to get a fix, or else the section itself was elusive, but it had an unnatural hue to it, not a color so much as a lack of color, and a diffusion of shape.

Susan tried to blink the distance into clarity, but it wouldn't cohere. *I'm out of my element here, way out.* She asked how long it had been there, but couldn't tell from the answer if it had been two days, two weeks, or two centuries. In Africa such distinctions were often lost. She'd seen many strange things since her first Mission here ten years ago, and this silent gathering and odd landscape was yet another she didn't understand.

The wind blew harder, lashing them. The rain fell like exploding pellets, making it harder to be heard. Around them the people in the tribes sat, still and silent. She shouted to Ambway, a struggle to be heard, "Ask them what it is." The rain streaked her dirt-caked face, drops fell from it to the muddy ground, her soaked clothes stuck to her; she ignored it like all else seemed ignored around her.

Ambway spoke to one of the men, turned to her, then turned back to the man for some more words, then looked at her through the downpour.

"Can't tell, maybe he's talking about the place, maybe the time," he yelled to her.

"Never mind, what's he say?" she yelled back, leaning closer to him, barely able to hear amidst the torrent surrounding them.

Ambway shouted to her, "He says . . ." he paused, looked towards the spot, "He says, 'It's the end of the world.'"

Chapter Two

Parts of the world were disappearing; nobody had noticed.

That's what the kid was saying. Antifermo hoped the kid would change his story, make it easier to file a report, but he wouldn't; he sat in the dark processing room of Precinct 19, staring hard at the floor, next to his sister, determined to tell his truth. The detective looked down at them, the black teenage boy and the younger girl, picked up an official incident form, and wrote "general purpose" where it asked for nature of incident. The crowded room cackled with the sounds of tired men typing behind beaten wooden tables, awash in the stories people told. The kind that get transcribed, not believed. There wasn't a window that seemed to look out on anywhere. The keys fell like small-caliber shots at close range, the paper ripped through the rollers like sad gears grinding.

Lucy's small chin jutted forward, but she nudged close up against the side of her brother in spite of herself. He put his arm around her. She wasn't used to big, dark-haired old white guys talking to then. Neither was he; they'd walk around an avenue block to avoid that. He could tell she could hardly follow what he was saying, and Tyrone, who could chatter nonstop for hours sitting on a stoop, was just muttering and looking down as if his sneakers had become so important.

Tyrone stayed tight and ready to move, to protect Lucy, because Momma had said to, and because he had more pride than fear, which was why the report was such a pain in the ass for Detective Sal Antifermo.

"Tell me again, Tyrone, just what happened." He held the form in front of him like a baton he wanted to pass, only the rest of the team had left the track. His bulk shrouded the paper; all the boy saw as he peeked up was the dark contour of a large man against the smudged gray walls that surrounded them. Tyrone started to speak; a phone rang, and he held his breath until it was picked up. When the words came out, it was as if they were being expelled from a punctured balloon.

"I awready tol you."

"I know you did, Tyrone, but maybe I missed something. That's some story you got yourself there."

Lucy finally spoke, her high-pitched voice cutting through the striking keys like a knife through cardboard. "Tyrone, I gotta pee."

"Lucy, damn you sit there 'til he say we can go, okay."

"Hey, that's alright, we can take care of her, hey, Patoozie, take this kid to the can, now would be a good time." He yelled over to a woman in the light blue blouse and darker pants of a patrol officer, who was sitting on a bench talking to another cop.

"That's Patous, you know, Sal, like it could kill you to learn."

Sal pointed at Lucy and shrugged. Patous walked over, looked at Lucy, pulled up the sagging belt that held her gun and radio and a dozen other hanging cop items, and said, "Awright, kid, c'mon. We'll take a leak and leave the boys to their BS, you know what I mean?" Lucy stared intently at the equipment so near her head, her eyes magnified through thick round glasses; she stood, barely taller than when she was sitting, and held out her hand. Patous looked down at it, rolled her head while Antifermo held back a laugh, then took the hand and they walked down the hallway. Sal turned back to Tyrone.

"Listen, kid, I know how it is, you don't wanna look silly in front of the little sis, but you wanna say anything different, you know, like what happened, it'll just be between you and me, she'll never know."

Tyrone stared at him and talked through the sounds of others in the room telling their tales, talked past the clatter and the rings, talked into Antifermo's eyes and swore, "No, iss like I tol you, jus that way."

==

Tyrone had been caught running off a stretch of Jones Beach closed for restoration – nobody went there or guarded it, so they didn't have to pay an admissions fee to get into the area. He and two other kids were stopped as they came tear-assing out of the dunes by a couple of cops trying to coop in the hot sun, who popped out of their cars like all hell breaking loose from the shouts and then had to stand tough to make up for the embarrassment. When the kids finally caught their breaths and looked at each other, this one blurted out how some section of the beach wasn't there anymore, gone. Well, of course, the cops said, that's the restoration. No, that's not it, he said. The cops reported the kid refused to state why they were running. They let the skinny one, Samuel, go and brought Tyrone and Lucy in for questioning, mostly to make sure the girl got home safely.

"Gomez," Antifermo shouted over to the duty clerk. "Anybody check this out?"

"Hey, Lieutenant, gimme a break, huh." Gomez didn't even look up, his head barely visible over the papers on his desk. Sal shrugged; he knew the drills, and the weights, the piles of folders and reports that pinned them in place. Anyway, what did it matter? In fact, he kind of liked this story. He'd heard so many, the kind involving cousins having sudden urgent needs to go to hospitals, but this was a new one, and he appreciated that. He didn't believe it, of course. He didn't believe any of them, not after twenty-six years. Still, he liked it, it wasn't the kind you heard every day. It was definitely a good story.

Gomez threw a report over to him about some wannabe biker who'd scared a yuppie near the meat market. Antifermo skimmed it, told him he'd get to it in a little while. He turned back to Tyrone.

"Hey, kid, let's go get an Italian ice, whaddaya say?"

"When Lucy ges back, den les go," Tyrone said, still staring at the floor, his feet swaying in big white unlaced sneakers beneath him. "An I don like lemon."

They walked near one of the local basketball courts, a cement patch that had once been used for handball. Remnants of a chain-link net still hung from the rims, giving a slight rattling sound when the ball made it through. Sal sent Lucy home. Tyrone was still jumpy, so when he asked if he could play a bit, Sal said sure. He was one of the younger players, although, as Antifermo had guessed, the kid moved well and easily. After a while he called Tyrone back; the boy came reluctantly, the big sneakers that seemed to propel him on the court became two white anchors he dragged towards Antifermo. The other kids melted away from Tyrone at Antifermo's call, and alone in the hot sun he plodded over to the detective, who sat on a cracked cement bench with rusted metal support rods pushing through where the arms used to be. Antifermo breathed deeply, ran his thick fingers over the rough cement. It was a tough place, a tough world, but Sal reveled in the solid stuff of this city around him. Others might not notice, even despise it, but for him it was the stuff of life.

Antifermo figured if he got the kid out of the precinct house maybe he'd get more of the truth. He bought Italian ices for both of them, his lemon, same as when he was five, the kid's cherry, and started. "Okay, Tyrone, what happened out at Jones, why were you running away?"

Tyrone looked cautiously at Antifermo, the perspiration from the game starting to mingle with the sweat from the interview, but Antifermo nodded. "Go on, kid, I don't care about your beating the fee, okay, I used to hit that beach a lot when I was a kid." Antifermo could picture the three of them as Tyrone talked: this kid, his little sister, and his friend...

It was bad enough, Tyrone thought, to have to walk the forever walk from the bus stop along the road far enough out to a place where no one would notice them. The day was hot from before it broke; the sweat started while they lay in bed, it built as they took three subway rides and then the bus with the air conditioning not working as usual, its windows open with the hot, clammy breeze that did nothing but coat them with more damp. It was enough to make this long walk yourself, ducking whenever a car approached, but to have to drag along a baby sister, that was too much.

It was Momma's fault: "Take little Lucy wit' you, I got nothin for her to do today, she'll jes drive me crazy," in her insistent high whining voice you'd do anything just to stop it. Right, so let her drive Tyrone crazy, cause he's such a good boy he can take it. Damn.

The kids walked towards an out-of-the-way place, so nobody would catch them. Tyrone knew Lucy was trying hard to keep up with him and his friend Samuel – not Sam, or Sammy, but Sam-u-el, lots of emphasis, even with him lookin so funny with his skinny legs stickin out of his old gym shorts, goin in every which direction. Lucy's light brown round face was set deep and forward, its shape repeated in her round sunglasses with the reddish tortoiseshell edges and purple lenses, all under a big white beach hat. A purple-specked white dress barely got out of the way of her fast-moving little legs, which like her dark arms stood out in contrast to the dress, floating limbs ending in clenched little fists and toes, her always puckered lips leading those wide eyes in determination. Tyrone and Samuel accepted the burden with practical resignation. It was rare to be completely care-free, and a whole day at the beach, or a day as long as until they got caught, even with Lucy around it was close enough.

Lucy hadn't done badly on the road, but it got tougher for her over the dunes, scrub grass, and sand, into a thickly overgrown path, vines and grass, sharp-leafed ocean's-edge plants snapping at their feet, the boys in big unlaced white sneakers that promised they could fly, but today wanting to get them off sooner than they could, Lucy in little flip-flop sandals that she kept losing in the mean crabbing vines.

"Tyrone," she called out, "one of these plants *cut* me." He saw a bloody scratch on her leg, but she didn't cry; she never did.

At last they were through the growth, at the edge of the beach, still hundreds of feet from the shore. With the goal in sight, Tyrone lost his patience.

"Lucy, I'm goin carry you now, I don want no argument." Lucy, who had absolutely refused to be lifted so much as an inch through the path, pouted and stood like she was trying to plant herself. She crossed her arms holding her little yellow towel up to her chest, while Tyrone picked her up and deposited her on his strong, rounded shoulders. She settled in quickly now that she could see over the bushes to the sand and ocean beyond.

"Thissa lot better than lookin at choo boys' big butts," she said, and they laughed.

In the distance was the big rec building with the hot dogs and the bathrooms Tyrone would want to trudge to only once during the day but he already knew Lucy'd have to go at least twice. Right now it was fine just to get her quickly closer to the water's edge; he would work the hurry out of his system playing in the surf, never going in over his head, though, because he didn't know how to swim all that well, none of his friends did.

They walked for a while, Lucy just looking, the boys talking excitedly about getting into the water, finding some type of tray on which to skim the waves, and about jumping the little ledge that the night's tides would have carved near the water's edge, a miniature of great canyon walls that they could swoop down, feeling like magic, like princes, enveloped by the sounds thunderous to whispering of waves approaching, crashing, pushing white, soft foam along a stretch of shore, greeted only by their brethren pausing here before turning round for the long march out.

The boys took off their sneakers at last, Samuel hopping around on one foot for a while before finally falling and removing them sitting down, Tyrone never losing his balance as he shifted weight onto each foot, even with Lucy on his shoulders. He teased Lucy about carrying his sneakers for him. She wrinkled her nose even more, making a sound like "euuu" while crossing her hands under his chin, tilting her head in silence. They walked towards the shore.

"Tyrone, what is that?" Lucy cried out, to press her little voice against the sounds of wind and distant waves, bigger noises even than the rumble of trucks constantly passing under their windows.

Tyrone had been watching his footing, the morning sand cool and rich around his feet, carefully stepping through washed-up rubbery seaweed and nail-studded planks and shreds of plastic containers, around big holes dug for beach restoration, talking to Samuel, not looking ahead. He was content to let the smell and sounds and the feel of his toes through the sand fill his senses without the distraction of the sights, still a bonus to come. Better to take in each sensation separately than use them all up at once. He had no idea what his sister was talking about, nor did Samuel, who was walking backwards to keep up conversation with Tyrone and his funny little kid sister. Samuel talked in a singing, continuous way, and Tyrone figured that Lucy was interrupting them because they were talking about girls, Samuel saying he wasn't about to run his hands through no braids on the top of someone's skull and Tyrone saying he didn't have to worry cause no one was about to give him the chance. She yelled out again, and Tyrone conceded in exasperation: "What is what, Lucy?"

She pointed straight ahead, a little to the right. "That. Iss like part of dat beach ain't there, jus ain't there."

"Well, they diggin the beach up, Lucy, you seen them holes."

"I'm talkin right by the water, they's no hole diggin there."

Aw, hell, Lucy, they laughed, it's just the mist, ain't you ever seen mist before, fog, haze, clouds, girl, from a distance at the beach you could almost get like a what was it, a mee-rage, that's all. They hardly looked.

"Dat don look like no mis' to me. And how come it's jus in dat one place if it's dis big mis' you keep talkin bout?"

Damn this girl can be a pain. Tyrone looked up to see her priggish always-right little face, a princess pucker when she felt denied. Man, he thought, she is goin to be a ball buster when she grows up. Like lots of the girls his age, fourteen, which is why he and Samuel wanted to come down by themselves to this empty place sometimes. But what was Lucy talking about?

"Hey, Samuel, you walk like a turkey, you know that? Take a look. Whatchu think of that?"

Samuel laughed with Tyrone at Lucy, never turning around. Now he spun, saying, "Ty-rone, my man, it is only the mind that is the prob – hey, what is that?"

They kept walking forward, but slower, slower, finally coming to a complete stop. Tyrone deliberately and gently lifted Lucy above his shoulders and put her down, his gaze locked ahead the whole time.

⩦

Tyrone's voice got softer, Antifermo had to lean forward to hear him as he repeated what happened, above the claps of bouncing balls, the honking cars, the incessant buzz of the city.

⩦

Off to their left, waves crashed onto the shore. Tyrone could see the sun reflected off the spray that jumped into the air like when they opened a hydrant in the baking summer. Far to their right where the bay turned inward he could make out a calm blue surface, small waves woven through dark green weeds that grew straight out of the water, like one of Momma's needlepoints, with the silhouette of the rec building past that. In front of them, as they gazed in silence, was… nothing. Absolutely nothing. No beach, no waves coming in, not even light; instead, a mushroom-hued curtain where sand, waves, and sky should have been. They stared at it, at nothing. It seemed to muffle noise, the distant caw of a gull, the far roar of waves on the beach, seemed to take their thoughts away as well, with all the sounds around them muted .

When they had crossed the dunes, the air had been still, a slight sea breeze wafting with the promise of a cool shore and tingling seas. The wind that had blown in their faces now swirled around them. Suddenly, it created a vortex pulling them in, an emptiness, sucking at them. Lucy, near fatally the most curious, was drawn forward. Tyrone, big brother, raced to catch up with her, pull her back, while Samuel, unattached when crisis came, ran off. The whisper of the wind turned incessant, from grandma's gentle hush to a train's oncoming roar; it whipped Lucy's pretty white sun hat off her head, the sound of the brim snapping like a slap from Momma's hard hand at the last edge of control. The hat hopped over the beach like a drunken marionette until it entered the strange space and then it was gone, gone like vision itself in front of them, gone like hope and fear, nothing left. Lucy went after the hat, on the edge of it until Tyrone grabbed her, turned her around, the sand grasped their feet as they tried to run, mocked their motions to escape, like the dream where legs didn't work, slo-mo until finally they were away from it.

"Sheeyit," yelled Tyrone. He lunged, seized Lucy around her waist; she kicked and screamed as they ran back the way they had come, catching up with Samuel, heading in the only direction that mattered – away.

==

The detective and the boy sat silent for a moment. Antifermo liked it, a great excuse – hell, none of the kids was charged with anything – but he couldn't see anything more to it. Who knows what even a good-looking kid like this was into. On a flash thought, he said, "So, Tyrone, whaddaya say we go back, check it out."

Tyrone jumped up. "I ain goin back there, no way."

Antifermo shrugged, his lips pursing. "Right, kid, just thought I'd give it a shot." He got up, told Tyrone to take it easy, take care what he got into, and walked away, to pick up another file, listen to another story. Tyrone ran back into the game, yelling for the ball, but when it came his way it popped out of his hands and slipped across the court.

Chapter Three

Would they skinny-dip, or not?

The great debate had already begun, and they weren't even off the boats. The issue had gone back and forth for days in subtle currents, Bill Robinson and the other boatmen regaling the tourists over the last five nights with stories of the great old times, of carousing, wild moments, freedom. Hell, they were down in the middle of the Guhrrand Canyon, one of God's great spectacles, one of the real places where when you looked around you saw the world – rocks, walls, water, wind – under original ownership, still untrammeled. Porta Potties notwithstanding. A natural place, suitable to being inhabited in that natural state, that precursor to innocence, a state of grace that shed away and was unimpeded by the cloistered social necessity of clothing. So, "Let's get *down* to it!"

But then, there was the Park Service. The Rangers. Nothing so distinct and able as a serpent in the garden, at least rejuvenating one of the fundamental themes, no, not so worthy as evil. They were more like clicking hens of bureaucratic morality, a morality that was neither personal nor concerned for the individual, but rather was a mask subtly concealing the face of righteous majorities, so that its enforcers could defer choice to authority and perpetrators were left with an inchoate body for recourse. The regs didn't reference morality, of course; that wasn't allowed. They established instead a set of boundaries and conditions in such a way that the moral underpinning was canceled out of both sides of the equation – precept and result, offense and law. Just a uniform to do the job, cluck cluck clucking the limits, a uniform of easily ruffled feathers ever preening in righteous indignation.

The Rangers could issue tickets – a ticket in the Grand Canyon! Might as well start nailing people for double parking on the moon: hey fella, get that module out of this crater, can't you see the sign, no landing seven a.m. to three p.m. No, these were not the old days – hell, some companies even brought down portable generators to make the biddies feel safe and at home surrounded by electric lights at night, colored lights strung on red, green, and yellow poles repeated like cheap Christmas ornaments left up all year in a Hong Kong bar, the sense of the ceremony stretched meaningless by constant ornamentation. As if the turkeys – the tourists the boatmen took down the river – weren't bad enough with their standard set of questions:

"How deep is the water?"

"'Bout twelve feet."

"How wide is the canyon?"

"'Bout a quarter mile."

"How high are the canyon walls?"

"'Bout a mile."

The answers never varied no matter where they were on the trip, and the turkeys were always satisfied with them, as satisfied as they were with the technological and spiritual comforts derived from their excess of equipment: their latest-design interlocking nested multiple fabric sleeping bag, good for sub-arctic conditions with additional liners available, and free standing, instantly constructible and collapsible double-decked tent with rain-splash cover and their propane-fired cooking burners and astronaut freeze-dried squeeze-tube gourmet foods instead of first night steak while the coolers were still cold and then, say, tuna casserole or chili or good stuff like that. Hell, on one trip organized by a preserve-the-environment club the boatmen calculated over two thousand dollars per person in equipment, more than the swampers – apprentice boatmen – made in a summer.

To top it off, each one of the turkeys had to show off their woods-person's skills – better get that gender thing right, boys – so that instead of one nice, big comfortable, cozy campfire burning a few old pieces of wood with everybody lying around it, passing the bottles one way and the joints the other, sharing, telling the good stories, no, they each had to make their own fire, a dozen isolated fires spotting the beach like glowing welts of insect bites on a smooth skin, the campsites scavenged of kindling and wood.

Well, if the turkeys were bad enough, it was a harmless bad compared to the biddies. The biddies carried with them down the river what the boatmen and even most turkeys left behind upriver at the put-in point, at Leah's Ferry or a few days below at Phantom Ranch – the biddies kept their judgments, their rush to distinguish right and wrong for themselves and to apply their standards to others. And the biddies, make no doubt about it, did not approve of public swimming in the nude.

A few weeks before, one of the biddies happened to be a Congressman, and if his own trip was righteous enough, unfortunately his boat had swung past the junction of the Little Colorado River with the Big Colorado River, a junction which often formed a deep, oozy, warm mud bank, a browned oval some forty feet by twenty feet, a lot of soft warming mud. Unfortunately the Congressman's boat swung by that junction just as Bill's last group had prepared themselves to reenact the great evolutionary step of animate matter arising out of the primordial ooze onto land. Eighteen naked boys and girls first completely immersed in mud, then slowly deliciously crawling, and then with a shout of glee at that glorious liberating moment of humanity's history for which they were giving thanks they arose and ran across the shallow water rinsing off the mud arms in the air with yes breasts bobbing and dicks dangling, a joyful shout for the Creator unfortunately just as the Congressman's boat swung around the bend to witness the much anticipated junction of the Little and Big Colorado Rivers.

Other biddies might have just clucked, or written a letter, but the Congressman had training in complaining, he was ever-poised to make noise, administrators were contacted, official notices sent out, licenses could be suspended. So now as Bill reminisced and the good old turkeys on this mellow trip, just working folks with no ideology to express, began to feel on their fresh-tanned alive skins the shackles of their clothes down to their bathing suits, in the background the biddie judgments stood to squash the tingly feelings, and the stopovers with plunges into little pools near the Big River were righteous ones, itchy but righteous. But day after day of sun and rushing water, unshaved beards and bodies washed with their natural fluids through sharp dips in cold cold water and hours of feeling the sun like it was another member of the trip, the one who gave everybody messages, had taken their tolls on resolutions, creating conflicts between permit and license. The turkeys were watching the boatmen for a sign, any small indication that the time had come to cut loose, what the hell, enough was enough, thumbs poised on waistbands, ready for the complete airing of their views.

If it was going to happen, it would happen today, after the run to Havasu Canyon, one of the most intense days on a Colorado River rafting trip. The rapids didn't let up, successions of great and small standing waves -- "holes," the boatmen called them, a cut of water downstream from the rock, curling around it as if to renew and deepen the acquaintance, an intimacy that bred jealousy towards an intruder, as water tumbled over rocks thrown down like a giant's jacks, shifting patterns read only by experienced eyes -- and even those sometimes deceived, as in the first run of the year when the river has enjoyed its prerogatives and fulfilled its obligations as a mover of earth, of boulders, trees, sand, to reshape itself, so that the path that once was safe down the right side leads suddenly to a crescendo of a fall, a boat poised headlong on itself ready to topple, an impossible moment of decision with the river deciding, and then it lets you go, a prankster, don't forget to say thank you.

A day's run in which one second you were high above the water, paddling air, and in the next completely submerged, like an oarsman on a submarine, too excited to feel the cold water. Most days they'd take a long stop for lunch, swimming, beer, sun. Making for Havasu they'd run straight through for an extra hour, to have more time, all the rest of an endless day, to tie up at the mouth of the side canyon, jump overboard, and walk and swim up shining blue waters cascading in falls and slides and pools like playful pups on their way to mother's teats, the sheer fun and sensual joy of it foretold by even the stolid boatmen, important to keep their image of looking at danger and thrills with laconic and steel-eyed stares, even the boatmen getting excited, pass the joints and rum, now's the time to play, here's the place, not a care in this world.

Havasu Canyon was clearly going to be the place if there was to be a place. Nobody could just happen by the pools they were aiming for. No cheap sitings – it took effort to get up the canyon, beyond biddie effort. The boats were tied into sheer rocks on the edges of the canyon walls. You first had to jump over to a narrow ledge, swing to the edges, hand food and gear back and forth, then wade upriver, a clear river with sun reflecting off surfaces so clear it glinted off the rocks at the bottom as well. You had to walk and swim up chutes and through narrow passages with water flowing past sheer smooth walls rising well above you, had to fight claustrophobic fears and stories of flash floods joked about last night now all too relevant, finally squeeze out the other side to a broad expanse where the water was broken by bulging rocks into rivulets and side streams harmoniously tinkling like one of nature's instruments in perfect pitch and rhythm. And the sun enveloping it with the imperative of now, it had to be now, it should be now, and you could almost see the shorts coming down.

Bill Robinson knew what was coming. Hell, they gawddam well were not going to take his gawddam license away, not after ten years, and it wasn't ten dull years, or one, or he wouldn't still be here. He was chief boatman of this crew, shepherd to these turkeys, part technician, part storyteller, a lot of good times, a lot of girls, and people had these bodies and here was their chance to feel 'em, be them, and gawddam if ten days of this shit wasn't enough.

Bill led the group most of the way to their destination – a wide series of mini-waterfalls, natural pools, gnarly vegetation, and sandy ledges that composed one of the great spots of the trip, on the earth that Bill knew, for sure. It was now just a few hundred yards straight up a single stream bounded by canyon walls, so not even a turkey could get lost going there. As usual then, he let some of the gung-ho ones go first, to have the expeditioner's thrill of discovery, part of what they were here for, and Bill sure as shit didn't care. He brought up the rear with some of the more cautious ones, while the others splashed by laughing and forging ahead to wait, as they all could sense, for some sign from Bill that here at last they could drop trou, boys and girls together, that anticipation superseding even the sense of their surroundings, like having to pee in front of a Picasso, no amount of beauty could overwhelm the body's imperatives, the essential human state. So when the first ones got to the top of the stream to where it all broadened out into playful possibilities, they hardly looked around at the diverse array of water and canyons surrounding them, waiting for Bill and the last stragglers to reach them. Bill finally arrived, walked up out of the stream grinning big, walking tall, and as he kept walking sure enough his hands went to his khaki shorts and down they started to come and with a shout the others followed with their suits, tops flying and bottoms descending, looking around, sure, but this really wasn't about the sex, you biddies, it was about the freedom, and off they ran around Bill, rolling and splashing and laughing, but Bill just kept walking straight, hardly noticing them, the grin still on his face but the sun creases of his eyes taking over until his whole face creased up, looking up the canyon, shielding his shiny bronze face and sunglasses for any possible glare with his hand over his forehead, as if saluting a far off commander.

The noise around him slowed down, quieted. Since the turkeys had never been here before, they couldn't tell what was usual from what was out of place, but they followed his stare and, well, it did seem strange. Bill, what is it, they looked to him for an answer.

Bill finally stopped walking, his wet shorts dangling around one ankle, standing at naked attention. "Hell, I sure as shit do not know, folks, but . . ."

He looked up the side canyon, one wall rising above them, heading back and up to the top of the canyon, but the other wall, it didn't take a naturalist's eye to follow the other wall and all of a sudden see, like a quarry's cut, two fuzzy sides in between which was . . . nothing.

"But . . . I do not like the look of it one bit." He tried talking around the fear, that maybe it was a new cut for water to come through, even as he knew it was something else, something off, that made his stomach rise and pulse within him uncontrollably, and he was saying, "Let us get the hell out of here," without even knowing it. Their nakedness increased their fear, no defenses; they dashed around quick as they could, picking up their suits and shorts and tops and they ran and swam like hell down the stream, scraping knees and elbows and shins fighting back to the boats to cast off, get away.

And Bill thinking now there, there is something for the biddies to complain about.

Chapter Four

Parts of the world were disappearing. Tell me something I don't know.

That's what Susan thought as she flipped through the files in her briefcase while driving up the Saw Mill River Parkway to meet with somebody who probably didn't have any more clues than anyone else. Nobody had noticed. Hello, she thought. If I'm missing a shirt, after a while I search the closets, go to the laundry. People just questioned the reports; everybody wanted to be staff now, nobody was willing to go in the field.

After sixteen months in dry, dusty African villages, all she wanted was to get to the beach, wash off the grime that stuck after showering. It had taken her two days to get from the deep brush where she had been stationed to an airport. After what she'd seen, Susan called in to her supervisor and told him she needed to go home. She got a call back, from deep within the UN infrastructure, the Director of Science Missions, Harold Upshaw. He ordered her to report to him immediately upon her return. She pleaded for some time for herself, but he insisted there wasn't any time for herself. She was too exhausted even to sleep, until just before landing, when the hard thump of wheels descending woke her to the gray-shrouded New York skyline; as in her dreams, the mist scared her.

Upshaw said, "Hey, you've got to do this; your experience puts you at the top of the charts. Go interview this guy, this physicist, we've gotten these reports, we need somebody who can tell us what's going on." After talking to Harold, she was terrified. Reports from China, Hawaii, Long Island. She had wanted to go the beach, but if that had disappeared . . .? She stepped on the accelerator.

There was another thing. Physicists did not make her comfortable. In college the "History of Science" course she had to take to meet her requirements had been taught by a physicist. He mumbled; when someone asked him a question he would write on the blackboard, then turn around so his body covered the answer, hold up his hands and say, "How's this?" For a French lit major, it had been a trying semester.

The car made a strange rumble. It was UN issue, no working AC, no CD, no GPS, and AM-only radio. She held the map up while driving, to search for a scientist, hoping that he didn't mumble. She tried spritzing the windshield, but the car was out of cleaner. The wipers made four passes across the dry glass, spreading out a big bug that had splatted in her field of vision. How's this?

She drove up the Saw Mill Parkway past fast food drive-ins and iron husks of old industrial plants, some sheathed in siding and converted to storage barns, small signs and sharp turnoffs pointing to the hibernating affluence surrounding the road. The sun was bright in her eyes, the sides of the road mottled green. She sped past sprawling restaurants that looked like they could accommodate whole tribes, past prefabricated office buildings built, by their square barren looks, primarily as tax shelters. She laughed to herself, thinking of the Land Rover she had been driving the week before, as dusty inside as out, over roads no better than leveled animal paths, to villages of scattered huts and impossibly thin inhabitants. By training and conscious choice she had become immune to culture shock – she was there, now she was here, each to be viewed by its own standards, in its own context. Still, she laughed. She swerved into one of the off-balance turns, almost missed the exit, ducked across lanes, and headed off the ramp's tight loop to meet a physicist.

She hadn't always laughed easily, not in the days when French literature had seemed so right for her, along with long hair that lolled in front of her eyes, dark plaids and black leggings. She had an intensity that decried laughter, left her ready for a serious older man who entered her with studied gentleness but left her with a swift cruel cut, swimming amidst a sea of black turtlenecks fogged in by Gauloises smoke. When the rudeness of postgraduate Paris overcame its charm, she came to New York. The Cliffie network landed her quickly in magazine publishing, where the early excitement of trying to turn her experience into erudition kept her preoccupied until she realized how bored she was. At a party she met a terrifically tall Dane who worked for the UN; he introduced her around before returning home. To his wife, it turned out.

She didn't care enough to follow up on his contacts until a TV show flashed images that nauseated and arrested her, of swollen stomachs on scrawny dark bodies. In Africa, she would discover that the images didn't capture the worst – the eyes of children without hope and the faces of parents who could not help. At first she was just searching for a way to get out of the string of articles she had to write on Gallic style imported to U.S. streets, and the allures of continental men, subjects that aged poorly for her. It was a break, to be assigned to travel with a United Nations team to Africa, to write a story on "People with Purpose: Men and Women on a UN Mission." It was a revealing chronicle, as it turned out, of the ferryboat nature of relationships in this particular world, as people shuffled back and forth between each other as easily as between continents. She took a few rides herself.

The men became trivial, variations on a theme. It was the eyes that stayed with her from that first trip, just as they had followed her when she walked among the bodies, only the eyes moving in their defeated bodies. She stayed nervous, energized by agitation, finding release only when she managed to get a job working as an assistant program officer at a small foundation that focused on "Providing grant support and technical assistance for supplemental developmental programs for the culturally bereft." It gave her time to get acclimated to the ubiquity of process that surrounded all goodwill activity, and the opportunity to make mistakes at home before going in-country, where errors could be elevated to major incident.

Tolerance hadn't come easy: not early, when it was trying to move through layers of officials each in symbiosis with the others to create work that maintained their jobs; and not later, as her responsibilities grew, when mountains of grain stood in warehouses not five hundred yards from those starving eyes, while a debate meandered five thousand miles away, letting the food slip into black markets under the watchful and knowing eyes of those just fed who wanted to keep it that way. No, tolerance didn't seem to be much of a virtue then, nor understanding, if it implied acceptance. But Susan learned to navigate, when to slip silently into port and when to blow the big horns. She came to live with the terrible simultaneity of taking satisfaction when some of the food got to some of the people, while suppressing the acid anger that ate at each such small victory while the fat dealers laughed, their very bodies an affront. But the eyes of those that didn't get followed her, first around the villages, knowing that she knew too, blaming and accusing silently, silent because no energy could be expelled in giving voice, no precious energy could be wasted in fighting what couldn't be won. Then their stares invaded her time alone, penetrated her along with men whose faces blended together but filled nothing, unable to keep those stares at bay, explain to herself that this was all she could do, that it helped, pleading that she deserved to be left alone sometimes.

According to the memo Susan brushed through whenever she stopped at a light, the man she was heading to meet, David Altaforce, was a physicist and mathematician noted for physical world applications with "an unusual ability to connect advances in particularly abstruse new areas of mathematics, such as theories of chaos and disaster, to tangible experiments or uses." She wasn't sure what that meant, other than that he didn't answer his phone.

Susan found Altaforce's house overlooking a small lake in Westchester. The front grounds were neatly parted by a winding path of red-gray fieldstones leading up to the door, an attenuated

S curve, narrow at its start and widening closer to the house, as if to give her more time to consider the decision to approach it. Tall pale grasses waved gently around their bases. Flowers, bushes, and bulbs seemed to grow randomly amidst the lawn; the effect was at first jarring but then somehow pleasing, an assertion that asymmetry could also convey relationship.

The front of the house was simple: two large windows set in a white cedar board wall flanked a brown wooden door with a brass doorknob. Susan walked up the winding path to the door without hesitation, rang the bell.

"It's open, come on in." She heard a voice that sounded close by on the other side. She tried the door knob. It was locked. "Come on in," the voice repeated. The voice was very clear, as if it was right there, right next to her.

"It's locked," she cried back to it.

"What's locked?" said the voice, sounding like she could touch it.

"The door, goddammit, let me in."

"Test your assumptions," the voice replied.

She tried the door knob again. It wouldn't turn.

"All right, play your silly ass game." She leaned back, and shot out her right foot to give the door the hard swift kick the voice deserved.

"Whoa," she heard him shout, as her foot seemed to go into the door. Off balance, she stumbled, nearly falling in.

"What the . . ." She glared at the door. Slowly, she stepped back up to it, then reached out to touch it. Her fingers met no resistance. She barely could see past her wrist, and then felt someone shaking her hand.

"Welcome – well done. I've had graduate students of logic come here and never get in." A slight tug and she walked through the door.

Altaforce stood before her, grinning, black mock turtleneck draped over a tall lean body, standing up straighter than she had expected of a professor of physics. He looked amused, which further irritated her.

She shook her hand out of his. "Explain."

He motioned her to turn around. She saw the image of the door, but could also see a series of what looked like lenses inset behind the top and sides of the frame.

"It's some kind of a hologram, right?" she said.

"Right. Although the density from the multiple array gives it an unusual sense of realism. Along with some light-sensitive variable programming."

"I'll say. But what about the door knob?"

He pointed. From this side, she could see that the knob was connected to a vertical wooden strip, shaded to match the color of the picture around it, running the height of the door, with another strip attached to the frame at the doorknob level.

"A little reality, a lot of illusion. Works quite well, don't you think?"

She laughed. "Aren't you afraid of burglars?"

"I like to live with the illusion. Once someone attempted to break in – so they tried to come through the windows. I have a rather interesting laser security system, by the way. No one has ever tried to walk through the door."

"Any special reason you have it there, or just general perversity?"

He smiled. "There's a viable explanation. I wanted to see if I could do it, when they first came out. Now I use it as a test for my classes – I invite them here and ask them to get in without breaking anything. Just say the same thing I said to you – 'Test your assumptions.' I've had platoons of deep thinkers – the kind that would be smoking pipes if they weren't more worried about their health than their image – wandering around the place, talking, talking until they run out of things to say, and never getting in. Not one of them ever moved as quick and mean as you did. I take it you're not a logician."

"No way. I'm more into deliveries – checking if food or medical supplies have gotten to where they're supposed to. I guess you could say I work with many elements, but that's about as close as I come."

He smiled. "Seeing things as they are is the essence of problem-solving, so I would imagine you're pretty good at it."

She looked at him. It was the first "professorial" thing he had said, yet somehow it didn't put her off. His door game had led her to forget her preconceptions about him, as well as his stature and profession. Was she seeing him as he was, or was he also telling her something else? She was used to sizing up people and situations quickly, responding to the logistics and the politics, the resources and the need, the short time available and the long time of what she confronted. She was used to doing it well, without looking back. Already he had created ambiguity in her, and all she'd tried to do was get through his front door. She took a deep breath.

"I assume you're David Altaforce." He nodded.

"I'm Susan, Susan Corporell. I'm from the United Nations, and ... well, we've got one hell of a situation, and we're hoping you can help us figure it out."

They walked through the hall to his living room. There was a large raised fireplace with ashes still in it. Underneath the couch in the middle of the room were indentation marks in the sandy rug, indicating a large sectional couch with pieces at right angles to each other had recently been there. The newer couch was bright, with a flowery print. He led Susan to it, clearing off a pile of magazines and academic papers, while he took the large red easy chair, a reupholstered Art Deco relic. Glass ran long the whole back wall of the room, sliding doors that showed a cluttered backyard with barbecue, picnic tables, and chairs. She was encouraged and disappointed at the same time.

"So," David said, "what can I do for you?"

She blurted out, "I'm here because parts of the world are disappearing.."

"What?" He almost laughed

"There have been these . . . disappearances, and the UN has been asked to investigate them."

"Sure."

"No, it's true, I know it sounds silly, but ..."

"And how big are these vanished parts, where are they?"

"You know, I didn't come here for no reason." She wanted to explain to him, and she noticed she wasn't angry.

"I'm glad you're here. Really. It's just, well, maybe there's some other agenda here. I'll bet money's involved, right?"

Now she was getting irritated. "There is a special U.S. appropriation."

"See."

"Listen to me, there's some kind of a threat out there."

He shook himself in a way she was familiar with, a man distracted by her looks forced to listen to what she was saying. "Like what?"

"Here's a picture, of Jones beach – it's like a part of it isn't there." She handed it to him.

He examined the picture, holding it at an angle so the light could hit it in different ways. "This could be a UFO photo, some kind of hoax, easy to do. You're sure this isn't the product of a hyperactive imagination on a cloudy day?"

"My boss, Harold Upshaw, he's got a lot of experience, head of missions, no pushover, he went out there and looked at this spot himself. You can see his report attached to the photo. There's nothing there. It's blocked off now."

"You've probably heard nature abhors vacuums – but actually it's rather fond of them. Plays with them all the time. This is awfully vague to get hopped up about. I've waited nine years for this sabbatical. Want something to drink?"

Susan felt a frustration welling up inside her, bad, like the early moments in her career, when arrogant men stood between mounds of food and hungry people. Not here, she thought, not now.

"Mr. Altaforce, you've . . ."

"David."

"Fine, David, please. Look again."

He looked, not at the picture, but at her. "You seem awfully convinced, concerned about this."

"Do you know why I'm here, why they picked me?"

"Because you're beautiful and usually get what you want?" He smiled. She wanted to object, but his manner was of someone simply speaking the truth, plain words, no editing.

Susan paused, turned a little red. "I wish that were true. It's just that . . ."

"What is it?"

"You'll think I'm crazy, another UFO sighter, but . . ."

"But."

"I've seen one of these places." She tried to still her body. "At least I think I have, it wasn't clear, but it was," she shuddered, "something very strange, horrible, insidious, I don't know."

"Tell me about it."

She told him what she had seen.

"He said – " she didn't even feel silly saying it " – he said, 'It's the end of the world.'"

In the silence that followed her story, Susan laid out the rest of her documents on a low glass table: more pictures of Jones Beach, reports regarding the Grand Canyon, Hawaii. The situation was urgent, she was sure, they needed answers, action, but she wanted to keep talking about it with him.

He offered coffee but then didn't have any; she said she preferred iced tea anyway. He squeezed lime in his; she asked if she could have the same, and liked it. They wrapped their hands around the glasses, the cold moisture refreshing on their palms. When they laughed it seemed as if they touched. The sound of ice cubes tinkling was like music accompanying their words. The morning continued, holding two people in its gentle, inevitable grasp.

Chapter Five

The clouds were not nominal.

Approaching Hawaii from the east, the pilot of Flight one-three-two-seven had been preparing for the end of a standard flight. Which was fine with him. For it was routine that Captain Hank Dawson had faith in, detail, series, double checking, and then giving it a final going over. It was the drill. As a pilot he believed in routine, in its power, its saving grace. In eighteen years of flying, he had spent a lot of "extra" time on the ground, making final checks, insisting on all repairs, rejecting aircraft that had not had the proper periodic inspections. A lot of extra time on the ground, but no problems in the air – which was Capt. Dawson's standard procedure, the one he believed he literally lived by.

A flight for Capt. Dawson was like entering a meditative state. Fully alive, aware and focused. His experience and his concentration enabled him to know the reading of each instrument while looking at the sky around him and being aware of the moods of his flight crew and how they might affect performance and reaction, like a basketball pro who is constantly aware of the shifting positions of the other nine men on the court, the movement of the ball, the flow of the game, and can tell what his girlfriend is eating in the ninth row. While Capt. Dawson wouldn't have described it as such, the feeling was exhilarating, it was completeness within a milieu. If home is the place where you can find the light switch in the dark, then the sky was home for Hank Dawson.

Flight one-three-two-seven, San Francisco to Hawaii, had been routine. Mostly tourists on the final leg of winter journeys that had started in New York, Dallas, and Chicago, Indiana farms and Westchester suburbs. A couple of honeymoon kids in first class, eager for and wary of the free champagne, excited, eyes wide open to each other, the broad seats, the stewardess's attentions. When he made his routine special introductions, they even giggled. The crew was alert, the mood solid and up, the passengers calm.

One-three-two-seven was on course and on time. All checks showed A-OK status, all instruments working, engines in tip-top shape, personnel attentive, passengers tranquil. Outside, the lazy, dense clouds surrounding their takeoff had yielded to over two thousand miles of clear sun, scintillating sparkling seas below, an unfettered horizon to the limits of sight, smooth sailing at thirty-seven thousand feet.

Three hundred miles from Hawaii a cloud bank had begun, first the shredded outskirts dangling like raw woolen yarns waiting to be woven, then as the wind played loom to knit the pieces together, a denser pack that now stretched under and before them for as far as they could see, cascading bulges and bumps, purest white and sun-spackled shadings, inviting the child's mind to come out for a walk. Dawson continually scanned the blanket before him – that was routine – but even he was swept up by it. He almost expected his radar to show a false bottom beneath him, like a ship's sonar giving a reading when passing over square miles of tiny squid, so dense and broad as to reflect back to the surface a misguided but demanding ping, defining the limits, defying the instruments, the abstraction that was the ship's reading exposed by untold tons of flesh acting as a unifying and uniting force. These clouds had even less consciousness, but they were no less a presence, and if the instruments didn't catch them, that only added to the evanescent reality they conveyed. Dawson read his instruments and talked to his crew; he watched the clouds. Routine wasn't the end, mind you. Routine was the preparation for the unexpected, a certain amount of which was… routine. Safe passage was the offspring of Dawson's routines, the well-behaved child of diligent parents.

One hundred forty miles out. Honolulu Airport reported the clouds extended far beyond the Island to the west.

One-three-two-seven would have to land through the clouds. "It ends as it began," thought Dawson. He liked instrument landings; in a way, they vindicated his checks and cross checks, his reliance on the machinery based on his intense scrutiny of it, his never-take-it-for-granted approach. He had confidence his readings would be true, and that he was prepared for each contingency.

Dawson, then, was not known as the wild man of the skies. His diligence was legendary – the Rock of the Skies, they said, he carries the ground with him. Even that sensibility helped him; ground crews snapped to with him, air traffic controllers conformed to all procedures. Dawson was coming in – do not screw up, he will know. Honolulu ground crews organized for one-three-two-seven, prepared for Dawson, prepared for by-the-book sequences and a picture-perfect landing. What they were not prepared for was to hear Captain Hank Dawson's startled voice reverberate through their earphones saying, "What the hell is that?"

"One-three-two-seven, please repeat, repeat, please repeat last request, we do not copy."

Dawson flashed back for a weather update. Unbroken cloud cover, they responded. "All conditions uniform?" he asked. They listed conditions: winds constant, pressure even, the great front defined the world around it. Any swirls, microclimate activity, say, eighty-five miles east north east, he asked. None. Any ground-level activity? It's all water, flat and even. No Navy testing, no recent flights, no plunges of multiple aircraft on maneuvers towards the water, Dawson asked, no tornadoes, no oil rigs spurting CO2, maybe a freighter or two circling, anything? No, they responded, no to each, no to all. They were looking at each other, shaking their heads, wondering, what in the hell was going on, this wasn't the Rock of the Skies, this was pie-eyed wackiness falling out of there, Chicken Little territory. "What data are you seeking, please repeat," they asked.

Dawson wasn't about to repeat. He pushed his mike aside and looked out his window. Now approaching, below and to his left, was – nothing.

An unbroken sea of clouds does not, by definition, have any breaks in it. Micro conditions can change the local pattern, the cloud's complexion, from glistening dense white to greener grays, its density, even, from an integral field in the skies to a lighter, moister-looking shroud. But Dawson had never seen a clean pip of a hole in the middle of a dense cloud bank. Well, he had first thought, anything can happen. His initial sighting had been during his routine lateral scanning from his instruments to the bright panorama through his windshield, a still figure on his throne, body upright and unmoving, only the head flickering, tilting, serenely regarding his domain before him, unhurried, unceasing. In front and a few degrees to port from his standard approach path, the continuous cloud cover seemed breached. It wasn't clear at this distance how sharp the delineation was, and at this angle it was impossible to tell how deep, but there was a discontinuity.

He went back to the routine checks, but the anomaly lay there, his mind darting to it like a tongue to an aching tooth. His motions became less even and consistent, more pointed, pausing longer a little to the left and down, and longer still, skewing his serial scan, kurtosis in the captain's consciousness.

A headwind had slowed the plane's true speed to less than two hundred knots, enhancing the stately procession beneath them. The break remained in its place as the plane approached like a cautious suitor, buffeted but inexorable. And, like a rapt lover Dawson abandoned his other cares; relinquishing control under the guise of a copilot training routine, he gave himself over. For as he got close and stared unblushingly he had begun to notice that he couldn't really focus on the spot itself, nor define the contours of this ephemeral infatuation. It wasn't just air between the clouds. For one thing, he couldn't see across it to the clouds that lay on its other side. As their angle of sight increased, he also could not see through it to below, either to any other clouds or to the ocean. Interest became intrigue. There was no routine for this observation, no memory, no drill.

He dipped the plane a little closer, the pull of curiosity, he said to himself, past the questioning look of his co-pilot who, having been given command of the landing from the Rock of the Skies, had wrapped himself around the wheel in his hands and the instruments before him too tightly to be aware of anything beyond that intense compressed world of his responsibility. But Dawson had awareness, he had seen, and he wanted to know.

He contacted ground control again. He pressed, a honed and directed intellect wearing away in sequence at the problem, moving from the vaguely possible to the probably absurd, a form of Holmesian dialectic – eliminate the impossible, and whatever remains, however improbable, is real – and still no satisfaction. He gave up on ground crew. All he could do was look, look at nothing, at a space between pretty white clouds seemingly unaware of a new neighbor on the block, at nothing now just below and to his left. He fought a sudden strong impulse to take the plane down and in. His craned neck looked down an abyss, a seductive invitation that summoned and repelled.

The sun shone down on his clouds and his plane, reflections abounded, but not in his nothing, which neither absorbed nor reflected, but taunted, called out to him as they passed, his neck distended, he got up and leaned out in front of the hunched copilot staring near bug-eyed straight ahead, nothing to port, nothing behind his wing, nothing a hole in his mind, nothing gone, gone from his view, obscured by the blissful bath of their cloudy descent, nothing had replaced routine, no cross-checking, no repeats, he let his wondering copilot handle it, what the hell did it matter, did anything matter when a piece of the sky could dissolve to less than sand beneath him, for the Rock of the Skies, however long suspended, had fallen irretrievably back to the ground, nudged by infinite nothing to a new and mortal resting place.

Chapter Six

"So why haven't I heard about this on CNN?" David asked.

He was still captivated by his first image of Susan. He'd been sitting in his big easy chair, critiquing the latest solution to Fermat's theorem, thinking that mega-computing power was a mixed blessing, sometimes an antagonist to thinking. He heard noise in the driveway, looked up to see a striking blonde woman get out of a car; he had no reason, but hoped that she might be coming to his house. Amazingly, it seemed she was. He studied her, intrigued with this unexpected gift. She wore ankle-high brown leather boots under a long batik skirt and a wide-knit white cotton sweater, partially covered by a leather jacket that matched the shade of her boots. As she stepped up to the house, she removed gray-tinted tortoise shell sunglasses. His eye followed the motion, seeing a tanned, slightly freckled face; as she got closer he could see the sun-bleached streaks in her hair. He'd been trying to calm his breathing since she entered the house, concentrate on what she was saying. He noticed the light shining through her hair as she spoke, picking up and differentiating the outer filaments loosely dancing over her head.

"So far the incidents have all been in out of the way places, perfectly isolated, or the people who might report something have no credibility. And no one's taken any real steps yet to study them, so there's no trail. Although I don't know how long that can last. Only Upshaw's command station had all the reports of the phenomena centrally collated and monitored.

"But you know," she continued, and he sensed she was going off script, "I can't help but feel that whatever I saw in Africa, if it was one of these weird spaces . . . well, how many more of them might there be, still undiscovered, places that are disappearing. It scares me, really scares me. Something's got to be done, soon."

"So what's been done so far?" David asked. Susan described how the UN was sending out investigators to discuss what was occurring with numerous noted physicists and mathematicians.

"You mean you've got lots of your people out there telling other physicists about these occurrences?" asked Altaforce, leaning forward in the chair.

"Yes we do."

"That could be a terrible mistake."

"Why?"

"I'll explain later, if it appears relevant." And with that he continued his gentle and relentless probing, deflecting her unspoken questions by filling the space between them with his own.

David Altaforce lived with a mind that made the abstract concrete, that could generalize broad implications and theory from a few, sometimes seemingly unrelated, pieces of data, that could derive real world behavior from abstruse concepts, draw meaning and inference from the dialectic between data and hypothesis. Once he started poring over Susan's papers and photos, a part of him was extrapolating. He could visualize areas of nothing, that shimmered and grew larger, delicate looking but unforgiving. If they were really there. He didn't fear phenomena, just explored them, but he understood Susan's urgency, could postulate a vortex, expanding, inexorable. He was ready to listen to her from the moment she entered his house, her beauty ensured that, but he also sensed a desperation in her that was all the more captivating.

Susan spent nearly five hours with him in his Westchester house near the water, and after lunch with wine – "the perks of a sabbatical, and it looks like I better enjoy them while I can" – eaten in a bright airy kitchen that did not have a single gratuitous modern appliance, the most elaborate mechanism besides the refrigerator and gas stove being a hand press orange juicer of ancient black iron, he agreed to look into the disappearances, with a rueful enthusiasm. He was adamant that if he was to do anything, it must be done his way, since, he said, the nature of an investigative process could have an effect on what was being examined. Susan agreed, while expressing her doubt if it really mattered.

"I'd just rather not have Upshaw send me out again to find somebody else, especially if you think you can find the answers." David hoped there was more to it than that. He was searching for a way to say something beyond the quest, when Susan asked, "Do you know a scientist, Dr. Mary Quintin?"

David was almost more surprised by the question than anything else she had told him. "Nobody gets to know Mary Quintin, but sure, I've run across her, why?"

"Well, she was on the list, lives in New Hampshire I think, and I'm supposed to visit her tomorrow."

David raised his eyebrows. "She's brilliant, no doubt, but really kind of a, well, wacko. We've got a lot to do, if you want something to be done about these areas. I'd skip her for now, if we're going to get started – I'll get us the right people, if we need others." She nodded agreement.

David asked Susan to play the role of taking care of all that he might need, acting as liaison with Upshaw and the UN, obtaining material, dealing with their staff and all the other necessities.

She bridled. "I'll see. I'm used to nearly complete independence in the field, running the show in remote areas, I'm often senior staff or the only staff, it's not my style."

Altaforce was fixed on limiting the number of people both exposed to the problem and involved in his activities. When they ran out of things to say about the project, Susan gathered her papers. He shook her hand goodbye, and for the first time in his sabbatical felt alone in his house.

⁂

Back at the UN, Susan daydreamed about when she left David's house, feeling like a sophomore in the English professor's study, trailing her pony tail like a wave of innocence. She remembered his voice, soft yet carrying, a kind voice that invited trust, a voice that would always accept and believe her.

She shook herself, checked her notes, and called the scientist she had been scheduled to meet next, Dr. Quintin, ready to cancel based on David's insistence, happy to avoid a long trip. It had taken Susan a while to track Quintin down, since she had left her university position and all other affiliations, and was living in a rural part of New Hampshire. Her isolation alone made Susan think a trip wasn't worthwhile; Quintin wasn't in the game anymore, it seemed, which David had confirmed, and it would take a long time there and back that could now be better spent.

Mary Quintin answered. Susan explained that she would have to put off her visit.

"Oh, and why is that? I had planned for it."

"It's just that we've been looking around for physicists to help us, and I hated to bother you, it sounds like you've moved far away from things. So thanks and goodbye."

"Didn't you mention there'd been some unusual occurrences, some areas that looked like they vanished?"

"Did I?" Susan had forgotten what she had said in the first call, was trying to remember.

"Well, aren't you concerned about these disappearances anymore?"

"We are, it's just . . ."

"It certainly sounds odd. You mentioned the first time you called that you're from the UN."

"Yes, but, anyway, we've found somebody to help us, so . . ."

"Oh, well good for you, who've you found?"

"Dr. David Altaforce, from NYU." She didn't want to say they were also contacting other people, that the list was still open.

"David? Oh, well, that's an interesting choice. He can be so sweet, can't he, when he wants to be."

Susan thought suddenly of David's admonition, unexplained but potent, not to tell too many people what was going on. She wanted to get off the phone. She shuddered, so slightly it was drowned by the residue of bigger tremors, the memory of places that might not be there, the one in Africa, the one in her heart.

"Ah, yes, well, I wouldn't really know. Look, I'll get back to you if it's necessary, thanks for your time." She said goodbye and hung up. Physicists, she thought; they can be difficult.

Memos on her desk indicated that in her absence Upshaw had scheduled her to meet the following week with two more scientists, Dr. Harry Gribowitz and Dr. Ismail Ramadapur, visiting from India. She wanted to just cancel them, but they were local, and she knew Upshaw wouldn't approve, so she made calls to change the assignments, warning her colleagues not to say too much, without knowing why, other than that David Altaforce had said so.

Chapter Seven

Two days after they met, Susan introduced David Altaforce to Harold Upshaw.

The meeting was interrupted by a security guard who told David that he had parked his car in the Deputy Under Secretary's parking space and asked him to move it. Susan decided not to describe her lunch with Altaforce to Upshaw. When a field operative makes omissions in a report, it is a sign of shifting loyalties. She knew that Upshaw distrusted mavericks, self-proclaimed gadflies who, he said, "would swim against the stream even if it was in the wrong direction." He had told her of too many missions, from small huts in the Antarctic to literally shiploads of technicians, endangered by people who thought they could park in the Under Secretary's space. The rules of Upshaw's world combined different teams and different games simultaneously, and they were very fragile. Susan could see Upshaw weigh Altaforce's brashness against the intelligence she had portrayed, and decide he had nothing to lose by taking a wait and see attitude. He directed Susan to stay with David, as his liaison to the UN team, take care of his resource requirements, and continue reporting back to him; he concurred that she could put off meeting other people. Susan got David out of the office.

They stood in one of the long green UN hallways, the staff and diplomats walking past them as if they weren't there. The first thing David wanted was space to work in. She asked if he couldn't work out of his New York University office, like many of the scientists they had contacted.

"No," David responded. "There would be too many distractions. Besides, nobody ever returns to their school during a sabbatical.

That would attract attention, just what I don't want. I'd also like to be near the UN, to know what's going on here."

"Well, how about getting office space in the UN building near Upshaw's investigative staff? I could probably arrange that."

"No, no good. I must keep exposure to what I'm doing to a minimum – if I'm right, that would be essential to what we're trying to accomplish. And besides . . ." He paused.

"What?" She was so unaccustomed to reticence in him that she jumped to fill a void in their conversation. He waited for three men in turbans to pass.

"Well, I guess you could call it a theorem, an Altaforce axiom: conventionality depends on mass, and the degree of conventionality increases in direct proportion to how close you are to the center of administration."

"Meaning?" asked Susan.

"Meaning, Upshaw will have his hands full trying to satisfy his masters, which requires showing progress constantly, when he's not explaining what he's doing to people who think management means oversight and involvement regardless of whether they know anything about the substance of the work. I've seen it before, and I really don't want any part of it."

"David, I've known Upshaw for a while, he's really a pretty good guy."

"I'm sure he is, but still, he'll have to justify budgets and expenses in ways completely unrelated to the actual nature of the work. They'll want creativity on demand, advancement on schedule, and since nobody can deliver that they'll all start substituting the trappings of progress – papers, reports, designs for bigger and better machines, then their purchase and testing, lots of time preparing for presentations, lots of time giving them, then the meetings, meetings to discuss agendas for the next meeting, progress reports, analysis of data requirements for a management information system, then selecting and programming it, real-time data monitoring, debugging. Months can get eaten up playing with these dummy variables; there's nothing real about them, but they're required to satisfy the institution's equations."

"But since you're so sensitized to this problem, couldn't you avoid it?" She wanted to move towards action in the most direct way, not cater to his stream of tangential concerns.

"Anybody near Upshaw or inside the UN would get drawn into – call it the irresistible gravitational force of bureaucracy, pulling anyone or anything nearby into its field. The only way to avoid it is to stay far enough away so that the pull can be observed and deflected; otherwise" – his hands extended towards her in a clutching Jack the Ripper spastic clawing motion, he hunched over and his voice got gravelly – "it's being swallowed by the black hole of bureaucracy, where nothing really lives except paper, see it now, this vast gelatinous abyss, watch it swallow whole cities before your very eyes, can nothing stop it, tune in next millennium."

"All right, all right, you win, let's get out of here." Her laughter echoed down the hall. His show had already stopped a delegation in kaftans and three frozen-faced Brits. Susan pushed him out of the building and into a high-priced coffee shop in a hotel across the street.

The first thing they needed, he repeated, was to get an apartment near the UN. Susan suspected it would be easier to distribute grain in Ethiopia. She could see that this assignment was going to be like a crash course in doing all the things she hated to do in New York City, other than looking for a job. Office buildings were immediately ruled out as being too open and accessible. David also vetoed any large building with a doorman. He wanted something inconspicuous, anonymous, where contact with others could be kept to a minimum, and he wanted Susan to find it by herself.

This man, she thought while sipping her iced tea with lime, looking over the top of the frosted glass at him as he talked, feeling the chill in her fingertips, this man could be exasperating.

David was asking, "These first reports are over a year old, and god knows how much before that these areas actually disappeared. How come it took so long to start moving on this? And also, how'd it end up at the UN? Seems an odd place for it." That, Susan thought, was a long story. "Order a sandwich, professor, and another iced tea," she said.

Chapter Eight

It really was a good story.

Sal Antifermo had liked Tyrone's beach tale so much that a few months after he heard it, when he accompanied the Police Commissioner down to Washington to testify before the Special Standing Committee on Urban Decay, he'd worked it up into a nice little punch line. When asked about trend-lines, he had said, "Hell, a while ago we got a report they stole some beach, I mean, whaddaya gonna do?"

It got a laugh, they got some money – and the Commissioner told him next time he had a cute story, to tell it to him first. Antifermo shrugged okay. The Commissioner walked off; he had a story he'd told for years, about walking along upper Broadway on December twenty-fourth when a voice and a hand came out of the shadows clutching a scraggly pine, saying, "Hey, man, wanna buy a tree?" From a hot Christmas tree to some stolen sand; a new tag line. A more productive hearing than most.

Antifermo was making his way out when one of the Congressional aides asked if he could have a word with him. The aides in faceless repetition over the years usually just knocked New York in the hearings, a quick swipe and then they moved on. Antifermo didn't know his name, because they always sat behind a placard with the name of their elected official, and he never paid attention if they said who they were. Who cared? "Detective, I'm Dan Smathers, aide to Congressman Luton."

Sal nodded. "Yeah?"

"Well, I was kind of interested in what you said about the beach thing, you know, it disappearing. What was that about?"

For Antifermo, it figured. They got every bad guy imaginable, crap laws that create the crimes and then not enough money to cope with them, and here's some aide in a sleek blue suit who'd puke if he saw a girl with tweezers coming after him, and after seven years of testifying before this Urban Decay committee, and the Crime subcommittee, and the Drug Sub-Committee, and the Police and Arms subcommittee, here's this snot-nosed kid from some state he didn't even know where it was, and the first thing they ever ask him about, with all the other things he would say if he had a chance, was about this bullshit story he just told for the laugh.

But this kid's guy had a vote, and the Commissioner depended on the guy, so Antifermo tried to tell him as quickly as he could, the oversized double doors in the back loomed like trap doors to his escape. They sat on one of the hard wooden seats and talked. Antifermo couldn't believe it, not even an hour later when they were still talking, all for this bullshit story.

Dan Smathers didn't know quite what to do with it. He'd spent much of his thirty-four years involved solely with process, how to get things done, who to talk to and what to promise – or threaten – who to avoid, what was the take, the spin. When he heard something different, he collected it for his Congressman; stories to knock New York City were always good for the Minnesota campaigns, chuckles over chicken. He figured he'd net Antifermo's story, keep it for the right time. Only he wasn't quite sure what it was about. He scratched his short, dark hair, cut every two weeks. This New York cop, Smathers had been afraid to get too close to him, the guy made him feel – fragile. But, he'd gotten a new story for his own repertoire, always valuable at the parties. Maybe there was another angle for him. He sat in the empty hearing room, until he realized he might be conspicuous, and hurried out, shortcutting through a maze of corridors back to his office.

Several months later, in another part of Washington, a few guys from the State Department had gotten their ears chewed off for not knowing why the Chinese were making oddball inquiries all over town, from the Library of Congress to the local hangouts. As near as the Pentagon intelligence people could piece it together, the Chinese were asking whether Stealth-type radar avoidance systems could be reconfigured for use in fixed ground-level installations. Nobody knew what that meant, but it sent off a flurry of worries that a. that was what the Chinese were doing, whatever it was; b. there was a potential Stealth-gap that could prove embarrassing, and maybe even actually dangerous; c. money had to be spent to address the problem; and d. it had to be spent in secret.

The Secretary of the Army wanted to create a Sino Strike Force, but the rest of the Joint Chiefs voted him down as being too retro. The State people didn't know what was going on, but didn't want to let Defense position them as either being unprepared or compromising the nation's security out of ignorance. Defense requested a special appropriation, which State supported, with misgivings first because they couldn't find a way to ask for a piece of the new pie and, secondarily, because none of it made any sense. They stayed in the briefing loop, but their indirect role left them frustrated, especially when Defense got an additional covert appropriation of one hundred seventy million dollars to analyze the situation.

Shortly thereafter, the Defense people determined on second look that they had no idea what the Chinese could mean – the Stealth system to avoid detection was in part based on its ability to fly very low, but hell, the ground was even lower, it didn't take much research to figure that out, and the ground didn't move, it was just there, wasn't it, once you had a position fixed it wasn't going to change, even if it could disappear, which was hardly possible. Satellite photos had shown a very tiny blurry patch around military activity in the Lang YaShen mountain range south of Beijing. For a while they wondered if the Chinese were developing something new and checking to see if the Americans had anything like it. Later they decided it was just a glitch in the photo – nothing supported it, and the military activity disappeared.

So the Stealth gap scare quickly began to evaporate into a lingering confusion with no clear way to spend money, and nobody was going to invest time in a problem that couldn't accrue some sort of resources, be they money, power, prestige, personnel. It occasionally popped up at interagency meetings; nobody knew what to do about it, nobody had a way to resolve it. As a type of problem in Washington, it was not alone. The world worked its disparate ways, and nobody did the sums.

==

Dan Smathers ran into an old buddy at a five-to-seven cocktail party hosted by the Defense Contractors Association. Among the invitation cards he had been dealt lately, Smathers considered the DeeCee, D.C. one a trump. He'd put on his best suit, stood in front of the mirror to see in which position he could hold his arms so the fabric would have no creases, look hand-tailored. He'd pulled at the rear of the jacket to eliminate any wrinkles around the back of his neck; the look needed to be upright, straight, crisp. He was wearing an Italian silk tie with stripes of different widths, a custom-made shirt, he was tan, confident, had a good new story, and he was going to the right party of the night.

He wasn't disappointed; in the four-story Georgetown townhouse, hordes of Vietnamese servers hustled trays of Cajun shrimp, smoked salmon, and teriyaki chicken on skewers that piled up on his plate. A crowd full of people with discretionary spending authority in the tens of millions really whet his appetite. While standing next to the iron railing over the steps that led into the main living room, he heard someone call, "Smaa-therrs." He looked around; once again, more sharply, "Smaa-therrs." The call came from Ron Hassey, a Department of Defense midlevel snooper he'd worked with three years ago when there was still political gold to be mined in exposing incredible over-expenditures in the Pentagon. Smathers had loved the action, especially since no enemies were made, everybody knew the game, and at the end, like the magician's assistant disappearing from the cage, the audience was satisfied and the performer intact. He wondered if he should spend this valuable time with someone he already knew, saw it was unavoidable, and walked down the steps.

Hassey moved his six-three rounded bulk over to Smathers. He was wearing a no-press khaki suit and was tilting to the right. "Man, I am tootin' – ain't this place a honker? Hell, it's the third time I've been here and I haven't repeated the same brand yet, this is serious bourbon."

Smathers felt as if he were holding up a drunken dance partner and wasn't sure whether she would turn into a barfing disaster or an easy lay. He took a tentative step, asking what ol' Ron was doing to keep himself out of trouble these days. Ron, it turned out, had mined silver, if not gold. The air safety thing was still a bother, and he was in charge of a team looking at equipment selection and protocols for the next generation of flight control systems. Smathers was interested; he decided to commit, to focus on Hassey. He'd learned long ago that the solidest strategy to score at parties was to focus, one contact, one woman. It was a gamble, but it could mean getting some serious business done, getting laid the first night, if the moods and timing were right, instead of "I'll call you," or a "let's have lunch": down time. Dan and Ron played catch-up, hoping to find some mutual advantage that fulfilled the night's expectations.

Like teachers who knew by instinct when the bell ending the class was about to ring, by six forty they had decided that the process of setting air traffic safety protocols raised technical, national security, legislative and budgetary issues of sufficient scope and longevity as to warrant a joint effort for the two of them. Since it could be considered weakness not to have dinner plans, they were winding down their conversation, Hassey three more drinks into it but seemingly no more tipsy than when he had approached Smathers in what now was a clear calculation, much like Smathers's to stay with him. Business done with, it was nice to be known as a teller of stories, part of the Washington aesthetic, and Hassey had a good one. It was about some idiotic Chinese ploy around ground-level Stealth, a small patch of mountain they couldn't get a photo fix on, and a shitload of money sitting over at DOD with no place to go, and by the time it was over Smathers and Hassey had each made phone calls to nonexistent dinner engagements, canceling nothing to talk about nothing.

⩵

The measure of a man may be the stands he takes, but a system is judged by what it can absorb. Spongelike would not be praise for Hank Dawson, but it suited the airline industry just fine. Keep the planes flying; that mattered. Cope with aberrational reports by smothering them.

Since Hank Dawson's approach and landing were otherwise nominal and A-OK, the crew at Honolulu air traffic control had already decided that the strange series of questions he had asked had nothing to do with anything, even if Dawson was convinced they had something to do with nothing. Dawson knew he had exposed himself, but he was not the kind of man to look for a big bandaid. While ground crew Hawaii had just responded to him with uh-huhs and gone back to their next flight, he wasn't about to let it go. Company channels were also out; there was no way they would encourage a senior captain of the fleet to exclaim publicly he had seen a weird patch of unexplained emptiness in the middle of a cloud bank while bringing two hundred and seventy-eight passengers in to roost.

He started slogging his way through the Federal Aviation Administration, filing a report with the local Hawaii office, personally taking it to the California District Office, then to the Western Regional Office, and finally, like a shaggy dog story, to the Central Administration in Washington, DC. It had been easy for him to request and arrange his flight plans to cover these locations; the hard part remained getting anyone to take him seriously. The skies had turned clear over Hawaii the day after his sighting, and no one else had reported anything unusual. That didn't help.

Neither did the nebulous nature of the incident. If Dawson wanted to talk about shiny cigar-shaped objects that could move and change direction with abnormal velocity, they could at least find a pigeonhole to put his report in, break it down for comparative analysis, hold some briefing sessions, notify sister agencies and interested parties, generate some paper and then ignore it. But when Dawson reported just seeing nothing – well, nothing was what he got back. How did you describe nothing, what could you file it under? For chrissakes, Hank, it was a bunch of clouds, couldn't it just have been the wind, the shadows, maybe a floater in your eye, a tiny blur magnified by the distance and the uniform background. He held fast. Dawson was a dogged man, and over the next several months, forgoing the milk runs and exotic stopovers his seniority afforded him, he stayed around Washington whenever he could, to tell his story to whomever would listen.

"Hey, Dan, you're not going to believe this." Hassey had called Smathers as soon as he had sobered up from the conference's last night gathering. Hassey had participated for the Department of Defense in a symposium between the Federal Aviation Administration and the Department of Defense to discuss coordination of civil and military flight.

"Christ, Ron, how'd you dream up that one?" said Smathers, not without admiration – getting military together with industry in one place could do wonders for the immediate and distant career, a nice double.

Hassey laughed. A few months back there had been one of those periods of frequent near misses and airplane crashes. "As far as I can tell, these new controllers don't even know it's unusual, figure it comes with the territory. Well, I guess it helps 'em sleep at night. So as usual, there's an outcry, passenger volume goes down, but then it goes back to normal pretty quick. It's like the chicken in the room with the snake. You know, first it dances around like crazy, while the snake lies still. Then the bird quiets down. Then it gets eaten."

"That's reassuring, Ron, make sure it goes in the press briefing. So why the fuss this time?"

"Because this time some military planes got shaved. And those boys like to keep their balls intact. They raised a ruckus, invoked the holy – 'it's a matter of national security.' That got Cartwright in California – all those aerospace contracts – to suddenly find he was taking leadership in this area. His staff put together the conference.

"So listen, anyway, it was the usual bullshit. Each group uses different computers, protocols, and whatnot to manage and monitor information, so they could barely talk to each other. After two days of nearly complete confusion, each group presented their final paper, which the other guys praised and agreed with, probably because it was so different from their own that it couldn't possibly have any impact on what they were doing. Everybody says it was a great success.

"So it's the last night, yesterday, and the government's still paying for the booze – you know, those West Coast guys, everything they order looks blue – and I'm cruisin', until I hear about – you're gonna love this – some air traffic guys laughing about some hot pilot who whacked out, they figure, reported that he saw nothing where there should have been some clouds," and Hassey sobered up with good speed while the rest of the guys were laughing about the story of Hank Dawson. "Remind you of anything, Dan?"

"Shit, Ron, what in hell is going on?" Smathers was getting drawn into thinking about the substance of something, and he didn't know what to do.

"Beats me," said Hassey. "I haven't got a clue."

==

Thus coincidence led to collation. It left Smathers and Hassey confused. Both men looked solely at a specific situation and its potential resolution. They hadn't attempted to grasp "the big picture" since their college days. For a staffer, displaying grandiose visions was as sure a way to get his nose chopped off as playing around with Congressional pages – worse, as it was a far less explicable sin.

"Well, I'm stumped," said Hassey. "I just don't see where to park this. Take it off the Hill and it's too weird and diverse – no one'll feel responsibility, so why stick their necks out when there's no reason to?"

"Yeah, but if we keep it here, we could lose a shot at a budget app, plus it gets out in some bullshit hearing – if it clicks, we lose control, if it dies, we look like assholes and I've got one angry Congressman to answer to – either way we lose."

So, for all their numerous discussions, they couldn't find a place to deposit their asset. It sat like money under the mattress, not earning interest, the desire to capitalize on it burning a hole in both their breasts.

Until a month later when they both were listening to the President make an announcement. Although his military spending increases had cemented his hold on the conservatives that were his power base, they had created a backlash of concern about war that was threatening to create a public opinion poll majority negative rating for him. Faced with mounting political pressures stemming from congressional elections in the fall, the President's advisers had sought a means to defuse the issue. Military spending cuts were out of the question, and they didn't have the time to launch a major new foreign policy initiative. Even at their level they had heard that the staff consensus was that the safest path was to pledge strong support for the UN, since it was unlikely that the organization could possibly interfere with their real policy objectives. Thus, despite having been one of its severest critics, the President found himself in the position of having to support publicly a stronger UN, to "solve those pressing problems of today which can benefit from international cooperation, and to prepare for that day in the not too distant future when the nations of the world can truly unite in common purpose."

As with many actions in Washington, this one had unexpected consequences.

Smathers and Hassey shared the light. While the announcement was ignored by most Congressional staffers, they instantly recognized it as Opportunity flung full force from the goddess of timing. They interpreted this pledge as a policy directive needing no further specifics to prompt action, providing an outstanding opportunity to dump irritating, no-win problems that otherwise wouldn't go away. The UN commitment was an ideal chance to further the President's aims – albeit not quite spoken in these terms – while getting rid of some real dogs.

Their page-and-a-half cover memo, plus a full report summarizing all the separate incidents with a two-page executive summary and supporting documentation, was ready in two days. Because he had gotten some recognition for helping pull together the civilian/military conference on air traffic safety, Hassey had a chip to play, and he used it to get them an appointment with a Special Assistant to the President, Chris Hawkes. It was a reach, but they both felt it was worth it.

For Smathers, the journey to Chris Hawkes's office combined bureaucratic culmination with childhood fantasy. Knowing that they had arrived at a certain level of power, he and Hassey took in with blasé indifference the quick glimpses of the legendary rooms – not just the tourist-trip look at the Oval Office, which itself radiated plush purpose on a day when it was a workroom and not a guided tour stop, but also at the conference rooms, the Situation rooms, the offices of Secretaries and very Special Advisors and Assistants, the loudest sounds being conversations muted by the background hum of space conditioning systems, but oh what those conversations might entail!

Smathers felt the confidence flowing out of him, as he used to feel when on his second or third level up he started getting invited to the fundraisers back home, sitting at a table for low givers, staff aides, and other freebies. He would watch the intricate dance of real estate developers and commissioners, public relations peregrines mixing with press secretary hawks, a waltz of power all the louder for its discretion. Men in black ties casually leaning over and whispering, tantalizingly whispering to each other with frozen smiles gilt-edged into permanently tanned faces.

He would come home morose and sweaty from those gatherings, his bow tie hanging open at his neck and shiny studs pinpricks of emptiness, a hollow feeling that he would forever be watching the game from the bleacher seats, so far away that by the time you could hear the sound of the bat hitting the ball, the player had already rounded first, the deal already done. The distances, from power and self, combined to create a void that left him empty beyond filling, while the next morning they recreated a vacuum irresistibly drawing him into it once more, to put on his tux again in the hope that someday some tanned smiling face would lean over to him and tell him whatever it was that they talked about, something he would know before the rest of the old table, something to enable him to walk around the room with a casual manner as people stopped to discuss it with him and he could smile and placate some, tease others, making lunch and dinner dates and jokes about getting it done, ever more casual remarks as the importance of it increased, until he could actually stay still and have people walk up to him, the greatest players being the ones who could stand in place and create movement by having the stream pass by them, the illusion of relative motion.

Now the Smathers-fish was swimming past the office of the Chief of Staff and past National Security and Domestic Affairs, escorted by an executive assistant to an Assistant to the President, past uniformed Marine Corps guards, the blue and red of their uniforms outlined by yellow striping, highlighted by chests of medals, mostly black men, stiff and taut, seeing and looking past them with the same glance, and into a tiny, crowded windowless cubicle where he learned immediately the law of White House Staff Inverse Proportionality, that the greater your power the smaller your office. Hawkes was on the phone, leaning way back in his wooden rolling chair; he motioned them to sit down, pointing the pen in his hand to the two faded armchairs that along with file folders stuffed the room. Smathers shuffled through the papers on his lap, listening furiously.

"No, Harry, if you even bring up the set-aside before mentioning the vote, he'll slap it as a quid pro before we get a damn thing. Hit him on the appropriation first, get a clear signal, then let him . . . that's right," a pause, Hawkes grimaced, "no, not yet, it's . . . right, seven percent max, right, good, that's it," a longer pause, a smile, "perfect, that definitely ought to do it, and it could leave us with a billion two for the other thing . . . uh, uh, he's definitely on-line for it," a long pause while he made notes on a pad in front of him, "terrific, Harry, call me back, gotta go, bye." He hung up with a look of satisfaction on his face, made a few more notes, and then with a deep breath refocused himself.

"So, what brings the two of you here, kind of unusual to get legislative and exec branches together without anybody doing the prompting, you guys trying to move on the air traffic appropriation?" Hawkes was tall, slim with thinning blond hair and a protruding Adam's apple that moved up and down as he spoke, punctuating each word as a separate item to be listened to. He wore dark-rimmed glasses of the kind Smathers had not seen since grade school.

"Not exactly, although it grew out of some of those meetings," said Hassey. He handed Hawkes the short memo. "This sums it up a bit, it's a situation that, well, we think might demand some serious attention." Hawkes took the memo, scanned it, reread it while Smathers and Hassey breathed silently and slowly, not wanting to distract their audience in any way during the crucial minute when they either could play the rest of the show or get the hook.

Hawkes looked up for a moment, scratching the underside of his chin with the eraser end of a pencil that said "The White House" printed on its side. He stared at them, one after the other.

"What the hell does this mean?" They breathed out almost audibly; scene one had played, they could go on. They handed him the summary of the incidents, told him how they had discovered them, while he read the memo, and explained what else they knew while making reference to the report.

The major part of their verbal presentation was not contained in any of the written material, in case it was not consistent with policy directives of which they were unaware: the diversity of the incidents, the initial encounter with them in several locations and their consequent housing in several agencies, which to be coordinated would require an entirely separate interagency effort necessitating a commitment of resources and funds far beyond what the actual issue demanded, especially as it was not a public issue and in no way could significant credit be gained by addressing it, indeed, points could be lost in trying to justify the unanticipated expenditure – all this coupled with the international angle stemming from the Chinese inquiry and subsequent rumors of a similar incident over there – well, it was a natural to put into the UN initiative. Plus they would have a strong ally if they could get State in on the action.

"You know the funny thing about bureaucracy?" Hawkes asked. They nodded no. "Like conspiracy, bureaucracy is best when its players act unbidden yet in concert." They nodded yes.

They got an unbelievable forty-five minutes before Hawkes said he had to go but would look into it and get back to them, forty-five glorious pinnacle moments at the top in a tiny office next to the biggest one there is.

And they had guessed right. Smathers was asked to get his man to support the UN initiative, in return for which they offered a small but to him significant reallocation of public works funds for a new bridge in his district over a creek they could say was swollen with global warming. For Smathers, there was the delirious moment of getting a call directly from Hawkes telling him what a good job he had done, letting him know – before it became public knowledge, whispering in Smathers's ear like a glowing man in a tux – that indeed the UN angle would work out just fine. Hassey was promoted to an international coordination position – budget oversight, travel, being considered somebody as opposed to just a low-level in seven countries – and Smathers was promoted to Staff Chairman for the Permanent – permanent! multiyear! – Committee on International Trade, with a large staff, interaction with top Corporate people, public/private ventures, heavy potential business contacts. All of which radically expanded their party circuit potential.

The President announced as part of his renewed commitment to the UN a special one-time appropriation of one hundred fifty-five million dollars, the amount allocated to Defense for the ground Stealth research less the amount for Luton's bridge and some Department of State special administrative expenses, especially monitoring trips to New York, making a lot of people happy for what was to Hawkes very little. The President pronounced that he was taking the money out of the Defense budget as part of a "Dollars for Peace" program, and called upon the other major powers to similarly take funds out of their military expenditures and redirect them towards "our ultimate greatest source of true security – mutual effort and trust." It was a propaganda coup, especially as it was so unexpected. Hawkes also got credit to the State Department by passing the funds through them to the UN appropriation. Defense was happy because it could back off from thinking the unthinkable – returning money from its budget. The President got lots of credit for a pittance of funds that had already been allocated but would not have been used anyway, so there was no one to complain about the program anywhere in the system – and it effectively deflated opponents who complained he was too military-solution oriented, which particularly delighted him. It was win-win all the way. All that remained was to call the Secretary-General of the United Nations who, as expected, agreed that for one hundred fifty-five million dollars the UN could take a look at pressing concerns suddenly well-suited to an international organization.

As for the odd little problems that gave rise to all these successes – neither Smathers nor Hassey, nor Hawkes, for that matter, gave them another thought. They had been useful in meeting various needs, and now disappeared from the agendas. It was as if nothing had happened.

And if each day there was a little less sand and water and soil visible on the face of the earth, since there was so much left, what did it matter?

Chapter Nine

When you drive one route, you never know if the other way would have been shorter.

In all of Harold Upshaw's years at the United Nations, he'd never had a meeting quite like the one he'd just had with the Secretary General. Form a Special Committee, to investigate disappearances of parts of the Earth. Jesus. Oh, there was some additional U. S. funding attached to it. Reports from a few places – New York, Hawaii – and some odd stuff from China. Enough to get it international, enough, he calculated, to get it off any of the backs in Washington, toss it to the UN with a few bucks, talk about how you're supporting world peace, and let them worry about it, it's no-win for us here. Look for some places people said weren't there. Report back, and get on with it. He'd heard the subtext of the Secretary General's talk – see if we can get some more funding after that. Alchemy must have been the result of politics mixing with science, thought Upshaw; make the changes happen, we don't care how.

He had known he was about to face trouble the minute he walked into the office and saw a smiling Secretary General. In his experience Secretaries General did not smile at people at Upshaw's level without motive. The smiles were held like flowers in a cooler, resting prettily behind the glass, a static depository waiting to be plucked to make a sale, buyer and seller each suppressing in their own way the certainty of tomorrow's wilt. The rest of the time the words and expressions were pursed out, brief to the point of being curt; generous looks and embracing gestures were bits of energy deployed for creating good will amongst equals, not obtaining agreement from underlings. The smile was a dart; Upshaw was the target, rooted in its path. It was an automatic bulls-eye.

Upshaw had met the S.G. in his office near the top floor of the UN Administrative building. This was the third S.G. he had sat with in this office. His longevity gave him cold comfort; he served at the pleasure of this current one every bit as much as he had the S.G.'s predecessors, a life in which politics and tact went beyond style to form a good part of the substance of his activities, a regime built upon the art of balance, in which the scales were multiple and the measures constantly shifting. Upshaw was part of a core of individuals who had come to integrate this fluctuating set of circumstances into their being, who read the day's varied moods and the long-term rhythmic changes instinctively as well as analytically, weathermen who stuck their necks out the window, didn't just read the maps, who understood that straight lines, of communication, of information, even of authority, were unnaturally short if they existed at all, that between any two points, people, memos, or even desires, there could exist many, many others, so that the paths between them were twisted and convoluted, evincing the extraordinary capability of a set of human beings to extend a decision point to the time of the horizon.

Sitting in the S.G.'s office, Upshaw looked out the window, not straight out into the views of midtown Manhattan but down to the curve of the General Assembly below, as always feeling that wall enveloping him, even as its edges beckoned an elusive freedom, smooth glass and steel with little to grip, delicate, implacable, escape always at the edge that lay just a little further along the curve. Behind the glass there seemed little between him and the gray, wet rain outside.

By now he hardly noticed the artifacts that filled the room as if the ultimate explorer/adventurer had taken roost, an oddly colonial hearkening in this most egalitarian of spaces. He had lost interest when he realized there were no stories behind these prizes, no dust upon them, they were imbued with the scent of disinfectant, not lingering exotic aromas mixed with cognac and cigars, there was no one present to tell how they had been won;

taken with passion, neutered by institution. A distilled sense of formality and sterility pervaded the room, it was a refuge of polished perfection and facile diversity while just outside lay corridors where faded paint might crack, where voices moved around each other in the circuitous dance of diplomacy, in which the partners never touched and each listened to different music.

The various totems and statuary were messages that society was the ego but humankind was the id, and that power transcended culture. A gleaming Japanese warrior sword lay casually next to a six-screen television viewing system, flanked by a Mexican mask of the Dead and a tall, lean, dark wood Nigerian sculpture of a nude woman. Upshaw sat on the plush beige upholstered couch, wary the moment he had been invited to sit, while the S. G., instead of sitting at his huge desk, took the darker easy chair at right angles to the couch, looking across the low burled redwood table, a polished single cross-section of a once ancient tree. Upshaw would have been more comfortable had the S.G. chosen the formal demonstration of authority rather than imposed this relaxed camaraderie. He waited through the small talk, the computer-generated briefing sheet reprise of his family and children, skirting around the debacles of those relationships; he waited through the sighs regarding current crises and rueful recountings of recent debates on the minutiae that were not extraneous tissue but were the veins and arteries of the world body, waited to see in what way he would once again be asked to preserve some aged and distant endangered organ with his own lifeblood to further the painted purposes of this man, the myriad mandates of this institution.

"Harold," the S.G. started in his smooth, caressing private voice of intense sincerity, playing with a primitive stone scepter that lay on the table, "we've got a situation and it is going to take someone of special talents, someone yes possessing excellent technical skills but who also knows his way around here, how things are working, it is a rare combination, Harold, and you did that superb job for us on the Polar Ice Cap business, in short, Harold, I feel there is only one man for the job, we are all of us feeling that way, and that man, Harold, that man is you." As he spoke his glowing almond skin seemed to blend in with the chair, as if it were the furniture, and by extension, the room and the building, that were speaking to Upshaw.

"Situation?" he gave back, keeping his wrinkled hands intertwined in his lap, resisting the temptation to pick up a geode that looked like a brightly colored egg cracked in half.

"Well, yes, actually it is a couple of situations, and then the US has tied some funding to it, and the Chinese are involved somehow, so," he sighed, shrugged, and smiled simultaneously, leaving Upshaw to wonder if there were some school for Secretaries General, as all of them seemed to perform this trademark triple, "so you can be seeing it has to be handled delicately, with caring, like perhaps as if the divorced father has his son over for the weekend and yet the mother's presence lingers," thanks, thought Upshaw, always an apt way to find communication across the barriers, "and I, we, know you can do it."

Upshaw had his obligations, and he knew them. "What are the couple of situations?" he asked, picking up the geode and cupping its weight in his hands.

"It's rather odd, all things considering, but there have been reports of, well it seems hard to describe, to even be imagining, but people have been reporting seeing, or maybe I should say not seeing, hah, sort of blank spaces or something where there should be, ah, well more like hard ground or beach or whatever." He gave a faint flick of his wrist, the extent of his motion magnified by the rough blade of the ancient knife held carelessly in his hand, a small gesture preserved for denoting tiny anomalies of human behavior in a world where large ones were just as common.

"I know it sounds odd but, well, there it is being, and with the Chinese and the US interested – and not just, I think, because the other one is, and the US has found for us some funding which maybe we can leverage for some more, and I don't know much about it but then I never really understood these international expedition science things anyway, and you are so on top of them I don't know what we'd do without you, all those wonderful reports and papers and things, really they're even better than the UNICEF cards for us, so could you please be taking a look into it, here's the file, let me know if you need anything." Dismissed. Harold stepped into a long corridor whose end he could not see, the building arced around him.

Harold Upshaw had last headed a UN Scientific Mission to the Antarctic, for International Cooperation in the Year of the Ice Cap; he was a survivor of three multicountry polar expeditions and innumerable bouts of head choppings in the US and UN governments, when at times it seemed as if connection with one entity's policies would mean automatic expulsion from the other. Now he was being asked to head up a Special Mission for Maintaining Earth, an ambiguous title reflecting equally, he suspected, the vagueness of the task and the instinct of the institution. By implicit instruction he proceeded first to hush everything up, collect all files, and second to start trying to figure out what to do, in that he was asked to commence an investigation with all deliberate speed, particularly as the U.S. budget funding cycle required requests to be made for the next fiscal year in three months, and the S.G. indicated he would be most pleased if they could show enough progress to justify further special appropriations.

Upshaw was at fifty-seven more organizer than scientist. He was told to pull out the stops and get things done fast. At first it was hard to take those instructions seriously. Nothing moved fast at the UN, not even the cafeteria lunch line, held up by a combination of pauses for spontaneous intense debates and arguments over change at the cashier's, which delegates insisted emphatically be in converted currency. One of his assistants said to him as they walked along an endless corridor in the Main Building, "How can anyone here get excited about a few bits of earth disappearing? Events have been vanishing in this building for years."

Upshaw read the files with a knowing skepticism, sitting in a small office in a sub-basement of the administrative building, ostensibly to be near the working staff but primarily because no room with a window was awarded without a purpose, and Upshaw was already totally committed; besides, he was American, and potential charges of favoritism usually put American staff in the basement. Glaring fluorescent light played evenly over the cubicle, giving a greenish pallor to the piles of paper and reports that lay everywhere, pictures of icebergs and deserts blending in with those of jungles and marshes, evenly tinting his skin and the plastic surfaced desk.

The one hundred fifty-five million dollar contribution memos lay on the top of the pile, followed by memos outlining outreach plans to raise matching funds from other nations as well as potential areas of follow-up for additional dollars, in addition to tie-ins to existing programs and a summary of the latest overhead charging rate, ending with the descriptions of the sightings. The ordering added a weight to what lay below that might otherwise have been lacking. Upshaw would have to search for the real mandates here, with this much money involved. He read on. Three black kids had been found, questioned extensively, brought in for testing. They discovered that all three were quite bright, the young girl especially was a terror, but as for the story, the kids stuck to what they had seen; the police and forensic psychologists finally just attributed it to three good imaginations with no outlet that formed a collective intrigue in the early morning sun and ocean reflections. The pilot's review was similar. The information from China was obscure.

The files consisted of interviews, reviews, psychological explanations with no real scientific basis for any conclusion, just some general hypotheses that maybe it could be explained this way, and if it could be then that's enough for now, and now's mandate was assumed to last forever. They all had one element in common – not a single interviewer or reviewer had visited a site where the strange pieces of nothing had supposedly been witnessed.

Upshaw was long past being a field man. He was an administrator. He was not a scientific problem solver, but a diplomatic organizational problem solver. He knew how to garner resources, keep together if not meld disparate groups to focus on problems of interest, problems whose location or breadth at least allowed for multinational cooperation. Not, in Upshaw's estimate, that it made the science any better to have to cope with organizing teams from five or eight countries to live together for months at a time, where press releases on how people got along were more intensely prepared and scrutinized than the technical papers stemming from the missions.

Upshaw had come with age to see that the accrual of knowledge was not straightforward, nor were the ostensible problems ever quite so urgent as to require immediate solutions; that there were tiny victories to be won in finding common process, as important over time as the science might ever be, and that easy judgments should be suspended. His vision blossomed, part psychologist, part ambassador, science had become a medium, the problems created method without demanding resolution, so much the better that they could frequently return to familiar if esoteric territories, ongoing enclaves that might vanish if hard answers were found; the critical questions were not always the obvious ones. He was an extension of the UN, it was a part of him as much as he was of it. He was a particular form of modern man.

After a couple of weeks of reading, organizing, assigning sections to aides, and developing a work plan, he thought, "Why not?" He hadn't been to the beach in years, before the split, probably, since Marge would always take care of those kinds of activities, with the kids and all. If nothing else, it would be a pleasant change for a day, away from the air conditioning. He requested a car, with diplo plates, to park along a stretch of sand with parking restrictions. No picnic, no thermoses. From the large, quiet parking lot under the UN campus he launched into the slow-moving bustle of the FDR Drive. He drove out by himself, because he wanted flexibility of response assuming he didn't find anything there. Hmm, he thought, even that didn't quite sound right. Hell, he considered, cradling his files and his memories, I should be pretty good at finding nothing.

Upshaw drove past the squad cars stationed along the beach drive, showing his credentials as he got closer, as if he had a pass to enter the concentric circles of hell. He followed in Lucy's footsteps, and Tyrone's, and Samuel's, and like them he came to a halt suddenly. He stood in the sand, wishing his feet could take root, feeling like he was being seduced forward, tempted into a hue of oblivion. He had once stood at the top of the World Trade Center, and no part of him was tempted to experience the jump, the flight. But here a conspiracy of wind and light pulled him forward, he wanted to reach in to what he could not see, more than anything he wanted to make it go away. He stared for a while, the sounds around him muffled as if all sounds were foghorns trying to break through, trying to warn. There was no one to say anything to, and after half an hour he turned and left.

⩦

Patterns repeating, predictable periods within welcoming chaos, clarity among randomness. The encounters had spacing; like error chatter on the lines, they could be adjusted for. Some, a few, none, many. Little sensibilities, big ones, observations keen and dull. Again, and then . . . again. Distant occurrences became intimacy, finally, nuzzling like the whispers of a breeze on skin. They had approached, and would again. Order and spacing, conducting the march; only they didn't hear it. Music, joyous as a sound wave propagating through a vacuum.

⩦

As shaken as he was, Upshaw formulated a plan as he drove back to Manhattan. Part of him was debating whether to stay on the Grand Central Parkway all the way in, over the Triborough Bridge and down the FDR Drive into the UN garage, even with the eternal construction around Sixty-First Street that always escorted him like a child hanging on to his arm, slowing his pace home, or to take the Long Island Expressway, hoping to catch it into the City before they shut the Midtown Tunnel down to one lane in, sharing the burdens of exiting rush-hour traffic by astonishingly creating it in both directions. He knew that whatever decision he made would probably be wrong but that even in that closed two-option matrix he would never know if the other choice would have been better. But today he didn't care about the traffic, the jam was like honey, the slow pouring giving him time to consider the tastes to come. He planned. The traffic was a distraction easily filtered out, compared to the usual bustle in and around his office. Home had no kids around now, it was true, but that was somehow the worst distraction, like city dwellers disturbed by the smothering silence of the country, that shattered the anonymity of a voice, a thought, a breath, a relentless emptiness that a single sound could fill with terrifying proportions.

Bumper to bumper he edged towards a plan, surprised that he needed one, but accepting the necessity. In an odd way he felt more alive; he didn't know what he had just witnessed, but he knew that he had to find out what it was, that he was uniquely empowered to do so, and that at long last he had a Mission with purpose. He was surprised, yes, but ready. He organized, and he drove. And every now and then he allowed his mind to review that lingering mushroom-hued image of a stretch of space that wasn't there, and transplanted that hue onto the blue-and-white sky, onto brown-and-green mountain sides, slowly seeing all the colors of the earth transformed into that plaintive enticing breach, a vision that was his alone, or worse, his shared with some vengeful force. Almost without noticing, he was back at the UN. He was scared, no doubt, and excited, energized in a way he had forgotten, leaning forward as he strode past rows of cars from his underground parking space to the elevators, like a golfer walking up the hill towards the distant green, his eyes on the flag, his mind on the selection of the club and the flight of the ball.

Upshaw followed his first reaction: to canvas the scientific community to see if anyone had either experience with or useful ideas about what he was confronting. He started with a list of local scientists with interesting reputations, while preparing to expand it quickly, and a briefing sheet and interview format for his staff. As he expected, he quickly ran out of scientific aides and technicians, and was forced to recruit experienced field operatives from other departments.

It was then that Susan called and told Upshaw about what she had witnessed. It was another bit of dismaying news, and made him realize: of course, why should we think we've heard about all the occurrences that are taking place? He ordered her to report to New York immediately.

Upshaw knew Susan Corporell from her days working on the Temporary Mission to Preserve the Ecosystem. She had recently spent well over a year trying to distribute food and medical rations over the objections, incompetence, and corruptions of various African governments; she had a right to fatigue. Upshaw was working through his list, one by one; when Susan came in he asked her to track down and interview the file that was on top: David Altaforce, a thirty-nine-year-old mathematician/physicist. She was not pleased.

"Harold, I'm tired. I don't know what I saw out there, maybe it was just fatigue. It was scary. I'd really like to take some time, I'd like to walk around, go someplace where nobody except children weighs under one hundred fifty pounds, okay?"

"Sorry, Susan, your search for fat will have to wait. Your experience makes you too valuable to waste, you can be more convincing than the other operatives I've got out there, convey the urgency of the situation. Find this guy fast and see if he can help. When you're done, there'll be other people for you to talk to. I've got to cover all my bases, and it's too early in the game to start discriminating."

"Harold, I don't know how to talk to scientists. They mumble a lot, roll their eyes and then fail me on a test. I never comprehended a response any of them ever gave me, now you're telling me the answers are important – and I don't even understand the questions I'm supposed to ask."

"Try this one, Susan, and get back to me fast. You look great. Bye."

"Harold," Susan said.

"Yes?"

"Get a window, will you?"

He smiled. "Hey, Susan, don't worry, I just went to the beach."

⁂

Altaforce was on sabbatical from New York University. The secretaries, most of whom giggled when she asked for him, had given her several phone numbers to check, including three National Laboratories, the Institute for Advanced Studies at Princeton, and his mother's house in Brooklyn, from whom she was finally able to locate him at his house in Westchester, forty-five minutes north of the UN, which no one had suggested because who stays at home during his sabbatical? For a Philadelphia girl who had gone to Radcliffe, done graduate work at the Sorbonne, been on UN assignments in eleven countries, spoke six languages and as many dialects, and had three almost-marriages, Westchester looked to be a snap.

Chapter Ten

There was nothing to be done.

Susan and David sat in a temporary office in the United Nations, barren except for a few metal desks connected by thick wires like flies captured in a spider web. They got a computer with an extra large screen. Susan went out to start the search for a place for David to work. She wanted to get started, get it done – the place, the equipment, the thinking, the answers. Like she used to want to get the people fed, all of them, right away. In her frenetic state she was forgetting lessons learned. New York streets were no more conducive to immediacy than African veldts.

It had been a dozen years since Susan had had to search for an apartment in New York. When she first moved to the City, finding an apartment was mostly a question of choosing where to live. The City was a pastiche of neighborhoods, and if a few, such as the Upper East Side and its building blocks of large, featureless white brick structures, were unaffordable – as well as unpalatable – still many more were within her newfound first-job economic reach, a heady, exuberant grasp relishing freedom, from school as well as home. She had moved easily several times, uptown and down, walk-ups and lofts, shares and solo, until without warning or notice a particular choice became, unbeknownst at the time, her last choice, as an extraordinary rapid rise in rents coupled with regulations that kept her "occupied" rent low, froze her and many others in place.

It reminded her of the game she used to play as a kid, "red light, green light." A child would stand against the wall with his back to the other players and shout "green light," and the other players would begin to advance. Suddenly, the child would turn around shouting, "red light!" and anyone caught in motion would be out, while the remaining players, frozen in their positions, could then continue to advance at the next green light, until someone either reached the wall or all the players were disqualified. The game was played on concrete alleys and driveways, the kids' shouts reverberating through the neighborhood, no cars but red lights and green lights marking the passage of time and movement, the near impossible tension of getting so so close to the wall and not moving too quickly, to be caught off-balance and midflight as red lights and green lights came in ever faster succession between her and her goal. She often won.

The difference with adult games, she thought, is that they also move the wall further away. There were so few fixed reference points in the shifting terrain of career and accomplishment. Once, she'd been certain that problems clearly seen would generate equally obvious solutions. On a winding street in Lower Manhattan, in a neighborhood that hadn't yet been named in order to get even higher rents, she had settled in to a five-story ancient building, once used as a carriage house to keep horses and store equipment for the rich merchants in the area, the building now more valuable than any other local merchandise. She had the top floor; it was a walk-up. She had moved in when a friend, an actress who had actually gotten work, a two-year road tour, arranged with the landlord for Susan to move in at the same rental, yet another human interaction that no longer existed in the current market; after all the years and travel, she still found it hard to accept how the interchange of money so easily warped once-basic attributes of a culture, a salt that overpowered any stew.

Susan's apartment had a large central room with a ceiling that sloped from about nine feet down to just below six feet, effectively limiting the height of any boyfriend. Coupled with long, exposed dark wooden beams and the view over an interior set of courtyards with gardens and barbecues in the summer, it gave the apartment a genuine feel of charm, irresistible when she had first seen it and paid five hundred sixty-five a month for it. Now her rent was twelve sixty, anything comparable was over forty-three hundred, and she was stuck with charm, a once sweet sauce that had congealed over her, the taste long since indiscernible, as well as a strong predisposition towards tall men. And that was home in New York. For hundreds of thousands of New Yorkers, the kid had turned around, yelled "red light" with exceptional enthusiasm, and then walked out of the alley, leaving the breathless, excited players to plant roots in random infertile patches neither chosen nor suitable for such long-lived purposes, immortalizing temporal compromises and foregone amenities that standard pay raises could never quite reach.

Occasionally she thought wistfully of lofts in Soho, of large kitchens, of apartments advertised in the luxury homes columns of *The New York Times Magazine* – often she only read those columns – with whirlpools and saunas, balconies and greenhouses, breathtaking views and a place to put her television other than in the middle of her living room. She put it all together – a high-tech art-deco penthouse overlooking one of the rivers or Central Park, Japanese interior design, the crisp tinkle of glasses clicking and people laughing on her terrace with running water, a little fountain, to obscure the sounds of the City, only the views and the powered discrete conversation of her benefit parties perched high above the City as she read the Sunday paper spread around her on a slumping couch with a faded floral fabric in a charming West Village flat in the alley of her life.

But this assignment, this man, had come down to asking her to find an apartment in which he could set up shop. Not just anywhere, mind you, not even that pleasure. Given a virtually unlimited budget, she had at first seen an opportunity to play out some part of her housing fantasies, a peculiarly New York phenomenon, like asking a stranger how much rent he paid. But no, it had to be close to the UN, not so close as to be in its organizational shadow, the bureaucratic gloom, but not so far away as to lose touch, the chance to shoot over with the latest finding or request for information or just to keep up with the news on the floors. David might dwell with abstractions, but he had seasoned, concrete ideas of how to work with institutions. Her directive from him was to involve as few people as possible, so she couldn't even use a real estate broker. One more daydream dashed.

⁂

There was a knock on the UN office door. It opened and swung towards David. A medium-height, stocky man walked in, almost cautiously, as if to avoid making contact, because when he made contact things tended to break. He was wearing a dark raincoat with areas of sheen to it, and the outlines of a few stains – you could almost see him fixed to a sidewalk corner eating a hot dog, strands of sauerkraut running freely down one sleeve because his other hand had a soda in it, elbows raised high too late, and a shrug. Rain or shine. A full face, round but not soft, dark short straight eyebrows counterbalanced by the hues of heavy growth shaved but not contained on the bottom half of his face. He walked towards David, his eyes darting around the room yet somehow keeping David fixed in their stare, as if you were afraid to stop looking and face the inevitable moment when his eyes would return to yours and find them not looking back. If he was impressed by the flashing screen, the UN, or David, he didn't show it. David had been reading reports, immersed in thought. He sat silently, waiting for this phenomenon, at least, to explain itself.

"David Altahfawce?" he looked, and continued in response to the nod. "How d'ya do, I'm Sal Antifermo, detective with the New York City Police, how are ya?" He stuck out his hand, first wiping it on his coat. David shook it, immediately felt engulfed in the strength of the grip.

"What can I do for you, Detective?"

"Hey, there's something about a beach, they say you're the guy to talk to." He shrugged, trying an approach – look, they sent me here, can't we work together, get them off my back?

"I thought they explained through the UN Liaison to your Mayor, that it was outside your purview."

"Pur-vue, huh, yeah, well, that's right as far as it goes, but – well, it's our beach, you know. We kinda like to keep track of it."

Antifermo's speech was punctuated by hard d's for th's, dropped g's, but it was as if he simply eliminated soft or unnecessary sounds, adding more strength to the points he made. David could recognize the implacability of a force, in nature and in man.

"Sorry. Right. Let's talk about some disappearing beach."

Chapter Eleven

He had to go back.

When the detective came by and asked Tyrone again if he wanted to go to the beach again, show the place to this other guy, David, Tyrone said yes. For months, Antifermo's question had stuck like a street challenge, taunting him: "Do you want to go back?" They hadn't been bad to him, really, not like all the stories he'd heard, even ended up with Lucy in a better school, once somebody paid attention to her. But they didn't believe him. He discovered his pride, his lower cheeks puffed out in silent affront. After a while it became the clearest thing in his life.

"Yeah, I'll go," he said, ignoring the looks from the guys on the rest of the court – you don't voluntarily travel with cops.

He'd see for himself, and then the rest of them didn't matter. Old goose-eyed Samuel could walk away, dream up some new line to hit on the girls, talk himself up with it, but Tyrone found a different spot. He figured that you cope with the things you grow up with, and that ain't much, but when something new comes at you, you either stand or run. He'd run, seeing that new thing, and he wouldn't do it again. Samuel, and the others, they could go on running and talk a streak, their words like shovels of soil burying self-betrayals; Tyrone had grown quieter.

This time he wasn't carrying a bathing suit, he wasn't thinking about the hot dogs or the girls, didn't have the weight of Lucy on his shoulders. This time he rode out in a car, David's convertible, not three trains and a bus. This time he wasn't sneaking on. This time he was going to take the same walk to look and, if it was still there like he knew it would be, this time he would stand his ground.

The day before, a flock of sea gulls had taken off from the Jersey coast. For one of them it was now hard going. Yesterday his wings had carried him wherever he chose to fly. It was an act of instinct, but also of confidence, no more thought to the choices than to the act of flying itself. Then, in a typical fight with another bird over a just-dying clam at the edge of the water, he had reared up with his wings, only to have one smashed by a waterlogged piece of driftwood hidden by the white surf, so that in an instant it appeared and slammed into him. The clam and the contest were both forgotten with the surprise, and then the pain, the other bird's victory squawk barely heard through his own cry, his beak jutting desperately into the wing, sinking into the feathers, as if to knit them back together, in-out the head, stretching the wing back and forth, but this was not a tangled sand fly or skinny piece of seaweed. He didn't understand the distinctions, but he was hurt, and he cried out.

That night the flock took off, heading north, lifted by a sweet breeze away from the Jersey dump and up along the coast. The wind carried them; the injured bird felt discomfort, but no threat, and kept up easily. Towards morning, squalls started, and the mixture of natural convections and urban heat swells added to the turbulence. The sky's night blue was never severed by sunrise, but gradually faded into a numbing gray in which the land and sea below were barely distinguishable, their features blended together.

The flock turned east and veered across the bay towards the end of a long and familiar strip of beach and dunes. They were moving across the wind now, pushing to keep from being carried inland away from the comfort of an ocean's nest. The injured bird broke the silent intensity of their wings flapping with cries it did not understand, nor even knew it emitted. The rain eased into a fine mist, and little beads formed on his head and back. Even the etched white markings on his gray body seemed to fade. The sky had no contour, and the regularity of the shore line below made it impossible to tell what progress they were making, so that time became irrelevant, swept away by the surrounding gray.

He was losing touch with the flock, old friends and foes alike. If only he had been able to rest, perhaps it would have healed. Up ahead, there was a long length of beach, with just a couple of people on it. Plenty of room to avoid them, set down for a while, catch up with the others later. The flock suddenly headed out to sea; tired wings stopped coasting and beat continuously, frantically. He didn't understand the change in flight direction; even if he had, his world had closed in on the necessity of driving a body that ached for the first surprising time. All at once he sensed something, something . . . wrong in front of him. The gull beat his wings in response to what lay there, a strange presence that inspired fear, not curiosity. But he was too late, and too weak, his wings like broken paddles in a strong current, his sudden squelched squawk muffled by the wind and stifled by nothing. The rest of the flock pushed into the wind, out towards the sea. A sudden calm and their momentum carried them forward. The injured bird was gone, and none of the flock noticed as they beat their wings towards the only place that felt safe – elsewhere.

The fog and rain had limited their vision, so Tyrone tugged David closer to the shore before he spotted it again, the empty space, barely visible against the gray sky and sea.

"There, d'as what I been tellin' you." He pushed out his chin, vindicated.

The space was still there, still rising into vision, still carving a blank coat out of its surrounding. There was no rain, no mist, no spray, no movement, but something that was pulling him in to it. He stopped, halting David with him, stopped and stood and looked, rocking from the wind and the pull in and his resistance, not feeling the rain. Here he would stand.

He saw a bunch of birds off to his right, and watched them, happy for the company. One was lagging behind, and when the others veered out to sea, changing direction on a beat, the last one continued ahead. Tyrone watched as the gull seemed pulled into the emptiness – and didn't come out. He waited. A second, then another, and another still. Come out, he thought, I'll count to three and you'll be out one . . . two . . . three, shit that was it and the hues shimmered and grew, maybe even reached out towards him, and Lucy and Samuel and the block and everybody, and this time he knew the fear for what it was – valid, with no shame in it, and if all those folks didn't listen all he would do was get as far away as he could, because not he, and not even they, he understood that now, could save him, no TV ad could create an image of hope, no movie gave a sweet ending, so he turned and ran, ran this time for ever.

David stood still. He was a theoretician, not a field man, he worked with the equations, not the elements. The rain beat patterns on his face, familiar patterns rendered ominous like a walk in backyard woods in the dark. He stared. The wonder of it. It must be like discovering a new virus, he thought; deadly, but beautiful in its complexity and efficiency; a mix of exhilaration and terror. It was like the Northern Lights descended, a monochrome curtain, near enough to seem as if you could touch it, sensing that touch could move you to the other end of the cosmos. It was like a vortex that drained life and energy themselves.

He stood firmly, not pulled ahead physically, for his mind had already catapulted forward. Amazement dominated his being. If this is a new phenomenon, he thought, I am here near its birth. An uncle, if not a parent. He didn't know what he was looking at, but at this moment for him it was the most extraordinary thing on earth. The wind whipped him, restored him to where he was.

He spent a few more minutes gazing at nothing, like not wanting to abandon a sunset when there was still a hint of red in it, then turned back towards the dunes and scrub grasses that lay behind him, tiny plugs gripping the sand as if trying to capture the memories of things the way they once were. Tyrone was waiting for him in the car, crying, crying against all his wishes not to.

A tremor. Nourishment Shaking, not unhappily; not exactly wanting the encounters, but they happened; like a tickle, hard to eliminate, hard to resist. If they stopped, it would be because . . . but that was still too much to think about. Things wished for and things had. A shiver of anticipation. Waiting.

Chapter Twelve

Susan took to the streets around the UN.

Her hands would interlace, release, in nervous excitement. She wanted to find this apartment, set things up, start getting answers. The tight set of criteria David had established put her in familiar territory. It was old tenement buildings with no doormen, no elevators, few apartments . . . and definitely no charm. It was, inevitably, Mrs. Pudanski.

The daughter of the original owner, Mrs. Pudanski was showing her around her building. A shapeless five feet three, she walked around in what might once have been called a pink shift, somewhere between a bathrobe and a wraparound dress, dirty yellow flowers melding into the faded pink fabric, as if some dull raspberry Jell-O with pieces of banana in it had learned to walk. Her hair was in blue and green plastic curlers. Was it *de rigueur*, Susan wondered, did they learn it from family or TV or was it built into the genes: as the lines of demarcation between breasts, stomach and hips disappeared into a single curve from neck to knee, did the curlers gradually appear, perpetually enshrouded in a cloud of smoke from a cigarette dangling from thick lips overgrown with lipstick that magically matched the ancient pink of the wrap? Mrs. Pudanski seemed to have solved a smoking problem, for somehow the cigarette in her mouth was always there, never removed, never, it seemed, changing length, always just enough ash to get Susan fixated on when it would drop, so that she kept having to shake herself back into the conversation.

The outside of the building was familiar enough. Three washed stone steps, now light brown, one side of an iron railing still up, the steps more worn on that side, or perhaps it was an illusion of shadow, the metal painted a rustproof shit brown. In places the paint had dripped and built up so as to close off the whirls and curlicues and spaces in the original railing design, leaving bulbous drops perpetually ready to fall. The building had two doors, with the buzzer system in the hallway between them. Only the outer door was locked. Susan banged on it for a while, and there appeared Mrs. Pudanski.

"Oy, is dat stuck again, dat schmuck Mannheim vas s'posed to shave it or somding, anyvay, c'min honey, in," she coughed, dangling the cigarette up and down like bait.

Susan's frustration had already increased from too many "Apartment for rent" signs up and no apartments available, and she didn't have the time. She asked if Mrs. Pudanski indeed had an apartment as the sign hanging from the second-floor fire escape had indicated. Mrs. Pudanski looked up to the ceiling, layering the skin at the back of her neck. "Vhy, it's jus' come on da market, it's lucky for you valking in here like dis before I could even put an ad in, c'mon, I'll show."

With that Mrs. Pudanski headed up the stairs. Each step had a different sound, the two of them together creating a chorus of creaks to accompany their passage. Up Mrs. Pudanski led, past faded green hallway walls running along the staircase, illuminated by bare bulbs nested in old light fixtures, all the glass covers gone, at least one bulb, often two, of the three in each fixture out. A brown line about four inches wide at the height of the banister on the opposing wall had evidently become a sacrosanct testimony to design, for successive paintings had sought to preserve it, each one encroaching on it slightly, so that now it was a wavy line with streaks and brush marks in it, surrounded by a pastel green that was lighter above the line than below, perhaps a tribute to yet another inspired interior decoration idea, let's give da place some more cless, make it darker lower down, Mannheim, like in da hospital. The banister itself was wood that seemed somehow soft, as if it had finally conceded its integrity to the successive grippings of immigrant hands grown old and replaced with softer, more affluent ones; in places it even seemed to wave like its afterimage on the other wall.

Following Mrs. Pudanski up the stairs gave Susan the opportunity to appreciate her slippers, polyester pink – of course! – fur encased in a suede-like plastic, the underlying pudge bursting through like clay squished between fingers, the feet never moved even a fraction of an inch higher than necessary to negotiate a step, as if they were fingers playing a beloved piano, each creak a note for the maestro, the foot rolling from the front of the step to the back, playing piercing squeaks to clunking bass, almost an organ under her pedals. Susan could only produce a single note as accompanist, the Pudanski setting the theme while Susan defined the contrapuntal. They reached the sixth floor.

"Well, Mrs. Pudanski, that walk must keep you in shape." Susan smiled at her, laughing nervously. Am I nuts, she wondered? She made better small talk with near-naked Masai chieftains.

"Call me Nat, hon – it's short fer Natasha, ya know?" Natasha! Oh, what a world is here o'er thrown, Susan thought, reminded of the hopes of parents of babies too skinny to walk; dead hopes could be fat, too. The climb had made Mrs. Pudanski – Nat – even more talkative.

"Yeh, dis sonuvabeetch jus valks out one day, tree months overdue and den he's gone, is dis vat da vorld's coming to, I ask ya."

They stood in front of a faded brown door, with several large eviction notices and a sheriff's order still pasted on it. Mrs. Pudanski took a large ring from a pocket Susan hadn't noticed concealed within her folds, the ring stuffed with keys. At no time did the cigarette leave her mouth. After laboriously trying several keys, keeping Susan pushed up against a banister she didn't trust in the narrow hallway, feeling the heat rise noticeably, Mrs. Pudanski unlocked the door of 6N – the letters must have been there for the last painting and since fallen off, leaving a stenciled 6N in faded yellow against the brown door. Susan walked in, and even as her stomach sank she knew David would find it perfect.

The apartment appeared to be carved out of a once-larger space. It had wooden floors, long discolored slats of varying shades, many gouged or with spaces between warped edges. The walls looked like they had been used for a combination of hanging dart boards and experimental abstract art – a mix of holes, brush marks, mostly in blacks and purples, peeling plaster and flopping sheet rock that might well have been accepted in an exhibit marked as "mixed media." The door opened onto a roughly twenty-foot square room that was introduced as the living room; one wall had half a fireplace in it, with another wall running neatly through the mantle. Perhaps, thought Susan, the fireplace was to encourage neighborly cooperation – it would take two apartments to build a fire. A kitchen with a small eating space was off to the left, and doors in the right side of the far wall and the right wall led to two fifteen-by-ten bedrooms, in between which was nestled a bathroom with a tub more green than white, a sink with separate hot and cold water faucets, and a toilet with the water tank near the ceiling, a frayed braided pull cord to connect to the once royal flush.

It wasn't simply that the apartment was grimy that gave Susan the shivers – it was also dark, amazingly gloomy for the middle of a summer day. The kitchen window was about three feet from the rear wall of a building from the next block, while both bedrooms each had one window with an equally intense view of the windowless wall of an adjacent high-rise, one that must have been built after the tenement, blocking what view or air that once might have been.

"Waddaya think, huh, honey. All dis space, ya cud even start a family here, huh, ya lookin like for dat," the Pudanski startled Susan out of her open-mouthed staring. "Now, look, honey, I like ya, and I don wanna rush, but dis is primo territory, ya know, so ya really gotta let me know like rideaway, de're gonna line up for it, ya know."

"Uh, sure, what's the rent again, Mrs. Pudanski?"

"Only thoity-five hunred a mont, such a steal but it's almost like regulated, ya know, I'm tellin' ya honey ya shud grabbit."

Susan was still wrestling with visions of duplex penthouses overlooking the river, all paid with someone else's money. Her fingers gripped each other. This had to be over. She sighed. "Give me a day, Mrs. Pudanski, I just have to have someone else look at it, okay."

"I unnerstan, hon, ya jus bring him aroun nice and quick, okay?" Mrs. Pudanski leaned forward, starting with her curlers and rocking to her rounded shoulders, and leered, her lower lip dropping with the effort. As they left, the cigarette ash fell off into a little pile in the middle of the front room. Susan broke a heel on the next-to-bottom stair, getting caught in a hole in the edge of the step. "Oy, dat Mannheim, I musta told him haffa dozen times to fix dat." Mrs. Pudanski smiled at her on her way out.

"David, you're all wet." Susan picked at David's jacket, trying to wipe off the moisture.

"Who've you been talking to?" Back at the UN, David had recovered enough to enjoy Susan worrying about him. He took off his jacket, slung it over the faded reclining chair behind one of the desks, and looked at her.

"I saw it, Susan. At Jones Beach. So close." His hair was slicked down from the rain, his eyes glowing. He described his encounter, Tyrone, the lost sea gull.

"It just disappeared?"

"Seemed to. I couldn't be positive, since I couldn't see to the other side. And Tyrone had run off, so I had turned around for a second following him; maybe I missed it coming out . . . The space – it's really something."

"I know." She paused. "You didn't feel like it was trying to pull you in, get tugged forward?"

He cocked his head in thought. "No, nothing like that. Just the emptiness, so stark against the rest of the beach and the sky. Think of the capacity to create this conversion: it's amazing. What a feat."

"Feat!" Susan almost shouted. "Are you nuts? You've seen what it does to a place, that horrible emptiness, what it could do everywhere. How can you call that 'a feat'?"

"Okay, I see your point." He pulled out his hankie, a red bandana, tried to dry his hair with it. "You just have to admit it's really extraordinary, that's all."

Susan looked at him. She was ready to respond to him, from the depths of how visceral her experience had been, stay engaged in the argument, and was hit with how consistent he was in his frame of reference, how embedded that perspective was in his approach to the world.

"David, how come you've never been married?"

"What?"

"I mean, you're an attractive guy, smart, nice house, no zits, don't smell. And still single. I'm just curious; how come?"

"Well, I don't know, I mean I came close a few times, but ultimately each one fizzled. To be honest, they were usually the ones that left. By the time I got around to asking, they were already out the front door."

"Ah huh."

"Hey, don't get any ideas, okay."

"Just curious. Let's get back to work, it's all right."

He already had, was picking up the photos from the files. He said, almost to himself, "It's unlike anything I've ever seen."

"That's for sure," she answered. "Speaking of which, I've found an apartment so awful you might as well look at it."

As she had foreseen, he found the apartment just right; at least it meant they could move on to the next phase, setting up their lab or whatever he needed. David even talked with Mrs. Pudanski about the old country, and was rewarded with a piece of noodle pudding that he likened to super-dense matter. He called her "Pudge," and the Pudanski took it as a term of endearment.

Susan got the UN maintenance staff to the apartment in record time to clean and repair the place. They fixed the flooring, scraped and finished it. They plastered the holes in the walls and repainted. They planed the doors so they would close, replaced the hinges, put in new closet doors. They rewired all the light fixtures and put in bright bulbs. It was still dark enough to make Susan shiver when they walked in, but at least it was clean.

"It's almost a shame to put anything in it," she said, looking at the shining wooden floor. "I guess I like this minimalist thing – it's nice without anything in it filling it up, open, calming."

"Hey," said David, "which would you rather have, the messy coastline or a stretch of nothing? It's too easy to say a room looks nice when it's empty. Sure – it's clean, open, uncluttered. It's like a meadow without a planting, the facile seductiveness of a young girl. No challenges given, none taken. Put in the furniture, live in it a while – then make it look appealing, real, full without clutter, ordered without boredom, surprising but not chaotic, a balance of space and filler. That would be far more attractive to me, because it would be trying something. This room is like an unlined face – no character. So," he rubbed his hands together, "let's give it a few wrinkles."

She wasn't sure what to expect in the way of his equipment requests – rooms full of it, or just tobacco, a few pipes and a blackboard. Instead, he first got her to have Con Edison hook up some high-voltage wiring – "it's for a visiting scientist from Sweden, Mrs. Pudanski, the guy's an air conditioning freak, what can I tell you?"

His material requests seemed simple. A few personal computers, powerful ones with lots of storage, color monitors with intense resolution, printers, scanners, lots of routers and lines, most of which plugged into the machines. He did in fact air condition all the rooms, connecting them to a temperature-monitoring system in one of the computers that controlled all the cooling. Coming out of the summer heat in the hallway and entering the apartment, Susan had the sensation of finding a Hollywood house with swimming pool and ice machine in the middle of the Sahara. It was beyond an oasis, beyond even a mirage. It was all real, and it was all for nothing.

Chapter Thirteen

This was not music to her ears.

Susan kept looking up the stairs, as if the connection would lift her into the apartment above. She had learned to play the steps, a deep groan from the back of the fourth step up between three and four, the high whine in the middle of the second from the top on five, her own creaking cacophony around which she invented rhythms to weave the noises together. She was carrying a newly purchased laptop computer, damned if she was going to be shut out of any game. The laptop was no longer as light as promised; her left foot hit an E sharp.

6N had a new lock, but as usual the door was open. She walked in, stood next to the door, shrugged the computer in its case off her shoulder, shouted "Hi," tossed her blue plaid blazer on top of it, stood a second to cool down from the climb, and headed for the kitchen, at which point she noticed a stranger staring at her from behind a computer table.

He was short, with short, dark hair, a dark, short beard, all thick curly hair. He looked at home in a white lab coat, a one-color dark tie disappearing into the vee of the top buttons uniting both its sides, him within. Each piece of him seemed connected to every other piece. There was nothing sharp to him, rounded shoulders, rounded eyes with perpetually quizzical curved dark eyebrows above, a rounded beard around a round lower face and a rounded belly, hands full yet delicate. He looked straight at her and said, "Hello, you must be Susan." The tones were soft, already familiar.

David came in from the kitchen, a half-eaten brownie in his hand. "Susan, meet Driscol Sebastian," he said. "If we're going to find out what we're up against, I'm going to need help, and Sebby's the best there is. We've worked together for a long time.

"In his youth," David said, "Sebby was a dual philosophy of religion/physics major at Berkeley." David defined him as the product of an old-fashioned family who believed in faith combined with a probing, analytic mind which led him to question it. "Lucky we went to school at a time when the explosions of ideas, from speculations on the origins of the universe to positing the existence of subatomic particles which could only be derived by inference, not seen, seemed to affirm that at the frontiers of physics it was a kind of faith that drove men's ideas."

Thus Sebby had resolved spirit within mind and pursued further training in physics. David met him at the Institute for Advanced Studies at Princeton. "We were simpatico from Day One," David said, as they had each sensed a sympathetic being whose diverse interests, and soul, would complement the other's. They'd started working together six years ago; the resonance of their interests and approach had kept them collaborating ever since, recognizing they were considered eccentric, eclectic and sometimes brilliant by their colleagues.

David found Sebastian's diverse background combined well with his own vagaries, a sounding board and a prod. Sebastian tested mercilessly, thoroughly, without bias or expectation, and if David was the source of new ideas, Sebastian, "reared them properly, toilet-trained them into respectability to meet the world outside." Sebastian for his part expressed content – as David said, it was his nature to be satisfied with what he had, even as he strove with David for more.

Susan was quickly taken by Sebastian's calm presence. He invited trust and respect, seemed to listen even as he talked, never yielded but was always giving. Like David, he had never been to a single place of her travels, never witnessed the specter of pain and horror that she had learned begrudgingly to live with, acknowledging thereby the impossibility of the instantaneous change she had felt a just world would demand. Yet he seemed to understand those places, and her in those places as well.

"When did you first come to hate them?" he asked.

Nobody had ever asked that before, had thought it or dared it. It was not offensive coming from him, for it was true; the victims became her torturers, she was tormented by them, their presence, their pain, their undiminishable grief became the pins and needles of her anguish, yes, in her love she hated them, how could she not and still return to them alive, come home from them intact. He asked, and she answered.

What a world these two men inhabited, she considered. Here in this dark, cloistered cubbyhole of an apartment, removed from the street below, from worrying about eating or sleeping or war or money, a few cubic feet of the planet's space, two people out of its billions, and she was challenged and driven more here than by all the rest combined; David and Driscol seemed to look over a canvas that stretched beyond her senses. Once, she was sure, that would have meant to infinity, remote and vast, comfortingly distant and without access in this world; now that boundary seemed closer, and she was not so sure.

David was alone in the new apartment, not all the equipment installed or operational, walking from room to room, thinking of the sea gull's final caw in the gray mist, Tyrone's crying beyond his ability to comfort, wondering what he had seen, what it could mean. He read all the reports, several times. He picked up articles and books, tossed them down, surfed online with quick scans of page after page, his mind racing down a hundred alleys only to plunge into reverse out of what were all dead ends. Finally, he went to lie in the bathtub, as he had done since a child, to shut himself away for hours with a slow, steady stream of water to insulate him from outside noise or distractions, to let his thoughts roam undirected when his conscious mind hit a wall. He would rest with a book over his stomach, stretch his legs so that his feet lay flat against the wall above the faucets. His tall frame was particularly compressed in the small tub of the old apartment; lying with his knees bent, staring towards the greenish tiles on the end wall, mottled grouting between them, seven tiles wide and fourteen high, he started to calculate the minimum number of movements it would take, starting in one corner and moving diagonally, bouncing at a right angle whenever hitting an edge, to get back to another corner, and which corner it would be, for a wall X tiles wide by Y tiles high.

As he thought, he flexed one thigh, then the other. Water rippled, to form a pattern of crests and troughs radiating out in fixed interactive positions, like a series of diamonds extending away, capturing his vision. He played with the timing, then rhythmically flexed both thighs at the same time, staring at the pattern for several minutes.

He jumped out of the tub, grabbed a towel but didn't stop to dry himself, dripping on the bathroom floor and leaving a trail of wet footprints with drops surrounding them towards the telephone next to the computers, where he quickly and excitedly made several calls. He had an idea, too strange to express, so that all he could do was call people he knew, locally and in China, and ask them to conduct an experiment. After half an hour, nearly dry, he stepped past clusters of drops outlining the shape of his feet, back into the tub, not noticing until he was immersed that the water was cold, so that he had to run the hot water only to raise its temperature to a comfortable level. He washed and for a second time stepped out; the soapy water drained out until the only pattern left was a slick residue crenulating the bottom of the tub, punctuated by a few more of his hairs.

==

Susan was reading a *National Geographic*, reaching for ideas, watching David as he sat in front of the computer screen. He typed the way he doodled – at times the picture in front of him would be still, reflecting a single key occasionally pressed; then it would explode in a series of rapidly moving numbers and equations, switching back and forth to grids, waving lines, mushrooming entities that began as a lot of points in the middle and then moved outward, sometimes uniformly, sometimes in spikes, occasionally pulsating back and forth. David would almost growl as he pointed at a screen to Sebastian, who sat at his own station on the table at right angles to David, entering single pieces of information into a more slowly evolving set of numbers and shapes. Often David would stop, stare at the terminal, or write something on a yellow pad.

They had set up a couch and chairs and a low table in the other corner of the room, where Susan now sat, tried to read, waited, and thought, about David, but even more about a world that could disappear beneath her; their inability to act, given such urgency, left her nearly frantic. She tossed down the magazine, expressed her fears to David, who left his terminal and sat in the chair next to her.

"Want to know my theory of afterlife?" he asked. She nodded.

"It's that you get the kind of existence after death that you believed in when you were alive." She scrunched her face into a question.

"So people who believe firmly that Heaven or Hell awaits actually get one or the other, or maybe both; posthumous penance is deeply embedded in these equations. Those who believed in nothing, in the Void, get just that, others with their own peculiar versions will find themselves in the places they imagined, or dreaded. So it makes sense not only to believe in life after death but also to decide what you want such an afterlife to be, and to fix it firmly in your mind." He asked what hers would be like.

"I'm not so sure," she said, and laughed, "but there'd be lots of chocolate." She thought a little further. "It wouldn't have anybody hungry in it – I can tell you that. But I can't see hanging out for eternity with a smile on my face, it would have to have challenges, too, wind in your face. Though they'd have to be risks that don't involve other people suffering. So I guess art, self-expression, exploration – yes, I'd want those to be a big part of my next world – not a world where you knew everything there was to know and lived in stasis, but a dynamic world that still had frontiers in it. What about you?"

"I'd like to see a world in which science and logic weren't corrupted by politics and bureaucracy." His jaw clenched.

"We *would* have to wait for another life to see a world like that," Sebastian said. They all laughed.

"It's what I'd want, anyway."

"You've kind of been burned in the physics biz, haven't you?" Susan said.

Sebastian spoke. "Maybe you're just tired of all the grants games, publishing hassles."

"I do get fed up losing games I don't even want to play."

"Because you don't really need to," said Sebastian.

David's head tilted slightly down while his eyes faced up and into hers, as if he could look inward and outward at the same time. "Well, I'm a mathematician, as much as a physicist – I guess because of that I think not so much of the specifics in the next world as the rules that would govern it, the basic precepts and conditions. Establish the structure, and then let come what may."

"So you'll pick some orderly world, all reason, equations, and principles?" Susan asked. "Sounds boring."

David laughed. "No, I like your idea of challenge. I like uncertainty, even chaos, the creativity that comes from it, the delight of surprise – God's greatest gift. Otherwise, what's the point? Anyway, I haven't picked my after-world yet."

"So you think–"

"Plenty of time for that," he said. She smiled in appreciation.

"I once told this theory to a bunch of physicists at a conference in Salt Lake. I think it was on multidimensional strings, or maybe a study of how many blondes could occupy the same town. Anyway, I made the mistake of revealing this belief, and was greeted with shock by all those rational types, each with their own religion; I was the guy who thought he could make up his own life after death – whee. For at least two years after the conference I got flack about it. Of course, it just reinforced my slightly flaky image – great for cocktail parties but not much good for raising grant money, that's for sure."

He stood up, hesitated next to her, took another moment. She leaned into him as if he were about to say more, but he returned to his computer, back to seeking nothing, a growing nothing that had insinuated itself between them in the apartment like the space between two stars that isn't there yet measures the distance.

In the three weeks since they had moved all the equipment into the apartment – just five weeks after Susan first met David – it already seemed to her like a space that had been in existence forever. Its insulation from the outside world added to that sense of permanence. Computers on table tops, overhead lights usually off, no intrusions of light from outside the central windowless room where they had placed all the equipment, and very little in the adjacent rooms where they slept, ate, and washed, the normal essentials reduced to support services for living, thinking, and being in front of computer screens. Piles of materials built up around the room, creating a maze of passageways; manuals and reference materials and notebooks all within quick reach, a composite of data to David and Sebastian, a compendium of longings for Susan, that within those pages all could be made well.

There was a couch in the computer room and beds in each of the two bedrooms. Each person slept in whatever was free at the moment, all three rarely being asleep at the same time. Although Sebby seemed to have a girlfriend or three he would spend time with, his presence lingered like a lotion that soothed long after it had been applied. For David and Sebby it was oblivion to non-essentials; for Susan it was no worse than being back in the field, where dust and dirt and bedding formed a continuum of experience, a crust day and night. Even their smells linked together as they followed each other, a uniform must of mind and body, oddly enhancing their state of extreme awareness.

The way David and Sebby sat in front of the computers reminded Susan of the ease of regulars at a bar, a slight slouch, bodies settled into the stools. Must have been a time when it was a familiar sight, she thought, barely remembering. She would shuttle back and forth to the UN, to Upshaw, insulating David from the bureaucratic requisites he abhorred, gleaning enough from them to keep a flow of satisfactory, or at least placating, reports in motion. David and Sebby communicated with each other through their computer terminals – wires connected every element of the room to every other, hard wired for security and speed, and even then there seemed to be some that led elsewhere. David told her how he used to walk around NYU with headphones whose cable was tucked into his shirt, seemingly connected to his navel, no iPhone in sight, to keep his students guessing. There was little talk, just the white-noise hum of the cooling equipment and the terminals. Material got printed out soundlessly on laser printers, was studied with equal silence; the screens said nothing to Susan, and neither, for a while, did the men.

Chapter Fourteen

Does God choose sides?

"I'm starving," David said.

He swiveled his chair around to look at Susan. She had been napping, lulled by the quiet hum of the hard drives. It was late at night, clocks long abandoned as a measure or a guide. His face, which had been illuminated primarily by the computer screens, reflections of green backgrounds or light-blue grids or pulsating red shapes, still seemed to be glowing – maybe it stemmed from his eyes. They had expanded as if to take in more, and they seemed not focused, as if through the screen he had looked across great distances, so vast they could only be comprehended by looking within. She had met explorers deep in-country whose eyes had that distant focus, seeing things without fear and having nothing to prove to anyone else. But such people, she had found, ruled out any sense of consequences in order to pursue their goals step by step. David was looking at possibilities of profound disquiet, seen primarily through his mind, yet still his eyes looked without fear.

"It's nearly midnight," Sebastian said. They turned to Susan.

"If there's one great reason to be in New York, it's for times like this." Part of her UN manual was all-night take-out places. They worked through the choices as she read from a pizza menu.

"What?" said David, "I figured you for broccoli and cauliflower."

"Not this girl," she laughed. "You go for stronger tastes after months of cornmeal paste." They ended up with sausage, onions, and anchovies. After they ordered, Sebastian went over to some large boxes stacked in the corner of the room.

"I meant to ask you about those, I don't remember that order, is it some of your hand-wrought gadgetry?"

"Variation on the theme," Sebastian said. "Vital enhancement for data flow and resource deployment."

"Say what?"

Sebastian opened a case, pulled out a bottle of wine.

"Wine?" Susan looked at the bottle, amused and surprised.

"Hey, this isn't just 'wine.' It's a Ridge Montebello '94. At the perfect height of its maturity."

"Someone has to be," said David, not surprised at all by the bottle or cases.

"Oh," said Susan.

"You'll see," said Sebastian. "A meal without wine . . ."

"Susan, you should understand . . . tell her about your second master's degree, Sebby. He's got three."

Sebastian rolled his eyes. "Look, I grew up in N'Orleans. Was making gumbo when I was six. It was all about taste, taste, taste.

"So when I went to Berkeley, it was sure drier and sunnier. But bland. Until I discovered wine. Taste, taste, taste. So in between the degrees in nanochemistry and physics, I wrote a thesis on Fluid/Gas Molecular State Exchanges in Wine Decanting."

"You didn't!" said Susan.

"He did," said David.

"How is it you're not married?" Susan asked.

"And give up the life?" David laughed.

"Hey, I came close once."

"What happened?" Susan asked.

"Well, when the aesthete she met turned more intensely to physics, she left. With a French vigneron, as it turns out. Taste, taste, taste."

They were waiting for the pizza, in the state where waiting for food distracts from any other pursuit. Susan said to David, "I got the impression from the way you were looking at your screens . . . I don't want to inject hope, but."

"Let's start with a working hypothesis," David said. "Something we can rebound off, at least, even if it's all wrong and we have to throw it out later. But I think we have some basic sense of what's going on out there, even if it's very, very limited, and doesn't give us an inkling of why. "

Susan flushed. "Thank God you've got something – what is it?"

"Well," he started.

"And remember," she interrupted, "I barely squeaked past History of Science as my science requirement at Radcliffe."

He smiled. "Okay, well, over the past hundred years or so there has been an emergence of the understanding that matter can take two forms – as particles or as waves. Which has led to a profound expansion of our notions of the way the universe works."

"Is that the way we got the A-bomb, energy equals mass times – well, something – squared."

"The speed of light squared, right, it was confirmation of a non-intuitive, startling sensibility: that mass can be converted into energy while the total amount of matter remains the same, just appearing in different forms, particles and waves are fungible, are two sides of the same coin.

"Quantum physics later furthered the explanation and began to quantify, even codify, this strange idea of matter as waves or particles, sometimes one, sometimes the other. It's been phenomenally useful, not just as a better understanding of the universe around us, but in all the speedier, smaller electronics that populate our world now."

"I'll take your word for it."

"Right. On an everyday basis, we don't observe any of these wave/particle transitions. It's always been an obscure area, a few people using vast complicated equipment, those billion-dollar particle accelerators, to create and study incredibly tiny bits of matter and energy that are observable only for extremely short periods. Most people – they can't see it, and they couldn't care less, because our experience of the world is the experience of matter as solid, as particles – the hard, tangible stuff we sit on, eat, wear, and so on."

"You're about to tell me what's going on out there, aren't you?" It was finally happening, so fast now that she didn't notice her excitement was nestled in her fear, like a short pole in a deep hole.

They heard creaks on the staircase, and a knock on the door announcing the pizza had arrived.

Sebastian opened the wine with a pop and poured it into the wine glasses that appeared out of another of his cases, while Susan set plates and David opened the boxes. "Ever notice how they don't quite slice all the way through?" he said, pulling two pieces apart, the cheese running between them, reluctant to let go. "It's some kind of a skill."

Susan had to sniff, sip, and slurp the wine until Sebastian was satisfied she'd fully tasted it. She pronounced it wonderful.

"The best wine I've ever had with pizza," David added, getting a look from Sebastian. They all took deep sips.

"Hey, tell her how you used to make money when you were a kid."

Sebastian shrugged. "Used to sweep up in the music houses. Heard lots of great music, and was able to eat all I want, tasted nearly every gumbo in the Quarter."

"More like whore houses, wasn't it! Talk about tasting."

"No, *mais non,*" Sebastian said. "Well, maybe a strip club here and there."

They all laughed. Susan blushed. David patted her hand. He held onto to it for a moment more, until they had to let go to pull slices. She felt a connection, more than just a pat, was surprised by it, didn't know where it could go. And where it fit in.

"You were about to say what you've found," she said.

He looked at her, ran his hand across his chin, wiping some of the oil from the pizza. "It's the state of matter. In these disappearing areas, the fundamental prevalence of particles over waves no longer exists. Waves have become dominant, leading to discontinuities – as we perceive things – where the interface occurs between that wave dominance and our usual world."

"You mean, the earth is turning into nothing? How can–"

"That's only what it looks like. More precisely, particles in these areas are converting to their wave state."

"But why?"

David stood up. In the dark room only his body was highlighted by the computer screens behind him; his head hovered in the darkness above it, a disembodied voice telling her of a nonmaterial world.

"That's where it gets more speculative. Lots more. One way to think about what's happening requires considering another fundamental tenet of quantum physics, the relationship between the observer and the observed. Basically, these theorems hold that the act of observing has its own effect – that in fact there is no reality until something is observed."

"Is this the answer to the tree falling in the forest question?"

"In a manner of speaking, yes – one can say that the tree is in a quantum state, neither upright nor down, until somebody observes it. What's important, especially in what we're looking at, is the notion that the observer affects what's being observed, fixes it somehow as reality."

"But what has this got to do with those – those areas that vanished out there?" Susan felt like she was swimming in an endless lake, all ripples moving away and disappearing soundlessly, leaving just a vast smooth gray surface surrounding her. She remembered Ambway's voice, shouting above the rain, "He says, 'It's the end of the world.'" She wanted to return to the blank ridge, shake it, hold it, bring it back. She hated it, and her fear of it. David's voice brought her back into the room.

"My lecture on the evolution of physics wasn't just to bring you up to date on the history. We've had decades of a changing set of beliefs inculcated in a growing, if still very small, group of people."

Susan was trying to keep her head above water by supporting it with rationality. It felt like it was floating, trying to separate from her body, disassociate from awareness, producing a light nausea. "If matter is changing over to waves, why isn't it happening everywhere? Wait, why is it happening at all?"

David paused, then continued, holding his hand in front of him. "It may be that for the first time in history, consciousness has entered the picture that conveys our reality – and consciousness is creating its own perceptions. Like a printer for your dreams."

"Perhaps not the first time," said Sebastian.

"Who… who was first?" asked Susan, spinning around at him, startled by his intrusion.

"God," said Sebastian. "God establishing the material particle dominance of the early universe."

"If that's the case," said David slowly, halting for the first time in his examination of what lay before them, "then man is now challenging God. The supremacy of the nature of the universe itself is at stake."

⩶

"Oh my," said Susan, as the terminals behind them silently pushed new images across their screens. "Oh my."

David and Sebastian went back to work. Over the next several days Susan floated in and out of their conversations, listening, reading, trying to keep up with at least the surface level of their explorations. Piles of half-full containers of Chinese food lay on tables and the floor, even the gourmet side of David subsumed by newer tastes, ceasing to care if his double-sautéed pork was spicy enough, or if the sesame chicken was soggy by the time it reached them. But at every meal, at least the ones that started after dark, Sebastian uncorked something he said was spectacular, insisting they maintain standards of civility, although Susan sensed or projected an undercurrent of carpe diem in it. Containers of rice, flat, cheesy, oil-drenched pizza boxes, greasy wrappings of hamburgers and tortillas, the detritus of take-out New York filled the room along with papers and journals, reams of computer paper, textbooks, and technical manuals. It wasn't the *New York Times* on Sundays with lox and bagels, but it was home, a world complete unto itself.

⩶

David and Sebastian were having an excited discussion. Susan looked up from her book. This time she got swept up in it without any explanations.

"Right," said David, "it would explain the emergence of a material universe. Not as a 'Big Bang' from phenomenally dense matter – unbelievably dense, I've always thought – but the simultaneous universal conversion of non-material wave aspects of matter to particles."

"Or through the God consciousness catalyzing the conversion," interjected Sebastian.

"That introduces the precept of a linear development of the cosmos, requiring a God to explain the original formulation of matter in either form out of a real nothing – impossible to prove or disprove."

"But that problem also exists with the puzzle of where did the matter come from to start the Big Bang."

"True, but at least this way we have a more palatable theory of the process of origin, the coalescing of particles out of waves, and then the universe isn't expanding so much as following the lines of the original waves outward. Besides, the math is so elegant. You don't have to go crazy, continually inventing new rules, particles, and effects to explain what happened. Just one 'thwap!' – the soft gook hardens simultaneously and at all points into fudge, and here we are."

"But guys," Susan nearly shouted her way in, "you're describing a continuum, a process; even if there was a cycle, could it revert back like this?"

"On its own? Doubtful. Even if a change has to begin sometime, which we don't know, this is too local, beginning on too gross a level. Something is interfering here."

"Well, that's a hope."

"Maybe," David continued. "What confronts mankind now is its own dissolution into waves. Given what we know about the relationship between what we see and how we see it, it may be that mankind's maintenance of its selves and its world as matter, as tangible particles, can only be sustained by its belief in that perception."

"Then religion itself becomes antimatter, for faith in God is faith in the non-corporeal," said Sebastian.

"If mankind doesn't believe in itself, we could disintegrate, into what we now see as nothing, chaotic; in terms of our own minds – nonexistent."

"Then let's hope God really *is* shaped in our image," said Sebby.

"It is a fascinating phenomenon," said David.

"It's malevolent."

"It's something to be observed, you can't ascribe intent to it, judge it."

"Oh yes I can," Susan said, raising her voice, emphasizing each word. "You haven't seen it, what it's like, the way it draws you in, pulling you, like a pedophile towards a child, wanting to take you away and you can barely resist even if you know it could be somehow the end of you."

"Whoa," David said. 'That's pretty strong. And I did –"

"You've lived in labs among abstractions. If you'd seen what I have, just what people alone can do to each other, then pile this on…"

"What you've done, I can see –"

"How can you be so dispassionate about this, this horror?"

"I have to be, if I'm to understand it, not be overwhelmed by it, let distaste or fear or bias interfere with grasping it in its entirety. If that's even possible."

"Distaste! Surely some part of you has to recognize how horrible, godawful it is."

"It is. That's the essence of it, Susan. It… is. I can no more judge it than the fusion that produces sunlight."

"How about the ant assessing the stomping boot?"

He laughed. Then stopped himself too late as she burst into tears. He reached out to her, but she pulled back, stood up, and walked out the door.

David looked at Sebastian, hoping for support.

"This is more than a theorem, David."

"You too? Look, I was just–"

"We're in a fight. Not a lab. I may need to understand my enemy–"

"But is it an enemy?"

"Hell, if it's trying to make this earth disappear, us, you, me – Susan – then yes. And yes, I have to try to comprehend it, but that doesn't mean I can't hate it."

"You've never hated anything in your whole life, Sebby. And now?"

"What it represents. Listen to her, David. For your own sake, and hers."

"Emotions get in the way of science, you know –"

"Oh hell, drop the Hawking act. Emotions drive science, scientists, as much as anybody. We need that drive, to win. And we have to win, David. We have to."

David took a sip of his wine, but didn't taste it. He looked at the door, still shaking slightly from Susan's slamming it shut.

=

Susan had to get outside, take a walk, anything. The room had begun to haunt her, even before the conversation threw her off. The glow from the terminals an ugly, incomplete light that left corners off a chair, turned walls yellow, corrupted color and shape. She wasn't like David, couldn't look at facts and face them with clear eyes calm. He hadn't looked at bones popping out of skins with no tissue to cover them, at staring faces with no energy left to move anything except the eyes, watching this full-bodied creature striding past them, she wanting not to see more than wanting to see, but looking anyway, on her way to the Head Man's office, the chief, the local bimbo, the stealer, the obstructer, obscenely fat, how better to flaunt your power than to be fat in a world of emaciation? And even that was better than the horrid shrouded nothing of a ridge, which could swallow up the thin and the fat and destroy even the chance of change.

Her leg ached, the way it did sometimes when she was fatigued. It was a wound from three years before, shrapnel from mortar fire. She wasn't supposed to have been on a front line; she had just been sent to monitor the distribution of food from a large warehouse. The food had accumulated for months, held up by the usual debates and red tape, as if trying to distribute it was grounds for a crime. So Susan had waited, and finally all the approvals came, and she went with her team to develop a distribution system to counter the enormous graft that would accompany such a release.

It had been pretty much business as usual until mortar shells started landing, and she was instantly surrounded by troops, dark arms in green uniforms and assorted berets that supposedly distinguished units and functions, friends and foe, minute differences to her, like the ragtag colors friends would use to tell apart the teams in touch football games on the quad, but here they were flinging death in ancient recognition. Engulfed by movement and noise, not supposed to be in harm's way, yet there were lines waiting and cartons piled to ceilings, so her team voted and kept at it, until the shells landed on them and there was a sharp pain in her thigh and lesser ones in her calf. Flames sprung around them, and the soldiers came in and pulled them back, then had to disperse the crowd that still waited with an unyielding silence that cushioned the bedlam of war noise around them. They stayed outside for Mission vehicles to come get them, as Susan watched in frustration as the flames destroyed the warehouse, the flames ate the food, the flames the only well-fed entity in town, while the line dispersed in silence and thin stupid soldiers whooped and made more war noise.

The field operation to remove the metal shards in her leg was less than perfect, and even when the pain finally went and the scars smoothed down she was left with a discomfort that became an ache when she was tired, and at times a slight limp. Still, it wasn't as bad as the memory that came when a whiff, of a fireplace or the acrid smoke of a candle extinguished, brought back being enveloped by noises and uniforms and the shattering silence that preceded the sure knowledge that for reasons none of them understood or cared about, for the whims of leaders far away, that more would starve while wisps of smoke carried away the last hope of sustenance.

She shook herself free of the images, the anger, the dread, and walked over to Fifth Avenue. Her disheveled hair blew past her eyes. She entered Saks, where just inside the door a slim girl with short hair and big eyes done up to look like a waif was offering free sprays of perfume. "Wanna try some, it's real nice," the waif asked.

Yes, said Susan, I wanna try some, she drew in the smell of it, felt even the cooling on her skin where it evaporated, walked up and down the aisles, touching: caressing silk, ruddy wool, yielding cotton, even the grate of polyester welcome to her. She walked up Madison Avenue, stopping in the trendy boutiques and Italian designer shops, trying on flowing dresses and chiffon scarves, wondering if David would like the way she looked in them. She went to a lunch place between Fifth and Madison, ordered a chili burger with onions and cheese and flaked red pepper over it, taste, taste, she wandered out in the warmth of sun on her face, noise and smell God bless it – no, God preserve it, please.

Without being aware of making a decision, she hailed a taxi to go back to the apartment. On its way downtown the cab stopped at the top of the hill on Fifth Avenue in the Seventies. She looked down the long straight street. There were red lights in front of her, and beyond them further down the avenue a sequence of green lights beckoned, like hopes undiminished that remain forever out of reach.

Chapter Fifteen

Some patterns bear repeating.

Sebby had returned from getting some reference materials at Princeton. David was scrunched in front of his terminal, his body poised in a way that told Susan he had found something of deep interest. They were debating what takeout to get when Sal Antifermo showed up at the door, carrying two large pizza boxes and with two bottles of wine tucked into the pockets of his raincoat.

"I've seen what you people are eating, and that's not pizza." They laughed. "This is from John's, the best in the city. They don't do takeout for nobody."

They opened the boxes, put out paper plates on the low table in the middle of the room, while Sal brought out his wine. "I seen what you have around here, time to step up to the real stuff, Italian."

"Hey," Sebby said, "the bottles I've got, from California, they're the best in the world."

"Brunello." Sal laid down one bottle. "Amarone, aged the right way, over twenty years," he said, putting down the other. "Drink these, I will rest my case."

Susan found some clean tumblers, which united Sal and Sebby in looking down at them. "Know what my housewarming gift will be," said Sal. "And what the eff happened with that kid at the beach?"

He opened the wine, poured the Brunello, which Sebby admitted was rich and complex, while not anointing it better than his stock. David walked Sal through his time at the beach, the disappearing gull, poor Tyrone, his sense of wonder and awe.

"What the hell, Doc, thing is for real, huh?

"Sure seems that way."

"Any idea what it's about?"

"Yes," echoed Susan, "any idea? I had a feeling you were getting somewhere."

David went over to his terminal, stretched his hands high up in the air, called them over. "Look at this." He held up several sheets of paper filled with black-and-white patterns. On two of them there was a dark, smooth, triangular line running along the right side of the page, peaking towards the middle and ending at the right top and bottom corners. On the other two, the pattern was a series of tighter, smaller curves running the height of the page, the ones in the center longer, peaking closer to the middle, than the ones at the outside.

"What are they?" she asked, sitting next to him.

"On a bathtub hunch I called several labs to request they each conduct the same experiment – projecting a small particle beam, of electrons, through a single hole and recording the pattern the particles made as they hit a recording plate on the other side. It's a classic quantum physics experiment."

"It was the same experiment in every place?" Susan asked

"Right."

"But," Sal examined the papers, "these patterns are different."

"You got it. These," he held up the two with the single large curve on them, "were performed next to the areas where there were discontinuities. They show the classic bell curve distribution of particles going through a single hole that you'd expect to see."

"How about the others?"

David pursed his lips, took a deep breath. "And these," he held up the other two, "were taken by shooting the beams through the areas exhibiting discontinuity, with the transmitter on one side of the area and the receiving plate on the other. They all exhibit an equally classic pattern you'd expect to get as a diffraction pattern from wave interaction. It's . . ." He paused.

"What is it, David, I don't understand." Susan's voice sounded squeaky even to her ear; David had never looked puzzled before. She thought of him as an abstract engineer, able to look at the universe and understand how it worked, the way mechanical engineers could look at some piece of equipment and do the same. If David couldn't figure out the machinery, then who had built it?

Sebby spoke up. "One of the central mysteries of the quantum world stems from the ability of small particles such as electrons to also behave as waves. If you shoot a stream of larger particles through a single hole – say throwing tennis balls through it – then the particles disperse pretty much as you'd expect on the other side, most of them in the center, falling off uniformly as they move away from the center."

"Like these patterns," Sal said, pointing to the papers showing the single bulge.

"Exactly. Now, if you put that hole down in water, and pushed waves through it, the waves would spread uniformly on the other side and you would see a continuously curved line as the waves went through the hole and continued outward from it, an analogous pattern to the tennis balls going through a single hole."

"The great mystery arises,' David said, "when you cut a second hole on the screen. If we fired our tennis balls through the holes towards a recording screen, each hole would let them through to land on the other side in a pattern that simply added up where they would land for each hole without the other being there – bulges across from each hole, and an overlapping in the middle between the two holes. Got it?"

"Sure, " Susan said. Sal nodded.

"Now, what do you think happens if we fire electrons through two very tiny holes?"

"Electrons are those little guys going in orbits around the center of the atoms, right?"

"Well – sort of, it's the way they used to teach it. But sure, that's the particle we're talking about."

"Don't roll your eyes at me! You've got your professorial tone, I just know this is a trick question. So, I'll give you the Socratic satisfaction of correcting me – I'd guess it would look the same as the tennis balls, since the electrons going through the one hole look like them."

"Reasonable – but, as you suspected, wrong. When we run a two-hole experiment, the pattern of electrons landing is like the pattern of seeing waves going through two holes. Think of two pebbles being thrown and landing next to each other in a pond. You know how the ripples interact: there are some areas where the low part of one wave – the trough – crosses the high part of the other – the crest. Trough and crest cancel each other out, and you see a flat, no-wave surface."

"Got it."

"That's the way our two-hole electron pattern looks. Like two waves."

"So you mean the electrons act like waves?"

"Sometimes."

"Well you just said . . ."

"This is like "Who's on First,"" Sal said.

"I said when we have two holes open, we get a wave diffraction pattern. But remember – when we had only one hole open, we got the spreading pattern of a particle. It seems like the electrons know if we have one or two holes open, and alter their behavior accordingly."

"That's . . . weird."

"Just think about all the zillions of electrons in our universe – and in effect perhaps each one of them knows what all the others are up to."

"That sounds like – well, like God," Sal said.

"God with one hell of a calculator," said Sebby.

"Do you know what this is like?" David asked. She shook her head, her hair brushing his shoulder. "It's like turning on a light bulb and feeling battered by a stream of particles being emitted by it. It's like a waterfall going up instead of down, like a teacup starting to dance. It's, well, it's impossible in the world we know."

"You're scaring me. "

"Facts ordinarily shouldn't scare us, but, yes. If these phenomena cannot exist in the world we know – but they do exist – it means the world we are in has changed – fundamentally, radically."

"How can you tell there's such a change?" Her voice sounded unsteady to her.

"The electrons passing through the vanished areas, going through a single slot, are already acting like waves, with no particle characteristics. And more, they are behaving as if they were interacting with other waves present, not just the one going through one hole – as if they know they're supposed to diffract as waves there under any and all circumstances. This isn't just God playing dice with the universe – what Einstein so vehemently opposed. This is like God has moved us from the craps table to the roulette wheel – it's a completely different game."

They sat in silence for a while, staring at the patterns.

"So when do we take this to Upshaw, the UN team?" Susan finally asked, not really knowing how to think about it, trying to tie it to a familiar pattern."

"You can't do science by committee. You have this tendency to the bureaucratic, that doesn't work when something new arises."

"Hey, Doc, take it easy, we're all just–" Sal started.

"And you have the lone-wolf-I'm-the-hero syndrome, don't you?" Susan said. "What happened to you, that that's your default?"

David and Sebby exchanged glances. "What matters is how to best deal with this, now," David said. "And blaring it to your offices isn't the way."

"Fine," said Susan. She picked up the paper plates, tightly folded them, crusts still on them, and walked to the trash.

"Okay, gotta go," said Sal.

"The wine, it was . . . pretty okay," said Sebby, nodding his head. "Thanks."

"You know what," Sal said, looking around the room at the detritus of take-out life. "Next time, you come to my house, we'll have a real dinner."

Sal left. Sebby said he had a date, and took off. Susan and David cleaned up the boxes and put the glasses in the sink; he washed, she dried. All in silence.

⩦

David finally broke it. "You have a slight limp, don't you? I hadn't noticed it before."

"Yeah, well, it's not on a screen, so . . ."

"Ok, ok," he put up his hands. "How'd you get it?"

They sat down on the couch. She told him, her story, the surprise, the pain, the legacy.

"Wow," he said, at the end. "I've never come close to anything like that."

"But, "she said, "you can close your eyes and envision the cosmos. That's, well, that's really amazing, I can't come close to that."

"They say when two people are the same, one of them is unnecessary," said David.

She moved closer to him. "Well," she said, "here we are." He moved towards her.

She pointed to the papers on his desk. "David, aren't people made up of these electrons?"

"Part of us, sure."

"Then what's to become of us?"

"I don't know. But, if this were to spread, we might wave goodbye to everything we now perceive."

"Soon?"

"How do I know? Sorry. So far, I'd guess not. These areas of discontinuity seem stable, for now. I think the beach one got bigger when it swallowed that seagull, but that may have been my imagination. I'm glad you didn't get to do a close inspection when you were in Africa."

She jerked her head. "You mean . . .?" A chill went through her body, reminding her she had one. It was Ambway who had stopped her; she wasn't sure whether she would have done so on her own. David was next to her.

"I don't know; just be thankful. And whether their growth is linear, or could change radically – I have no idea. What I'd dearly like to do is to figure out if there's a source to them, and, if so, how to trace it."

"But I thought you said it might be God who was changing the rules. Are you going to try to track Him down?"

He shrugged. "Well, that's one hypothesis – I have a few others to work on first. My fear is that I have to find it before we get other sources."

"What do you mean?"

"Remember, I was concerned about all your peers talking to so many of my colleagues about these phenomena. My request to set up this lab away from the folks you've got working on this at the UN."

"Demand, you could say. I kind of thought you were–"

"I wasn't sure it was important until now."

"You are now?"

"Another element of quantum physics is that it's not possible to determine simultaneously both the position and the direction of an electron – the observer interferes with the electron while trying to observe it in such a way that he affects it."

"Is that what they call the Uncertainty Principle?"

"Good. Yes, right. Well, one offshoot of that theory is that perhaps it's the act of observation itself which creates the reality, establishes the fact that is seen, that without the act of observation we can't really say what exists. What we see isn't just what we get – it's also what we've created.

"If that's true, then we've expanded the belief in the possibilities of this tilt towards matter behaving as waves over a larger and larger scale – of belief. It's hard to swallow, but when these formidable intellects your people are talking to start accepting it – and they'll soon see or hear about the same data I've got here – we're creating a wider and wider circle of a different consciousness, and yes, Virginia, maybe faith can move mountains. Actually, it won't move them, it will convert them to waves."

Susan thought of so many UN personnel talking to other scientists. Like her conversation with Mary Quintin. "So what can we do?" she stood up.

"Act as fast as we can." He got up next to her.

"David." Susan looked at him.

"I'm sorry, I'm not trying to alarm you, it's just . . ."

"David."

"What is it?"

"Oh, nothing."

"Don't say nothing unless you mean it." He moved closer to her.

"It's only, if we convert to waves – would we be able to touch?" She was close enough to him that she had to look up into his eyes.

"You mean, like this?" He ran his hand along the line of her jaw, down to the small scar in her chin.

"Yes, that would be one way." The touch shot another chill through her body. It was the first time they had made contact not out of necessity or accident.

He cupped her face in his hands. His voice got lower. "We're now a particle manifestation of matter, maybe we could also be a wave manifestation." He ran his fingers over her hair. "I have no idea. But as particles . . ."

"Yes." She put her hands on his shoulders, felt him like the pull of gravity near a sun, essential, impossible to resist, hot. She paused, on the precipice of irreversible change, one last look and then, she knew, the jump, the biggest she'd ever take.

He looked at her with the thrill of recognition, an altered state, hers and his.

She ran her hands down his arms, he cupped her back with his hands. Close, now, close, each moment, time distended.

Then they kissed, first quickly, their lips finding each others, again, more slowly, but with an urgency born of the intersection of time immemorial and first time possibilities. No space between them, no space to be threatened. They shuffled into the bedroom, not wanting to let go of each other, pulled each other's clothes off, when they could break from kissing, from stroking each other. They had abandoned their last thoughts, of changing worlds and the indifferent power of consciousness. As he entered her, she felt joy, a thrill that connected from her sex to his mind and all points in between, at long last to his heart, and to gratitude, the unspoken thanks when the universe works. And in that fleeting instant between consciousness and ecstasy she thought, knowing he did as well, what a wonder of possibilities the quantum world truly was.

Chapter Sixteen

Nothing like holding a hearing outside of Washington.

It was one of Dan Smathers's favorite things to do. A long way from his boss, he could be the center of attention, run the show, the hub around which all the spokes had to revolve. He could piss them off, and they had to cooperate; he could be gracious and pleasant, so they could comment openly on his charm. It was always a win, and there were often women around, local aides that got a rush being close to someone with the power. When the chance came to hold a hearing in the Grand Canyon on the pressing subject of nudity in the national parks, he jumped at it. The nature of the issue guaranteed a salacious atmosphere with potential; he could take a few days, work on his tan, come back on top of the world.

The impetus for the hearing had been the collectively offended eyes of one of those old-lady preserve-nature trusts, well-heeled and contributors all, who evidently had witnessed more of wild life than they cared to see on a trip down the Canyon, and whose censure was enough to create prompt action. Smathers's Congressman's subcommittee position made him the man to go to, and he was only too happy to accommodate them with an opportunity to vent righteous indignation. Indeed, the Congressman had himself witnessed an outrageous public display just a few months before, on one of those government-business bonding trips. The Congressman was doubly offended that his subsequent and specific admonitions regarding public nudity had been ignored, while the memory of the offenders rankled in his mind – well, at least some of them, for there had been some moments that he could cherish in private. Smathers got the nod to hold the hearing; he was riding high these days and deserved a perk, so he packed his Ralph Lauren plaid bathing suit along with his light khaki suit and headed west.

The hearings were held at the public information lodge at the entrance to the Riverlands National Park area. It was a large brown building filled with exhibits about the rivers and their ecology, including dioramas of a few stuffed mountain goats jumping up a wall surrounded by some marmots looking on in a captured gaze of perpetual wonder, or perhaps amusement. There were Indian petroglyphs with conflicting explanations of their significance and meaning, and slight allusions to the extraordinary level of indigenous trade and activity that once took place in the tourist lands, the movement of goods and people, the insistencies of commerce mixed with the constraints of available tools, thoroughfares and routes now gone, leaving traces only for the rare experienced eye, and no glimmer at all for the rest, silencing the echoes of history in the din of changing worlds. There were cross sections of the strata at various places along the river, pictures of the plants that could be supported there and how they managed to survive, exhortations on the fragile nature of the ecology and the care that needed to be taken with fire, waste, and feces.

There were no pictures of skinny dipping.

The building itself was a demonstration project for solar energy. Over three million dollars had been spent on analyzing solar influx, designing and installing a system of photovoltaic cells that produced electricity that primarily powered the dryers for the laundry at the lodging for park employees. It was considered a successful project, another reason why the building was chosen for the hearing. The employees had rapidly discovered their clothes still dried faster in the hot, dry air, and were routinely rebuked for the panties, T-shirts, and graying shorts hanging outside the building. No laundry appeared the day of the hearing, at which a succession of local officials, state and federal employees, and three perpetually disgruntled townspeople spoke. They all had their chance to talk in tones of sincere outrage, to the Smathers-fish at the head table, happy to connect his Congressman to their pleasure in venting.

At the end of the day they called Bill Robinson, the boatman for the offending trip. And while a boatman could steer down a roiling river of rapids with calm, he could sweat like hell waiting in a puke-green corridor for some tight asshole who couldn't paddle a fat boat across a pond to tell him how to run his river and shit, he had to tell this damned story, which didn't help when they finally called him in. Smathers sat on a raised table in front of the room normally used for nature lectures, and with stern stuffed owls looking down on them he tried to sound like fury as he spoke to Robinson.

"And isn't it true, Mr. Robinson, that you gave the go-ahead to the people on your trip that they could disrobe completely, and in violation of Park orders as well as the recent memorandum from Congressman Luton concerning standards of decorum on public lands, specifically the Grand Canyon waterways?"

"Hell yes, Mr. Smothers." The crowd laughed, until –

"That's Smathers."

"What I said."

That more or less did it. A chance to do some more venting, then get to the river beach. Except Smathers was curious about one thing. "If you did permit this public display of nudity, then why were you and all the members of your trip running down the canyon when you were spotted?"

Robinson squirmed in his seat. "'Cause we was up near the top of Havasu, they's a part of the canyon wall up there, Chief Henry's notch we calls it, only it wasn't there."

People were laughing, good old Bill telling a story, stoned again, to the gills, say anything to keep his license. They hardly heard Smathers saying, "Wasn't there. What do you mean, wasn't there?"

"It was just gone, that's what it was. And when we saw that, we got the all-fired hell out of there, faster'n a Kaibab squirrel duckin' an eagle."

There was still some tittering, but it was hard to keep it up as Smathers grabbed the microphone hard and sounded like he was gasping for air. He declared the hearings over, right then and there. The Parks Department suspended Robinson's license for sixty days, which in the middle of the season effectively meant a year, which is why he ignored it and went right back on the river, avoiding Havasu Canyon, and spread the word to other boatmen to do the same. The rest of the Committee staff and aides worked on their tans before heading back East, where they passed around the story of the naked boatman who must have been really zonked to think saying a part of the canyon walls had disappeared could calm the biddies' righteous wrath.

Smathers, however, was frantic. He brushed out of the meeting, leaving the assistant to the Park supervisor, a young blond, surprised and almost disappointed. He didn't know who to call. He couldn't can't get Hassey or Hawkes involved, they'd gotten what they wanted out of it, wouldn't appreciate him bringing up old news, turning something clean into something messy. He thought of that greasy detective from New York, Antifermo. He could call him, no danger of any repercussions in Washington, just keep it out of the loop. After everything had gone so well, there was nothing more for him to do. He'd unload the story and get back to the safety of Washington as fast as he could.

==

Antifermo got the call, and immediately went by David's apartment to tell him. The first thing that he noticed he just filed away; he was too experienced not to sense a change in the mood between David and Susan, it was like all the edges in the apartment had gotten softer. He looked at Sebby, who smiled at him.

The second thing he saw was a ramrod-straight man in a commercial-flight uniform talking to David. He was introduced to Hank Dawson, and when he understood why Dawson was there, David having tracked him down and Dawson welcoming the chance to talk, Antifermo said, "Wadisdis, like a support group for people who've seen nothing?" The moment they heard about the

Grand Canyon incident, Dawson told them he could arrange to fly them there faster than any other way they could manage, and could also pilot a helicopter to get them in close. Antifermo said it was out of his jurisdiction, so David, Susan, and Dawson followed in the Smathers footsteps.

David had made several Grand Canyon river trips years before, in his wanderings between college and graduate school. He'd hooked up with a crew of mostly Viet vets, who liked his apolitical openness and willingness to do the grunt work. He knew the river, a bit, then, the feel of paddles long gone from his hands, the dull recurring outboard motor sounds washed away by the constant rustle of water. On the plane he'd described to Susan his memories of the area where the incident had been reported, recalling wonderful sensations, both of them still exhilarated by the powerful rush of information flowing between them in the first moments of their intimacy.

Shacks and warehouses were scattered in dusty lots along the river's edge at Leah's Ferry, the starting point for Grand Canyon river trips. Dawson had landed David and Susan on the ridge above the beach area, red sand swirling like dried drops of blood beneath the helicopter blades. VIPs happened, so the sparse group of boatmen and dogs spread along the sand below looked up briefly and then returned to drinking beer and chasing cottontails. A raft of tourists about to embark, already excited about the trip, kept chattering about it, thoughts of movie stars descending confirming that this place was indeed special, until the appearance of three unknowns walking down the trail led them back to their more piquant concerns, of the stories of big water that had attracted them here and now terrified them, in just the right proportions, while husbands reassured their wives in between pissing off the side of the boat, laughing and blaming it on the beer.

David and Susan headed directly to the put-in point for Big Canyon River Trips, the company that hired the boatman who had testified about a disappearing canyon wall. They located Bill Robinson in a warehouse filled with equipment, motors, and food. He was thin, a scraggly beard over his naked chest, wearing ratty jeans with holes and grease spots in equal measure. Susan sat with Dawson on a big gray rubber pontoon, while David asked Bill to tell his story.

Bill Robinson was trying to recapture it, as best he could, and it didn't hurt his storytelling that he'd already toked up for the day, fixing a sputtering motor, mending boat holes with rubber patches, tying spare oars in place, tanned, hyped up, and fit for the part. Hell no, he didn't mind recounting the story, not now, it was like he had immunity! He led them to a quiet spot under a rack of stacked rubber boats and jumped into his tale like the best outdoorsmen, broad and at the point of interest.

Of course, they'd been caught. Scrambling down the side canyon, not a whoop, eerily silent in their nakedness, their intensity, they quickly made it past the ponds and rocks, down the stream and on to the ledge that ended in the big river where their boats were tied up. The nearby rapids drummed out any noise anyway, so since they would not have been heard had they been hooting and hollering, their silence went unnoticed by the people on the other trip that had parked across the river, already piqued that their anticipated lunch spot was taken, and how the ladies and gents of the Board of Directors of the Preserve the Wildlife Fund were put to the test, for the type of wildlife they saw running at full tilt towards them across the river apparently did not deserve preservation, in the eyes of the biddies munching their tuna fish and salami sandwiches and the lemonade whose pucker was lost in the pursed lips and tight jaws that accompanied the surreptitious glares across the way, never mind that those... bodies had put their clothes on as fast as they could, in the face of propriety felt no doubt even across the river, and had cast off and gotten out of there with astonishing rapidity and purpose, thinking – wrongly, the biddies vowed – that in doing so they could avoid the inevitable consequences for their actions, and the Fund's boatman knew just who it was, and while reluctant to say, also knew that his tip didn't come until the end of the trip, for services rendered, and each member of the Board had his or her own means of working the moral channels when they got back, a plan that did not diminish as they cast off down the river, several more days till they could get off, the Canyon walls acting like a funnel concentrating their festering fury.

The turkeys went their own ways, but the boatman could be found, and it didn't take long for the collective might of the Board of Directors of the Preserve the Wildlife Fund to get its story heard, and pressed through the Congressional Committee with National Parks and Preservation oversight, leading to the dork who flew out and held public hearings on Park conduct and ethics. And that left Bill with a suspended license, a series of serious headaches, and a memory he'd just as soon forget. So no, Bill Robinson said to them, he didn't really care to join them in any flight over to Havasu Canyon, there wasn't enough rum and dope to excuse that excursion. No way.

She lay in a space that was less than a space. She thought, or dreamed – it didn't matter, there was no matter. She had memories, there were places. She knew how to do certain things. She had learned on nearby little bits and pieces, first those she could see by looking at, then those she could see by the remembering, then the thinking or the dreaming. The wanting had power, like breath on coals buried under ashes, an incessant stroke that finally found the dormant heat, a constant, insistent trigger, a way to touch. At last. She lay in a space that transcended the space, and more and more the seeing was touching. She wondered if there was an end to it.

There was more now, she could tell who was approaching her extensions, the knowledge whetted her appetite, she could be more discriminating, not every course the same. And the recognition bred other hungers; like the girl, she'd come close before, almost, almost. And the bright boy at the beach. They were drawing nearer, and now she knew…

Insider, outsider, once there was such a gulf, she couldn't reach out, she wanted to, they looked at her, but no one breached the distance, no one could, and she stood stuck in her space, a tiny space then, no bigger than herself. Inside her, outside her, there was once a void between. But not now, she'd found a way, the crashing tumbling need she poured into her looking, what was within was without, no difference. You could have heard her laughing, if there was anything around to carry the sound.

By following the river, they couldn't miss Havasu Canyon, Bill Robinson told them. Its characteristics were distinct, and David would probably remember. David and Susan piled back into the helicopter with Dawson, David in front and Susan in the back, and they took off.

From above, the muddy waters of the Colorado moved with deceptive speed. Boatman were constantly warning the turkeys not to go swimming where the river looked tranquil, David said, and nearly as constantly having to pull people out, often way downstream and exhausted, who ignored their warnings. Every year some drowned. Through the rapids white water roiled over the brown base of the river, great rocks jutted into the air, and the water sprayed up in gushing, powerful fountains. It was only beautiful, and as the helicopter wound through the canyons following the curves the river had carved in its centuries of wandering, they were virtually hypnotized by the scene below.

More varied than the river itself were its sides, from steep red gorges to broad, rocky flats, canyon walls rising in steps that ranged from a few feet to a few thousand at a single sweep. Bordering the river were side cuts, canyons in which tributaries, many now dry, fed the great central Colorado in its unyielding southern journey. Waterfalls dotted the side canyons, built like people, some short and powerful, others long and slender, erupting out of rocks or nearly blending in with paths of vegetation. Bighorn sheep sprang from one seemingly impossible position to the next, roaming the canyon walls at will.

They got to Havasu in late afternoon. The side canyon was unmistakable, a sharp, gray-stoned gorge with narrow jade and aquamarine pools running up the notch and finally opening up into a broad expanse of shallow water rushing over low rocks and down little esplanades. "There," shouted David. There, unbelievably but unmistakably, was a vague inchoate curtain where red walls should have lined the canyon.

"Christ," said Dawson. "I knew it. Like the clouds. What the hell!"

Dawson waltzed the chopper up the cut like a mountain goat of the air, springing from a series of relatively stationary positions, gradually approaching the emptiness. They hovered around eighty feet above ground level. The sides of the vanished section were easily discernible, a fuzzy outlined notch amidst the red walls of the canyon. From the air, the top of the space was harder to define. David urged Dawson to move the chopper in for a closer and closer look. They slowly got within two hundred feet.

All of a sudden the chopper's nose dipped forward sharply, so unexpectedly that David, who was sitting next to Dawson, was thrown against the glass front while Susan was slammed into the back of Dawson's seat. The chopper jumped fifty feet closer.

"Whoa, what's going on?" David spoke through his headset.

"We're being pulled forward, I don't know. Hang on." Dawson pulled hard on the chopper's guidance stick. The chopper's nose came back up, then down again. The navigational instruments were spinning as if there were no up or down, no left or right for them, nothing level and smooth.

"It's almost like a vacuum effect," Dawson shouted.

"Or a strong gravitational well," David said, almost to himself.

Dawson had gotten the nose to point high, but the helicopter was being pulled forward. He pulled the stick back and to the left, then right, but couldn't establish a line of motion across the path they were on. The distance between them and the space closed, one thirty, one twenty-five, one fifteen.

"You better do something damn quick," Susan shouted. Her shoulder felt like a mule had kicked it. From the middle of the chopper, the space filled the windscreen. She had a feeling, similar to the pull she had felt in Africa, and also to something else, more personal, a seeking, but she couldn't place it, make the connection.

"God, it's like before, only stronger." She shuddered.

David pictured the sea gull at Jones Beach. He turned to Dawson.

"Reverse the stick."

"What?" Dawson was fighting, yanking the stick back, his arms feeling the strain. The chopper was bucking underneath them, as if two hands were wrenching it in opposite directions.

"Push it forward," David repeated.

Pushing the stick forward was not what Dawson's instincts told him. The best pilot in the fleet didn't send a chopper smashing into the ground, or for that matter directly into a massive forward tug.

"We'll use its pull like a slingshot, like a return from the moon." David explained.

"Will that work?" Susan shouted in their ears.

David looked back at her. He brought his arm around the seat, held his hand next to her cheek. "I think so," he said, "but I can't be sure. It's better than our current state, don't you think?"

Eighty-five feet away, a dank, tinted non-space sat like fate. The chopper was sixty feet off the ground, and bucking under Dawson's efforts to turn it.

"Okay, I'm convinced," he yelled. "I can't hold this much longer, and it's not working anyway. What do I do?"

"Jam the stick forward, then as you pick up speed pull back and sharply left. Wait as long as you can." David sounded like he was explaining a problem in class. Susan watched in silence.

The Rock of the Skies said quietly, "What the hell," and pushed forward on the stick as hard as he could. The chopper plummeted ahead and down. It looked like a contest as to what they would hit first, the ground or the wavespace discontinuity; they were aimed at where the two met. The sudden acceleration lifted them up in their seats, Susan nearly blacking out from the pain as her shoulder hit the side, but determined to see it through.

In the space of seventy feet the chopper had accelerated at several times its normal rate. David said "Now," not shouting but not low-keyed, and Dawson pulled the stick back and left, to the closer edge. The chopper pivoted and rose like a cannon shot. A shudder ran through the cabin as they passed within a few feet of the upper edge of the area, then continued straight forward. The chopper was above its maximum speed, still bucking; within seconds they were a thousand feet away, and Dawson slowed it down and started turning it, so that they were moving backwards away from the space.

The three of them whooped into their head sets. Susan leaned forward and gave David a kiss, while Dawson reached over and pounded his shoulder.

"I was always curious about that effect when I read about it in astrophysics," David said, smiling. "I never thought I'd get a chance to experience it. But the only way to create that pull must be that the wave space can vary in density. It really is amazing."

"You and your 'its so amazing,'" Susan said, pounding him on the back, still exhilarated from their escape.

"Bring on the black holes, right, David," Dawson said. They all smiled and whooped again.

Susan pointed forward. "Guys, look. Look at that."

They turned their attention back to the wavespace. It looked darker, somehow angrier, and as they watched the red canyon walls next to it started disappearing, as if a giant claw on a huge bulldozer had cut them out, vanishing without a rock left behind. The space tripled in width, a whole stretch of canyon wall was no longer there, replaced by the same sick-hued emptiness, as if the anger was simply in their beholding.

They watched in a silence all the more stark for its contrast to the joyous sounds that had filled the cabin a few seconds before. Susan thought, at its new size they would not have escaped.

Dawson instinctively backed them away, further, insurance distance, routine. Susan took David's hand and squeezed it. The space had stabilized, its new size now a grotesque mockery of the splendid canyon walls and rushing waters around it, for there was no variation in it, no texture, no nuance, only the callous indifference of uniformity; nothing was not subtle.

The chopper felt like a bruised fighter to Dawson's hands, game but battered nearly to a knockout. Susan's shoulder felt similar. Dawson, exhausted, pulled them up, out of the shadows surrounding the canyon, up to where the sun glinted off the helicopter's swirling blades, where the horizon was no longer defined by the canyon walls, towards what remained of the comforts of home.

Chapter Seventeen

Susan felt like a planet caught between the pull of two stars.

Upshaw called an all-hands meeting at the UN, not just his people but pulling from every department. Susan sat in the front towards the side, in a mini-amphitheater that mimicked the layout of the General Assembly, as if to remind the people in it as to there location in the way of the world.

She watched as all the faces screwed up in confusion when Harold mentioned they were facing something urgent – heard that before – requiring immediate action. This was the Scientific Mission of the United Nations, an organization that was still trying to find a mechanism to determine if global climate change was real, given the mandate that no finding could have an implied negative economic impact on any member. Urgent was a once-pungent spice whose over-use had numbed the palates in these halls; imbued by David's perspectives, she now was fidgeting to get away.

It was only when Harold mentioned that funding was involved, to establish a Cross Department Priority Effort, that the faces unrolled into clarity, pens up and notes taken. It was one thing to talk about the survival of the world, which pretty much ran on its own regardless; it was another to talk about survival of the organization. Funding was a clear imperative, whatever it was connected to.

But when Harold said that the people in the room were getting packets of information, to make contact at every university, research institute, and scientific journal they could find, to explain the situation and recruit where appropriate to help them study it,

Susan began to squirm, trying to catch Harold's attention to make him stop, too late.

At the end, when all three hundred twenty-six acolytes had filed out, and Harold stood still at the lectern, Susan went up to him.

"Harold–"

"I know, I know," he held up his hands. "But I can't just hand in a report a page long every week or two about one guy, it's too flimsy. The SG wouldn't hear of it. We mobilize, involve, get as many of the best minds as we can, build hypotheses and consensus, serve process, it's what we do here."

"But if there's a real danger–"

"Altaforce's theory of consciousness affecting the world? It's too far-fetched to base policy on, make decisions around. We have a massive international operation going, that's the best way to yield results."

"Or generate reports."

"Susan, please, I've been there too."

"I hope you're right." Susan saw how tired Upshaw looked. He just stood for a moment.

"I wonder," he said, "what Andy and Eileen are up to, in their Brooklyn brownstones. Even Marge. I always treated time as an endless commodity, I could dip back in and recover all those lost moments. Now... You look pretty happy, at least."

She smiled. "I've met a good man, Harold. It turns the future into a comfort zone."

"I'm glad for you." He pulled switches under the lectern, dimming the lights in the room until all that remained was the dim reddish illumination of the exit signs.

==

Susan returned to David and the work in the cloistered atmosphere of the apartment. They had been stunned and motivated by the view from the Canyon up into an emptiness that couldn't exist but was a presence nonetheless. She told him about Upshaw's speech, the other forces at play in the UN, with its problem-solving-by-committee approach to the disappearances.

"I'm not surprised," David said. "It's the usual. Call everybody up; don't discriminate. Better way to cover your ass."

"Upshaw's not like that, but he–"

"It's okay, he's stuck."

"He's tired, David, I could see it, for the first time. He used the best way he knew to motivate them. Funding!"

"Get that grant dollar, even if it's the last! He does know his audience."

Susan ferried back and forth between the buildings, glowing with many excitements. She used her relationship with Upshaw to maintain contact with the activities of the multitudes of scientists either transplanted into the UN or in direct contact and under the direct control of the UN team. Intellectually, Upshaw recognized that diverse approaches might be the best means towards finding a solution, as uncomfortable as he had become over the years with uncontrolled pieces of his puzzles. He was also under great pressure: the work had actually cost as much as the total budget, further appropriations were required, no slices of the prospective pie had gone to anyone else's table – and he had convinced the Secretary General that the problem they faced was very, very serious, which only led to further requests for progress reports, and demands that progress itself be made. He had to find some way to take the heat off.

Susan came into the apartment and approached David with a mix of excitement and trepidation.

"David, Upshaw's picked someone to head up the UN Special Investigating Committee. He'd like us all over there for the announcement."

She wasn't sure how he would take it, afraid he might be disappointed. That wasn't his style, she was sure. He ended up troubled, but for other reasons

"Who?" He was sitting on the floor with his back against the couch, going through papers, didn't even raise his head. "Not me, obviously, just as well, but who is it – it would be nice if it's someone we can work with."

"I don't know, someone big, is all he'd say."

"Look, you go, you know how I feel about being involved with all that. Just a distraction, let them put someone up on a big screen, doesn't solve a thing."

"He'd really like everybody there, asked specifically." She paused, thinking him through. "He's pretty good to you." She waved her arm around the room, all the equipment. "Just this once."

Upshaw walked to the front of the stage. Susan laughed; indeed his image was projected on a big screen behind him, like it was a new Apple product announcement.

"So many people, I hadn't realized," David whispered to her. The room was packed with hundreds of scientists, physicists classical, electromagnetic, particle, theoretical, and solid state, programmers, mathematicians, geologists, astrophysicists, engineers mechanical, electrical, and quantum, molecular biologists, chemists organic, inorganic, and analytical, acoustical engineers, cosmologists, nano technologists, computer and knowledge experts. They could launch a thousand ships of any sort from here, Susan thought, across the known universe. But could they traverse the unknown, she wondered, looking at David squirming behind her. "Look, the astrology section," he whispered to her. She poked him with her elbow.

People were waving to David, she noticed. Colleagues and professors from Princeton, Berkeley, MIT, Caltech, Beijing, Stanford, Cambridge, Chicago, Tokyo, Sorbonne, Michigan, Oxford, Wisconsin, Columbia, Zurich, and Harvard. He looked shy as he waved back. Susan turned to Sebby on her other side. "He's helped most of them solving frontier problems," he said. An assembly of the greatest minds on the planet, now each just a chair in an auditorium.

"... and I'm pleased, proud, very excited to introduce you to the first head of the United Nations Special Committee for Maintaining Earth ..."

Susan had never seen Upshaw so flushed. A man walked onto the stage from the side, a large man, with droopy jowls, like a sagging LBJ, large heavy earlobes, a rolling gait like he'd just gotten off a horse and owned the ranch as far as the eye could see. A buzz went through the room, he nodded his head, not a smile, waved, his hands large, with big pudgy fingers that seemed barely to fit together. Upshaw beamed, applause broke out.

"Oh, Christ," said David. Sebby put his head in his hands, unable to look.

Susan was torn between looking at the stage and at David. "What?" she said.

"... proud to introduce Nobel Laureate, Distinguished Scientist, Knight OBE, awarded the Royal Society Copley Medal and the winner of the Fundamental Physics Prize, well, you all know of Anthony laDoop," and a larger round of applause broke out. David sat on his hands.

The meeting ended after an exhortation from laDoop. It was interminable to Susan, who wanted to ask David what was the matter, but he was surrounded by colleagues as they made their way out, shuttled to a reception line in the adjacent ballroom. David and Sebby were trying to get sideways to the main flow, but there wasn't room, and then they were in front of Upshaw.

"Ah, David, our resident maverick. Let me introduce you to –"

"So, Tony." David said.

"So, David." laDoop looked at him with squinting eyes.

"Still sucking up other people's ideas and calling them your own?" David said.

Susan gasped. Upshaw looked like he'd been stabbed.

"Still doing psychic physics in other dimensions?" laDoop said.

Upshaw shot Susan a look. She grabbed David by the arm, murmured "We have to get going nice to meet you," in the direction of laDoop, and pushed David through the crowd to the outside hallway.

"What was that about?" she asked, feeling breathless.

"That? Oh, nothing." David said.

"That wasn't nothing."

The three of them left the building, away from the UN campus, back into the bright, noisy city streets. She led them to a Starbucks, waited on line, David and Sebby ordered teas, she got a double macchiato which she wished she could spike, sat down amidst a sea of young people staring intently at their computers as if the world depended on it.

"So," she said, after they'd sat in silence for a while, sipping. David and Sebby were engrossed with their cups. "Look, I can't say I'd ever really heard of this guy – but then I'd never heard of any physicists other than Einstein until I met you."

"What good company I keep." David's normally easygoing expression was now pinched lips and tight eyes. "It figures," he finally said.

"I gather you know him."

"Tony 'Big Bang' laDoop." He rubbed his eyes. Sebastian groaned.

"David, what is going on? Why do you call him 'Big Bang?' I know you're hot stuff – but I didn't think all physicists were."

He clanged his spoon on the table. "This particular big bang has to do with the origin of the universe."

"Okay I would have guessed that next. What's the problem?"

He looked at Sebastian and put his lips in a grin that his face didn't match. "Twenty-five years ago laDoop did some work on super-dense matter, which he parlayed into a Nobel Prize five years ago by connecting it to the period of time just after the Big Bang that supposedly is the beginning of the universe."

"Wow, a Nobel Prize. You don't sound . . . respectful."

"Umm. After his selection but before the award was officially announced I put out a small thought piece on considering a four-dimensional interpretation of that period. It indicated that since time wasn't yet in existence, as least as we know it, it allowed for a transitionary fourth dimension that explained the coalescing and dispersion of matter, as well as chaotic perturbations in the dimension that explained the non-random distribution of matter in the universe. The math was clearer and better than Big Bang's, I feel safe to say – " Sebastian nodded " – and there was a flap about whether he should get the award. He'd been around a long time, and the intimation was that the Prize was sort of like one of those honorary Academy Awards that they give out to the stars that never received a regular one, like Cary Grant. So he got the Prize, but he was plenty pissed at me, and he has spent a lot of time justifying his position – getting deeper off the track, in my opinion – while knocking me at every opportunity."

She leaned forward. "Gee, it sounds to me like you deserve the Prize."

"Oh, no, you get that for more than a thought puzzle. I think that's beyond me, I'm afraid." He looked across the small table at her, and the rest of the computer geeks in the room didn't exist. He poured some honey in his tea, finished it, and continued. "Most of those guys do that really intense transcendental work when they're quite young, all that energy from sublimating and channeling their sex drive." He pointed around the café room. "I took those years off."

"– and didn't sublimate a bit, I'll bet."

"No complaints, I guess. When I came back I brought, I hope, a broader perspective, but not that intense abandonment. Maybe developing a taste for wine is inconsistent with living in the fringes of your mind." He nodded towards Sebastian. "Anyway, laDoop got the Prize, and because of the dispute – ours is really a small community – it was generally assumed that I was a flaky newcomer whose time had passed before it ever arrived. I got shunted off – no big grants, big guest-lecture fees, and so on. laDoop carries a lot of weight in this neck of the woods. Maybe it was for the best – I've had to be awfully resourceful, and have a number of good people who know my work and will talk to me any day of the week – so long as they don't have to admit it."

She reached over and laid her hand on his arm. "Well, I don't think it's fair, no matter what you say. This is too important to let those kinds of things get in the way."

He took her hand in his. "Hell, Susan, and kids dying isn't? Nothing on this globe is too important to keep politics and personality and institutions and conventions from getting in the way – you know that. We're changing the global soup that created us into a hash that could consume us, and it's still business as usual, the last two people left will go out rounding up votes for who will be class president. Besides, I was never the guy who won top of the class, you know, grades plus service plus all the intangibles that gave the selection committees the chance to pick whomever they wanted. My handwriting was lousy, I got bad marks for conduct and effort. No regrets, Susan, not now, not ever."

They put down their cups and walked back onto the street, jostled by the crowds, assaulted by the grit and noise, blinking in the harsh sunlight, relishing every bit of it.

Two

Fractal Shores

Chapter Eighteen

The Altaforce Odyssey.

That was what they called it, he told Susan, after he showed up at Princeton one fall to take advantage of the open invitation he had been given from the physics department three years before. A professor who had been part of the committee that gave the invitation, upon learning of his arrival, had greeted him with, "So, Mr. Altaforce, I see you have returned from your Odyssey. Pray, what bounty have you brought?" David had smiled, opened his hands, and formed them into saucers. "Some more pieces of the world, professor, for our enlightenment," then raised his hands in turn, blew a puff of air into each, opened the hands wide in front of him, said, "Easy come, easy go," and enrolled.

For a while he had lived on a Buddhist retreat in Colorado. It was both totally new and sheltered at the same time, generously supportive of his search, for despite his enthusiasm he was unskilled in living outside of his old milieu of colleges and scholarships; he needed a new vocabulary before he could ask questions of, let alone understand, a world he could only intuit he was seeking, one that had come through on television screens and through music, movies, and newspapers, strange apparitions on the streets, hair and garb like nothing he had ever encountered.

He tended the community garden. For the first time in years, the Institute had to buy vegetables. He was apologetic, offered to pay. Instead, at their suggestion, he stayed through a second growing season, and contributed the money he raised from selling the excess vegetables he grew from the same plot of land. When he had

had to go shopping because of his crop failure he would be sent out to get lettuce and come back with cabbage. He cooked. He spent hours learning about the chemical dynamics of cooking, only to produce a cloyingly sweet stew and flat, dry, lace-like cookies with little humps of raisins rising up: he mistook the flour for the sugar. It was the first time in the history of a Buddhist institute that they sent out for pizza. The monks loved him, even as they were grateful when he left. Seldom had the teacher's precept of acceptance been so tested by a novice, for which they thanked him. He laughed halfway down the mountain, whereupon he bought a banged-up dark-blue '53 Ford pickup, a tape deck and tapes, and a black-and-chestnut mutt who answered to the name Chico, and headed off to Mexico.

The old engine was strong enough to withstand his frequent attempts to fix it, and besides, he had a ball everywhere it broke down, a quasi-random event generator to set his itinerary. Several weeks in the forests, contact with small villages where joy and beauty were a part of everyday life, peyote that immobilized him for days in wide-eyed wonder, a sultry beach and a French diplomat's wife, hands raised at midday atop the Pyramid of the Sun, a thankless time in a whorehouse that doubled as a rectory somewhere in the Yucatan near the southern borders, endless stoned hours on beaches, and he was lured with the siren's call to California. As he drove through it he often muttered to himself, "Of course, of course," much like a physicist finally observing a particle whose existence was previously only deduced through mathematics, a thing that had to exist, and then did, the confluence of his needs and the nature of the environment so perfectly matched. He gravitated quickly, though, from the glitzy madness of Venice and L.A. through the surfing beaches and easy pickups along the way, some who just lay there and some who devoured him in glee, with him happily if unsuccessfully trying to predict their behavior in advance, to end up, as if ordained by the natural order, in Berkeley.

His Berkeley was endlessly exhilarating, where he integrated the monk's teaching of living without judgment with his existential quest to exult in experience itself. He participated with activists and wrestled with whether process and style were as important as, or even distinguishable from, substance and cause. He took courses in economics and philosophy, lived first two blocks from the hubbub of Telegraph Avenue with a disenchanted law student with whom he hiked and climbed and skied until she decided to make Law Review and he was deemed extracurricular and too frivolous; then in the Hills above town with a modern dance major – another newfound creature – spending his days playing tennis, drinking mai tais and modifying the latest space games at the University's computer center, writing multiply interconnected versions in which the aliens almost always won, much to the distress of the center's young visitors – games so complex and demanding of computer memory that they finally banned him from access to their systems.

Oh, California! Sensitivity training to heighten his awareness of how others reacted to him; immersion experiences, wherein he was first surrounded by other people, flesh of the flesh, and then left in some gelatinous mass approximating his body temperature, to get in touch with his true self, always emerging with a big grin and ideas of things to do; people to read his handwriting, massage his feet, press Mazola between their chests, people solely into the music, the war, the waves; tripping in mountain shacks where he saw more colors than he had dreamed of when he was analyzing light by looking through prisms and spectroscopes, affirming that the mind was greater still than the tools, never a really bad trip for David, for he lacked fear and indeed had learned acceptance. He took some math courses, first to see how he would react, then with an intensity he had not previously experienced, especially when the math was connected to physics and oriented towards analysis of worldly situations, applied pure mathematics, they allowed him to call it. It was the end of the circle. Tan, perpetually smiling, lean, much loved, he headed east, to Princeton, now years behind his former classmates, no breakthrough at twenty-six, a different dreamer, he returned to the studies he had rejected. He had succumbed to indulgence, and found in it discipline; searched for his self, and discovered the world.

David hadn't talked about his early days for many years, but the passage of time and now Susan's vibrant interest, the exchanges on all levels flying back and forth between them, gave him a different sense of his life than he had before, like rereading a book after years and experience give a changed perspective. Life was, he mused, an extraordinary source of data. One could take the facts of one's life and give them a thousand different interpretations, complementary and contradictory, each somehow containing a kernel of truth. And that for just one life, out of billions. Makes relativity look easy – at least all the quadrillions of particles and movements were governed by some common rules that provided for understanding across time and space.

There must be a pattern to these events, something to link them together, he thought. And why these particular places? So far the areas, now under continuous observation, had changed little, occasionally growing slightly, sometimes retuning to their previous normal state. It would have been easy, lying in a lover's arms, to be lulled into a sense of "that was all," we can live with this, it's even kind of pretty, turn it into a tourist attraction, like the haunted house where the balls roll uphill, do a Disney special, invite it on the Jimmy Fallon show. How fragile the world would be then, he thought, a world susceptible to dissolving at any moment. He thought of wind in his face, of driving a car, he smiled and thought of being held by someone, intimate touching, aroused, sweat, handball, bare arms, a sailboat capsizing, laughter. I like this, he thought, not all the time or in all ways, but I like it, I have friends, people who care, I care. I care. It was that thought that led him back to the terminals, reluctantly leaving Susan's side.

The areas defied definition. He first applied variations of catastrophe theory, math that worked with discontinuous events, sharp breaks from a regular pattern that had been useful in describing epidemic outbursts, major earthquakes, microelectronic equipment failure, with the hope of being able to predict such events. He built paradigm equations simulating as best he could the conditions occurring within the phenomenon, then attempted to work backwards to see if he could establish a set of conditions that would yield the result. Even by bending lots of physical laws and precepts he couldn't replicate the final conditions.

He worked with topological shapes as variations on the disaster theory, but couldn't produce anything that injected the energy to create or sustain a wave phase-out of matter at the surface of the discontinuity. The attempt did make him realize that among the things he didn't understand, he didn't have the faintest idea of the kind of energy that was involved, and absolutely no sense of how it might be transmitted.

Day and night he and Sebastian searched for new ways to approach the puzzle. He called friends, enemies, strangers, hours of continuous conversations on the telephone, with no introductions and no goodbyes, entering on a thought and leaving on a question, seeking any ideas, any new, untested theories, hunches, hopes. The phase-outs grew a bit, retreated, taunted, threatened.

Sebastian led the way to the first breakthrough. He had put the test condition equations into his computer, his fine hands seeming to paint on the keyboard, never hitting a wrong button or making an extraneous stroke, and was idly playing with them. He was looking for irregularities, to magnify or pinpoint them, some handle with which to grab hold of the larger piece. He couldn't find any. The definitions were unyielding to a probe breaking them apart. He described the behavior to David. Midway through the explanation, David stood up and started pacing amidst the clutter of the room, almost hopping over piles of periodicals, mountains of memos.

"Christ, man, I can't believe I've overlooked this," he burst out. "Think – what types of entities exhibit these characteristics – replication across scale, random within certain boundaries – mountain edges, clouds, sea shores – classic. What a dummy."

Sebastian looked at him blankly for a moment, then his round face lit up, the curve of his smile parallel to the contours of his jaw. "Of course. Fractals."

"Right. Fractals. All the areas affected are characteristic fractals. But why?"

Neither of them had any idea. They talked in bursts, between staring at their screens, as if they could coax an answer from the terminals. They quickly decided they wanted access to the more powerful on-site computers laDoop had running at the UN. They woke Susan up. She was sleeping in one of the adjacent bedrooms – to her amazement, she actually enjoyed the dark, quiet space and the hum of the machinery next door. The charm of her apartment had long ago worn thin; now it seemed a mockery of an outside world run amok. Here she found greater insulation from that fear, buttressed by trying to do something about it. She had brought a number of the tribal prints she had collected, strong designs of oranges, blacks, and browns she draped around the room and on the beds, their symmetries congruent with the patterns on the screens next door, repetitions in different media as she moved within the apartment.

David and Sebby raced around the small room, as if trying to break through its walls, explaining their need to her. She found their enthusiasm infectious. So this is what it's like at the frontier, aroused again by David in this new state. She was also, however, an experienced field operative, and she did not act hastily when confused.

"Right – what's a fractal?" she was finally able to inject into their back and forth statements. "C'mon guys, how can I ask Big Bang for something I don't understand myself?"

David sat at the end of her bed, balling up a piece of the print covering it, stroking her calf, while Sebastian walked around the room, explaining, "Fractals are a relatively new branch of mathematics. They describe conditions or phenomena that are similar across different scales, that occur on a small scale and replicate in similar form on a bigger one. Like if you ran a little stream of water through clay for a while, you'd get a tiny version of the Grand Canyon – shape, form, patterns. Yes, like sea shores and clouds. In each of them, the shapes along a given scale occur in the same ratio as they would on a larger or smaller scale, as you vary the length of the measurement tool. If you look at a coastline from a passing airplane, with that perspective, or instead are standing over it, with the correspondingly smaller ruler of your height to measure the variations, you would essentially see the same form of line – inlets and channels, curves and reversals. It would only be your knowledge of where you stood that gave you a sense of the size of what you were looking at. You could divide a fractal shape up and each piece would mirror the whole, like a small broccoli floret reflecting the whole head of broccoli.

"By plugging in fractal equations the Hollywood animation jocks get those amazing clouds for movies," David added.

"So what's the meaning of these areas being like fractals?"

"We don't know yet. But it's the first link we've found," said David.

It was a lot to be hit with just waking up. "What do you want laDoop to do? I thought you couldn't stand him."

"He's not creative – but he is a bulldog. Get him to start running correlation analyses on these areas with various fractal equations. See if he can link any of the areas to specific references in the literature. Also, check if the four areas are exhibiting the equivalent fractal behavior as waves as they do as particles. I don't know what that means, but maybe he can come up with something. It'll certainly tie his tubes for a while and keep him from bothering us."

"You're such a sweet bastard." She shoved them out of the room and dressed, putting on loose fitting green linen pants and a beige linen blouse, kissed him goodbye, and walked over to the UN, leaving two men, a quiet dark room, and a pile full of humming electronic equipment. The bright hot day, crowded streets, and smelly traffic seemed peaceful in comparison.

laDoop agreed to meet with David, with considerable prompting from Upshaw. Sebby tried to mediate, but it was an uneasy alliance that fell apart at the first stress, data that fueled some of Altaforce's ideas that laDoop found anathema.

They were in one of the high-floor conference rooms at the UN, surrounded by artifacts of the world, elongated sculptures and intensely colored paintings, the city far below them, all its sounds subdued by thick glass.

"Tony, you know David has for several years been trying to challenge assumptions with regard to order and uncertainty. Just hear him out," Sebby said.

laDoop sighed, big and large, his fingers swallowing a pen he held. David pushed on.

"I've been convinced that in the first flush of quantum understandings over eighty years ago numerous implicit assumptions had been left unchallenged, and since the results were working on a practical level nobody was driven to reexamine them."

"If it ain't broke," laDoop said.

"It's dimensionality, Tony, that's what troubles me, especially now. There's the potential that patterns that looked one way in one set of dimensions could have an entirely different character in another set." He looked out the window, the skyscrapers lit in sharp contrast to the sky.

When David came back to study physics it was after his years of travel, during which he had coped with all kinds of people, wars, sex, drugs, adolescent moments his early brilliance had shielded him from. It was also after a lot more math. He reviewed all the wave/particle experiments and was struck by how all the explanations literally fit neatly on a page – three-dimensional events reduced to two dimensions. He was convinced that that was the basis of a trap that kept thought from fully encapsulating a truer nature of the reality being examined.

"Tony, think about the so-called 'proofs' of uncertainty, will you? We take as faith that it's impossible to determine precisely two conditions of a fundamental particle simultaneously, such as location and momentum. But the flaw lies in measuring a four-dimensional event with four-dimensional mechanisms."

"Oh Christ, there he goes with the dimensions again. Look around, it's not enough for you?"

David persevered. "Just as three dimensions are required to observe an event on a two-dimensional plane, such as the intersection of two lines which, if one was actually on that plane, would be impossible to measure or even comprehend, isn't it reasonable to posit that five dimensions are required to observe fully an occurrence that had length, width, height, and continuity over time?"

Sebastian asked, "What would the fifth dimension be?"

He pursed his lips. "Perhaps the spirit," he replied, softly. It was where his analysis had bogged down, standing on the precipice of awe.

laDoop rolled his eyes. Upshaw patted him on the shoulder.

"We can't understand these areas of discontinuity, because the shortcomings of looking at wave/particle interactions with two-dimensional descriptions, let alone three, four, or five, are now coming home to roost," he raised his voice, trying to break through the wall sitting before him. "How could what were supposedly random uncertain events on the quantum level, which by its very nature is not observable on an everyday scale, have built to such discrete, tangible, and controlled new environments?"

"Goddamit, you take the equations we have, the ones we know work, we adjust them to fit the data, apply the adjustments, we don't have to fully understand them, just use them. You don't win wars with theories."

"But you can lose them with ignorance. Think, maybe what we see as ordered is in fact random, just as what looks uncertain might not be so, depending on the dimensional framework you're observing from.

"Sure, turn all the accepted ideas of quanta upside down, just for the hell of it." laDoop looked at Upshaw, exasperated.

"Take light," said David, pushing on. "We think of it in its wave function as orderly, that nice neat sine wave up and down, a quite remarkable way for the photon as particle to behave, if you think about it. But suppose it's actually a random distribution in four dimensions, and it's only our taking a slice out of it across three dimensions that makes it look like orderly waves.

"It's the act of observation in any given slice, imposing a two-dimensional perspective, that leads to perceiving a three-dimensional cohesiveness and uniformity, according to a probability distribution curve, when in fact we could just as reasonably infer that the action is random in four dimensions.

"So," David considered, "as photons are quantum particles that can purportedly be 'anywhere' from one moment to the next, then it's possible they are grouped so as to give the appearance of continuous waves by the nature of the attraction of one to the next."

"When fish fly and birds talk," laDoop said. He turned to Upshaw. "You want to support this crap, that's up to you. I've got a team to manage and one big motherfucking problem to solve." He stormed out of the room. Susan was roiled up, but David seemed quite calm.

They walked back to the apartment, where David continued as if nothing had happened.

"If that's the case, then, these areas of discontinuity are created by a force that understands – or at least can manipulate – the linkage of one photon to all others, and by extension other fundamental quantum particles, and can somehow extend itself to the wave phase areas from somewhere else, through a medium we have yet to discover.

"I almost get that, but where does it lead, practically?"

"We might be able to pinpoint the source by discovering a pattern to the areas of discontinuity. Actually, they should be called topicalities of wave/particle contiguousness"

"Jesus," Susan said. "No wonder you piss laDoop off so much."

David laughed. He turned to Sebby, serious again. "Let's take a three-dimensional pattern, impose it on a model of the globe, and see if we can find a distribution pattern that could logically emanate from a single source to the other locations."

"What if we can't find one?" asked Sebastian.

"Then, Sebby, we're back to your God."

"Or maybe the Devil."

"Well, if it was God that first set up both waves and particles as a potential state for matter, then maybe this is His way of reestablishing an alternate pattern."

"Maybe the Devil is rushing His phases."

"Whoever or whatever, let's see if it can be fought. But first we have to understand it better, starting with – why fractals, and why these places? And it looks like we're on our own to do that."

'I'll talk with Upshaw, I'm sure we can get some help," Susan said.

"Tell him, if we can't solve those problems, then our species, our world, could land on the other side of these fractal shores, in a place without context, shape, or meaning."

They sat, quiet and still, contemplating a future they almost beheld, each challenging the terrible foreboding of prophecy with their own mix of faith, science, and love, that carried them back to aching terminals showing patterns that did not connect and would not end.

Chapter Nineteen

So far it was all for naught.

In the midst of hectic, intense days that ran for days, they still had time for nights or their equivalent, quiet times together when the world collapsed down to a small room that was world enough, for it was filled with their selves, past and present, alive and well. Sebby discreetly – Susan wasn't even sure how – made himself scarce for their times of intimacy. During one of these times, sitting next to each other on the couch, Susan asked David how he first became interested in physics and math. He lay back for a moment, staring at the ceiling, and started talking after a smile had come to his face.

"When I was around fifteen I was at my desk one night doing math homework, finding factors in binomial equations, and sitting there working with the numbers, I started to get this erection, this enormous erection. I was thinking about breaking the equations up into their parts, and, well, first my penis started pushing up against my jeans – the ones with buttons – soft, old, faded jeans, it was pushing bent over, trying like a straining weight lifter to straighten up, pushing and making the streaky faded blue lines bulge against the lower part of the fly until I couldn't take it anymore, I had to reach down and get my hand under my belt and jeans and shorts to uncurl the poor thing, flip it up and over so it was straight at last.

"It was enormous, running under the whole length of the fly and up against the waist band, compressed there like it was ready to push its head out from under the covers with a 'Hi, remember me?' – as if I could forget! – its whole length radiating a tingling sensation and still pushing up, pushing up the sensations too up into the head feeling it more and more like there was a heater in there turned high splaying its warmth full bore, a radiant tingling heat source that was me. I was finding factors for negative numbers, my first real encounter with imaginary numbers, and playing with the square root of minus one, known as *i*, while playing with the root of I, I reached down again barely in time to unbutton and release it. I stroked my equations and came in an epiphany of understanding of how negation forced an alternate hypothesis and overflowed in my hand and tummy and shirt and papers and books, God was I full.

"And that's when I decided to become a mathematician!"

=

Susan walked into the room packed with terminals and heard Sebastian singing lightly to himself.

> "Believe not those who say,
> the upward path is smooth.
> Lest thou should stumble on the way
> and faint before the truth."

He saw her, stopped. She smiled.

"A ditty from my momma's church-going insistence," he said.

"No time to faint. Isn't there something about hope later in there, keep it thy chief delight?"

"You too?" Sebby asked.

"African churches," she shrugged. "Had to show respect."

"Ah. Hey, come look at this."

He pointed to a screen with two gently sloping lines rising from the lower corners to meet in the middle. David hovered over it.

"We're seeing what we can simulate using fractal analysis, compared to the areas we've discovered. Maybe we can work our way backwards to figure out what's happening and what we can do about it. Watch the screen."

Sebastian hit some keys, and the two lines became four, breaking into two figures each roughly half the first, one slightly larger than the other, creating two connected mounds on the screen. The lines subdivided again, and again slightly unevenly, so that the smooth earlier shape broke into a more complex, rugged one.

The screen came alive in front of her, until the smooth lines had disappeared, replaced by a jagged one of slight edges, roundings and juttings, uneven, yet now looking familiar to her.

"Remind you of anything?" asked David, smiling.

"Yes, but I'm trying to think of what. It's like, not a roadmap, oh, looking from above, it could be – why, David, it's like a shore line!"

"Right. A fractal simulation of a shore line. We subdivided each section into smaller sections, but randomly moving a distance from the midpoint of each section to determine where the focal point, or angle, of the next subdivision was. While random, each movement took place within the limits contained within the previous situation. That can establish order within chaos, creating a pattern that repeats in a way that becomes identifiable even while it contains random elements within it.

"Okay – cool. So what's the point, really?" Her patience was based in love but her habits were honed in the field.

"Well, Sebby, let's show off for her. Run the next demo."

On the screen, a triangle appeared. It divided into four triangles, of uneven size, by inscribing an upside-down triangle inside of it. It divided again, some triangles folding down or up, it divided again and again, taking an overall shape with increasingly tiny pieces within. The subdivisions filled in, denser in some areas, lighter in others, creating texture, giving a three-dimensional appearance to the shape . . . "And, presto," said Sebastian, snapping his fingers while he hit some more buttons, and the shape took on color, lighter and darker browns, greens of different hues, a white top. It was a mountain, not a mountain she'd ever seen, but to Susan it was the essence of a mountain, a wonderful and true shape that distilled and captured her notion of what a mountain was about, the way she would draw one if she were able. She gaped.

"Guys, that's one hell of a PC you have there. I sure couldn't do that with mine."

They were almost beaming. "This is the souped-up version – overhead hemis, dual carbs," said David. He showed her some thick cable connections into a large router. "We built a high speed Ethernet, to connect to a powerful advanced graphics computer at Cal, used for creating special effects in movies. We're also plugged into a supercomputer at a research lab in Michigan."

"And I'll just bet you could do that with clouds and canyons, couldn't you?" she asked.

"At the head of the class as usual. Yes, they can all be simulated through fractal analysis."

"I'll know where to go when I make my next movie, but isn't what we're facing a little different? I mean, we already had the whole fractal thing in place – by nature – and bingo, they disappeared. Can you do that?"

She looked at David expectantly. "That's, well, not possible," he said.

She felt worse for him that she had asked, sensing his disappointment in saying no, deflating his feeling of accomplishment with the perspective of the practical, and possibly insurmountable, task they still faced. Well, that's what love is, she thought.

"But," he said, "I think we can use this as a basis for understanding what's happening. As you say, we already have our fractal shore in place. So, what happened to it? Let's work backwards – if we start with the final shape . . ." He started pushing buttons, in effect reversing the process, reassembling the initial, simpler drawing from the minute detail of the final version. Gradually, he worked back to the initial shape, now altered, each side of somewhat different length due to the random displacement that had been used to generate the patterns. "You know, actually, I'll bet we could get it back to the exact original shape, for all practical purposes, by halving the distance between the point of each angle and its non-random midpoint, to successively eliminate the displacement, but . . ."

He looked at Susan, who said, "We need actual purposes," a field operative impatient with an intellectual game. He abandoned the effort.

"All right, this doesn't get us anywhere. Sebby, any ideas?"

Sebastian shook his head. "Not really. It seems like once we get past a certain point on the screen there's nothing further we can do to alter the shape, let alone dematerialize it, if I can sound so occult."

They stared at the screen. David set it for automatic cycling of the iterations, from mountain to triangles and back, each different, yet each mountain so much like a mountain, more infinite than the world itself. The glow of the screen reflected lighter and darker off their faces, like separate frames of a movie, dusks and dawns dancing in quick succession. They stared from afar at pieces of their world forming, paring down to some abstract essence, reforming, a sparkless fire dying and coming back to life in front of them, endless embers to oblivion, created, broken apart, rearranged.

David broke the silence. "You know, Sebastian, what you just said" – it had been over a half hour before – "maybe you're on to something." Always gracious, she thought, ingrained even in moments of great pressure. "What if we keep pushing down, keep subdividing, what would happen?"

"Well, we'd reach a certain point at which it wouldn't matter, so to speak. The regression is theoretically infinite, but past a certain point our ability to measure it would stop – indeed, as I think on it, according to the Uncertainty Principle it would have to stop, there would be a point beyond which we could not measure because we couldn't actually observe it."

"Or more precisely, where our measurement would interfere with what was being observed. Right, that's right. Now let's suppose, though, that somehow we created an observation method that could push past that point – somehow."

"Isn't that like saying, imagine going faster than the speed of light? It just can't happen."

"But what does it mean here to say it can't happen? Perhaps such a stress would force a fundamental change in order to preserve the integrity of physical laws? Maybe pushing down to the subatomic level and somehow pushing beyond creates a total inverting, the particle can't exist as matter anymore under these conditions, so it collapses into a wave, in effect to preserve its energy, its very existence. And since we're still looking for an origin for all this, it would be consistent with the notion of the observer interfering with what was being observed."

"That's pretty wild, David, even for you."

David's excitement was visible, his eyes wide, breath coming quickly. Susan's eyes were drawn to his crotch, wondering. "Take it as a working hypothesis, if you like. But think of one thing. What we're facing seems like the ultimate step in the observer having an effect on what is being observed. Whatever the explanation, it lies frighteningly close to the – well, to the heart of the matter, our matter, a manipulation of the basic forces of the universe at a level we never before even thought of, let alone can comprehend. Whatever this thing is, it's not trivial – it's a direct challenge to our very existence."

Susan found it amazing how often she felt ill after a conversation with the man she loved.

⩧

David and Sebby went back to the terminals, while Susan sat on the couch and searched for materials about fractals, seeing the two men only in outline, the contours of their bodies framed by the light emanating behind them. When she walked over to them, she noticed that their skin pallor increasingly resembled the color of the screen before them. Susan asked what she had forgotten to pursue the day before. "So why are you connected into the super-duper-scientific computer in Michigan?"

"I created a mega-hub linking multiple systems, we—"

"Here?" said Susan, looking around the small apartment.

"Sebby can be quite efficient in bootstrapping resources," Davic said. "We need more firepower to see if I can use quantum mathematics to portray what that stretch of beach looks like, in the sense of seeing it from the perspective of waves, not particles. If I can do that, see it – through the computer, at least – as a wave-oriented observer would, then maybe I can understand what's different about that patch of beach or stretch of mountain, and find some way to jumpstart it back to our own reality."

There was nothing for Susan to see on the computer that day, no mountains made of math. She looked at numbers and equations for a while, staring at symbols about which she didn't have a clue as to what they meant, wandered listlessly around the apartment, went out, came back, exhausted by their efforts, her inability to function usefully, the perversely abstract nature of the problem they faced, a world disappearing, yes, but nothing to move, nobody to pummel, unending. All the while the two men hovered over their screens, typing, talking quietly, constant, the room illuminated by the twin green eyes of the computer screens, staring out at them, cold, unblinking, unfeeling, yet a gateway to all the compassion they would need in this world. She slept.

When she awoke she saw both men slumped over their screens. They had sat in front of the computers for over thirty straight hours. She also hoped it wasn't so, but knew, because she had not been awakened, that they had not discovered anything helpful.

David confirmed her fear. They had, indeed, constructed a wave equation "picture" of the beach space, in far greater detail than anything even implied by the fractal pictures, since the math was not limited by the screen's resolution. They had then plugged in the equations from the fractal analysis, to try to overlap the fractal approach with a wave orientation. They made some headway in the overlap, but found the whole approach a dead end, since they still had no idea what was causing the switch. They had analyzed some spectroscopic readouts taken in the space that disappeared in China, which the Chinese had prepared, for reasons David could only guess at, not happily; the actual analysis matched the theoretical, with no indication of any variation that could cause the switch from particle to wave, no extra or different energies. And yet . . .

"There's something there," said David, staring straight ahead, hoarse with exhaustion, his hair lying flat on his head. "I'm convinced of it. What we're up against is the limit of our ability to measure. We just don't have the tools to see everything that's going on there."

"So what do we do next, if we've reached our limits?" she asked, sharing their fatigue, no sleep could diminish it, almost in tears with fear.

David spun around, took both her hands in his. "We do what we've been doing since the dawn of relativity and quantum – we throw out the rulers and use our heads. And since I'm not sure a conscious mind will be any better than a subconscious one for figuring out what in the hell is going on – goodnight."

Chapter Twenty

So . . .which came first – an uncertain universe, or the theory of uncertainty?

After sleeping for over twenty hours, and making love for several more, Susan and David lay in the tiny bedroom, talking sporadically about their problems and frustrations in coming to grips with an issue so rooted in the world around them and yet so ethereal in the analyses it demanded. David sat up, wrapped his arms around his knees, and looked out the window, to the comforting solidity of dirty gray bricks. She tucked in alongside him.

"Why did you leave physics for all those years?" she asked.

"Like I said, to find myself."

"Seems like a long ways to go."

He stared out the window for a while. "It was because I was afraid."

She looked at him, startled.

"Yes, afraid I didn't have it, 'well, sure, he's a bright one, could have had a shot at the Prize, maybe, some real breakthrough in him, but that's past now, he gave it up to search for his soul, like a tennis player who breaks his leg skiing, romantic, we all make our choices, still . . .' I hear it in the corridors, buzzing gnats I can't spray away, I think it myself sometimes."

"David, Sebby told me that what you contributed, that pissed laDoop off, once it was understood, it's now considered part of the foundation of understanding quantum-relativity intersections. Seriously."

"Well, I had intuition, I could look down deep and see that electron shift orbits, emit some light, jump back, beyond the clunky model into the sense of it. Even when I was a kid, I understood a nanosecond at the level where small particles make big use of tiny bits of time, I lived the algebra, the numerics of it. Hell, I was a cool date, I could look up at the sky and explain why the light from all those stars didn't fry us, whistle a Doppler shift. But there comes a time when intuition isn't enough, couldn't carry me through, for the first I felt fear in a math class. I tried to stay with it, through it, like if I could just lay there close I could skip step ahead to my visions, working on my acceptance speech, maybe a spot on Letterman, they would have put Einstein on if they had the chance, I can just hear the intro –

" 'And now, ladies and gentlemen, here's a man you've all heard about lately, he predicted light would bend around the sun and sure enough, during that last eclipse – say Paul, did you notice the eclipse or just think it was another day at the office, under the table, uh hah – but seriously, he made this prediction and – um, what was it, say Paul, you've worn a few suits that bend light, what was it called – that's right, relativity, the theory of relativity, which predicted the light would bend – um, relativity, that's sort of like the measure of sincerity when you say 'I do' – uh hah, especially the third time or so – anyway, they had a chance to do the measurement of this prediction, and sure enough, a star was moved to where Professor Einstein predicted it would be – boy, could NBC use him to do programming,, uh hah, here's, and please welcome, Dr. Albert . . .' "

She would have laughed, but he was so serious, she nestled against him.

"Look, you get the picture," he said, "I had my fantasies. When I got back, I could see the value of those years away, but uneasiness sits like a former addiction inside: cured, but once you've had it you can't ever be really sure, it lies within just out of reach, and in moments of doubt it turns reason into a hoax, a thin veil over an endless hole. I've climbed out of it, and I know, I know I won't fall back, but it's not like never having been there at all, and that's so scary," and she held him and talked to him and shook him through that murky night, a sea anchor to keep course through the gusting winds.

==

"Why are you so sure the areas are linked together by all being fractals?" she asked, later, to return the professor to solid ground. She sat cross-legged in the bed, the covers draped over her legs, while he lay propped up on several pillows. "Each of the areas,"

David said, "represents a clear characteristic of fractals. Clouds are a perfect example of similarity across scale, a section of the cloud was like the whole cloud.

"Jones Beach – well, you've seen a fractal shoreline, it shows how the nature of measurement and the length of measuring devices are important elements in what we see.

"As for the mountains and the Canyon, they're examples of fractal dimensionality, that the distance from the observation affects how one perceives dimensions. The masses were two-dimensional contours from afar, three-dimensional textures from closer up. Fascinating, really."

She listened, attentive in her focused way, and asked, "But why do you think fractals are involved, what could the underlying purpose be?"

He thought for a while. "Well, fractals are simple and organic. They also tie in closely to parallel, fairly new areas of study in chaos theory. Once you understand the basic geometry, the repetition of events or characteristics, you can manipulate the data, and, it seems, the space. And they're a frequent natural occurrence, from the organization of systems within the body such as the bloodstream or the lungs, to the rhythms of events such as species population growth or market price fluctuations. Fractals and the repeating evolution of order and random behavior in chaos are a recurrent and persistent pattern in our lives."

He stood up in his paisley boxer shorts, but she could see him in tweed jacket standing in front of a blackboard in a lecture hall. Animated and focused, sure-footed yet spontaneous. A teacher like this, she thought, and I might have gotten past arithmetic.

"And if you can learn to use them," he was saying excitedly, "it would really put you at the head of the class. Once you could shed the perceptual state you grew up with – not easy –and train yourself to the discipline of observing events through their fractal nature, then the bright glow of consciousness could highlight fractal systems and organizations around us, like an injection of dye highlights an organ in an X-ray. Their frequency and commonality make them a tool as easy to employ as basic addition, symmetrical organization across scale and time, and just as fundamental a building block in perceiving and manipulating the world around us. And if you could utilize them on a small scale, maybe just for practice, their replicability would make fractal-based activity easier to enlarge upon than a purely random-based one, since the understanding lies in the relationship, not the scale. If you got it down for a small area, it would just be more of the same for a big one, the road ahead defined, not like having to find yourself a new path for each additional space. Expansion would be a matter of energy, perhaps, or time, but that's all, not of understanding, no more insurmountable problems."

Susan poked him in the stomach, forcing out what little breath he had left.

"Whew," he exclaimed, and they both laughed. It was as if he were coming back to life and had regained the pulpit of his classroom, and in Susan the congregation of his students.

They looked at each other, thinking of a few little spaces that had disappeared, and all the big spaces around them. And time and space were less abstract, as real in this tiny room as either of them had ever known, and in greater jeopardy than anyone had ever conceived. Small spaces growing like continental brush fires, with no water left to douse the flames.

The joined Sebastian in the main room and caught him up. "But why should the universe be fractal in nature," he asked, "as opposed to linear, regular, or some other ordering mechanism? It seems so arbitrary."

"It's just the world we inhabit," David responded. "Forget using a name to define an order, and think of the essential nature of what's being defined – the Universe, its underlying principles. To understand its order you need to determine a mechanism that can encompass random events as well as orderly, logical, predictable progressions. The universe oscillates back and forth between these two poles of deterministic phenomena – I drop this glass, it will fall and it will probably break – but where will the pieces land, this time, and next time, knowledge to probability to the unknowable, the world of human activity, the future that is gloriously mysterious.

"Fractal order is simply a name we've given to a description of the way the world works. Today's phenomena are echoes of an original state, of the only Big Bang we know, can know. Who knows what elements passed through the other pole, the breath of chaos. Fractal geometry, like science itself, isn't a creation, even a discovery, it's more like a description, the cosmos contains order, and it contains chaos, and if you want to play in its park you have to accept both, the biggest yin and yang there is.

"It's as if we live on a bridge hanging between the pillars of order and chaos, predictability and randomness. Probability is a measure of where you are on the bridge, which direction you're facing, even where your last step took you. Our lives play out on lanes of that bridge, progressions of the obviously-going-to-happen and of chance events, encounters. Each actor plays out his or her role based on the initial conditions of their genes, the quandaries of their environment. Quantum leaps of tiny particles occasionally accumulate enough weight in a direction to create real change, big unexpected change, for the random maelstrom deserves as much a place in our view of the world as does any certainty, of dawn and dusk, death and ripples of water when a stone falls in it, the sinking of the stone in that water, into love and leaps of faith, of events that transcend reason, of particles that aren't there blipping on the screen. Maybe God himself is on the continuum, at times knowing what he's doing and how it will turn out, at others birthing the craziest of notions with no idea of what's going to happen, some ninety-foot three-toed vegan dinosaur."

"Makes you wonder from which vein man was born. Was He deterministic or random on that day?" Sebby said.

"Down deep, at that last level, you can't place anything exactly," David said. "If it's true that if you add enough of the possibilities up you get statistical probability bordering on certainty, it's also true that if you lay them end to end and multiply you can get some hellacious deviations."

"So we have no idea of that the outcome might be, from the disappearing areas?" said Susan.

They sat for a while, the dim room evenly illuminated by light reflecting off the wall across the alley, muting any contrast or shadows, joining the three of them together and melding them with the room itself, with the uniform background noise from the air conditioner, a cool isolated room, like coming in on a too-bright hot summer day to a dark wooden bar, sitting towards the back while the sweat dries, and a drink or two, and only a little middle-of-the-day background murmur of other travelers' voices blending together to smooth the wrinkles of another day.

At that moment, Antifermo walked in the door, looked around the room, the piles of papers sitting amidst remainders of too many take-out meals, and announced that tonight was the night they were coming to dinner, his place, no arguments, the car was downstairs.

A ride made quicker by the flashing light that cut through civilian traffic, confronting Susan's egalitarian instincts with the convenience, and they were at Sal's house, in Brooklyn, a single-family brick home with a few steps up to a raised small lawn crowded with trees and bushes, a porch above that, a driveway running the length of the house to the side.

Sebby had had just enough time to grab a bottle. They got inside, and Sal introduced them to his wife, Rosie, "my mui Latino princessa," he said with clear delight.

Rosie rolled her eyes. "Latina, baby, Latina." Sebby handed her his bottle of California pinot, which Sal quickly intercepted and placed on the counter. "Maybe later," he said, pulling an Italian from a rack of fifty or so that took up a large portion of one of the kitchen counters. He opened the bottle and they sat in the living room, brightly covered couches and chairs covered in plastic.

"We met at a dance," said Sal, answering Susan's question, "my Catholic school held with a local PR congregation, showing inter-faith good will, I guess. You can imagine how much I wanted to go. But there she was."

"Only I heard about him, didn't want nothin' to do wit chu, did I?" said Rosie.

David laughed. "Why was that? He seems almost respectable."

Sal raised his eyebrows. "Back then, I used to run with the bad boys. Lunchtime, we'd go in a pack up to the kids around the deli, say, 'Hey, you gotta nickel for the cancer fund?' That was to buy us cigarettes. We'd roll the packs in our T-shirt sleeves."

"Chu thought you were so cool, dint chu, Papi?"

"Well, I met her, she straightened me out."

Rosie said it was time to eat. They walked through a hallway to the kitchen. Behind some hanging coats were rows of plaques and medals. "Wow," said Sebby, pointing to them.

"Nothin' much, really," said Sal. "Last long enough, just an everyday cop, they come with the job."

"Yeah," Rosie said, "just the most decorated detective on the force, the last seventeen years. Crazy guy." She punched him, hard enough to move him a step.

"Call the kids, willya," Sal said.

Down the staircase came Bennie and Hector, fourteen and twelve, their Italian and Latin features combined to create faces with delicacy and force, wrapped in skin of a burnished umber that seemed to glow. They took their seats at a large old wooden table with thick legs.

Sal said, "Okay, so Rosie's made carnitos con spaghettini with tomato salsa sauce." He laughed. "Our version of fusion, Docs. Latino/Italiano."

The meal was lively. The boys spoke easily, but when Sal spoke they stopped and listened. Which was when Rosie took him on, telling him to let the boys speak. Sal put up his hands. "See, I think I'm king of the mansion, but princessa here keeps me in my place." He opened a second bottle. "Nothing goes with food like an Italian, eh, Sebby." Sebby held up his hands, then his glass, smiled.

Over cannoli, Rosie said, "So tell me, what's keeping my Sal up late at night, and he can't get up in the morning, never happened before for nothing."

Sal looked pained, glared at her. "Like I said, it's about nothing."

"Oh please, will you stop with the games awwready?" She turned to David. "Whas this about?"

David paused, then went into a brief explanation. The boys had been pulling out their video game players, but stopped, listened, as did Rosie.

'You saying we could all end up like dis nothing?" she asked.

David warmed to his audience. "I suppose there would have to be an upward limit on the fractal dimension comparable to the lower limit governed by what is observable, like resolution on a screen. A swirling gust of wind may be a tiny hurricane, and a regional hurricane may be mirrored by large-wind patterns, but at some point the globe itself places a limit on what can take place within its boundaries. Thus the scaling up would also have its upward boundary, dictated by what in a sense could 'fit in' to the space."

"He's saying, plenty of room for everybody, not to worry," said Sebastian, looking at the boys' worried faces.

"Imagine if you had a hurricane inside a box, how big could it get relative to the box before its interaction with the sides of the box would distort and diffuse it so that it ceased to be a hurricane? At that point of maximum size, would there still be some areas in the box untouched by the maelstrom? People do survive plagues or catastrophes, somewhere, somehow, something survives."

"Not the dinosaurs," said Bennie.

"True, but we have no way of knowing what patterns we're plugged into, maybe there are some structural limits placed on these areas of discontinuity, at least at this moment, as they're currently produced with the energy now infused in them. So Rosie, we don't know, some parts of the world might be preserved from the wave maelstrom we are threatened with. Some hope, tiny as it might be."

He turned to the boys. "Pretty interesting, huh? Weird stuff, but..."

There was a silence, then Rosie stood up. "Whas wrong wit chu, talk about this so easy? Can't chu see you're scaring the kids?" Their faces did look pale, they sat with their arms at their sides, motionless. "I'm sorry," said David, "it's just, you asked, and –"

Susan interjected. "Rosie, I'm so sorry. These guys live in a world of abstractions, don't realize the effect they can have. Don't worry, boys, there's a solution, David, your dad, Sebby, they'll find it. David!"

"Yes, yes, we will."

"Let me help with the dishes," Susan said.

"Let's see what that thing you brought tastes like," said Sal. He grabbed some glasses and led them out to the porch, where he lit up a cigar. Sebby joined him, David declined. Sal swept his arm in front of him, holding up his glass to all the single-family homes with porches and well tended lawns, the occasional statue of a rabbit or a boy peeing. "Look around, Docs. Been in this house twenty-seven years, just four blocks from where I grew up. It's safe, solid, same as it always was. The house, family, neighborhood. But this business about nothing, well..."

He took a puff. "You should see this place Christmas time, the lights, you can see the glow in Jersey."

When they were kids, he said, they used to call it "Bay Ridge for the newly wed and nearly dead. Made fun of it then, now that's a pride we got. My mom could walk her schnauzer two in the morning, no problem. Only danger was, every now and then, some house got a buzz cut from semiautomatic fire, a Mafia misunderstanding."

"Really?" said Sebby, backing up a step.

Sal laughed. "Those days are long gone." He knocked some ash off the end of the cigar, watched it fall into the trimmed privet below.

"My kids go to the same schools I did. Place like a sanctuary, didn't get that when I was a kid, but now... I don't understand it, you're telling me somehow this, all of this, is threatened." He took a deep pull on the cigar, slowly blew out the smoke.

"I don't know how I got involved, but fuck, somehow I am, and somehow I am going to fix it."

They watched the smoke gust sideways, until for all intents and purposes it disappeared. They went inside to join the women and children.

When they got home, Susan said, "I'm sorry for butting in, but you –"

"No, you were right. Sometimes I get carried away, you ground me."

"I don't know about that but now, with us . . ."

"This is more than the way I've lived my life 'til now, way more. There are attachments, interconnections, and that makes the risks, beyond . . . There's you. I don't want you disappearing on me, in any way, so say what you think, but don't ever leave."

Susan flushed. "I won't then, if you don't want me to. You can count on that."

Chapter Twenty-one

It was Susan who got them going in another direction.

They were eating lunch in the gray dim kitchen, which looked like it had been sardine-canned as an afterthought into the apartment, "newly renovated," as the ad said, meaning a shallow stainless steel sink five inches deep, seemingly designed to hold take-out containers for the presumed fast-track occupants of the City's hot neighborhoods, a narrow refrigerator with a little plastic-enclosed freezer compartment holding short half-inch-square ice cube trays, and an electric range so small that the only way it could fit two reasonably sized frying pans or pots would be to place them diagonally across from each other; neither its length nor width could otherwise accommodate them.

Munching on cold cuts and bread, Susan spoke about Africa. "I saw villages built of dung, the only material available, wet as well as dry. When the flies were done with depleting the dung they moved over to the people, children covered with flies, helpless to avoid them, adults long given up on even trying, brushing them away as futile as building houses of shit, everybody too tired from hunger to even try. To an outsider it was as if a system had been developed solely to perpetuate disease, an experiment to transcend the known limits of suffering, where the people were conditioned to patience, patience was equivalent to death, and death was the only freedom."

She looked at her sandwich, holding it in her hand as she gesticulated, so that after a while piles of little pieces of the sandwich fell and lay ignored on the burnished wooden table, a trace of the movements of the hands above.

"You know guys, the key – and it was really a burn – was that it was never a problem of not having enough food, there's plenty of that out there. The problem was distribution, of getting it to the people who needed it, past the people who were keeping them from getting it. I mean, you can lay it all on institutions, on bureaucracy, on entrenched interest groups, all the jargon that divorces us from really feeling what's going on, but in the end it's people who keep other people hungry, able to stuff their faces and wipe away the excess while other people die for lack of crumbs. Just people."

David and Sebby listened. Eating seemed an abstraction for them, a way to keep fuel in the body, to get back in to the game, listlessly chewing the rare roast beef and Westphalian ham sandwiches on semolina bread with herbal mayonnaise and roasted peppers Susan had painstakingly constructed, and which she was eating with relish. She knew the stories of her forays startled them, but David always said he sought to connect the abstract to the concrete, and her experiences served as infusions of a real world into the cloistered one they typically inhabited and had recreated in the apartment. She had pinned her hair back, and with her hands brushed away some strands that had fallen out of their restraint across her face.

"What I'm trying to say is, well, let's face it, you've kind of dead-ended looking at all the math and physics of these things. No offense, I'm just going by what you've told me, that you get so far in understanding them, being able to explain them, replicate what they look like on your screens, in equations, but you can't for the life of you figure out how they switched into being so different, right? I mean, I know this is the lay perspective, but there it is. So how about looking for the people behind it, the person who might be able to perform these miracles, surely there must be some way of taking that approach."

David sat mid-chew for a while, then grinned. He swallowed. "Look for the throne behind the power, huh? Maybe you're right, we sure are stuck doing what we're doing. What do you think, Sebby, somebody out there doesn't like us?"

Sebby shook his head. "Hey, you were the hippie. If this isn't anti-materialism, what is?" He paused. "I'll throw out the God hypothesis for a while, sure. If that's the answer we're just spinning our wheels anyway. Maybe there is a person behind what's going on. But how would we find him?" He looked at Susan. "Or her."

"We must have five hundred names from the list which we used to contact you. How about starting there?" asked Susan.

"That's the modern style," David said. "I call it the categorical exhaustive approach. Generate all options from all variables, because the computer lets you do it, then use the computer to screen them, do anything but think about them. God forbid someone should first exercise a little judgment, excise the irrelevant, no, instead we have to have an affirmative action program for all ideas, no matter how ludicrous, covering your ass in case anybody challenges you, and then use all those extra resources to sort through options that should never have been created in the first place. That UN list was bureaucracy generated, it has a built-in limit. And besides, whoever is perpetrating these scandals is out of the mainstream – waayy out of the mainstream."

Susan waited until she swallowed most of what was in her mouth, and washed the remainder down with a dark Mexican beer. "There were names on that list that we never reached. And anyway, it turned you up, it can't be all bad."

David smiled. He held up a half-eaten sandwich, impressions of his fingerprints in the middle of the bread, saying, "I can't even make this disappear. All right, let's start with your no shows. What the hell, it's better than reiterating what we've already got, maybe it'll even jog our poor numbed brains a bit." He put his sandwich down on his plate and used one hand as a brush to scoop all the crumbs on the table into his other hand poised just under the table's edge. He tossed the crumbs in the garbage, left the remains of his sandwich on the table, and went out of the room.

They started their search, looking for a clue to a who that might be capable of dissolving their known world, some combination of ability and desire, to be able to create the weapon and then want to play with it, restraint overthrown by – what? need, recklessness, simply being oblivious or darkly purposeful. Sebastian began wading through the thirty-four names not contacted in the initial UN survey, while David and Susan toured the technical libraries, phoned friends of David's and friends of the friends, around the globe.

They reconvened in the apartment thirty-six hours later, sitting on a burgundy Persian rug Susan had happily splurged on for the occasion, and tore through a generation of scientists.

They had a list of over sixty names, plus numerous articles and references to others. Susan suggested running through them on a first level to weed out the clearly improbables, then get a short list to examine more closely.

"Yes," said Sebastian. He seemed the most adept in getting to the heart of the people they were reviewing, bringing discipline to Susan's ideas and David's energy, their intense need to find an answer. "We need an organizing principle; we're looking for a fringe player, an outcast, some offbeat oddball none of the major league teams picked up who's now striking out the sides on some sand lots with a new kind of curve ball that none of the coaches could recognize, maybe even an undetectable spitter."

"This from a Little League dropout," said David.

"I didn't like the Marty's Hot Dogs uniform."

They began winnowing, surrounded by folders, files, and articles, leaning against the couch and chairs, folders between their knees, piles to rest their arms on, scrunched up and lying down, tossing through the papers like confetti at a parade.

"What about Morton Crankowitz?" David called out. "Czech, post-Soviet breakup, did research on very-high-temperature fusion interactions, looking at the possible particles that might serve as intermediary binding points, to speed the fusion process, release more energy."

Sebby did a quick search. "He'd be pretty hard to reach; he's over eighty and sitting under his gray hair in a sanitarium near Prague." He held up another folder.

"Here's a paper on 'Potential Replications of Early Particle Formulations in Existing Super-Gravitational Fields,' by Charles Schlumpelpfinick – whew, there's a reason to get even with the world that made you – about how the kinds of tiny, short-lived particles supposedly present only in the early instants of the creation of the universe might in fact still be being produced closer in to the center of the universe, in random accumulations of super-dense matter." David and Sebby quickly read the article, made a few calls and put Schlumpelpfinick on the short list.

They worked through a catalogue of modern physics and math, discarding the dead, ignoring the conventional. Names and ideas were strewn about the room like a melee in a supermarket, a spree that cast papers and names into different baskets rolling around the aisles, a large mess of discards and a smaller one of possibles. It went on for days.

=

"I sometimes wonder how we know what we know," said David.

Wandering through the mazes and disparate pursuits of thought had set David to musing that night as he and Susan grabbed their quiet moments together, talking in bed.

"What do you mean?"

"That there's a random nature to what we know, that the order in which humankind has accrued knowledge is not linear, but chaotic, fractal-like. Random within certain bounds, the boundary of what is already known establishing some set of possible branches at any given time, not an infinite set, but not a solitary limb either. That the path followed is a quasirandom interaction of the people then bringing their talents and personalities to bear with what they're exposed to and what they are trained to tolerate. Why Freud in his time, and not one hundred or one thousand years before, or not until yesterday or tomorrow?"

"Don't there have to be underpinnings to knowledge as it evolves?" Susan asked. "You have to know about bacteria in order to treat disease."

"Maybe. But. . . why Newton before Einstein? Why that solid, causal, deterministic linearity before a more fluid sense of time and space, which could have fit comfortably with the sense of mystery with which people confronted their worlds? Why fix matter hard and fast instead of building around its other possibilities? I don't think it was written in concrete how we got here knowing what we know, I think it could have gone a lot of different ways. We so often look back and say, 'Oh yeah, logically the one thing followed from the other, such and such was a reflection of his times.' But if we were really good at reconstructing the past then we'd be a lot better at predicting the future. We'd know the growth in GDP in advance, instead of having economists dissect it so authoritatively after the fact, only to be wrong again the next time they made a projection. It's easy to take a whole picture and cut it up into jigsaw pieces that all fit together. But really that's just narrow hindsight, an attempt to impose order because otherwise the shifting paths and byways would be just too hard to follow, nobody likes to set out on a hike with a map that explicitly says, 'and here's where you get lost, LOL.'

"Ever go to a museum of natural history and see the chart that shows the evolution of the horse? First there's that tiny little thing, some fur in places that look odd to us, sort of cute. And in the picture to its right it's a little bigger, leaner, more horsey, each successive picture a little closer to what we know today, nice and orderly, linear. Only if you look closely at the dates, in fact the horse didn't evolve in that way at all, it went bigger, then smaller, hairier and fatter some times, leaner at others. But the curators and the public just had to impose that sense of moving from one of their logical steps to the next on the data, otherwise it didn't fit in with their model of what they think Darwin was talking about. Knowledge could be quite coincidental, its evolution non-linear.

"I went to a dinosaur exhibit once and saw all those odd protrusions – dorsal, fins, sails, horns, mantels – and different shapes, skins, sizes, and I thought, it's as if someone was playing around a bit with creation to see what works. Yeah, let's add a couple of big nails to the small front feet, or make the legs longer, hey, why not try bigger teeth, let's see how they work. It was all the signs connected to the exhibit that said, 'It is not clear what was the purpose of the long, tiny row of scales running down the back to the lower left leg, although speculation is that it was used as a means of radiating heat or even a solar collector, while it may have been related to distinguishing mates, or detachable for picnic plates.' They have no idea what the purpose was! For all we know, neither did the dinosaur. In fact, I heard that they even stuck the wrong heads on the wrong bodies in the exhibit. But maybe they were an evolutionary testing ground for different designs, all kinds of add-ons and shapes and means of interacting with the ground and water and the sun, of collecting and digesting food, protection, attraction, interspecies relationships, maybe it was all just a hodgepodge of ideas the creator put down to see what would work out and what was not viable, and when the tests were over . . . bye bye dinos."

"You sound a bit like Sebby," Susan said. "That creator thing."

"I'm not immune to uncertainty. I may tease Sebby about his faith, but I don't dismiss it. Whatever is causing these disappearances seems to have stepped aside of the track we're now on, the understanding of fractals not just intellectual knowledge but a freeing up of new processes, opening up a brain at a different level so that it can pursue some of the old roads not taken, some of those branches that existed as possibilities yet for some reason were not followed, ones that were buried. Burned volumes ignored. A potential spark stillborn in a sick mother's womb, or destroyed in a car's careening. Maybe it can illuminate those darkened alleyways of lost opportunities, false dead ends that could have led somewhere with a bit more pushing, and now has come up with its own physics, based on different assumptions. Clearly there are alternative ones regarding the stable and existent nature of matter, as well as the relationship between the observer and the observed, between us humans and our world, a notion of interaction, control, and understanding that makes Yogi masters look like Shirley Temple.

Susan listened, enthralled, herself a tingle with the intensity, his words sweeping her in their scope and fire, whacky and enchanted at the same time. And he still wore the button jeans. She thought back to her high school classes, memory spurred by desire.

"Hey, care to factor A squared plus two A B plus B squared?" she said, and reached for his thighs.

"A plus B times A plus B," he grinned, and pulled her towards him.

Chapter Twenty-two

Simulating reality was easier than living it.

They continued going through the literature the next morning, looking for the offbeat, outcasts, scientists not initially contacted. Deep in their stacks, Sebby found an old, yellowed paper from the archives at Princeton, by Mary Quintin, titled "Self-Fulfilling Prophecies in Sub-Atomic Particle Detection."

"Hey, I think I spoke with her," Susan said. "Wasn't she the one you said was crazy, wacko I think was the term you used?"

Sebastian shot a look at David, who held out his hand for Sebastian to continue. "It's the usual about how if you mathematically determine the existence of a particle, you can create an experiment in which the particle will appear, especially when coupled with a perceptual state in which you expect to see it. She bypasses – with some snippy asides – the infinite worlds/infinite possibilities notion, by referencing limits to the imagination, of all things. But here's the interesting part, tucked in at the end:

"'Considering the initiating energy of such a particle, or rather allowing parity between notions of self and absolute creation, it may be possible through the focused intimate observation surrounding birth to enhance the perceptual state in such a manner as to interact with such particles and, by extension, particles with which they interact, in a cascading effect whereby self-fulfillment stems not only from the intellectual impetus to observe but also from the organic desire to direct.' Well, her syntax is properly Germanic, anyway."

"Did she do any follow-up, anything clinical?"

"Nope, seems to have dropped out of sight. You know, she was dismissed as wide-eyed and frizzy. Remember Kasselman's comment, 'the "me" generation doesn't belong in physics, they couldn't even do classical astrology.'" Susan laughed.

"Yeah. Hey," David said, "how about that Harold Kasselman? That S.O.B. would love the power."

Sebby shook his head. "He loved it too much – died crashing his Ferrari two years ago. Besides, he would be sixty-eight if he were alive. It seems to me this is a younger person's game we're playing."

"Younger, but not a kid's game," said David. "This degree of knowledge and control wasn't inherited, it was derived. It may be driven by some adolescent fantasy or fear, but it's a mature intelligence at the source.

"Wonder where she is now," said Sebby. David looked at him, frowning. "Mary. Remember her at the faculty house gatherings? God, she was something else in school!"

"You went to Princeton with her?" Susan asked. "You didn't mention that when –"

"Yup. She was something. Anyway, Sebby, how about –"

"What a case, Mary!" Sebby said. "I can still see her perched two rows higher than anybody else in the lecture hall, like she had eagle eyes that could see more clearly what was going on down below, big eyes looking intently in front of her, never turning, jet-black hair. Even the total physics jocks, the guys whose idea of sex consisted of moving their slide rules up and down, even they wanted her, she aroused sensuality at a fundamental state, so to speak. She was dark and deep, hazel-grey eyes seemed invitingly opaque, like if you could get into them you could get lost inside, but behind were steel shutters that clamped down hard. She laughed one time at a faculty/student party and we talked about it for weeks. But I sure never got anywhere, far as I know neither did anybody else." Susan had been leaning back on the couch; she now leaned forward.

"But she was sharp! Not one of the quick, instant-response types. But she was never off the mark when she spoke, always on top or ahead of what was going on. She was so isolated, though.

She never bothered with peer review for her papers, technically very sound, just, well, always a little askew from the rest, who were all pretty much loners anyway, so you can imagine how far out she must have been. I'm not even sure she finished her degree."

David took the papers Sebby was holding, skimmed them quickly. "I suppose we could look for her, might be interesting."

"I'll bet," said Susan.

David looked at her, started to say something, stopped.

"Okay – that brings the short list to nineteen," said Sebby, taking Quintin's paper back from David and aligning it on a short, neat little pile standing out as an oasis of order amidst the tossed documents, phone messages, computer printouts, references, and reports that filled the room, as if special care and nurturing might grow one of the little seedlings into something fruitful at last.

⁂

Sebby went off to do some interviews. Susan said that was a good idea for her as well. At her UN office, she told herself it was in the interests of solving the problem. That's why she called back Mary Quintin. David's deflection in talking about her had nothing to do with it.

It took several messages before Mary picked up, and considerable time to overcome Mary's irritation at being cut off in their previous talk. Susan kept reiterating how important the quest was, that she would come by Mary's, make it totally convenient for her, take up so little time.

"Oh," said Mary, "you don't want to come by here, it's so out of the way to get to, and there's really nothing to see."

"I don't–" Susan started.

"I'll tell you what. I have to go to Burlington, the University of Vermont library, doing a little research for the fun of it. There's a wonderful Chinese place there I go to when I can. Let's meet there."

"Okay." She was already piecing together the logistics. "If that's the best for you."

It was a small wooden building, painted blue and yellow, large Chinese ideograms on its walls, its interior a maze of rooms. Susan found Mary in the far back, a tiny room with a small water fountain providing a continuous backdrop to their conversation. Susan entered, extending her hand to Mary while thanking her for getting together. Mary didn't take the hand, instead beckoning Susan to sit.

They ordered quickly, paying little attention to it. Susan tried to obliquely indicate they were facing unusual conditions, in space and time, and David was one of several trying to assess the situation. Mary listened. It was, Susan thought, as if she absorbed the words, the thoughts, and shrouded them with a field that held no emotion or feeling. Susan finished.

Mary sat for a minute, playing with the lazy susan in the center of the table, rotating the food plates, uneaten, that they had ordered.

"David should be good at understanding disappearances," Mary said. She laughed, a sound like ice clinking against glass. "And you?"

Susan was trying to remember what she had told Mary, on the first call, and now. She was wishing she hadn't made this trip.

"Surely you know how out of it I am," Mary said. "Haven't published in years. That does you in, on the old all boys' network."

"Actually, I don't understand. You had such a stunning early time of it."

"Why do you say that?"

Susan pulled back at the unexpected attack against what she had hoped would establish a bond.

"Well, everybody says, and that paper you wrote, it was clearly brilliant."

"You don't know that. You can't, on your own. I don't mean to be dismissive, but really. You're just regurgitating what the boys said. That's not knowledge, it's words, words rattling in a void of incomprehension. That's so much of what passes for clever."

"But still . . ."

The food came, some dim sum. Susan politely picked up one.

"I got so tired of them, their overly attenuated traditions, archaic forms of conversation, diddling on their blackboards, all that enthusiasm, leading nowhere. Let Marie Curie die for their science, not me."

Mary used one of her chopsticks like a spear, skewering a dumpling, raising it to her mouth, a swift, suddenly angry movement. So that's what's underneath, thought Susan, so much for the gentility.

Mary looked up as if she were suddenly noticed, smiled unapologetically.

"I just tend my garden, tinker a bit. It's . . . well, it's what I do."

"And that's enough? For someone like you, so, well, so smart, once at the vanguard."

Mary gulped down her dumpling. "So, are you lovers yet? Oh, yes. I can see. He can be what he needs to be, can't he?"

"I'm not, that's not–"

"No matter, Susan. No matter at all."

"What's happening, what's important is–"

"I wouldn't know."

"Then what–"

"Of course, I would have to say, just the basics, I'm sure you've gotten that far. Matter must remain. It doesn't evaporate." She spiked another dumpling.

The check came. Susan quickly paid. Mary picked up her fortune cookie, smiled, and put it down unopened.

They said goodbye, without even the pro forma of they'd see each other again. On a whim, Susan went by the University library. They had no record of a Mary Quinton using it.

Upon her return, she found that David had gone to work with intense energy in the spare bedroom, filling it up with newly ordered equipment. Susan recognized long, narrow tubes of lasers, but amidst all the wiring, more computers, and other material, she had no idea what David was building, and he, working virtually round the clock, was not about to release the energy of creation prematurely. He just said wait, every time she asked him what he was up to. She bought some manuals and was teaching herself computer programming when after four days he finally asked her into the room, in the mid-afternoon of a cloudy day. They walked into the dark room, its windows all shrouded, David threw a switch and they looked in silence for a while at the void he had filled.

Susan saw a box-like array of intersecting lasers defining at first simply a hazy box of light, a shimmering more noticed by its contrast to its surroundings than by any property it yet possessed, gradually taking on greater definition until the boxed area had become a range of shapes that were peaks, mountains, valleys, ranges.

"It's almost like I can feel them inside me," said Susan, "more even than when I'm actually seeing them."

"I know what you mean, it's like they extend into the subliminal consciousness. There's some comfort in the recognition of a primal, fractal shape, isn't there? Interesting."

"You and your damn interesting." She laughed. "Although I have to admit..."

"I was almost in a reverie when I built this. We needed to look at the events in three dimensions. Remember the problems I felt we had with dimensionality? Fractal geometry was more enamored with visual depiction at its birth than any form of geometry in history, but they were all nonetheless two-dimensional depictions. We saw them on paper or on the screen, on two-dimensional surfaces only, and so powerful a tool were they in explaining and replicating our view of nature that they drew us in. So that in those science fiction movies we completely accepted that those clouds we were seeing were three dimensional.

"We're so trained to look at the surface, such as if you were to read what I am now saying, it would be the two-dimensional physical printing of the word on the paper, but how could I create a three-dimensional quote 'page' for you to read that could capture the color and depth and tone of not only my imagery but also the philosophy and meaning behind it? Words themselves impose this two-dimensional compound on us.

"Think of all the richness lost, of nature, of the depths of man. So I used the calculus to rotate my matrix around itself, like generating a football from a flat oval, and programmed it to portray these images, three-dimensional fractals using a holographic array – three-dimensional fractal holography – the beginning of a three-dimensional way of communicating across scale."

They looked at the images he created, the laser light slightly reflecting across their faces and hands, like a pale-hued TV set the only illumination in a dark room, communicating a late-night stationary image, a test pattern.

"It's beautiful, compelling even. But what does it do for us?" she asked.

"They say observation is the first step in therapy."

"It's not where emotions begin."

"For me, well, I have to establish some basis for understanding. This display may be only a beginning, but virtually nobody in the world has seen anything like it. Including our friend out there. I think we have a weapon, although I'll be damned if I can figure out how to use it. At least the light's coherent, even if I'm not."

They walked out, closing the door on mountains shimmering in the unlit room behind them. Susan tripped over a cord, shutting down the display. "No big deal," said David. He rebooted it, and the world rebuilt itself behind them.

⁂

"Okay," said Susan, "so what's up with this Mary Quintin? Really."

They were lying in bed, having made love, normally a time of intimate conversation they both enjoyed as much as the lovemaking itself.

"Ah, what do you mean, what's up, we told you about her, she –"

"Come on, David, her name comes up and you start talking about Schimmelpfennics, or whatever. You don't think I can tell?"

He sat up in bed, propped some pillows behind him.

"Remember that party Sebby was talking about?" She nodded. "Well, as it was breaking up, I found myself walking next to Mary, really as close as I'd ever gotten. We decided to take a sneak peek at Einstein's classroom, something we did now and then, imagining him, then ourselves, in front of that board, those equations. It's, well, it's a turn-on.

"So somehow we went from a heated dispute over quantum exchanges to a heated exchange of bodies."

"Aha," said Susan, "I knew it."

"Well, yes, but. It was odd, and then weird. Look, I was young, horny; she was something else. So I didn't notice at the time, but later – it seemed almost like she was forcing herself to go through the motions, more an experiment she was detached from, observing, than any real involvement, it was like she was overcoming the sensation, not enjoying it.

"When I entered her – it's okay to talk about this, really?" Susan nodded. She raised herself next to him, stroked his arm as he spoke. "So then, she shuddered, and, well, like I said, I was a young guy, moved to my own rhythm, only afterwards, when I'd gone and was lying back in my bed in a dark-of-night recreation, I realized, or thought I did, that she was more watching me, more enduring, more simulating the motions than actually being driven to them. Look, I came, as young men do, under so many circumstances, but . . . As soon as I did, then left her, I suddenly felt chilled, cold, as if my bones had turned to steel and were chilling me from within, draining warmth, inside and out.

"One moment she was lying there, calmly, at least; the next she must have sensed my sense, she pulled the duvet around her, stared, those eyes a gray opacity that seemed to open into her mind, opaque, cold, an abyss you could fall into with no bottom. A distance that was unspannable.

"I swear, it took me a moment to remember, was this my place or hers, then I got up, terrible I left her, still naked and wet with me, I crumbled any clothes I couldn't put on quickly, mumbled something that released me, got out of there.

"Over the next two and a half years, we never spoke again."

They lay next to each other, quiet, lightly touching. "And that's Mary," he finally said, to break the silence.

"I should tell you, I met with her."

"What!"

"Well, you got me so curious, and besides, if she knows anything that could be helpful."

"Whatever she knows, she's not going to be helpful."

"I see that, now, and what she said, I can see – anyway, that's done with."

"She, she kind of scares you off the whole thing, actually. Men, women."

"I'm not Mary, David."

"No, you're nothing like her. And everything to me."

In the morning, Susan woke up to David muttering about a dream he had in which he invented an all-purpose piece of furniture. On her way to the kitchen, she found a sheet David had printed out and left on the couch where she usually sat, titled *David's Doggerel.*

> The world is a fractal filled with desire
> Sometimes an ash, sometimes a fire.
> If the outcome of love was always known
> The spark would diminish, we'd end up alone.
> Life's excitement is what we can cram in
> to moments exquisite because they are random.
> Determinacy's not just beyond the door
> It would also be a colossal bore.
> Each aria is a different rendition
> of the notes of the initial condition
> And if a voice might sometimes crack
> that possibility adds piquancy to the great song's
> back.
> It is the chance of either by which we are touched,

for which we should say, "lord thank you so much."
Twixt the twin poles of linear and chaos
Lie the media that will forever play us.
Our footfalls like rain on muddy roads spatter,
The choices we face, the sense of the matter
But still it's a continuum in which our lives play
The constancy of moments that urge us each day,
The fight that we make from start to finish
To give our lives meaning that does not diminish.

Her eyes skimmed the screen and read again more slowly. She stood up, still for a moment, then a movement crossed her eyes and lips at the same time, a smile that filled her body. She headed back to the bedroom.

Chapter Twenty-three

He thought he knew every path and piece.

Shen-ya had walked these hills and mountains of the Lang YaShen mountain range most of his sixty-two years. He hadn't always needed permission to walk them, as he did now, but his skills and knowledge were such that he always got it, and besides, those puffed-up party officials and other uniforms had grown up on stories of Shen-ya in the mountains; many had walked with him, as children anyway, before the correct behavior of the moment kept them glued to seats below, where they forgot the freedoms the hills implied, even resented the implication.

His was introspective on this walk today, worried it might be his last. He looked around. A great mountain range has its own way of encompassing all emotions, he thought, eliciting with its indifferent will fear, love, respect, hatred, awe, a cushion of comfort and an implacable edge. The YaShens held all of these, from peak to peak across the range of feelings, made more special still by the difficulties of access and infrequency of contact. He passed the rough leather of his gloved hand over the light beard covering his face, looking, thinking. Consider a mountain path. It starts as an interplay between a microanomaly in the hill, some random shift giving texture and line along a direction. Animals exploit it, leaving spoors, feces, a leftover kill, small game ironically laying out the map for the hunters, among them, finally, men. Other men come, the next stage of hunters whose prey is movement, view, virgin crossings and ascents, conquest. Others follow, different if not wiser, hoping to breathe or bask along a well-marked trail, seeking to combine existing markings and their selves into unique experience. From ecstasy to tragedy, the mountain path leads its following, giving the newcomer the joy of surprise and the experienced walker the richness of old friends rediscovered, always the possibility of seeing a new line, new angles from each day's special light, eking out the riches within the limits, the unchanging core of the mountain. His mountains, his happiness and sadness.

So it was not easy for Shen-ya to come down to the flat town to the District Party Office and make his report. The day was cold and damp, his worn boots sticking in the mud as he walked to the regional offices, pulling at him like an unwelcome message burdening his usually solid pace. The enveloping grayness and incessant drizzle depressed him further, fearful as he was that with the news he carried they would take away his right to walk his hills, even perhaps incarcerate him for fear of a mental aberration. Still, he had done his duty always all these years, and he had survived, and that was the strongest habit of all. He was in fact held in far too much esteem in this small village ever to have any of his fears befall him, but it was a part of him that he didn't know this, and he was quietly concerned as he explained what he had seen.

"Yes, that's right, Comrade Commissioner, I had turned the bend of Wengfa Pass, it's a popular walk for tourists, we used to even take foreigners there when that was allowed, not that I am questioning the current policy, which I understand may be changing." He always found himself talking too much in official Presences, the energy of his natural warmth and good humor finding an outlet in this prattling. He was never obsequious – the life of mountains ran in him too deeply for that – but he did blather. Comrade Commissioner, for his part, would have been more concerned by the absence of such behavior from someone sitting across from him than by its accustomed display.

"Yes, I know the spot, I've been there myself, wasn't that with you, Shen-ya?"

That made Shen-ya more uncomfortable. Yes, they had gone, with comrades who had been this Comrade's superiors, so that Shen-ya had had to defer to them over this one, then a fawning pup, who now had power and might remember some affront or humiliation unless he just remembered having a good time, which was still possible in the hills, when the altitude, rugged terrain, strenuous hiking and climbing required complete concentration, no ideology after a few days in the mountains, which was why Shen-ya stayed in them as much as he could.

"A wonderful trip, unique with such men, you foremost, Comrade Commissioner, such strength on those hikes, you'd think you'd been doing it all your life." It was so hard to tell a story under these conditions, maybe it wasn't worth it. But he persevered, up this height like the others, a step at a time.

The rain rattling on the windows looking out on the inner courtyard, grayer still than the day, reminded him further of the contrast between being in the hills then and in this office now. There had been wall carvings of the deities nestled on the courtyard walls once, now just shaven stone like where a branch is cut from the trunk, smooth but unsettling. "It was a beautiful day, clear and sunny, as brisk as when we – I – was younger and bounced on days like that, seeing as far as you wanted. And then, around the pass, which is not so easy to find since the Triplets Peaks have so many similarities, there, that's where it was."

"And this it, as you say, it was . . . ?"

"Nothing, Comrade Commissioner, nothing."

"Nothing," the local Party leader repeated. "But how do you see nothing, Shen-ya?"

"It's a stretch I know like the back of my hand, Comrade." Shen-ya spoke with some force now, on familiar ground. A piece of his soul resided in those mountains, and was being tampered with. "It's lovely, as you know, and, well, you look across at it, and there's a section of the peak, jagged as always, and then lower down the same, sloping to the lake, and in between . . . is nothing."

The Comrade Commissioner knew Shen-ya. Like most men who climbed mountains, he had no imagination. He could look straight down an abyss of one thousand meters and mark only the contour at the bottom, where other men would picture their own crumbled, bloodied deaths. Shen-ya could walk across a four-inch plank over such a drop without stopping eating his snack or talking, and wait patiently at the other side to rope in his followers, who even with such protection inched slowly across the board, ashamed they could not hide their quaking, their sewing machine legs trembling as they loved for the instant this calm ruddy man who held and talked them over. There had not been much room for ideology on their trip, the Comrade Commissioner remembered.

Moreover, strange phenomena were not unknown in remote parts of the Chinese Republic where testing by any of a number of military and secret organizations could be going on without the knowledge of the other ones, let alone the locals, who were often treated with contempt and always shut out. So the Comrade was surprisingly inclined to accept the possibility that Shen-ya's strange tale had at least an element of truth in it. For what it mattered.

He told Shen-ya the truth. "I don't know of any special army activity up there, or blasting, or whatever they might dream up, but that doesn't mean it hasn't happened. I'll try to find out, Shen-ya, and if I do I'll try to let you know, if I can, so stop worrying about it. Take some other passes for a while."

That Shen-ya had already decided to do. He had peered into a nothingness that set even his stolid self to thoughts of mortality, a vaporous ending, and it was not an experience he cared to repeat. There were many paths through the mountains, and he had reached the stage where walking itself was the pleasure and the reason. Some peaks were already denied him, but that was natural. Eager to leave, he stood up and made for the door. Relieved once it was opened, he couldn't help asking, "But what if no one knows anything, Comrade?"

The Commissioner sighed. It so rarely happened, he might almost welcome it. But still . . . "Then I don't know, Shen-ya, I really don't know."

==

The Comrade Commissioner of the regional party office found that nothing could exist in many ways in many places. He found it when he began asking for any information about any activity by any agency in the hills nearby. "Nothing" wasn't the answer based on research, knowledge, or analysis; "nothing" was simply the answer. He had worked in and accepted the system and its mandates for so long that this quest marked the first time he had ever asked a question of it, and the results were disturbing. At night he began to see Shen-ya's vision as the embodiment of the organization around him. He had nightmares, of caverns and caves, of endless queues and questions.

He waited six hours a day in the District Commissar's office, shunted from Local Military Preparedness one day to Community Liaison the next, then to the Office of Integrated Planning among the Republics, finally to Strategic Deployment and ending up in Systems Testing. Always it was the same:

"Have you had any unusual activity going on in the Wengfa Pass, near the Triplets?" he asked.

"Nothing, Comrade."

"Would you perhaps check with your colleagues, since the area is so vast and the Chinese Republic's activities even more so."

"Nothing is there, Comrade"

"Precisely, Comrade."

"Why do you ask about nothing, District Commissar?"

"Because it is my duty to discover and control those activities taking place within my region which may affect the productivity of the local populations and the security of the nation."

"We have done nothing to impede these admirable and important efforts, Comrade."

"And that is most appreciated, Comrade, but nothing may be impeding them, and I would like to find its source."

And nobody checked, nobody in the Comrade District Commissar's review asked anyone else in the Department, and after a week he still had not found all the Departments or compartments within them, and he returned to tell Shen-ya that he, moving in his own way, had also found nothing.

It wasn't until several weeks later, at a regional meeting in Beijing which he had worked three years to be able to attend, on new advances in Chinese science, their potentially glorious impact on all citizens of the People's Republic and how they might be implemented at the local level at as yet undesignated times through appropriate channels, that a few vodkas, a custom remaining from the days of visits from their former cousins to the North, loosened his grip, and he told the story, a feverish confession that drew many nods of sympathy and at least and at last a little serious attention from those who could recognize when a man was genuinely troubled.

Chapter Twenty-four

Thoughts of the world vary.

"Field work's not my thing," Sebby said to Susan. He looked tired, unusual for him.

"What is?" she asked, partly in jest.

He took the question seriously. "I like taking the abstract and making it concrete. David's a fountain of ideas."

"That he is," she said.

"But they need testing and assessment, to determine their place in the rhythm of our models. And . . ." He paused.

"And what?"

"And my eschatology. For me, there needs to be a framework for what we study, a metaperspective. I really did think about becoming a priest; I just couldn't reconcile all the obvious nonsense with my sense of how faith should operate, the intersection of the rational with the notion of the divine. I hated that loss, but found something more."

"With David?" she asked.

"Yes, he's played a big part in it. But also –"

"Your wine!"

"That too, the meaning of taste, not as an indulgence, but as an experience of experience itself, self-awareness, in the moment and transcending time. Isn't that what our equations do, our principles, help us grasp moments within a longer view? I wanted that to encompass several worlds, of the human imagination, really. But now . . ."

"Now?"

"What we're dealing with, it challenges too much. Destroys faith as much as mass. I suppose I'd never thought the end result of imagination and possibility, the exploration of physics and faith, could end up in something so evil."

She patted his hand. "It doesn't have to, I think. Not with people like you and David involved."

"Thanks. Now I wish I had your faith."

"Well, I wish I had your physics!"

David came into the room, sat next to Susan.

"Speaking of people," Sebby said, picking up a file. He had wandered from research facilities in nearby universities, to libraries, roamed further through the network of computers centered at the UN, and made a few visits. They sat amidst the couches, chairs, and papers, which had melded into a unified multitextured and leveled piece of furniture. An arm could just as easily be on a stack of files as on an armrest, a leg could be aloft anywhere, it all seemed to mold around them wherever they sat. "I'd knocked out a bunch of names – dead, retired, recent contacts indicating full lives with no time, energy, or inclination to wreak havoc. Then I really thought I was finally on to someone who could be doing it.

"Major Daniel 'Don' Englehart, runs the high-energy labs for the Department of Energy outside of Albuquerque. I arranged to meet Major Don on the pretext of doing research into fusion at Princeton – that opens any door, bless the place, and given all the various approaches surrounding the efforts, nobody would have the audacity to suggest you're spouting nonsense, everybody wants to get in on the act. Out into the desert I roamed, looking for the disappearance of the burning bush!

"He sure had the right set-up, access to all kinds of data and equipment regarding high energy particles, even the ability – are you ready for this? – he has authorization to personally sign for up to forty million dollars for a project. Forty million dollars! He could more or less run his own private shop and it would take years, if ever, before anybody would catch up with him. Seemed perfect.

Sebby straightened up, pushed out his chin. "Only Major Don would not, repeat would not, be your candidate for precipitating the disappearance of the world, certainly not a world which gives him the discretionary authority to spend forty million dollars, and all the sucking up of vendors and staff that implies. I met him in his office in the middle of nowhere, a long, dusty jeep ride past three consecutive fences warning off those without 'authorization for further transit' into federal wild horse preserves to desert conservancy projects until finally through the inner gate which mentioned in passing a little government research going on."

Susan said, "Sounds like the concentric circles –"

"Of the Inferno, yes, that thought crossed my mind. Sure was hot enough.

"People were actually pretty relaxed once I got into the place, felt like a combination think tank, experimental lab, and corporate campus. I had the feeling parts of it would glow in the dark, they have some pretty big equipment, nothing I could get close to, massive electricity lines, stretching like mirages out of the desert above the boundless balls of sagebrush that dotted the landscape far as the eye could see, the lines seemed to grow out of the plants at the horizon, shimmering in the heat ionization, it looked like wavy lines of power sprang from the heat itself, as if the facility tapped into fundamental power, all surrounded by a big sign saying 'Do Not Disturb.' I tell you, folks, there is yet religion out there.

"Most of the people wore shorts and short-sleeve shirts. Imagine, David, a gaggle of physicists and they were all tan! One guy had a setup where he could light his pipe using concentrated sunlight. They drove around in souped-up solar-powered golf carts and dune buggies. Every now and then the lights would all dim and intense rumbling noises and hums would emanate from the hangers, which is what they called the big buildings. Just another day at the office.

"Then I met Major Don. Snap-to, brisk! His office was immaculately clean and neat, as if not even sand would risk bucking the force of his regimen. His desk had a few piles on it, all stacked flush on all sides; if there's a regulation on the number and position of pens and pencils on the desk, I'm sure I was looking at it. Everything neat and ordered, and there he was in pressed khaki uniform and a tie, the crisp jaw, tight lips. He called me 'Mister'! Did you ever feel tainted by being a civilian? That environment. After some discussion on his research, I widened the topics a bit. The guy does not believe in fractals. Seriously. First of all, there is no room in Major Don's mind for consideration of chaos. He believes in order, and orders. So to allow that there are random, unpredictable interludes in patterns is absolutely not tolerated, mister, it is simply a question of lack of knowledge which it is our mission to gain and we will gain it, I repeat, we will ascertain your so-called unpredictable periods and we will be able to know what the weather will be like anywhere at any time, and that is that, end of discussion on chaos.

"Folks, Major Don would in no way mister cause any part of his wonderfully controlled world to disappear; he has too much at stake in it, he genuinely likes it, and he doesn't believe in anything that would give him the tools, let alone the desire, to activate a dissolution of anything material. Besides, it wouldn't be in his budget, that would end it right there! So I went out for a hyper solar dune buggy ride and shared a six-pack with an old classmate who was working out there on weapons storage – they have a critical mass concern, you'll be reassured to hear – notice my tan, if you two didn't spend all your spare moments inside maybe you could also lose that wan, albeit it flushed and happy, look, and I came back east."

David and Susan squeezed each other's hands, which they had come to hold as Sebby went on.

"Figuring I could still rack up more frequent flyer mileage at the UN's expense I flew to San Francisco, Seattle, down to Houston, up to Chicago; everywhere it was more or less the same. Above all, nobody I met had the inclination, let alone the ability – whatever it takes – to initiate any of the phenomena we've been seeing. Lots of grants, niches in corporations, dedicated yes, and also coddled, not about to foment a revolution of dissolution. I did take one more trip that I got a kick out of.

"Remember Edwin Forrestor? He was a guest lecturer several times at Princeton and I ran into him again at Cal. He certainly could grasp the issues involved, his specialty was macro/micro analogues, the similarities between studies of things very large – the universe and galactic systems, say – and very small, the quantum understanding of which is required for analyzing theories surrounding the origins of space and matter. Strong math too, fractals would be no problem for him. He also dabbled in economics, whacky abstract ideas about distribution vectors, that there were directions to income flow and motivations to those directions which could be captured mathematically and altered by small intrusions at the base of the vector as opposed to large ones at its head, which for him was virtually any government interaction.

"Which is a riot because Forrestor is probably the richest physicist around. His family was big in retail chains – you should see his lawn furniture. So he never needed to be establishment in any way, unconventional, like certain other physicists in this room, but more because he never had to be anything else, not because he was intellectually driven in that direction, but because he could afford to be and wanted to let you know it.

"I went to visit him at his estate in the Berkshires. There was a longer distance from the front gate to the main house than from here to the UN. Huge lawns, groves, a small lab adjacent to the big Tudor house, really lovely. He met me on the front steps, small, natty, his Van Dyke a little grayer, just so, matched to his old-world manners, at home in the parlors of Vienna. Tea served in the rear garden, overlooking an immaculate hill, part controlled plantings, part natural but . . . just so, pretty and perfect."

"Sounds like your front lawn," said Susan.

"You noticed?" asked David.

"Of course I did, it was like something familiar rearranged. Until your stupid door."

David laughed. "It's all matter of scale."

"He was as usual slightly haughty, aloof, but very entertaining," continued Sebby. "Teaches courses on an occasional basis at colleges in the area. There are so many of them that they provide him with a never-ending stream of bright research students. He said he preferred undergraduates because 'their minds are less fettered with what is known so not constricted by preconceptions of what is possible or not.' That was important to him, as his approach is built primarily around thought experiments concerning the nature of reality."

"What are thought experiments?" asked Susan.

"They are," said David, "a method of thinking about reality without being limited by what you can physically examine. Einstein, as usual, was well known for using them in his work. You're probably familiar with the one about taking twins and sticking one of them on a space ship moving close to the speed of light, while the other one stays home on earth and runs the family bakery. Since time moves more slowly when you're travelling at or close to the speed of light – should you ever have the occasion – relative to its rate on the slower-moving earth, when the wandering twin returns he is now younger than the twin who remained. The approach was revolutionary in the context of classical physics, which rested upon tangible validation as part of its methodology. Utilizing the laboratory of the mind opened up whole new dimensions of areas of study; it's one of the reasons physics today can be so divergent in its approaches to issues, and so seemingly personal in the way material is analyzed and presented.

"I have a favorite thought experiment of my own. Want to hear it?"

Susan smiled. "Of course."

"Imagine a mirror around the universe, a gigantic mirror that lies like a great box around the borders of everything. Now imagine yourself inside the universe, looking out. As you know, light bends according to gravitational fields."

"Okay, I know that," said Susan. "Now." Sebby laughed.

David stood, opening his arms as if to encapsulate the universe he postulated. "At the edge of the universe, you could look in and effectively consider all the matter of the universe as existing at a single, massive central point, for purposes of determining its gravitational effect. Such a point would generate a field so intense that it would bend light back in on itself. So there's our mirror sitting at the edge of all the space and matter of the universe, and since no light would reach it, what would a mirror around the universe reflect? Here we are, we and everything else there is, and what would we see if could look into that mirror around us containing everything we know and feel and touch and see? Nothing, absolutely nothing."

"Jesus, David, you sure now how to paint a pretty picture," Susan said. "Maybe that's why Sebby's god or the gods don't know what's going on around here."

"Good an explanation as any," said Sebby.

They sat for a while, looking off into nowhere. In their stillness they became almost a part of the papers and chairs, letters and colors, that surrounded them, chameleons of the mind, changing with new information, adapting without even knowing it.

Finally, Sebby shook himself and continued. "Well, Edwin and I had a pleasant chat over tea, scones, clotted cream and wild strawberries picked in front of us. He was very good company, and I could have stayed for days, but after a few minutes it was clear that, as unconventional as he liked to think of himself, he was firmly grounded in his life and estate and adoring students, and that nothing was not about to shake any of that up for him. He'd heard about our problems, but suggested we were misinterpreting data, that matter simply didn't disappear, so perhaps we should look to perceptual states. I thanked him and drove off. I didn't get twenty miles before I had to take an enormous pee. All that tea! I stopped by the side of the road, feeling like I was back in school, having been lectured to and my ideas dismissed. I took a long time relieving myself in a cool breeze blowing down out of the Berkshires, and headed back to New York."

≂

The UN computers and investigators continued to work on the seemingly mundane task of trying to locate the whereabouts of the remaining people on the short list, ones whom Sebastian had not seen or found, as well as some who had been added to it through further research efforts. David, Susan, and Sebby stayed in the apartment to see if a few days respite from the analytical side of approaching the problem had given them any new perspectives. For a while, David and Sebby went back over the equations, while Susan read through some of the articles strewn about the room, bypassing the equations to get a sense of the text where she could. As usual, she was fearless in leading the charge, but it's not always possible to avoid the dangers of that approach. Apartment 6N was their world, but the world was not their apartment.

Chapter Twenty-five

Absences live on.

Two days later, Susan pulled David over to the kitchen table and sat across from him, nestling her chin into her folded arms. "David, when we first met, you said the essence of problem solving was to see things as they are. Remember?" He nodded, resting his head in his hands, elbows supported by the table, looking at her, a soft smile giving new contours to his face. She continued. "And you've also said that a fundamental tenet of your quantum bits and pieces is that you can't see them as they are, that if you try to measure one aspect, you can't pin down another." He nodded again.

"Well, how about if you try to measure direction of something in these spaces, and I'll shoot for position, or whatever, both of us at the same time in separate ways. Couldn't we sort of triangulate in, then compare notes later?"

"Hmmm . . . hmmm." He looked at her. "That's . . . Let's see – well, it couldn't really be done at the small particle level, because we don't have – or more precisely, it's theoretically not possible to have – instruments that can measure one without disturbing the other."

"David, it's not itsy-bitsy particles that are going ga-ga right now, it's bloody Jones Beach that we're trying to find."

He sat for a while, then doodled. First it seemed almost a random outpouring of numbers, circles, then a long rectangle with arrows shooting around in all directions, like an aerial view of Custer's Last Stand.

He looked up at her. "Maybe I should call you Susie Q – for quantum," he said. "On this gross level, where the events we want to observe are experiential and directly accessible to us, while somehow exhibiting quantum behavior … it could be a sort of simultaneity trap. And if we could through observation measure both momentum and position of the equivalent of a particle introduced into the phased-out space, at the same time, which would otherwise be an impossibility, maybe we could force the phased-out space to retreat from the impossibility, to remain as particles. Some way to fight back, hell, even … "

"What?"

"Well, I've been wondering. If we ever encounter the source of all the discontinuities – how do we fight it? Remember the old saw, 'I've invented an acid that can eat through anything, now what do I keep it in?' How do material beings go up against something that might be able to convert us to waves? I wouldn't have much of a right cross if my fist vanished, would I?"

She smiled. "It's your intellect that guides you, that'll enable you – I just know it – to prevail over something like this wave phasing out business."

"Thanks, but there's more than intellect required, I suspect. To withstand something like this assault, it will also take strength of will, preparation, god knows what." His voice trailed off.

"Okay," said Susan, walking back into the living room, "so when do we spring our simultaneity trap?"

"I've been thinking about that. I see two levels of experiment. One, to see if we can pinpoint the location of the source of all our problems, which I haven't been very successful at so far. The other would be to force a particle interaction in wave space under controlled circumstances. If we can control that, then we'd know we had a shot at controlling the source."

Susan, Sebastian, and David went to the beach. They went to look at a small stretch of vanished shore that had propelled Lucy, Samuel, and Tyrone to run from a free day by the ocean into an armful of skepticism, that could not exist but did, that with its counterparts pulsed like a potential plague still festering unknown in the sewers of the planet, that had swept them up in Harold Upshaw's setting in motion the most massive scientific effort in history. They had gone an hour in advance of the technical team they would coordinate, in order to get the feel of the place, of the curtain that defied penetration. Standing in front of the space, Susan remembered David's elusive door, as if it had been a precursor. Only the space on the beach was not done with lasers, it wasn't a holograph, it wasn't there, she didn't dare kick it, and it was infinitely more real.

In the end, they just stared in silence for a while, then walked along the visible shore for the rest of the hour. Susan took off her shoes and ran in the water, dragging her feet through the last of the surf and sand and pebbles, slowly, not smiling or laughing, her head bowed down, her hair framing her head like blinders on a horse, as if that was what kept her looking so intently at the movements through her feet, occasionally raising a foot and watching the sand slowly drip down between her toes. David felt like an old man absorbed by his frailty, but could only get himself to walk along the edge of the dry, hard sand that was the remnant of the last full tide, a happenstance of the waves that might once have served some evolutionary purpose, a different terrain to foster movement, perhaps, he feared, was doing it again.

We only studied the dinosaurs, he thought; we never considered what it would be like to be one, in those closing, dumbfounding days of an era that must have seemed eternal. He would sporadically talk quietly with Sebastian about a technical point to consider, Sebastian taking notes, the sun in their faces on the way out, and on their backs as they returned, a long, steady breeze blowing across them towards the land, so that Sebby had to hold on to the paper with one hand as he wrote with the other, as they walked back to an amorphous spot that remained unchanged. They met the technical team, plotted equipment location and the placement of portable generators, and drove in silence back to the apartment. Other than around the construction at the parkway turnoff, there was almost no traffic, but they didn't notice their luck.

Three days later, they returned. Signs had been put up blocking off the area, which was between two of the more popular beaches. The signs said "Rebuilding New York – Bird Sanctuary and Playground." It listed the Governor, the Mayor, four other elected officials, two federal grant programs, three government agencies and as many commissioners, as well as a date when the beach would be reopened, in six months. Such signs were common enough on roads and subway stations and parks so as to not attract attention; also they could be there for an indefinite amount of time, since nobody took completion dates seriously. Indeed, most people who passed it only wondered how New York City would get a beach to crack, like everything else the City bought or repaired, from subway cars to stadiums. They also cursed at the cars sitting in the "No Parking" area, assuming that their owners were probably sitting on what had become their private section of beach; there's always somebody more in. The only difference between the sandy restricted stretch here and most construction sites was the absence of Mercedeses and Jaguars with New Jersey license plates, but the dull grey and blue Chevrolet and Dodge sedans with their windows rolled all the way up neither aroused suspicion nor alleviated indignation. And then the large trucks started rolling in.

The experiment David devised to use Susan's idea was simple. Normally, particle accelerators require tremendous velocities and energies to get particles to collide with the intensity necessary to mimic the conditions when matter was superdense, such as at the beginning of time, to create new, short-lived particles such as bosons and quarks to study the innermost workings of subatomic activity. Thus the need for the gigantic machines with fifty miles of tunnels lined with magnets and driven with the power of suns, to drive particles that could not be seen in experiments that could not be witnessed, to review the records of the events and push back the fringe of knowledge.

It was easier at the beach. The shore line was – not there. Instead, there was a shimmering of hues, delicate fadings, the edges of the area hazing the incoming waves when one looked out at the water, while from the other side they shrouded the contours of the beach. The curtain ran for barely a hundred feet, then the beach returned to its normal state. It was small enough to be viewed in its entirety, big enough to conjure images of an endless hole that could swallow them all.

David had the UN team build two ramps, one on the beach tilted down towards the shore, the other built on stilts on the ocean floor, a mirror image of the first heading in to the shore. Where the two met, in the middle of the discontinuous space, the team had slowly and cautiously installed a barrage of sensors and recording devices. The data from these devices went out on two trunk cables leading up the beach in a vee away from the center connection. The first contained all data relating to location, tracking position instant by instant. The second measured momentum. The two cables fed into two computer stations, banks of screens and data processing equipment each continually monitoring data as fed into them. By comparing the timelines of both data feeds, David reasoned it would be possible to determine the two aspects of matter as it collapsed within the distorted wave-oriented space, taking advantage of its unusual properties to use those properties against it. By establishing these two aspects at the same time, he expected to be able to fix the particles themselves in a particular place with a specific momentum, and in a reverse feedback the observers could create what was being observed. Through the detailed knowledge of the particles they were monitoring, they could maintain them in their own reality, challenging the source of the distortions, and, he hoped, perhaps negating the source's ability to phase these particles into waves. He was excited; after months of absorbing blows, he was finally throwing a punch.

"So what particles are we observing?" asked Susan, expecting an ethereal discussion about the relativistic extrapolation of quantum properties.

"Bowling balls."

"What!"

"Sure – why not? We can easily get them to collide, we have an intuitive understanding of the nature of that collision, which will be useful for later applications, they're easily observable, the data should be . . . striking, ooh, I know, you'll say spare me the puns, oops . . ."

Susan sighed. "You just split me up, David. So this is how you'll pin down the data? I should have guessed, it's right up your alley."

"Okay, okay. Anyway – it's bowling balls. Care to watch?"

"You couldn't keep me away. Aren't you?"

"Oh, you know, I'm a theoretical player, not a lab guy. I have a helicopter so that I can observe the whole thing. It may give me some insight in how to encapsulate this simultaneity of observations into my consciousness."

"For when you have to go up against the Source?" She stopped smiling.

"Well, I'm hoping to avoid anything so direct – but yes, just in case."

"I'm staying on the ground. I want to watch the position monitor, since I can at least understand that."

"Good enough, see you after the show." They kissed briefly, excitedly, eager to start the experiment, eager to get back to each other. David marched off to the waiting helicopter. Susan watched him, a familiar lope she could now recognize from any distance, the sun and wind injecting energy into her awareness of her love, expanding it so that she felt she could see beyond the horizon, and understand the place; she smiled and ran off to the platform housing the position-tracking equipment, her feet slipping in the deep sand with each step.

From above, David looked down on the two ramps aimed towards their meeting point, each just wide enough to accommodate the ebony sphere poised at its end. David had suggested that the lab teams get purple silk bowling shirts with "United Nations Alleys" inscribed on the back, but nobody would approve the budget. Instead he named the position team the Beach Boys and the momentum team the Ventures. Upshaw had sighed and laDoop snorted. He had not been happy about the experiment, but Upshaw had insisted. At the junction point where the two ramps met was a large enclosed metal box, housing all the monitors. He couldn't see the box itself, it had been preassembled, with enough width to span the fractal shore line, then pushed into place from the beach and connected on the ocean side, the technicians carefully avoiding placing any part of themselves in the fuzzy part of the world so terrifyingly close to them. Nobody knew what the personal consequences of entering the space would be, and nobody cared to find out, not even the sea gulls and sandpipers, who also seemed to avoid scrupulously the emptiness beneath them.

The area where the box sat emitted a different, darker, more forceful set of hues, glowering in the odd reality of its surroundings. Out of a seeming nowhere appeared the feeder cables, like the antenna of a giant lobster whose body lay concealed under the water, running along the beach for fifty yards to the two monitoring stations, situated on platforms in the scrub grass marking the end of the sandy beach. Each station had a dozen technicians at it, as well as video and audio recorders and cameras. Anyone who had ever brought a portable music player or box to listen to at the beach would have thought he had encountered the heaven of sound, in a supercharged high. The Beach Boys Team was to the left, looking down at the ocean, monitoring position. Susan stood with them. The Ventures Team was to the right, maintaining a constant analysis of vectors, momentum, and shifting environmental factors, including temperature, pressure, and sunlight intensity, to determine direction and related energy. The data was relayed by radio transmission to the central computers at the UN for back-up.

David's helicopter circled over the junction box, around one hundred feet overhead. Through his earphones, he could communicate with the two assistants at the ends of the ramps. He had purposefully shut himself off from the two observation stations. He would read the data later; for now, he wanted to focus his attention on the physical world beneath him, a boxer looking at films of his next opponent. The churning roar of the helicopter drowned out all other outside noise, so that as he watched the scene below he heard only the communication between the technicians, and nothing of the waves or the chatter among the people on the teams, as if viewing a screen with the sound disconnected, and all the noise of living was stifled.

When everyone was in position, the two computer-monitor teams each signaled they were ready. He could see Susan hovering over the screen. He knew she was proud of her role in conceiving the basis for the experiment, and was treating it parentally. Pretty, smart, tough, and cute, he ran through his mind – quite the package. He smiled, then shook himself and said into his head phone, "Okay, let them go on my signal, three-two-one-now."

The two bowling balls, their shiny black surfaces reflecting a crescent of sparkling sunlight, were automatically released and began making their way down the chutes. It would take about eight seconds for them to reach the junction box and each other. Sensors along the ramps were already recording place and velocity. Halfway there, two Brunswick Beauties moving towards the shimmering apparent nothingness which obscured millions of dollars worth of hard equipment, labor, and thought sitting within it, no polished wooden lanes for them here, caught in a different reality, hoping to be extruded from it, hoping to pierce that vanished space, to impose on it the order of all that lay around it, of perception and particles, the balls picked up speed, governed by the old laws, faithfully obeying them towards their own dissolution.

The balls entered the junction, leaving at the last instant a trail of dark shadows behind them. Instead of the resounding crack of two balls hitting, there was a burst of light across the spectrum emanating from the place where the two ramps met, lightning without thunder, rainbows springing outward, distorting the waves, the ocean, like a world viewed through a prism moving in front of the eye. The shoreline shifted in and out of the spectrum, at times visible as a shore, at others completely vanishing in a radiating series of lights and movement more sensed than seen.

Both teams were hunched over their screens, twenty-five people taking notes, pointing furiously at their monitors. David saw Susan look up, hold her hand over her head triumphantly. She caught his eye and gave him the thumbs-up signal, the sea breeze blowing her blonde hair behind her, her face glowing from within and burnished from without. It was a way he would always remember her.

For as the teams recorded and she looked up, almost a frozen tableau, he watched as a focus of shimmering lines began emanating out, first expanding the area around the junction box, sending out spikes in different directions, then, suddenly, seeming to seize the cables, converting them to its own peculiar form of nothingness.

"Get out of there, away, run," David screamed into the headphones, knowing how useless it would be. A haze of steel-blue and sparkling violet hues, of emptiness, ran quickly up the length of the cables, into the computer stations, converting, distorting, craziness of waves eliminating the matter, disappearing, the cables, the computers, the platform, the people, Susan.

Gone. She was gone, just gone. Caught for a second looking radiant, beautiful in triumph, then puzzled, before any nonawareness could impinge, overwhelmed by the conversion, gone, the station gone, the Ventures and the Beach Boys, gone, leaving two ramps facing each other meeting at a point that wasn't there, watched by people who weren't there, in a time that couldn't be.

The two assistants still stood at the ends of the ramps, looking around in desperation, then jumping back, away, away. The helicopter pilot instinctively pulled back on his stick, bringing the machine up violently. Blood rushed into David's head as he yelled into his headset, "Susan, Susan, my God, Susan," but there was no answer, only the sight of waves he could not hear crashing into a shore he could not see. The trap had been sprung, and he was caught inside of it, forever.

Three

The Sense of the Matter

Chapter Twenty-six

The sixth story lay shrouded in shadows, as if it hadn't paid its bill.

The sun was obscured in the morning by the UN building and stayed hidden the rest of the day, behind less purposeful structures. David sat throughout, nor did he note the transition to night. The delineation threatened to become as artificial as the room's cold light flattening his features in the dark, dreary apartment, his intense stare, usually focused on a computer screen or paper, now replaced with an equally unmoving, rigid, dull look at nothing. Like Lear before the pageant of his fallen graces; a shattering mute roar. Occasionally he would go out, disappearing for hours.

Sebastian piled papers, cross coordinated data into equations, moved from one computer program to the next, interconnecting them, at times getting lost in the sheer game of manipulation, only to come across an algorithm or a memory that shocked him back to his task, feeling like he was cleaning up after a party that had gotten wildly, horribly out of control.

Finally he broke the silence, asking, simply, "What happened?"

David slowly looked up at him, stared for a while, and began talking, his voice flat and with no cadence. "It's almost easy to see, in retrospect. Masses had been introduced into the wave spaces before, but none in collision, and generally at the surface of the intersection between normal space and the wave area – molecules of air, small particulates, the feathers of a bird. Surface intersection is a well known and thus easily integrated aspect of fractal geometries, one that could be accommodated within the normal bounds of fractal activity by whatever is causing these spaces to exist. The shock of all that new mass violently interacting inside the center of the area and suddenly converting into waves sent out a dominating wave function that couldn't be contained within the existing wave space. It had to go somewhere, so it found the densest local medium to propagate in, all that nice metal in the feeder cables, and followed it up, converting everything it touched into waves in order to neutralize the imbalance. Hell, it wasn't the fault of whatever it is that's causing all this mess, it was ours. We added the unknown factor that put it out of control. It zapped all the machinery, and . . . and the people in contact with the metal, that damn platform probably didn't help any, and the rest dissipated in the sand. There's still a little shimmer left on that part of the surface of the beach – about all we've found – although it all seems to be changing back into particles. Except, of course, the original converted shore line, that's still gone."

Sebby had thought David had wandered aimlessly in his absences; now he saw the sand in his shoes.

"Why wouldn't the newly converted area remain in a wave state?" he asked.

"My guess is because it lies outside of the current power of the source to maintain it as waves. The sand is evenly but randomly distributed, with no fractal symmetry to provide guidance, unlike the shore line or the mountains. It's a small blessing, but at least the source can't control an area of random matter distribution. Yet"

"Isn't it possible then that the people who disappeared are still coherent and conscious, retrievable, the way other items are that go in and out of the wave space?"

"Like a transporter, Scotty? Nice hope, but I don't think so. When objects go in and out of the wave-dominated areas, they maintain a point of reference and are acting out of volition, entering a previously defined area. There's not a trace of those people, or the computers, or anything else, left on that beach. The violent shock of the collision being channeled into a tight path just overwhelmed the cohesiveness of the entities it touched, wave or particle, spraying their energy – Christ, anywhere, anywhere in the damned universe, I suppose. I'd like to believe – God, how I'd like to believe – there was a way to retrieve Susan and the others. But this wasn't a Star Trek beam, with some reconfiguring mechanism, this was a shattering maelstrom of the quantum energy of those people in all directions. I don't think they knew what hit them. Damn . . . and I was being so clever, the bright rebel gets a chance to stick it to Mr. Big Bang and the rest of the pompous creeps.

"She asked how we'd go on touching. I reassured her, as if I could, so flip. I was so fucking clever." He started to turn back to the emptiness in front of him, his lips drawn tightly, the mask of his face compressed like a flat plate to contain his bitterness. Again, Sebastian asked a question.

"David, what in the hell are you going to do when you confront the source of all this?"

He sat for a while, one hand against the side of his head, waving away the question. "That's not . . . I don't . . ." Looking down, another silence.

"Why ask, anyway?" His voice rose in anger. "We still don't know where it is, who or what it is. We thought we were on the right track, look where that got us."

He turned his head completely, and from this judgment Sebastian had no appeal. Whether he walked away and David sat motionless, or whether he stood still and David retreated from him, he could not tell; the relativity of emotion. While within David there lodged an inescapable distance, the gnawing distance, the ineffable capability of two lovers to be anywhere when they are apart from each other.

==

While David sat numb in the apartment, Sebastian also mourned, but he was restless, not consumed by physical grief. His sense of the universe sustained Susan's presence for him. The energy of his sorrow drove his effort to determine who was causing these now-horrific phenomena, searching for any link of the catastrophic escalation at Jones Beach to some trail which might lead to the source, regardless of whether they were now aware of it as a possibility. While he did not have David's intuitive leaps of intellect and imagination, he had a way of absorbing ideas, even David's wild new ones, of soaking up their implications and possible manifestations. If there was some... thing, particle, extension of consciousness, whatever concept, linking the progenitor of dissolution to the areas themselves, then perhaps it left a mark, was in some way traceable. The question was how to look, what might be a path. It was a mammoth undertaking, but driven by manic energy he was prepared to tackle it.

Large chunks of the earth were under virtually continuous observation. On any given day New York would be observed by airplanes, helicopters, satellites – military and civil – cameras and videos. It was crisscrossed by fabulous streams of waves, the communications industry, immeasurable amplitudes of frequencies and frequencies of amplitudes, voice, picture, data; any given point could contain a totality of activity that measured at that point would be like a spot with hundreds of lines drawn through it, the overlay turning black with successive coverings, a piece of transmission space near full to its potential, transmissions tracking through town towards their myriad purposes, all the reasons that sum New York into New York.

Sebastian searched for clues. He examined the reception patterns of radio and television bands at the moment of the event, comparing them and correlating timing with the back-up transmission data that had been received from the beach to the UN. He wandered through the logs of GPS tracking systems, sifted through airplane pilot reports, hoping another Hank Dawson had spotted something and had the courage to tell. Traffic helicopters, even automobile traffic in a radius around the beach. Nothing, nothing haunted him, no reports defined a variation in that day.

He hit it a few days later. He didn't fully understand it, but it was there and it pointed in a direction. He gathered the material.

" David, I've got some stuff to show you, it's–"

"Not now, Sebby. Maybe I'll take a look later."

"David, get up, point your nose in this direction, and look at these pictures, or I will switch off your terminal – you'll go off-line, David, I mean it."

David stared at him as if at a new apparition, the very act of looking hard jarring him out of his shell. Sebastian was determined to shake him and, as David looked at the photos he was spreading out on the kitchen table, he hoped David could understand he had something potent to back up the punches he was throwing.

"All right, Driscol, what have you got?"

Sebastian had satellite weather photos, a complete sequence taken at the time of disappearances on the beach. The day had been mildly cloudy over large areas of the northeast, patches of clear sun, light mists, and clouds. He had arranged key photos around the time of the event, so that a few photos at one-minute intervals gave way to increasingly frequent shots, down to several per second shortly before and after. Each photo had the time inset on the photo face. The early photos showed the normal stately succession of clouds providing evidence of the vast circular wind patterns that were the macroelement of weather across the planet. Immediately following the instant of the event, and for several photos thereafter, there was a faintly marked line that appeared across the swirling cloud patterns, almost like a shading following a stick as it's pulled through paint, more a delineation of contour than a difference of color or shade. A line, faint but straight.

David was by now very interested. "What do you make of it?" he asked, his eyes not leaving the photos in front of them, his dry hands shuffling from one to the next, like an ancient kinetoscope giving birth to the movie, seeking to connect separate still moments to convey meaning over time.

"I reasoned that if there was some sort of connection between whoever or whatever was causing the phenomena and the events themselves, then it might be a two-way connection, or some form of feedback between them, maybe not under normal conditions when we wouldn't have any context against which to identify it, but when the overload occurred, a dramatic shift in energy and control, then maybe it would precipitate a link. That's what I think we're seeing."

"What's next?"

"I can't say I can explain it, but I can look at it. The line heads north and east to when we lose it."

"All right, Sebby, let me think about it a bit."

==

Grief's obsession converted from consuming lethargy to continuous restlessness. David had to move, pulling his body from terminal to kitchen to bed, covered always with a light layer of sweat just short of frenzy, to move his mind from memory to conjecture, from images so vivid he could feel them to concepts so abstract he could forget what he was thinking about from one moment to the next. Grief ironically enhanced awareness; he could smell the garbage in the streets below, which he had never noticed before, catch the lingering scent of perfume on a pillowcase that otherwise would have lain undiscovered, then berate himself for past indifference. He heard the whirr of electronic machinery, different components distinct from each other, catching each separate instrument in the orchestra around him where before he had not even heard the whole piece. He lost weight, his appetite gone, gagging on taste, his body choking on the excess of sensation, Sebastian forcing vitamin pills upon him, as if he had become a machine existing on the essential ingredients, rejecting the middlemen of preparation, the inducement of taste had run amok.

The UN had put an embargo on all news of the event. Susan's vast network of people she had touched around the world, Ambways in a dozen countries, myriads of coworkers, whole tribes that had survived famine and despair thanks to her, were told if they inquired that she was on Mission. Her parents were dead, and her few cousins didn't keep up. There was no public opportunity to voice his love, his loss, to join with others in that expression. A world of less matter now held no hugs. So he cried, in private, then held himself back, his eyes a drawn red squint that stopped even New York City passers-by with their mono-focused intensity. He had never, ever experienced anything like this heightened state of pain-induced awareness that controlled his being, eliminated his filtering mechanisms. He was hypersensitive to taste and light and touch, retching on the incessant pricklings of feelings. Emotions looped in his brain so that a single sense once here and gone in the normal moment of awareness became instead an hours-long exploration without control of states that knew no bounds, holes without bottoms, the loops themselves not constant but like a system receiving with each iteration a tiny new burst of energy at its resonant frequency, so that the energy was added, not absorbed, over and over until the vibrations threatened to tear the bridge apart, the bridge between himself and the world around him, and the world within him.

And yet... there was that part of him, which while submerged still ran its program. The part that was always a step aside and considered what he was experiencing through the habits of his training and the mandates of his calling, aware of new phenomena and data, recording and analyzing it, even, God help him, unheeding of that part of him that felt pain, pushing to obtain more information, as if it were assessing the rock strata on the fall down the cliff, the thrill of a unique view, to capture if survival lay at the end of the plummet, to piece out each atom with the concentration of the doomed. He drove the obsession of grief onto the road of analysis, plunged into examining the data, that one day's data, reworking it as if his disbelief could somehow alter the outcome, a lonely batter reswinging his ninth-inning strikeout, looking for the connection.

And that part of his mind gnawed at a question, that subsumed memories, a vine of concern that became so intertwined with the trunk and limbs of his obsession that it became after a while indiscernible, body and mind flitting back and forth between the question and all others, the one part of his mind linking with all others. The learning of a lifetime and the information of the intense instant combined, beyond the state where there was food and drink and talk, where love existed but had been denied, its memory lingering behind a door that he would knock at with a separate hand set on automatic so that it would go on and on until it was only a bleeding pulp of exposed nerve fibers. The most painful moment possible yet giving way to the most painful that could be conceived, and again, and still, no way to stop its pounding beyond the reach of his controls, controls set in the normal course of existence and unable to cope with conditions that had never been anticipated, contingencies beyond awareness. But even this painfully exposed part of him sent in new signals, spurred by Sebastian's pictures, into a synthesis unlike any other, aimed at a thought repeated over and over:

"How does the source exercise control?"

There were ways to think about the areas that disappeared, pieces of physics to mend the mind's misunderstandings, but David saw them as small salves covering the real wound. Yes, they could establish a wave/particle linkage, reach back into a comprehension of the duality of matter, but these were understandings more like following recipes than knowing the ways the basic ingredients themselves behaved, the effect of a little more egg white, or heat, or yeast, fine for the meals prepared so far, but now the meals had lost their nutrition, the table itself was taken away; now a challenge appeared which cracked the easy utility of apparent understanding and lay bare a foundation of confusion, myth, and ignorance.

In the middle of an empty night, covered in moisture, David sprang out of an empty bed and sat with Buddha-calm, looking as if for the first time at the light-blue sheets and the separate grimy black dots and lines in the streaked window and clothing strewn about the room, at the flowing grain of the wood in the bureau and the enormous city on the other side of the wall, sat riveted on the center of his being as if a rod within him connected the earth below to the sky above. It didn't matter any longer that they were unseen, for now they were there. His mind had hardly dared to articulate fully the question, and now it could not contain the exuberance of his conclusion.

Now he had an answer.

He woke Sebastian, framed the question, which was a restatement in Sebastian's mind of what he too had pondered, and then jumped to his answer.

"All along," David began, "we've taken for granted this notion that the observer affects what's being observed, let it sit unexamined as a fundamental tenet of quantum physics. If you get in there to really see what's going on, then you have an effect on what you're looking at, fixing something in its position, say, which otherwise would not have been set, would remain undetermined until the attempt to measure it.

"But hell, that's action at a distance. When we see the light coming from that bulb overhead, our seeing stems from our reception of photons emitted by the bulb, streaming at us to create a visible effect. Action at a distance is an interaction which requires a means to propagate it; whether its light or electromagnetism, there is something that conveys it. If the observer affects what is being observed, there must be something that connects the two. So, imagine a particle that emanates from the observer to the observed, and maybe even creates a feedback in the other direction, in either event connecting them in some way.

"Call it . . . an observatron.

"Since it seems untraceable in our four dimensions, it would have to exist in a fifth dimension, one which may have to do with will and spirit."

"Maybe it's the gateway to the resident dimension of our souls." Sebby shook himself, like a child eating ice cream for the first time.

"The observatron emanates from the observer, towards an observed event that it fixes – or desires. Ordinarily, it must be very weak, so weak that it can't accomplish anything, or just affects the tiniest of tiny particles in a way that nobody notices. Maybe it was once stronger in parts of the East, Asia, where material items hadn't intruded so comprehensively as a basis for organization, but more than a sensibility, it could be a fundamental means of establishing relationship and formulating understanding. The last outposts of the ancients, when we conversed with the gods and they spoke back, in our own voice."

"So maybe we can trace the stream back to its source?" Sebby asked.

"That will not be easy. It has to be a massless particle, with its force and ability to reach its target proportionate to some quality in the sender, its potential impact related to some probability function, plus the random interaction with all the other particles and forces it has to encounter on its way. Since none of us knows of its existence, we're hardly in a position to find such particles, let alone use them in any way.

"But suppose you were the first to discover them, the first kid on the block with a new toy, or the guys with guns finding an enemy armed with bows and arrows. Think what your temptations would be."

They contemplated the impact: in an age where graciousness was subsumed by self-interest, integrity displaced by rationalization, value by desire, who would resist, what crimes to commit with the certitude they would go unpunished? Someone had opened a new gate to the fascinations of Hell, and peered in without an anchor.

Chapter Twenty-seven

What you see isn't what you get.

David sought to assimilate his observatron concept into the problem, reviewing all aspects of it in light of his new concept. Sebastian stuck to his material, looking to mine it for further information. But trying to trace a massless particle was like trying to track a thought in a room of conversations. He kept getting lost, trying new algorithms.

Neither slept much. They occasionally passed each other on the way to the kitchen or the bathroom, but besides intersecting through the basics they had had virtually no communication. They huddled closely over their terminals, as much holding on to the keys as hitting them. Finally, David lifted his shoulders up and swiveled his chair to face Sebastian, ignoring the empty couch.

"The effect you discovered in the cloud repositioning. I think it was a temporary alignment of normally random events, giving the illusion of a bend in the clouds. In fact, what we saw was a bend in the light passing through the clouds, an effect that did not have a physical analogue but gave the appearance of movement to the observer. A glorious phenomenon, you have to admit."

He stopped, punched by the memory of how Susan reacted whenever he said such things. He had to go on.

What he believed had occurred had to do first with the path of observatrons interacting from source to affected area. "Presumably once a wave-converted area has been established, it takes only an occasional follow-up of much less intensity to maintain the state, and in effect also monitor it. The affected area is established through the consciousness of a human being, I'm sure of that now, and as such has become in effect an extension of that consciousness, so that what occurs in the area would be registered in that consciousness. Probably everyday phenomena, the interaction of air or small bodies into the space, are not even noticed, in the same way that normal people screen out large parts of their environment in order to make their way through it. But when thirty-two pounds of relatively dense matter collided at over eighty miles an hour, that was an occurrence which precipitated a sharp feedback back to the source, and a sharp response from that source."

"Okay," said Sebby, "but what caused the effect?"

"Think about the seemingly random motion of small particles and photons. Theoretically, such particles can from moment to moment be anywhere, it's through statistical probability that the overwhelming bulk of them behave in such a way as to maintain the form and substance of our world." Sebby nodded.

"Well," David stood up, started pacing, drawing diagrams in the air, "suppose in fact that it's not quite true that they could be anywhere. Maybe they can move to many places, in a random way, but not an infinite number of places. Their movement is bounded by certain conditions, and behaves in a manner that is at times straightforward and at times goes all over the place, according to a theory of chaos, alternating periods of order and randomness, sensitive to the initial or previous state. In a sense, space, and history, might themselves be quantum, like energy, not continuous, but with discretely defined possibilities flowing from each other, maybe why history does tend to repeat itself, as the planes of these possibilities jump back and forth from one state to another, never transcending the core system. The possible places a particle might travel to would be discrete, not continuous. Bounded choices, not endless ones. It points to the shortcomings of the theory that there could be infinite worlds based on the infinite possibility of choices at any given moment, each possible choice creating a different branch of reality. In fact there could perhaps be many worlds, but not an infinite number, the possibilities bounded by the conditions precedent. A digital, not analog, frame of reference.

"Imagine this sudden concentration of observatrons and feedback between our beach and the source. The observatron is a medium of exchange between its creator and what is being examined. As we've seen, it can affect things, change their nature. So here's this whoosh of observatrons caused by an intense interaction between the dissolute beach front and its creator when we disrupted the area. Like a gaggle of geese, an oomph of observatrons–"

Sebby laughed, despite how serious it all was. "An oomph of observatrons, yes."

"–focused, powerful, sweeping across the country. Everywhere along its path, even though the intermediate points were not the target, they were minutely affected by the unusual intensity. Shows the power of what we're facing. So these affected points were aligned, the observatrons created a vortex of displacement along their way, briefly forming a nonrandom, consistent movement among the tiniest of particles they encountered, the ones that could be most affected, particles without mass – photons.

"What we're seeing is not something that physically happened, not, I'm sure, that we'd be able to tell the difference. To our eyes the clouds were pulled along a path, when what more likely happened was that the photons were aligned for a brief moment through the feedback effect, the normal random nature of their position choices instead narrowed down to a consistent single choice, so that a coherent nonrandom line appeared among the general spread of photons that normally give us the picture of smooth, fleecy clouds. The effect of this energy alignment was to force all of the photons along the path of observation into one choice, dictating the same choice, a fierce imposition of will that this struggle is all about. What you see doesn't have to be what you get, but it's all you can know."

Sebby was already at his terminal. "Alright," he said, "so then let me try…"

He pulled up a data set he had extracted from a compilation of the photos that first showed the line of distortion. He went through iteration after iteration, trying one set of equations after another, each failing to find a way to devolve an ethereal wave into something tangible, something they could grab a hold of and shake back to their form of reality. Over and over, with no luck.

He incorporated David's assessment that the pictures themselves were not depictions of something real, but rather an illusion of some other force. So he pulled in other data sources which he had previously not had a way to connect, searching what he could not see to find what he could not find. Here was the test of his life, the integration of his science and his faith, in a quest that mattered.

Five days later, he woke David up, looking like he had not slept in the interval.

"You were right, it wasn't in the photos themselves, but I searched the satellite mapping data used to power all our phone maps. I was able to detect a signal, and overlay it."

"And?" David sat up, tense, rushed to the screens. "Is it real?"

"Very definitely real, but you're not going to like it."

"By god, if we've found something. Of course not, I'm going to hate it, if it's real, hold it by the neck until . . . what have you found?"

"If you nurse that data stream, work it into a meager little line, barely perceptible but there, take that line, follow it to its end, and overlay it on a map of New Hampshire, you follow a swath north of Keene towards the White Mountains until you come to a few back roads, and at the end of Annie's Mill Road, in a little isolated hollow . . ."

"Jesus, man, get on with it."

". . . you'll come upon the home of one Mary Quintin. "

David fell into his chair, stunned.

"She's our source, David, there can't be any doubt about it."

Vivid memories of Mary poured back into David's mind, filtered into this new harsh light. He shuddered at the thought of that piercing cold intruding on the ways of the universe. He remembered Susan recounting her conversation with Mary: "No matter, no matter at all . . . nothing to see around my place."

That miserable, cruel bitch, he thought. And she, she of all the pieces of the world, she had taken Susan from him, excised her no doubt without the slightest sense of feeling or remorse.

"That bitch," he said, now out loud.

"I know, I know," said Sebby. "But regardless of who, the question is how, and what do we do about it. Please, David, get back to that state, you're the best in the world for this, maybe the only player in this world that can hit back."

"Mary Quintin . . . She must have developed an extraordinary understanding of what we're just groping with, coupled with intense belief . . . and desire, heaven help us from her desire, which enables her to emit observatrons of great strength. She has expanded, then, maybe even become aware of the fifth dimension."

He thought some more, fighting to replace his immediate anguish with his scientific habits. "She must have combined deep knowledge of fractals with places that are organized along fractal lines, to build on her new ability, pushing these observatrons around the globe, now able only to control certain pieces for some reason, based on what she understands."

"Maybe this is all she wants," Sebby said. "She is just a person. Not a god."

"Maybe that's where it started; she probably was as surprised as anybody would be. But as her knowledge and awareness and confidence increase, she'll be able to expand the sphere of her control, to spread with impunity the conversion of matter, instant conversion without faith, not in her image, but in its altered, distorted reflection, according to her desire, which unchecked will grow and grow, and who would be able to stop her? Isn't that a deity, Sebby?"

David and Sebastian steeped themselves in the history of Mary Quintin. They went back to her schools, talked with colleagues, no friends, really, people who had accumulated contact, usually by chance. None considered themselves close, by choice, memories of azure eyes that beckoned but were as changeless as a cold sea without even tides to sway one further in or even condescend to push away. Reticence had evoked no sympathy, its covering flint scraped too harshly, the brilliance also harsh, nonforgiving, incommunicative, and so she passed through and left no marks, nor did she receive any, they would say. David and Sebastian walked the same streets, read her papers, followed her paths physically and intellectually, placed themselves within her mind and body to see without judgment with her eyes, her feelings. David summed their conclusion:

"These areas aren't simply some local oddities. They're linked back to her, given the strength of the line, a part of her consciousness, external organs already providing her with more visions, knowledge, strength, grasp. It may in fact be only that hesitancy which she always displayed to get involved, mix it up in life, covering god knows what, that is keeping her from rapidly expanding what she can create – or uncreate – into the world right now."

David lay in bed, half-asleep, running through what he had learned and pieced together of Mary Quintin, his own memories, pictures, thoughts mixing with dreams in near feverish succession. Remembering how captivated they all were when they got a supercomputer to produce so fast and clean the Mandelbrot set, a simulator of fractal patterns, endless and fascinating. How she reached out to touch the screen as if in dialogue with it. He pictured her as he had last seen her, at their graduation ceremony, surprised she had shown up, wearing a turquoise dress with red flowers on it, with blue centers. He saw the fabric of the dress sweeping out, flowing with the wind, to land; on the side of a beautiful mountain seen on a dare of a walk while attending a conference with Chinese counterparts, a yearning towards a mountain away, escape, not possible, not then, certainly not there; across a canyon of red stone where she heard the roar of the river and drank enough with a boatman to commit one act of love as graceless as it was unforgettable, a hint, a whisper carried away by the river; on dreams flying over what should have been Paradise, hastily seen once to and from another conference, a place to stay that had to be left; and a soft and flowing billow of turquoise and reddish flowers rests lightly on a shore line, on a beach, a girlhood secluded spot to hear the waves, let the sound envelop her, away, away, he pictured her yearning.

Away, away from the dirty staircase to a dirtier room, four others and her and the touching, the godawful always nearby touching, asleep and touching, in and out of the bathroom, eating, cooking and touching, lying and touching, shitting and touching. A beach to lie on when dreams still looked for places to land, each length can be built up and down in the same proportion, variations, quasirandom pattern, she knew that, *lived that, her mind affixed, imprinted with an understanding that permeated and surrounded it, finally held it out, took her knowledge and her memories and thought hard and believed harder. First a pop in the desert, a cactus glow in the dark outside of Vegas where who-the-hell cared, then another pop, a fir tree, scared the bejesus out of him on that old stretch of road along the Coast, bingo, but she couldn't quite hold on to it, and then she saw herself as flowing, billowing out on her own energy and now she had more, so much more and still she was unfolding, her mind springing, springing out. She didn't know why, but she didn't want it to end, stretching outward, away, occasionally a touch of another being, usually a short dab, not untasteful, a stirring, a longing and then came the barrage, uncontrolled emissions at her beach, scaring her back to the dirty touching house, no! she cried out a flash and then engulfed, no no a nausea not like this and flashed and made it gone and she was wide open but hungry, hungry.*

Fractal geometry came along at a perfect time for Quintin to utilize, David mused. Or, she came along at a time facilitated by the development of fractal awareness. Working with a random model, or one that only replicated itself on the same scale, it would have been impossible for her to ever get beyond a very small, probably undetectable level. It was presumably size alone that was more difficult and took more energy for her, especially to maintain. If it was that factor that was limiting the growth of the current areas, he thought they faced a near and serious danger. She had moved from the very small to the level of the observable – itself a vast, exponential leap. If the next scaling up were to occur on that same ratio, it would be enormous: entire shorelines and mountains. And after that . . . much of earth would be in jeopardy. It would be difficult, but only a question of time. In fact, each scaling up might be easier as she got accustomed to and grew her understanding of the process. They didn't know how long it took her to go from the first scale to the current level, so it was hard to predict when she might commence the third. Also, David feared that as the consciousness of the possibility became more widely known, as more people heard of what was transpiring, the climate might become more hospitable to observatron-linked interactions leading to the particle-to-wave conversion.

It was a theory-shattering conclusion; even David had some cherished beliefs. For maybe this was beyond mere discovery; maybe through observatrons man had actually changed the physical laws of the universe. When Newton established his laws of motion, he was reporting on what he saw and experienced. Maybe he left out relativistic effects not just because he couldn't measure them, but because *they weren't there.* It took generations of changing thought patterns and creating tools of finer and finer measurements, and consciousness driving these efforts, great intellect-driven consciousness, Lorenz, Einstein, Bohr, Rutherford, Born, Dirac, Planck, Heisenberg, Pauli, to create the new worlds of relativity and then quantum; perhaps awareness created, or at least boosted, a new set of physical laws. When Einstein studied the various data and related equations that were springing up around him, and melded them from his central Swiss position into an extraordinary new set of explanations and precepts, he was more than just revealing more detailed stitches in the fabric of the universe. He was himself the torch, the bright intense flame of his consciousness not just illuminating but also soldering a new set of laws onto the old, of motion, of light, of gravity, of worlds now ripened for measurement and divination. The world created what it was ready to create. Perhaps that was the order imposed on an otherwise random process, that was the boundary of possibility for what came next; it wasn't a learning process but a creative one.

It led him to think about why there are no prophets now, no visions rewarded, no Bibles in the making. Once, humankind might have been more connected to its observatrons, to a spiritual dimension as tangible as the touch of soil, as equivalent as the experience of gravity. As physical science grew and succeeded in controlling and using the world around it, it drowned out the quieter sensibilities, and the world forked; cheap money drove out the dear, while wisdom became what was measurable on written tests, paring away dimensions of the mind. Was the evolution of forms of knowledge governed by survival of the easiest, whatever brought the most obvious reward for the least work? What fools long lives dedicated to spirit would then look like, no Yogis at the fast-food express. Even if knowledge proceeded in quasirandom steps, as David believed, what once had been was no longer, and now that sensibility was returning, with a vengeance, the wailing of a forgotten child become old enough to strike back. Mary would not leave behind a newer testament, he thought; there'd be no way to read it, nor worshippers remaining intact.

Knowledge was an accrual process, bits and pieces came together, through early consciousnesses emanating their sensibilities, until some kind of critical mass, aided sometimes by a powerful consciousness, one that could leap and coalesce and reproduce itself, brought together enough like thoughts and souls to effect the transformation.

This perspective offered an explanation as to why there was the extraordinary burst of great physicists and new understandings commencing around the turn of the twentieth century for a few sparkling decades, unparalleled, never reproduced. The answer was not rooted in coincidence. The great consciousness of Einstein and others had emanated their observatrons in such a force as to trigger a resonating response in other minds, creating in turn a chain reaction of explosive power, a vast barrage by a new consciousness triggering receptive minds into a new world created by understanding

And the growth of fascism and Hitler, of fundamentalism, was the instinctive response of an older rule; action must spur reaction.

Just as the extended periods of enlightenment of ancient Greece and Rome led to the protracted Dark Ages, so the explosive burst of understanding in the early nineteen hundreds gave rise to an explosive burst of reaction to it. It was a desperate grasp of those seeking to maintain an old, non-relativistic order, their order, their childhood understanding of the way things work, fighting the terrifying new premise that understanding could no longer be absolute, comfortably complete, but instead rested on shifting principles of time and matter as fungible, inconstant, the betrayal of the ground beneath your feet, a mother's womb, the passage of the hours, your life's span no longer sacred. If time or length could alter, if there were limits to our ability to know and control matter, these were terrifying limitations, desperately fought by those insecure and in need of assertion, seeking to dominate and control, to deny this new order by extending the old beyond its natural life, pumping demented energy to raise the corpse. Its indifference to death stemmed from it being already dead, a grotesque aberration of a system that was no longer vital.

It may even explain, David thought, why we have been unsuccessful in discovering a unified field theory, linking the great and weak forces, gravity and electromagnetism. It's not just that it's hard – maybe it's *not there yet.* Einstein had poured, literally, his mind into relativity, establishing both the new world *and* its boundaries, perhaps he and others simply didn't have enough energy left after their astounding fresh leaps to polish off that extraordinary creation, a whole other highly energized stream of observatrons in great mass necessary to make this bridge; and when it is built, in the glorious way that man creates worlds, it would look like it had always been there.

Periods of discovery themselves were fractal: apparent bursts, periods of inactivity, the dawn of fire, speech, the use of writing, electricity, some fractal related cycle. Was Mary Quintin and her dissolution of matter simply, for all their threatening aspects, another step in that process, the next great consciousness weaving together the glimpses of what was known and the borders of what was seemingly being discovered into a different sense of the world, driven by her consciousness, created as her observatrons established a new way in which the world worked. And might she be bombarding and tempting other minds into aiding and abetting this change.

No, David considered, compelled back to the moment. This change was driven by malevolent intellect, not by a mind open to wondrous possibilities. Mary Quintin's consciousness was not resonating within the world's, no gentle Einstein whose net was compassion, but rather a harsh despotic goddess seeking control, even revenge, for her own needs; this new way of the world stemmed from madness and despair.

Or was he just a maudlin, petty judge of an evolution that would so dwarf him, alter the substance of his world so profoundly, that he had abandoned scientific objectivity, an appreciation of the wonder of it all, and become merely a total reactionary to this terrifying new force, a Neanderthal gaping at an airplane?

He heard Susan, chastising him for abstract fascination. "To hell with philosophy," he thought, "I won't be Hamlet, I'll fight for the world I believe in, and what will be left or created in the end is by definition the appropriate outcome, a spirited defense against the prosecution, and let judgment be left to the Court of the Creator."

Chapter Twenty-eight

There had to be something beyond nothing.

David sat alone in the apartment. He had sent Sebastian off to find out about local topography around and transportation to Mary Quintin's house – make-work tasks. When the time came for contact, he already knew, other people wouldn't matter, and they would have to find their own quiet means of getting near her. He sat looking at lines of force converging on the computer screen. He played the lines out and watched with unsought awe how they could grow exponentially as they gained strength through mass controlled over time. The lines reflected like a spider web across his face, relentlessly riding every contour.

He had to enter their epicenter, to face an opponent who fought with her mind, who could strip away any other weapon before it reached her, convert a bullet or a warhead into a harmless set of wave functions to dissipate around her. He had to face her with his mind, and that meant he had to expunge his grief: no mourning period, no indulgence, no memories, only will, he had to employ his will. The sole means to keep him intact long enough for the battle – as for the aftermath, he didn't care – was through consciousness, a Zen weaponry, a calmness at the center that arose from accepting death before the battle began so that one would know no other fear. However selfless his motivations, in the end the rest of the world, as much as he professed to care for it, would be outside, and he would reside within.

He heard noise at the door. He wanted more time, dammit, needed space to relieve this low-grade nausea that enveloped his every moment, his body driven by his mind, turning on his soul, the regret he could not displace. He needed to find a way to eliminate it from his system, space, and time.

In walked Sebby and Sal, loud. He remembered a phrase from his monk mentor: if you want to mediate in silence, you can't keep the dogs from barking.

"We're going to settle this once and for all," Antifermo said, holding up a bottle in one hand, while the other held a paper bag full to its top. He turned to David.

"Ya gotta understand, this is a Sassicaia, 1989. It doesn't get better than this. Saved up a month for it, had to give the princessa two extra visits to the hairdresser in exchange."

Sebby had walked directly to his cartons, pulled out his own bottle. "Heitz Martha's Vineyard '86. I refute your thesis," he pronounced. "There's a reason they call it Old World, you know. Gone are its days."

"Hah. Some things you only get with maturity, you oughta know that."

They both turned to David. "Look guys, I'm sure this is vital, but right now –"

Antifermo held up the bag. "Mui princessa made us a couple of things. Spaghetti con sugo di cinghiale – that's wild boar, ya know – and pernil, pork shoulder she's been slow roastin' for the last day. I mean, Doc, ya gotta eat, right?" David glared at Sebby as if he had betrayed a secret. "And ya gotta wash it down with somethin', might as well be great somethin'." He held up his arms, bag and bottle, shrugged his shoulders, and managed somehow to look sweet and appealing.

David held up his hands in defeat.

"Only, I'd made flank steak with Cajun onions," Sebby said, going to the kitchen.

"Okay, we'll have it all," Antifermo said, and they pulled David to the kitchen table.

David said little over the first bottle, trying to be overcome his queasy stomach, its toxic mix of grief and anxiety. Sal and Sebby ate enough for all three. When they were half done with the

Sassicaia, Sebby popped the cork on his cabernet, and the two of them started discussing the ins and outs of soft tannins, fruit forwardness, and the length of the finish. David kept sipping, nibbling at bits, a bit more and then a bit more of each. And suddenly he found himself crying, sitting at the table trying to contain the convulsions that ripped through him. The other men quieted down, with modest sips and occasional comments about how the breathing time affected the taste. David felt their presence warm and comforting, appreciated their silence, gradually stopped his tears and his shoulders jumping up and down.

Sebby gathered the plates and brought them to the sink.

"Look, Doc," Antifermo said. "We got a bit of a situation. You know, with the beach, well, it was so weird, nobody really connected, no big deal, we could keep it on the QT. But now, well, a bunch of citizens disappear, there's more to it, people are getting a bit curious, ya know what I mean?"

"I thought we could contain that with the UN connection to the Mayor"

"Yeah, well, that's right as far as it goes, but – folks checked. A lot of those people lived here in New York, ya know, had families here, there's the insurance stuff alone. And the City Counsel he says there's no diplo immunity for it, Antifermo, you should find out a little more of what the hell is going on here, which the Mayor has to agree because losing a part of the beach is bad enough for the image, losing a bunch of people don't help it more, ya know what I mean?"

"I guess we finally fall in your purview, huh, Sal?"

"I guess you could say that, Doc. In fact, I think you once did."

David started laughing, and Sal joined, Sebby as well, until they were all laughing hard and long, letting David combine those tears with his others, and wipe them all away.

"Okay, Sal, I get it. What do you need?"

"Frankly, you could start by telling me what the holy fuck happened out there."

David looked at him for a moment, surrounded by his calm and quiet, found solace in it, thought about the alternatives, and started, finding a relief in the telling, the explaining, the sorting out and organizing. He poured it out, telling more than he realized, urging like a lecturer explaining the science to a nonscientist. As he did, the lines of Antifermo's grimace lifted as if squeezed from within. He listened, only occasionally asking a question to enhance, but never interfering with the flow, or the reasoning, or the feeling.

"Wow, that kid, Tyrone, maybe he was lucky. You're saying that there's no hope of recovering these people?"

"Even if we had a theoretical basis, we don't possess the practical means. Plus, the indications are that in these areas of discontinuity matter behaves according to another mode, closer to pure quantum. Thus the possibility of an electron, say, being almost anywhere, in contact with any other electron, across the universe, from one moment to the next, is statistically less remote in those areas. I don't know whether on some other level of reality, one with lots more dimensions than ours, those people," he paused, swallowed hard, "even the objects exist somehow, but we can't know – I doubt if even she knows."

"She. Ya mean this Mary Quintin, the one ya suspect caused all this disturbance."

"Right, the one we suspect."

"And what are ya going to do about that suspicion?"

David made a sound between a laugh and a sigh. What are we going to do? he asked himself. The lioness in her den, with talons to reach out and destroy intruders. At least Daniel had his faith, and even he had to be thrown in; he didn't walk in by his own choice. Might that arrogance, if he had so exercised it, have undercut his strength, to become one more among the shredded souls? David sat quietly with his thoughts until the detective interrupted him.

"Well, it seems to me what we got here is suspicion of murder. I'm gonna get out a warrant for the arrest of this Mary Quintin, bring in this piece of dynamite for questioning."

At first David, still wrapped up in his mind, couldn't assimilate what he was hearing. He shook his head sharply, played it back in his mind. "Sal, are you crazy? Haven't you been listening? How are you going to bring her in? You can't even reach her. Don't you understand, she could literally blow you away?"

"Hey, you don't know that for certain – hell, you don't know anything for certain, isn't that what you physics guys go by these days, the principle of uncertainty? So then, what are ya going ta do about her? Let these things keep growing, let more people join Susan out there in never-never land?"

"Hey, who are . . . no, dammit, no. We do have to get to her, but unless we think through how, it will never work. I've already made this mistake once. It could lead to her anger and her power surging, and we lose any shot at her at all. You can't just charge at her with guns blazing; you'd find your bullets evaporating before they can hit anything. I don't even know if you could see anything to aim at. This is a different world we're facing, you have to understand that."

Antifermo listened. He'd heard it before, every situation its own special peril. A guy on top of a bridge, no ropes allowed, wind pushing you like a hustler about to take your wallet, so's you'd only notice if you were looking for it; or the mean ones, the planners, a calm drop in your tea, something you couldn't trace for certain, so they thought, then cornered, a cobra full of venom lashing out; or the worst, some street punk junked out, a random variable, the worst, arbitrary death, no matter, staring 'til the rotted gray pitted teeth, chattering to the beat inside, looked like they could swallow you, the stench overpowering, no move, no move, and bang, one last look of surprise and you're writing up the report. Fuck 'em, he'd faced them down, survived, not a scar on his body, no fool, but no dent in his confidence. He respected Altaforce. Liked him. He had a murderer to catch. He needed to resolve the conflict.

"Okay, Doc, you know what your driving at better than I do. But I got some lady making citizens disappear out there, and I have to try to stop her. When do ya plan to make a run at her?"

"We're still assimilating data," David said, "how can we tell?"

"Figure it out now, Doc, or it's off I go."

"All right, two weeks, there's no indication of the potential for serious expansion within that time frame. I'll take the walk in two weeks."

"Great, Doc – and I'll take it with you."

"What? You can't possibly – you don't understand, and that lack of understanding could be fatal to you."

"I believe in myself, Doc, and I'll hold your hand if I have ta. The White Rabbit and Alice, right, Doc. But hey, forget about it, we don't go for citizen's arrests here, I've gotta be with ya."

David wanted to believe, that here was an immovable force of will to meet the irresistible one they faced; he knew it couldn't be, but wanted to believe, and hoped, and gave in.

"Okay, we go together. And God help us both. Assuming he's on our side."

Even Antifermo started at that. "Assuming? Hey, Sebby, is there something he's not telling me here?"

Tragedy may stop one person's world, but it did not stop the whole world – not yet. Reinvolvement with the world is made grudgingly. The mourner fears that by starting to live again without pain, to enjoy a meal, laugh at a movie, work without the intrusion of memories, he is somehow giving up love for the dead. So often the biggest hurdle is to allow a letting go of grief, giving grief leave, to permit grief's bittersweet departure, to admit the void left by grief, that living is to fill in the hole, the mud of grief's time cakes and melds into the soil around it, a quaking landfill amidst rock-hewn boundaries, sodded over solid on the surface, soft and susceptible from within. Grief simplifies the world by filtering all its input through its sieve of limited emotions, and grief's departure leaves one open again to having to deal with the full and awesome set of possibilities, with no quarter given, even when asked. Despair or dismay – David felt his choices were limited, and events increasingly were making them for him.

His purging was his first training for the encounter, and the necessity of it lent a new emotion to his anticipation. Before, he had felt almost exhilarated in astonishment – that such things could come to pass! – and even respect for a colleague who had so incorporated belief in her world view, no matter what the reason for the ability, that she could extend it to the real world, beyond the screens and the equations, directly, to manipulate it, control it.

Now waves of disgust spread through him like stains in linen, displacing his amazement, that a new universe could have its seed contained in its progenitor's warped frustrations: of desire cramped into loathing, of hope turned bitter, a spiteful goddess of dissolution, no seven days of unfettered possibilities, no intimations of paradise somewhere in the scheme, glimpses to preserve hope and prompt moral structure, no joy in the wonder, no acknowledgment of an order of beings worth preserving, not the love with the wrath, only a promise of emptiness. He had thus added to his set of feelings: hatred. That, too, he would have to eliminate.

A Creator, he mused, for the first time thinking through the implications of the thought. Whose world would he be fighting for? He had to work on his feelings, he recognized, and one way to purge was through involvement, staring at the screen, a volatile set of lines the most absorbing movie of his time, its reflection shining on his forehead, expanding lines of power and energy drawing him back into their inevitability.

Chapter Twenty-nine

It wasn't pleasing to be right.

A fifth incident occurred.

It created panic that others might follow shortly, that perhaps some critical mass – wave – had been reached, that the world was approaching a crossover point. The UN teams and investigators felt a sick apprehension, helpless observers. The jolt was that the fifth area was not fractal. It was a block of concrete pavement, with a uniform, random texture. If the conversions were not limited to areas with fractal geometries, than the sky was indeed the limit, and the land, and the waters. That terror was stark.

One of the top physicists at the particle accelerator in Illinois, Dr. Arnold Janson, had studied the data, like hundreds of other scientists enlisted worldwide at the UN's request. Janson sat for days watching particles collide, collapse into waves, move forward and, in reflection, backwards in time, hints of endless possibilities, explosions reflecting off his glasses creating a moving screen of concepts taking shape before him. The windows of his apartment high over the lake in Chicago seemed to echo those visions, no longer looking out, but, as he stared at them in sleepless reveries, possessed by energy without eating, feeding on himself like a bleeding piranha, the windows seemed to vibrate, shimmer with colors, move towards him and away, a noiseless siren beckoning to him.

His observations at work and his visions at home melded. He studied the data and wanted to believe in the possibilities, the promise of a different world, believe in the beauty of the colors in stark contrast to the harsh grounds beneath him, rough mean pavement and cold ragged people enrobed in gloves without fingers, jackets with shredded arms, layers of clothing that in total barely added up to a complete cover, dark visions best left to the edge of sight, yet still an impingement on consciousness. Was there no avoiding them? He just wanted to work.

At night he lay in bed pondering the origins of the universe, that there might yet be a boundary to this universe, that perhaps it had been created out of a local epicenter of anomalous fluctuations in an even broader space. Maybe there were other universes similarly formed, older even or in formation, perhaps out in the fringe, where our first particles of twelve billion years ago inhabited, the universes themselves overlapping, and what did that mean, that vastness, how could it be that beyond everything there was . . . there was something. Something beyond nothing beyond something. He lay in bed alone as he had always lain, no other worldly body to give him balance, to hear his cries, to offer humanity against those fears, a touch to dissipate them, like a child alone with facts beyond his understanding, learning that today's parent was tomorrow's visitor, so frightful, a pout on an almost sleeping face, nearsighted eyes better able to see clearly the phantoms within, nothing to touch him, nothing touched him.

Without human contact to ground him, Janson built up a nervous system charge, like a laser's light looping before it develops enough energy to burst forth, looking with increasing fervor at the data before him, the possibility. Like a generation of milers faster once the four-minute barrier was broken, he looked at Mary Quintin's work and saw that possibility had become reality, she broke the tape and he followed, sensing her at the edges of his awareness, Mary, Mary not contrary. He reached for her, or what he thought of her, she smashed in his mind the barriers of numbness and disconnection that had accustomed him to sleeping alone, eating alone, talking alone, now he wanted her with an adolescent hunger all the stronger for its gnawing years of going unmet, unheeded. He wanted wanted wanted her, and he knew that to link he had to match her pace, as he stared at the data at work and the reports and the windows, hating the mean pavement below.

Until ahh! it shimmered beneath the gaze of his mind, dissolved into the soft hues of waves, nobody could be hurt by the waves, nobody cold among the waves, no concrete to scrape your shins on while running away, they always chased him on concrete, tough growing up smart but slow and fat and glasses at four years old, brilliant, yes, now soft clothes, even a beard to cover the anguish of his little jaw, but the scars were still on his shins, his knees. Not anymore, no, no, the concrete converted under the fervor of his belief; with the zealousness of a convert he transcended her limits, he could look at the underlying structure of that concrete, had his face wiped in it he knew it that well, and whoosh, gone, like yesterday's sperm held in hand and washed down the drain, gone like paper decomposed in the wet earth, gone like a preschool picture of a world that would work in all ways for you, gone like the edge where smoke disappeared, no matter how hard you stared.

Susan had taught David to look for the people. Running a correlation analysis of major variables, he quickly discovered the proximity of the disappearing pavement to Janson's address. Janson himself had not been seen for three days; people had just assumed he was sick, or taking a few days for himself, as most top scientists did without warning from time to time. David selected some junior technicians who had not been exposed to the data, and went to pay Dr. Janson a visit. Up thirty-seven floors of a circular high-rise that reflected the lake and surrounding buildings on its exterior glass frame, looking down on the Navy Pier hearing the echoes of joyous shouts of children on its Ferris wheel, a knock on the door, Janson, Janson, are you in there? No response. They obtained a passkey, and entered.

Janson sat, gaunt and fixated on the distant window. He heard them behind him, chasing him little fat boy that slept alone in dark nights, ready to catch up with him, pull him back and the window beckoned, one last fat boy run, through the glass unfelt – already immaterial – and down into the pavement one last time, to evade his tormentors, and even as he plunged a small patch of concrete that had briefly shimmered softly in the distant air snapped back into the hard crust of his reality where the cold, ragged people layered themselves to combine into something whole, never succeeding, nor knowing they had touched an Arthur Janson, for what it mattered. And David looked down through a glass plate, wishing he could have restrained Ulysses from the sirens' call, but understanding the seduction, while a cold Chicago wind blew in through a smooth-edged new hole in the once seamless side of a tall glass building.

==

With Janson's death the spot of concrete rematerialized, but the fear of the contagion spreading did not recede with that memory, it infected the whole UN team. Looking down on Janson's body and the city beyond it, David thought that it was not just artists and scientists heralding the next society, avant-garding culture, but as Rome in decay it was the outcasts foreshadowing the future. If he hated Mary Quintin even more, still his once total loathing of what she represented softened like the edges of a patch of beach that wasn't there, a barely perceived shimmer.

Upshaw didn't see the shimmer. He greeted David at the airport and escorted him back to the apartment.

"I'm sorry, David, I didn't get it."

"An unhappy vindication, I admit. The spread of knowledge can abet the changes stemming from consciousness affecting the physical world."

"It's like a mentally transmitted disease. An MTD, just what we need!"

"I looked down, the hard concrete, the indifferent city around it."

"Look, with Susan gone, maybe you could connect more with the rest of my team?"

"Uncle Harold, she called you."

"God knows I miss her."

"You want to make sure if something happens to me, there'll be some repository of what I know. Don't worry, Sebastian will be there."

"No, no, it's not that. But can't the spread of knowledge be good for us as well? Just talk with them. I can't face a life infinitely multiplied by her loss, devoid of meaning as we know and feel it."

David's lecture was in the same auditorium where Upshaw had first briefed his teams, until the fusion process of their disseminating knowledge had created links that snapped into the nastiest chain letter there ever was. Upshaw turned all the lights on bright as he could, beyond the last row of chairs, trying to fill in the space at the end of the world.

"Before I start, I'd like, among us, to acknowledge someone. Someone who brought me into this place, and let me tell you, I was reluctant. I think she was the only person who could have done it." He looked in Upshaw's direction, who nodded back at him. "Susan. Susan Corporell."

"Even before I'd met her, she'd touched the world in so many places, deeply, always with insight and compassion, with a sense of humor that never left her. She walked through horrors, but was always guided by love. She could dream with her eyes open." His voice broke, briefly.

"And it was that insight that gave me, us, repeatedly, breakthroughs, in how to understand what we are dealing with. She understood that circumstances are driven by people, and led us to find the person. She had the clarity to see beyond my limitations a way to test the hypothesis, to challenge the person. And it was that clarity that led to her ultimate sacrifice, leaving us behind in her wake."

Upshaw had looked surprised when David began speaking. He was openly crying now, as were others in the room, UN staffers who had worked with Susan over the years.

"I cherish her memory, and will not rest until we have met the challenge and the person she fearlessly faced, and restored our world to the one she so beautifully inhabited."

He paused for a moment, in a room silent other than the soft sobs of others who had known her. And then it was time for him to go on.

He touched on the elements of fractal geometries that related to theories of chaos, that there were alternating periods of order and chaos that appeared to vary randomly but were sensitive to and bounded by initial conditions. He moved on to the many worlds interpretation of quantum physics, that the sum of all choices creates infinite parallel possibililties for past and future universes.

"Maybe different solutions, different worlds, do exist simultaneously. If there are or could be many worlds, perhaps the many branches of possibilities converge periodically, to create a particular Big Bang or derivatives from it. We, humankind, live by definition in the path with the set of phycical laws conducive to our existence.

"So what about Mary Quintin? Maybe the wave/particle integration she's encapsulated enables her to shift among worlds, pulling up energy from different paths, even those not taken, infusions unlike anything in history."

He saw some people raise their hands, including one of laDoop's assistants vigorously waving like a third grader with the answer. He waved them off, not interested in diversions. laDoop was not in the room.

"But what different world does she now straddle? Is her mind a wire short-circuiting two currents, or could she be accelerating towards one of those points of convergence, destroying the universe of possibilities which like biological diversity produce evolutionary results. Including us! Is she rushing us against our will towards a point beyond which we literally have no way of knowing if we will come out the other side? Maybe she's hypothesizing a return to infinite time. But I fear she thinks she's drinking from the grail of the sources of the universe, drunk on the potion's power, so inebriated she's inured to the possibility of crashing, or worse, doesn't care, a grip on the wheel of reality that could bring an end to all that we perceive. Or hold dear. So very dear.

"Or maybe we're just a bunch of old cops on a new highway."

Even with finite worlds, David thought, his eyes moving with a focus that barely saw the walls around him, the possibilities were very, very many.

As he walked off the stage, Upshaw held him at arm's length for a second, as if examining him, then wrapped his arms around him, saying, "You had me going there, as usual, but . . . welcome back to the fight, soldier. Lord knows we need you."

Chapter Thirty

Many roads lead to one place.

David's math was coming together, making more and more sense as a description of the phenomena. But as an explanation, it did little, told no more than was known as to why there was a Big Bang or some other initiating precept to start the universe off, told as little as he knew about the Original Organizer and Its Principles and Reasons for Doing Things. It was fine to generate theories, research papers, or analysis. But how helpful would they be to step into the fray, if they could not encapsulate the world spread before him, a world of relationships beyond thought, without shortcuts, embedding patterns in flesh and spirit, that could be thrilling still, yes, but also so so sad, and sadness was a dimension without a boundary.

He pulled himself away. He was preparing for a fight, a slugfest using the fists of matter, with an outcome that had meaning, not just for him but also for the world around him. If he had wandered in that world primarily to taste it and feel comfortable in abandoning it as the place in which to establish his goals or manipulate elements, he had through his journey come to love it deeply, the very disorderliness of it, the eccentricities and confusions a spur to his own intellectual development, but more, a grounding of his self in happy appreciation. It was his self that was going to battle for that world. He was preparing for a fight, and he needed to train.

Without being aware of it, he stood up and left the apartment, as if taking his mind for a walk, a little boy on his way to school, screening out distractions, moving through crowds and traffic on automatic pilot.

An observatron. A link between the observer and the observed! His mind swam with the thought, taken along on a current it produced yet could not control. The particle was a bridge between man and his world; producing it was perhaps a definition of consciousness. It united the internal focus of Eastern philosophies with the West's orientation towards science with physical applications and explanations.

Observatrons would have to move through a fifth dimension in order to move at all; it was only from a fifth dimension that the other four dimensions of the familiar universe could be fully observed, like reading a piece of paper. He tried to imagine a realm that peered in at his own, to which he himself was perhaps a contributor, pushing pieces of his consciousness out towards hopes, desires, intentions, casual wants, and deep-rooted needs. Was it a constant barrage, or did it take a certain threshold energy simply to release the particle? Did it stem from his active mind, or was he host to a fifth-dimensional sphere which when properly activated gave forth bits of itself?

And how had Mary come to use it? Through training and belief, dedicated and driven, now a soul had found its abilities, worked on how to control them, coupled them to the sphere of fractal knowledge where she felt most adroit and which had so many applications in the material world. She was a head of the class, the class of the species surrounding yet separated from her, pushing out this newfound and ancient skill to challenge man and God. Isolated, incomplete, yet existing at an unfathomed depth of awareness, Mary Quintin lay in royal repose, a fifth-dimensional state of grace, her four-dimensional subjects unable even to see her means of subjugation, let alone challenge her rule. If she limited her realm, it was more through indifference or lack of full understanding of her weaponry; she was no simple despot, content to tax the subjects for grand comfort of an earthly stay, not rape unpunished nor whim fulfilled her petty historical antecedents. Hers was a new and old old threat, of complete dissolution, even a pillar of salt would look good to our composite particles as they evaporated to flow out beyond their material and concrete limits; beyond the fire was the smoke, and beyond the smoke was the empty ether.

She connected to her fifth-dimensional self, he thought, emitted observatrons of a strength and multitude the like of which had never been seen on the planet before, aimed at areas of the planet whose type and contour were best known to her. She incorporated the wave/particle duality into her consciousness, which directed these particles out, out to convert not just people but matter itself, to proselytize an unwilling, unwitting, and unaware collection of animate and inanimate matter towards her will, her world. She was an evangelist of waves: Come follow me to nothingness from whence you sprang, you don't even have to believe, for I will lead you to me and away from yourselves. She would convert them to infinity by taking away their moment. It would be an end, but could it be a beginning? Was he protecting what really mattered, or fighting the next inevitable wave of evolution?

He crunched his feet on the pavement, inhaled the fumes of a passing bus, heard the screeching nasal New York of a mother restraining her child, "Get back offa dat street or I'll kill ya wait heah till it's green like I toldjya," he bought a chili dog loaded with sauerkraut and mustard. He drank in the smells and sounds, grounded himself in this earthy reality. He remembered Susan, and her touch, a feeling stronger than any other. He would not let that fade; he would stand in his ground to keep his ground, to battle this disintegration and desolation driven not by love but by hatred and fear.

Dusk wove into the streets, bringing him back to more practical matters. He wondered how he could communicate with Mary Quintin in a way she would respond to. Her language now existed in the quantum interstices between cells, faster-than-light responses, exponential interaction with a base of billions of cells each with billions of particles, connecting and travelling with a speed and movement unlike anything in the universe, dwarfing that universe while demonstrating its incalculable potential. To combat it was to give up all his self, conscious, unconscious, deepest and beyond self into absolute freedom, each particle here or anywhere else in touch with any other time now, then, or later. He had to move beyond language, for language was formed and finite, beyond thought, for thought was conditioned and learned, beyond instinct, for instinct was fixed and embedded, transcending into a state of absolute comprehensive matter, retaining a personality in the way Saturn has a personality distinct from Mercury, the Sun from Alpha Centauri, the Milky Way from the Andromeda Nebula, elementally vast, cold at the heart, endlessly, heedlessly, human needlessly cold . . .

Chapter Thirty-one

By our habits, voids seek to be filled.

David surfaced from his intense meditations and, as he had done so many times, found it most helpful to present his findings to Sebastian. Sebastian sat in his chair in front of his computer terminal, swiveling to follow David as he wandered around the room and talked.

"It's not enough for Mary Quintin to be able to emit observatrons better than anybody else. She has to have some sense of the matter she's controlling. We've looked at these areas and seen their gross manifestations of fractal symmetry. Maybe she looks at them and also 'sees,' in that she senses and understands, the interaction of the fundamental particles connecting the surfaces of these shapes, first to each other, a teeming subatomic world of bumps and holes, continents and rivers, of real and temporal pieces of matter sitting in fractal symmetry, which bounds and guides their relationships with each other.

"And then she governs the interactions of her wave world with our particle world, yet another surface meeting surface. We can't fathom or understand that intersection, but she's so far ahead of us she can actually control and define it."

"But David," Sebastian interrupted, nearly bursting, "what you're proposing is a whole new look at fundamental particles and how they behave."

"Yes, exactly. What the hell! I'd call it . . . Fractal Quantum Dynamics – FQD."

"As in, we're fuqued!"

"Royally! Now let's see if we can use anything I've just said to combat our increasingly extraordinary foe. We can leave the full ramifications of FQD to the physicists we hope will survive the war it might help us fight."

FQD was a scientist's nightmare. David was trying to apply the principles even as he developed them, building the plane as they were flying it. Sebastian kept trying to fill in the gaps, create a coherent framework for the concepts. After several intense days establishing fractal equations governing fundamental particle interactions, David contacted the scientists running the particle accelerator at CERN, in Switzerland, to examine the data from their particle-smashing experiments through the filter of his equations. They fit. He then sought permission to conduct an experiment there. laDoop objected – reserving interaction with anything that big was part of his fundamental nature – but David spoke with Upshaw, who set it up. Upshaw had first suggested the accelerator in Illinois, but David rejected the proposal, for fear of the site's greater potential to trip another incident, and because of the memory of a cold breeze blowing through the thirty-seventh floor of his soul. Upshaw was by this time feeling like a man caught in a maze that made his previous bureaucratic tangles seem like simply keeping a yo-yo at the end of a string; now he had seemingly endless interstices with constantly shifting material. He hadn't been this happy in thirty years, nor had he ever gotten along so well with his children. He dreaded the resolution of the crisis nearly as much as the crisis itself, and was without fear for anything else.

David's experiment for CERN was a variation on the standard method of accelerating particles and colliding them to study the new particles, their respective energies, lifetimes, and characteristics formed by the collision. David proposed to smash an array of one set of similar particles against an equal-sized array of a set of different particles, two distinct sets homogeneous within each set but heterogeneous as compared to each other. It was the equivalent, as close as could be arranged, of a fundamental particle surface interaction, which David theorized would best be described by his fractal quantum dynamics, applying distributions expected from fractal analysis instead of classical quantum descriptions to the behavior.

If David was right, he had given a new dimension to the study of the conditions in the universe in its first moments, and, as the quality of time itself evolved, seconds and minutes and years following the Big Bang. David also suspected they would apply as well or better to his concept of a wave-to-particle transition at the time of the origin of the universe. He didn't care about any of that. He was confident enough in his theories, in his intuitive feel for their *rightness*, that he didn't really need to see the outcomes of the experiments. More than anything, he wanted to be near the collisions themselves, observe them as close up as possible, sense the power of the interactions, feel within himself the surfaces collide, become familiar with how they behaved, putting his nose literally against the thick glass of the shielded rooms and esoteric photographic plates, as if to take in the phenomena by osmosis, into the core of his being.

Forty-six hours later, he was in the main control room at CERN, painlessly brought there through what was one of the UN's true capabilities – travel arrangements. If the Swiss loved order, they must have worshipped at CERN's shrine. Its long, high walls were filled with monitors of various sizes and hues, ranging from six inches in diameter, looking more like a meter to read the gas, to screens eight feet wide that could have proudly served as the center of any aspiring mogul's home media room. Buzzes of numbers ran down the screens in columns, turning along the bottoms of the screens, the numbers themselves forming patterns as they flipped over and over, the changes too subtle for any but the machines or the most monomaniacal of watchers to catch. Other screens to display fiber optic transmissions, conveying the visions of man-made interactions that were yet beyond the eye of man to witness, filtering and interpreting them so that the scientists could view their offspring, taking the energies of suns and turning them into tools for decay, so that the gods themselves were no longer immune.

The center of the room was filed with individual work stations, computer terminals, high-tech rows like library carrels for students of the cosmos, a space terminal ready to launch tiny astronauts on suicidal missions, set up to study in detail the moments of their destruction, extend that wrenching distortion, feed on their demise, new ephemeral players to bring back the secrets of the stars. Particles died and were born in the great vaults of CERN, and their parents thought not of individuals but generations, not of specific characters but the evolution of knowledge. It was a lofty perch, reflecting the relative size of the participants if nothing else, and few who occupied it ever paused to think who might be looking down on them with a similar perspective.

David was warmly greeted by CERN's director of research, Anton Buongiovi, who had by setting up the conditions for David's experiment become more excited than he had been since his arrival at the facility. A round man with a short beard, in his exuberance he easily tolerated David's brusqueness and focus, which barely stood out in the room of scientists. After a final briefing session, they set up positions in the control room. David got a place where he could have direct lines of sight to the visual transmissions sent from the core of the accelerator. The experiment began.

David stood, unmoving, his stare fixed. He wore protective goggles, and on their surface was a display emanating from the viewing ports of intersecting lines varying with bursts of intensity: long, thin, smooth lines crossed by other, thicker ones, some jagged, a latticework marked by occasional bright dots looking like bulbous growths on a plant's roots, glowing brightly for an instant and then slowly fading away like an afterimage in the mind, nearly immeasurable short lives that harkened of eternity. Looking at David standing immobile in front of the visions of his vision, it was impossible to distinguish if the dance of the universe that unfolded on the lenses was a reflection from without, or was projected from within. David was convinced that to contain Mary Quintin it was not enough to formulate abstract equations. The understanding stemming from these equations would have to be wielded by a human instrument. There was no high-flying pilot who could deliver that payload.

The experiment began, accelerating the two particle sets in opposite directions. When they got as close to the limit – the speed of light – as possible, they could be set on collision paths, with all the available machinery of the universe to track the interactions. Plus David.

Buongiovi nodded, and they hit the switches to start the movements. The air in the room took on a different quality, a hum below the level of hearing but audible to the body nonetheless, a sense of vibration denoting power, the power of humans harnessing their ultimate tools. The room itself seemed to start shifting slightly underneath and around them. It would carry a sense of foreboding if they all didn't know it had been done many, many times before, and was under good, orderly Swiss control.

Ninety-five million pounds of superconducting magnets kept the particles in place, moving at just a few meters per second less than the speed of light. The circumference of the collider was seventeen miles, and when they reached their top speed a particle went around it in ninety millionths of a second, eleven thousand times around in the blink of an eye.

The vibrations grew, the hums increased, the entire room was enmeshed by the dynamics: intense, extraordinary energies at the boundary of the universe. David stared.

"Are you okay," Buongiovi asked? And asked again, David so absorbed in the room and the feel of it he didn't hear.

"Yes, fine, thanks." He watched, trying to contain his excitement, match the sangfroid of the scientists around him who'd been through this many times before, just one more notch on their belts.

The lead engineer nodded. "We are about to initiate collision, using your parameters for size and distribution," Buongiovi shouted to David over the background din.

There were the terminals, and the small screens, and the larger displays with direct views of the collision points, not that they really mattered with one hundred billion particles colliding in a billionth of a second. The eye wasn't meant to observe this, just to know where it took place; only the computers and the machines could assert that something had happened, tell what had happened.

They initiated the collision sequence. David watched, transfixed. He was drawn into the walls of the collider, surrounded by its magnets and two hundred thousand pounds of superfluid helium cooling them to within a fraction of absolute world-shattering cold, minus two hundred seventy one degrees centigrade. The space was unique, rarified, inspiring, and monstrous, a world of its own.

Or normally of its own. With the initiation of collision, David sensed the dawn of his fractal dynamics coming into being, felt the impact, the billions of his brain cells corresponding with the particles in contention. For the first time in the collective scientists' memory, something tangible happened, something that didn't require post hoc assessment to experience. At the collision points, visible first on the screen and then emanating outward through the walls and tunnels and magnets and super-cold helium into the offices and rooms five hundred feet underground and then the earth around them, there was a shimmering, a radiance, a glow, preceding a vanishing, a void growing, growing around and underneath and above them.

Alarm sirens went off. Lights dimmed, then flared. From a distance there was a smell of electric wires fusing. Then a silence, louder than the sirens, filled with the shudders of a great beast expiring.

"Shut it down," Buongiovi shouted, and again, pointing. Frantic scientists driven beyond their adrenal limits first froze, then pushed, pushed every button they could, like kids playing a shoot 'em video game laying down fire as fast as possible, not bothering or able to aim, just hoping for a hit.

And still the shimmering grew, the void enlarged.

Buongiovi shouted to David, "What's happening?" But David was not only transfixed; around him grew a filament, an aura, a replica of what the screens were showing, what they were seeing in the tunnels of the collider and beyond.

"Altaforce," Buongiovi yelled, then again, to no affect. David felt his body becoming elongated, stretching towards a place he could not name that seemed to lack an end to it. With the walls around them starting to dissolve, Buongiovi jumped over a railing and tackled David, bringing him down, knocking the goggles off his head.

David looked up, out of a daze, pulled himself standing. As he did so, the world restored, the shimmering dissipated, the void vanished. Buongiovi looked at David, his face a question composed with fear.

David shook himself. "Well," he said, "that was positively smashing."

While the staff at CERN was left buzzing about FQD, they weren't sorry to see David leave for New York. It would take months for them to get back online, with a level of apprehension none had ever felt before.

David had a growing sense of creating within himself a bond between the abstractions of physics and the essence of being alive, being human. He didn't quite know what he had experienced at CERN. For him it was all just being immersed in what he was witnessing; he never saw the manifestations that the others did.

But it was as if he had come full circle. He had left physics because it appeared divorced from Truth, from what Nietzsche said, and David had accepted, was a necessary precondition to create truth from fact: the interaction of a human value system. He had wandered in search of such values, and returned to physics because he had come to realize that at the boundaries of science analysis was indeed made up in good part by subjecting data to one's values, which influenced the formulation, acceptance, or rejection of new theories and interpretations about fundamental states, the origins of the universe, the nature of matter. And now he felt that he had indeed integrated that duality in his science, within himself. He felt a great calm, more thorough than any he had ever known, encompassing his love and loss of Susan, disturbed only by the awareness that another had by her own means walked this path before him, and that she now lay waiting for him beyond the realm of known reality, in territory she alone defined, bearing weapons only she possessed.

The universe itself is fractal in nature, he now knew with surety, once you get the scales and dimensions right. If so, she may, without even realizing where she's heading, first convert Earth itself into waves, then be able to replicate outwards in all directions in scale, to the sun and other planets in toto, to all the suns and planets there ever were or would be, quantum jumping from next door to the furthest reaches of the universe from one moment to the next, or the one behind, until all of space and time become converted, hallelujah, no mass, no mas. And the possibility that was human would not even be an ash or a piece of kindling for some future fire, but just some pulses indistinct from all the rest, for waves would not take separate form or change or grow, they would vibrate across eternity in glum repetition, and God himself would ponder what happened to all the souls.

David now existed beyond the caring of the bits and pieces around him. Two warriors, transcending the limits around them, moving with powers beyond anything the world had ever known. One driven by fear and indifference into an obsessed exploration to control a world whose touch she could not bear. The other stolidly leaning into the hurricanes that flattened whatever stood around him, driven by obsession too, of grief, and love, hatred he could not tolerate, and yes, the wonder of it all. Each exhausting the limited resources of mere tangible earth and its derivatives around them, she feeding on the sources within and beyond, he following until he could pull out of the sodden imprint of her footsteps and start his own march, circling around until destiny, as it had to, as it had with massive congruities of circumstances before them, would loop them into each other, a convergence micro and galactic, momentous and endless.

He landed smoothly at Kennedy well after midnight. Upshaw was waiting for him.

"Jesus, David, when did you go from being part of the solution to part of the problem?"

"A soldier has to have training before going into battle, with the weapons at his – or her – disposal. Can't face her without understanding."

"But the risk..."

"Better a little bit of Zurich than the whole planet, don't you think?"

Upshaw was silent for a moment. "I don't know, it's too much to grasp."

"And yet I have to, if we have a chance."

"laDoop wants to go in guns blazing."

"That would be like the bow and arrow against a missile. It won't work, Harold, you can't let him. It will only make things worse, and get her defenses up."

"We have to do something."

"Even when you can see the power of nothing?"

"It doesn't work, the clever and funny thing, not anymore. Not with her gone."

David lowered his head. "All right, let me develop an approach."

They barely waited for his luggage, and were whisked off by a long limousine into the inky night ahead, alternately illuminated and darkened by the lights and traffic, reappearing one moment only to be swallowed up in the next.

Chapter Thirty-two

Keeping it together is different from not falling apart. David appeared at the apartment door, disheveled from his travels, unkempt, weariness expressed in every part of his face and body. Sebastian picked up his bag, walked him in. They looked at each other, taking a breath.

Sebby's hug was restorative. His words were not.

"I ran a simulation, using your new fractal quantum equations, inputting the CERN data for base case."

Exhaustion peeled off David, to be replaced by an even deeper fatigue, that went beyond mind and body. "And?"

Sebby led David to a terminal screen. It showed a map of the world in projection. A few flashing pinpoints were on it, the sites of the existing areas of wave discontinuity.

"What's with the one in China?" David asked, pointing to the largest point.

"They tried to fix it."

"Christ," David said.

"Exactly." Sebby hit a few keys.

The areas shimmered, grew a bit, retreated, then began to expand, remorseless and inevitable. On the screen they took on a clay terra-cotta color, as they covered more and more territory, until they stabilized, covering a large part of the map.

"As more people become aware, there will be more propagators, like Janson. And once the media picks it up, well, if every storm nowadays is the storm of the century, then imagine what they'll do with this. Opening it up for others. The brilliant but disenchanted.

Next generation of hackers, skip the computers, go to time and space itself. Particle terrorists."

"How long is this simulation?" David asked.

"Two years."

"Two years..."

"Half the planet, David. Three billion souls."

David shook his head; despite all his immersion in the math he was still capable of being shocked by the reality of the outcomes. Sebby went on. "And in this scenario, there seems to be a natural delimiter, like your analysis of how a plague doesn't infiltrate into every corner. But..."

"But what if she changes the playing field again, creates new rules. She's done it before, doing it now."

"Then it could be everywhere, and god only knows how fast."

David shivered.

"Get a hold of yourself, man," Sebby said.

They looked at each other and started to laugh, hard and harder, until they couldn't stop.

==

Sense yourself.

The process to select his method of training had been necessarily quick. Through his earlier wanderings, David had already encountered a variety of tools, philosophies, whackos, and practitioners of what was billed in those days as self-fulfillment, holistic healing, sensitivity training, or, on the garbage side, rationalizations for radical egocentricity, make way for the primacy of the self, the rest of you be damned. His memories and a quick research scan led him to use self-hypnosis as a primary tool. He had first analyzed the problem and defined his goal – how to use his will, his mind, to keep body and the mind it contained intact in the face of an unknown yet potent capability to create a different context which could eliminate any distinction between himself and his background, his body and what lay outside of it, in which he could be assimilated, overwhelmed by sensory transformation which could invade and destroy him.

He had to etch a fine and distinct line between himself and his surroundings. Then, too, he had to avoid the seduction he had felt amidst the bedlam at CERN, a pulling towards a sense of the kind of power and control that could only be achieved by letting go completely, a sensation he only became aware of much later. He had to believe in his self and, through his will, channel and maintain the profound worldview he now encapsulated, out of will and necessity, which found Mary Quintin's shimmering states of dissolution an antithesis to all he cared about – or most. And that, too, he had to face, no room for grief and mourning, not as a soft spot in his mental armor, where a reminder could dissolve him, in a world where the figurative became the literal, actually dissolve him if he indulged in a precious grief, so that Susan's legacy would be in his preparation, saying goodbye finally in order to say hello successfully.

He had to imbue in his essence a sense of immersion in each moment, of acceptance without judgment of what had happened and what might follow, without becoming so absorbed with the outcome as to lose touch with the moment, to enable the scientist to fall in love with the experiment itself, not either the previous theory or the hope of new discovery, when the experiment was life itself.

If David's assessment of what he faced was correct, then it was imperative that he confront Mary and whatever she threw at him, or drew out of him, not with a defensive posture of combating an elusive and perhaps unknowable weaponry, but rather by establishing the core of his being as an assertive presence in the equations, so that that core would remain intact and in doing so make itself known. Thus David's task was not to be distracted with a shifting set of external circumstances, and especially not to focus, with inevitable fear, on what might happen if he failed, and became nothing, joining, truly unconsciously, the enemy. Rather, David had to concentrate on keeping himself intact each moment, without fear, moving towards her while staying internally whole.

It reflected David's theory, derived from when he moved more in these worlds years ago, that therapy was most effective if it focused on the solid core of an individual's personality and strengths, rather than spending lots of time looking at the soft mush of problems and fears, remembered and current, that lay like a limp mantle surrounding the solid core. If David was correct in his concept of the relationship between consciousness and actuality, and that the medium of such relationship lay in a fifth-dimensional particle, the observatron, which could be a bullet in the upcoming struggle, then it was critical for him to remain literally in touch with himself, with the strength that was an elementary part of his being, and use that determined force as both an insulation from what might otherwise render him non-material and as a weapon in and of itself. Both men hypothesized that if David could remain intact against Quintin's wave-conversion observatrons, the feedback of that solidity would unquestionably affect her and the space between them. If David was correct.

Over and over, David sat and sensed himself, felt his energy and strength flow within him, filling up all the parts of his body and mind and into his soul. For surely that was where the energy and faith needed for the battle spilled into, seeking the confidence to move to a new depth inside himself, sit with the realities of a new universe within him, binding himself with his self to resist the sirens' call that had destroyed Arnold Janson and had corrupted Mary Quintin ultimately. He called up memories of the love he had enjoyed, the life he had loved, the elements of that life, the particles of those elements, grounding himself in a litany of sense and awareness. An hour became a day, a day became a week, while Upshaw fretted, laDoop fumed, and Sal knocked on the door, while David sat, and sensed in silence the infinite space within him, where possibilities resided in an endless act of becoming, grooming himself for a date with Mary.

A drive out to the beach. Before David would keep that date, he wanted to take another walk on the beach. Through high school and college he had rarely had time for "such things," connecting them to a perception of less serious intent, a child's imagery made sadly and inevitably inflexible by a longing for self-differentiation coupled with a lack of experience to modulate its certainty, held onto for years as a block of identity, until time and turmoil and the jackhammer of living, the contradictions of belief with experience, the repetition of untenable situations, erodes the once-fixed belief and a new hill, smaller perhaps, but more solidly grounded, can arise. During his odyssey, David used to go to the beach, get stoned and lose himself to the sun and wind and sand and smells, to movement and laughter, to closing his eyes and the red views fading into forgotten memories, creating rapid elastic imagery to the music in his earphones, epiphanies where symbols expressed what volumes of words could only hint at, his hunger aroused with bodies the only food in sight, fantasies from the next blanket where three teenage bikini'd girls pranced and talked and smoked and turned over and over from tiny breasts to oh-so-slim hips around and around in his mind and then the air and sky and water joined to ease and take his body, accept and absorb it, gently sleeping, at first more tired and then refreshed, burned back to life. To go to the beach and lose himself. A luxury then, today it would be a fatal indulgence.

Antifermo said he wanted to come along, as part of his investigation, "for the files," he called it. David arranged to meet him at the beach. He wanted time to prepare, he wanted the solace of unbroken time to sink into and move out of, to go through such times fully and come out without looking back. One legacy from his wandering days he had kept was an Alfa Romeo sports coupe: metallic green, sleek, it had carried him like a glowing comet down the California coasts, along the Oregon beaches, through the Utah deserts and Colorado mountains. Just getting in the car was a resurgence of that freedom, top down, then the radio had been louder than the wind, preceding him down the highway; today it was the wind alone, the wind and thought, a fast slow drive out to the beach.

David, even though seeking a neutral and accepting state of mind, laughed when he saw Antifermo waiting for him at the side of the road next to a beat-up old Plymouth Valiant of a generalized dark color. His pale hands and face blended into the sand behind, so that it seemed like a dark-stained raincoat with a sheen at its edges stood over a pair of protruding black shoes, some urban idea of a scarecrow to keep the kids from sneaking in.

David greeted Antifermo with a thought that he had while driving out, that justice and the courts were an aberration of the principles of quantum physics – an act unobserved was not real; indeed an act was real only after the court officially observed it, pieced it out, and passed judgment on it. "Even physicists aren't that presumptuous, Sal." The shifting tides of moral and personal perception were injected by the system to determine that day's reality. What really happened at a murder in Central Park? Only one person alive knows, perhaps, and he won't say; thus the case, the law is in essence a question of observation, knowledge is derived in bastard form from an observer with a stake in the outcome, and is finally deemed by the court, as observer by proxy. Since the outcome of Sal's world was so often circumscribed by the limits of what was knowable, or bizarre but inevitable limitations, he should feel right at home in David and Mary's world of quantum uncertainty.

Sal listened, shrugged his shoulders. "Dead is dead, Doc, this even I have observed. Shall we dance?" As they started walking his heavy feet would slip and slide in the scrub and sand, but he didn't seem to care or even notice. The area revived memories for him, and if his pronunciation remained hard, it was here an overlay for the soft and bittersweet time when they were all younger.

The one thing at the beach that had ever attracted Sal Antifermo, it turned out, was the hot dogs.

"Yeah, we used ta come here when I was a kid, ya know, take a train and a bus from the city, took fuckin' forever out and longer back. The guys would all sit together and the girls someplace else, mostly so that they could put their hands over their mouths and giggle, either in embarrassment at something we was doing – you know, like throwing a moon out of the rear window of the bus with the driver not knowing what was going on – or else at whatever they was talking about, probably like who was cute and who was dumb and who had said what to who or else asked somebody else to, ya know, it was pretty clean back then, the guys had bathing suits down to their knees, just about, none a those little teeny European jobs now with your balls scrunched up, ya know, and the girls, even though they had good meat on them still they packed it in, no bikinis then although man when they stood at the edge of the water and scrunched up their shoulders and took little jumps cause it was cold and shivered as they tried to get in laughing and knowing we was looking at them, man that was a sight!

"I remember this one time, I had a crush on this girl, a blond fair-skinned Nordic type, hoping opposites could attract, ya know. Pederson, Sarah Pederson. And we came here early in the season, maybe our last year in high school when it was all a lark and getting away from it all didn't mean what it does now, ya know, for us, nothing serious, a few grades and teachers, acne and erections, but not like real money or work, ya know. So a few of us come out, I'm driving the old man's big, big Olds, what a piece of work that was, we hit the beach and Sarah she gets in that water like it's a fucking bath, let me tell you. You woulda thought to look at her all fair like her skin was thin over that body, it was a nice one too, full and slim the way kids are built, she was wearing a white bathing suit with red stars on it, surrounded by that blonde hair and light skin, like water with a little beer in it, and right in the water she goes, no bullshit, and it was *cold*, let me tell you.

"So what am I ta do, ya know? I'm trying like hell to impress her and she was smart, in the SP class – you know, that's Special Progress, where they do all the advanced work quicker and more of it, guys like you mostly, okay, I was there too but not getting the heavy grades like her or you, I'll bet, and now we're out at the beach where I figure at least I can flex a little, not like those limp dick nerdy guys in the rest of the class – no offense Doc, you look pretty fit too – but I figure here at least I can show her something the other guys can't. And she's in the water cold as ice one two three and staying there! So naturally I gotta do the same and I'm there next to her and smiling all the time, we're jumping up and down, throwing a tennis ball back and forth, some ratty thing a dog would've passed on but it was all we had, and she's swimming and I'm swimming, and everybody else is long since outta the water back on the blankets, towels wrapped around them, talking away, it looked real good to me but not to my Nordic goddess, she's jumping through the water and talking about math class and whatever and finally, just when I think my balls have shrunk so far in they ain't ever gonna come back out, in protest ya know, finally she says 'hey, you wanna go out?'

"'Hey,' I say, 'if you wanna,' and I'm outta there.

"So we get back ta the blankets and I start ta shiver, I mean, I'll bet I was bluer than a cop's cap, shivering away, so they wrapped me in towels and a blanket and still I'm shivering, and I'm looking up at all these faces in a circle standing over me, peering down at me and talking and laughing and there's Sarah – she hasn't even bothered to dry off! – and she's nicely worried about me and I'm seeing a look like it's for a kid brother – shit! – but there's nothing, nothing I can do about it but shiver, I'm shaking all over and I can't stop.

"So one of the guys, Henry, says, 'I'll go get a cup of hot coffee, maybe that'll help,' and he runs off – he was kind of a crazy guy, always trying to be nice in a real exaggerated way but always whacking up, so he's gone a long time, 'cause it's early in the season and only the main stand is open, not the one near us, but he doesn't think about getting the keys and driving, no, he's gotta do it on his own power or something, he runs like a banshee maybe two miles, gets the coffee, runs back holding this one cup, without a cap, they didn't have plastic covers back then, so he's running like you see those waiters' races with the guys holding the trays up so as not to spill something, and finally he makes it back about to spill his guts he's so tired, what a crazy guy he was, and I've been shaking uncontrollably the whole time, it must be forty-five minutes he's been gone. He gets right up to me and in an exaggerated way – he has to fuck around, see, so he's playing real exhausted – he collapses down to his knees – and spills the whole cup of coffee all over me! Luckily I didn't get scalded, though, because he's been running for so long the coffee was about cold, so now I'm shivering and have this lukewarm coffee getting sticky all over me, and everybody is totally cracked up laughing except Henry, who keeps saying, 'I'm sorry, I'm sorry, should I get another cup?' Which really makes everybody, Sarah included, absolutely hysterical, while I'm just lying there looking up at all of them."

David had started laughing halfway through the story. They were walking from the cars across the broad grassy knolls to the beginning of the beach and down towards the shore. The day had started cloudy, then intermittently sunny, and now a bright mid-afternoon glare reflected off sea and sand into their eyes, concealed by dark amber sunglasses. David could have stepped out of a men's fashion magazine, khakis, knit shirt, tennis sneakers, his hair blowing in a steady breeze from off the water. Antifermo looked like he was knee deep in yesterday's garbage and didn't even smell it. He sidled along David's stride, managing to keep up while giving the impression he didn't even notice they were walking.

"So it's not like I'm saying I don't like the beach, it's just, well, it's got . . . memories, ya know what I mean. Later that day we played a game of touch football. I was real fast those days, so I'm lined up across from Henry, ready to go out for a pass, really make my moves at last, ya know, no one could keep up with me, and there was Sarah watching so I'm set, staring at him ready for the ball to be hiked, and he has this idea which I guess was a bright one to him, so just as the ball is hiked he throws sand full right in my face, figuring ta slow me down, not really thinking, ya could say, and now I've got tons of sand in my eyes, have to stand around for half an hour while they scraped my eyeballs, one more time surrounded by the laughing crowd. Driving home, I missed the goddamned automatic toll booth with my change, which was all we had – it was a long fucking day, ya know what I mean? Then when we get out to find the coins a cop comes and . . . Jesus, Mary, José, what is that?"

Chapter Thirty-three

Nothing was real now for Sal.

A slight mist, distance, and the spray from the waves combined so that the whole shoreline shimmered as they approached it. They walked over the final low dune to where the scrub grass ended, with a few final plugs like implants trying to combat the baldness, the sand now a wide strip, several hundred yards, ending with the water. The sand itself was a mix, patches still pristine in color and texture, a strip of dried seaweed and the miscellaneous detritus of an ocean's housecleaning, empty husks of shells, tiny clams to large horseshoe crabs, simple serrated ovals to gnarly gray prehistoric complexities, pieces of Styrofoam from old floats, grayish-white and pockmarked like a man-made transplant of an oceanic organ, bulbous black kelp and hard rubbery pods, strange alien designs, repetitious hints of the live inhabitants descended from these few no longer living.

And then the strips, patches, random and uniform remains of the people, the shore a memory mechanism teeming with the live and what they left behind, of soda, kids' plastic pails, grown-ups' liquor bottles, once-shiny bags that held chips and Doritos, laden with sand and rooted in place, beer, faded aluminum cans indistinguishable now by brand, an occasional swatch of red or yellow leaving hints like a mummy's sarcophagus. Ozymandias's dreams driven by commerce lasted no longer than when driven by other lusts, plastic plates and aluminum foil intact when all else will be gone, ready to last a millennium, containers for one adult portion of fruit-flavored and -colored imitation juice, a condom washed clean of love's fruitless juices, now as parched and empty as a gutted building or the grey candy wrappers it was perched on. They walked past tire tracks, deep wide wheels to collect the garbage, narrower jeeps to pick up and deliver the lifeguards in their summer glory, balloon tracks of buggies on forbidden rides, still an occasional mound where Ralph was buried in the sand or Lisa and Teddy built that huge castle with turrets shaped from packed and inverted little plastic pails.

Oh the hours spent here, the millions of people-hours between that last scrub of grass and the water line, eroded to traces, they walked past it all, sand working into Antifermo's black shoes and clinging to his black polyester socks, David too bending his legs, pushing off, Antifermo interrupting himself (the only one who could) – "Jesus, Mary, José, what is that?"

It was and it wasn't. It was a piece of the shore that wasn't there. For Sal Antifermo, the abstraction devolved into a reality that was an aberration. His life was built around nabbing someone, grabbing hold of them by the collar like a cat with her kittens, steering them towards incarceration with the organized machinery of institutions behind him. He moved always towards a physical act. The questioning and the verbal barrages, his intuitive pondering of why the crime occurred, the sifting through evidence, turning lies inside out, locating whereabouts, computer-generated printouts, pictures, the board game of rules and steps were for him incidental, pebbles crunched on a path that led to a firm, hard grip on a suspect, the entity within whom motivation coincided with ability into a package, to bring to trial. The real culmination was no mere idea, no simple utterance however built of logic and thought; no, it was a hand shooting out, the grabbing, the tightening fingers of justice that were his, his alone to touch, these were his moments.

But here, on this beach, more winded than he let on from their walk from the cars across the yielding ground, already losing purchase with each step, now finally to be confronted with this eerie bit of inapprehensible shimmering . . . for the first time, Sal Antifermo understood – this case was different.

David had his own walk memory. He had last seen this piece of shoreline from the air. From above it had looked more distinct, containable, with finite if fuzzy limits, able to see the good, solid earth on both sides of it. Now it loomed like a filter, straining more and more of the world as they got closer to it, until it threatened to blot out that comfortable world of matter once taken for granted and leave them, if they could be left, surrounded by its seductive haze.

But even as they closed in on the shore David barely saw it. He saw instead Susan, head up, determined chin, her beauty stranded – by him? – forever on this spot. He saw the cables and the platform, in his mind almost heard the sizzle like the fuse on a firecracker, little sparks and then the noiseless boom, she was gone, they were gone, he was gone.

It took the mind of man to create noise in a vacuum.

He felt a brief, familiar tear. If he had done nothing, accepted nothing, Susan could still be here. The thought convulsed his stomach: oh god, she could still be here, and she is gone forever. If he left the space alone, would it have gone away like the tides it obscured, returning the shore to the way it was? Maybe Mary would have grown up, or gotten tired, or too old, or consumed herself, someday? Had he presumptively produced this dragon, and caused his love to be swallowed up by it, when otherwise they could have lived indeterminately after? He had grown up on action/reaction; had he lost his knowledge when he needed it most, or simply accelerated a more subtle process?

For the first time on this long walk his steps felt heavy, his breath shortened by a constriction that kept him from inhaling fully, and the mist coated his eyes. He stopped, forced a few deep breaths, and looked around. The beach was restored, the winds had carved again bumps and snakelines in the sand where the platform had been raised and never lowered, where the crews had entered and not exited, where she had stood and never yielded, and still no traces left.

Antifermo was pulling his arm, a handle pumping his mind back to where they were, in time as much as place. "Man, Doc, I gotta admit I wasn't sure about all this stuff you've been telling me, particles and waves and what not. But, now, I gotta admit," the usually incessant pace of his words slowed into a flat accentless tone, "that is one weird-looking mother. It's like the, whaddaya call it, like the fuckin' aroara boris landed down here."

They walked closer, sliding down the last ridge undercut by the day's waves, past the point where the sand line was smoother, darkened temporarily and periodically from the water running up to it, harder, odd to find firm footing in this last close instant. They stood with all the world in front of them obscured, and in the whole world what they wanted to do most was turn around, look at the familiar terrain behind them, walk that terrain away from this fathomless creature in front, back to a hot dog stand or highway, into the car and away, turn on the radio and act like it never happened, until the nausea dissipated and time buried it away. Neither man moved.

David noticed that the breeze, which had been blowing in from the sea, now appeared to be coming from the side. He stood at Sal's left, and his hair was blowing to the right. He looked at Antifermo, whose darker, shinier hair had a few strands blowing towards David. He pointed it out to Sal. "The wind must not come through completely, some of its energy is absorbed, and there are no particles to transmit it. So on the back side of the discontinuity a partial vacuum is formed, and the wind blows around the area, like on an airplane wing, to fill it in. Interesting, huh?"

Antifermo put his hand to his scalp, hunching his shoulders as he tried to put his wayward wisps back into place, as if that might arrest the phenomenon that was blowing them.

David cocked his head. "And also, the sound of the waves, it's, yes, it's louder coming from there. I guess there's easier propagation through a wave-oriented environment, less inertia to overcome."

"Yeah, neat, real neat," Sal said without conviction, patting a few more hairs down. "Well, we're here. Now what?"

"Now, copper, we see what you're made of. And I mean see."

David viewed this trip as a warm-up for directly confronting Mary Quintin. He reasoned that if he couldn't handle contact with an area of discontinuity far removed from its source, he certainly couldn't handle direct contact with her. Conversely, if he familiarized himself with this strange, elusive surface before him, he could be better prepared for meeting Quintin and somehow coping with her. It all began here, and he had calculated it began with his self.

Quintin had somehow converted this strip of beach into its wave functions, extending it upward and preserving the area in that form as consistently as it had once remained intact in its pure particle state. His goal was also preservation, of the integrity of his own being, of his self as he knew it, embodying a world he cherished. Quintin caused this change through her control of this matter at a distance; in her way she was like one of Antifermo's perpetrators, the coincidence of motivation and skills, the opportunity being an area she knew well manifesting that fractal reality she had so thoroughly incorporated that she could extend her understanding into actual conversion. David had postulated a medium of control, the observatron, and believed that while they had their fullest impact on inanimate or unsuspecting animate objects, they could be nullified by a countervailing consciousness, so that he could come in contact with the barrage of fifth-dimensional particles streaming from her and remain intact. His brush at CERN increased his confidence, even if he had been taken unawares by it at first. He'd touched . . . something . . . and he'd come back. He explained this underlying concept to Antifermo, whose doubtful yet determined gaze shifted back and forth between David and the wall of non-matter that stood before him as he scrunched up his jaw.

"Well, Doc, it sounds kinda reasonable, all things considered, as in this is actually here in front of us. But, let me ask ya something. Didn't you say you was mostly, before this, and for all these years, a theory guy, not a lab guy, not one a those guys who actually does it, more like the guys who think it up. So I mean, well, here we are on the fucking beach, not back in the think tank. Don't get me wrong."

David smiled. "What the hell, Sal, it's just some sand and water and air, only it looks a little different."

David was counting on his explanation, combined with Antifermo's fierce natural strength, to provide Antifermo with a shield that would keep him together, armor David had had to consciously strive to possess. From the stories of his work Sal had told him, David knew how solidly put together the man was, by personality, experience, and training. At first he had resisted his presence here, but now, after all his self-conscious striving to achieve a state Antifermo inhabited naturally, he was glad for the other man's presence. It filled a void where Susan had been, a void he knew could, if left alone, swallow him up, the hole of the doughnut devouring its rim, some topologically valid if freakish domain that could, in the even more freakish space around him, translate into the physical reality of his literal undoing.

He outlined his plan. First, better prepared mentally and with greater understanding of the actual phenomenon, he would induce his self-hyponosis, and with his eyes closed sense his hand fully and completely. He would then gently put his hand into the discontinuous surface before them. It would be, he said, "a real hands-on – or rather, hands-in – experience." Antifermo would go to the other side of the wave area, and the two of them would shake hands through it. A simple handshake; that was all that was required.

David closed his eyes, took several deep breaths, and started the routine he had worked out. He relaxed his whole body, sensed it, and filled it with energy, moving through his trained responses. He pictured himself standing on the beach, seeing his body and the inchoate shape before him. He pictured the energy flowing within himself filling his body, his mind, etching his hand in sharp relief against its surroundings. He cast aside the layers of his past, the attachments and anxieties; some elements shed easily, others hugged like steel barnacles molded to his flesh, bolted in with the seamless dowels of emotion. He concentrated on that moment of being there, accepting the noise of the sea and the birds, the subdued sound of waves crashing in the distance, the smell of the ocean, the feel of the breeze mingling with the light of the sun so that he felt irradiated with the energies around him, elemental yet human, each and together not distractions from his awareness but incorporated into it. Accepting of the noise, accepting of the time and place, of what he was about to do, that he would do it in the fullness of his self and accept whatever outcome occurred as a result of his actions. He even pictured Antifermo next to him, stolid, and saw him joining with him in this action, in this battle, as he cast out hatred and desire and knew only a peace that did not judge.

With a final exhalation of breath, David opened his eyes, for an instant wider than their sockets, warmer than the sand and kinder than the whispering grasses. His face looked relaxed, reflecting the sun and wind and noise around it, his voice seemed to come from deep inside him as he again went over his plan with Antifermo. They walked to within a few yards of the right end of the dissolved space. From there they carefully paced and measured the distance to the end of the shimmer, and then continued walking well beyond it to ensure that they would not prematurely enter it. Standing now well to the right of the edge of the wave-space, Antifermo took off his shoes and socks, rolled up his pants, and entered the water. He looked like a kinetoscope of a bather in the twenties, his dark looks and clothing and the trousers absurdly rolled up.

When the topic of who should enter the water first came up, and David started talking about his concerns about distractions from the water and the temperature differential and the different orientation, Antifermo listened for a while and finally said, "Doc, what the fuck, I'll go in the fucking water. Let's just get on with it."

When the two men faced each other, David on the hard packed sand near the water's edge and Sal in the shallow water a few feet out from the shore, they looked at each other for a while, then shook hands, memorizing the feel, paused, let go, and without another word paced an exact distance back along the edge of the area of dissolution.

As they walked to its edge they began to lose sight of each other, at first as if through a mist, a fog, and then completely. The effect was unbalancing, each feeling a tendency to be drawn inwards as if to compensate for the vacuum of sight in front of them, each resisting in his own way, like the seduction of standing on the edge of a great canyon wall and looking to the mysteries below, to know them once and fully, uniquely.

Alone now, David marched fifteen paces, reached the spot where they had agreed to stop, turn towards each other, and shake hands again. David couldn't see Antifermo, could only assume he was on the other side. A few more deep breaths, a face that beamed with a glow, a look without fear into nothing... and slowly, David let his hand enter the dissolved and dissolving space before him.

For his part, Antifermo stumbled along the water's edge, cursing the rocks and other unknown sharp objects his feet kept hitting. He was in fact not crazy about going into the water, hitting some slimy creature to rub against or that would bite him, cursing each step, counting his way towards his appointment. If he had had his way he would have walked right through, a fullback going down the middle, with his coat buttoned. He got to the spot, faced inland, balanced himself against the waves and wind nudging him from behind by bending and bowing his legs, eyed the perpetrator, and thrust out his hand.

David sensed it before he felt it, a darker mass inside of the lighter shades, an aura of anticipation. As he entered the field, he could feel his hand as if it were being barraged, like a dry mist was pummeling it, a local cyclone enclosed it. He alternated between keeping his eyes open to remain fully aware, of his feet on the ground, of smell and feel and noise, and closing his eyes, picturing the sharp outline of his hand as it reached in front of him.

A wave came up within him, a nausea of fear that this wouldn't work, that none of it would work, that Mary Quintin was untouchable by her very nature, that this is the way the world would end, a terminal transformation, the angst of anticipation brief, pungent, and then he returned himself to the moment, breathing, sensing, accepting, the barrage against his hand subsiding, and then there it was, he clasped around Antifermo's hand, around a bedrock of simple straightforward resolute matter.

Their hands touched and the shrouded hood of uncertainty lifted from them, carving a circle as if the sky had reached out to follow their arms in gratitude, into a club where it had been excluded, a bending pipe at their elbows following in, a patch then of bright blue, a cylinder that connected each to each other, and both to much more, the world that mattered and the world that hoped, a circle moved by the calculus of their beings to elongate. The old math worked again, connecting them, surrounded by a dark-toned shadow, while beyond the obscuring hues persisted, still intact. They could not see each other's faces, saw only their elbows and forearms disappearing into it, not even knowing of the light that shone between them. From afar it looked like a tableau of man with arm extended, arm circled in light against a free-standing muted wall surrounded by all the blue there was.

They held on, then shouted, unable to hear each other but feeling the vibrations up and down their arms into their hands, increasing the strength of their grip, two grown men whooping like boys, a romp on the beach through space and time, alone, then finding themselves in each other, holding on until the feel of it was enmeshed in their memories, until they let go because this little touch was simply a peck on a lover's lips, and they knew that it was their bodies that were next in line, and they could not help but anticipate.

Antifermo sloshed back through the water, joined David, stared at him with a smile, even dragged his toes through the sand, and without speaking the two men crossed the gulf of rippled sand and mottled grasses that lay between them and their parked cars, pointing on the road to their next appointment.

⩵

What was this?

A touch, part familiar, part quite new, and different. She had trouble pushing back, but then it relented, and she was surrounded by her comforts.

Chapter Thirty-four

Nothing could stop Tony laDoop.

Tony laDoop had clout. He hadn't just taken over the computer facilities at the United Nations. There wasn't enough scientific capability in the UN machines to really crunch out the big data apps, do the mega calculations. So he'd gotten together the best of the supercomputers, springing them loose from the military, from the big corporations, from the Japs. He had a bank of twelve machines, had overnight gotten the best programmers to develop software so that the machines could talk to each other and he, laDoop, could talk to the machines.

He assembled his team, he organized them, delegated, had assistants to collate, filter, cross-check and summarize. Meetings didn't start until he arrived, focused on him when he was there, ended when he left, Banks of men and women stared at him across long, shining conference tables, the glare reflected in their faces, pale stares waiting. He was in command, he was witty, he made urbane references that left his colleagues shaking their heads in amusement, he was calm in the face of danger, he was collected as they looked to unlock the unknown. He was the link to the higher-ups, who deferred to his judgment, he was the key to public pronouncement, he was the foundation and the pillar, the probing analysis and the determined conclusion.

He was plenty pissed. "Where the fuck does Altaforce get off? First he gets twenty-five people blown away, now the almighty Altaforce is planning to go meet this Quintin on his own – walk up the front door, howd'ya do, could you please give us back those pieces of our world you took away, they're tiny but we got fond of them. Hello, cowboy. One-on-one doesn't cut it today."

He was pulling at his puffy earlobes, looking at his three Executive Assistants, PhDs in physics from MIT, Stanford, and Princeton, each there to serve as an extension of his manifold self; to him they all had the same personality, the one he gleaned from a mirror. He expected efficiency, crispness, and complete subordination; they were the three rings of his circus, and he was the big top. There were some who suspected they were also the real show, but they carried out their assignments with relentless efficacy, and left the limelight for laDoop. Years of schooling had trained them well for their role, that and the confidence of obtaining gratifications deferred which came with degrees and pedigrees.

"Well," EA2 said, "he did guess right as to the type of origin for the discontinuity fields. And it was his experiment that gave us the data to trace back to Quintin. Er, which you were instrumental in achieving." He was a recent graduate, inclined towards speaking what he saw as a reasonable probability of a fact, although he was becoming increasingly aware that perhaps such statements to laDoop should be tempered by consideration of his boss's position on innumerable grants-awarding committees. If he hadn't yet learned to bite his tongue, he was beginning to click his teeth.

"Right," said laDoop, "exactly, gave us the data to trace back to her. Okay, he got lucky – more, all right, he's smart, I'll give you that, but if it hadn't of been him, it would've been somebody else. You must know the work I've done with Hamigoto on the statistical probability that any bit of knowledge discovered by one person would be discovered by someone else within a standard deviation time period of less than fourteen months. We have all kinds of experiments in progress, plus wildcatters tied into the network. Nobody's that unique anymore; we would have gotten it. And the point is, when he found some leads, he had to bring them in to us. We ran the correlations to get the fix on her, we filled out the equations for the wave dissembling, we've got the power to understand this thing fully, and we've got to be the people to move on her."

"Right, but it's time, Dr. laDoop, it's time now," EA1 injected; the Senior assistant, closest to establishing his independent setup, he was normally the most cautious and buttoned down of the three, but time was rounding out his thin body and soul, and the buttons at times got close to popping. He was old enough to be swept away by the immediacy of their needs. "Our own algorithms show the instability of the current fields, the growing statistical potential for expansion, and the non-fractal-based move in Chicago shows the threat taking new dimensions. I guess that could be literal." He was about to laugh at his cleverness, but saw laDoop's unsmiling gaze staring at him. "If Altaforce hadn't found out what he did when he did, acted when he did, then by the time we might have determined it it could have been too late to do anything. At least he's given us that window of opportunity."

laDoop looked at him sharply. "That's not a window any damn fool should jump through. Remember Janson's window? It needs organization, a team, feedback." His words spoken, EA1 quickly agreed with his boss, tucking in his stomach.

laDoop let it pass. "By God, it's too great a risk for him to go gallivanting out there. Set up a senior staff meeting – for a trip I'm going to take."

The implication was clear to all of them. EA3 interjected, surprising the rest of them. He was the oldest, albeit newest, member of the team, recently recruited for this project. Not much was known of him; indeed, he was somewhat suspect in being available at such short notice for such a position at his age. He had received good references for intelligence, naturally, and a few asides with regard to personality which laDoop ignored, since they were not relevant for his purposes.

"Couldn't we just let her be? I mean, see what happens," EA3 said. "We don't interfere with other scientists' work."

"What the hell," said laDoop, as the other EAs cringed. "Are you out of –"

"Isn't she just an extension of the way the world has moved, why not leave her alone?"

laDoop shouted "I'm not about to sit by and let a threat to my world go unchallenged."

The other EAs agreed, and EA3 stopped talking, his cooperation assumed. As always when he got excited, laDoop's large stomach heaved up and down, making his tie curl up, mesmerizing his associates, like a snake doing its dance. His accent lost its refinement, his students would call him duh Loop in those times, for the das, disses and dats. But his mind was a disciplined, if conditioned, one, his presence forceful enough to carry dissenters before him like rag dolls whipped in a dog's mouth.

EAs 1, 2, and 3 coordinated, each contacting the Group heads for Division input. All Senior Staff were polled in an iterative Delphi technique, which had been established as the optimum decision-making process for the geographically dispersed group involved. Each scientist was asked to rank his top choices for responses to the threat of Mary Quintin. The scientists were polled, and the overall rankings were then distributed to all the scientists, who were again asked to rank their choices, in light of their new information on their colleagues' ranking of the options. The sequence was continued until a broad consensus was reached, imputing a high degree of certainty to the outcome. The process was broadly used by the government, to predict economic growth, for example. The results were then cross-polled, matched to computer-generated decision trees mapping out all possible combinations of variables and options. Those possible actions were then cross-checked against the polling, using weighted criteria to assess micro and macro situations, incorporating a probabilistic expected value analysis to analyze courses of action one at a time, in combination and in series. The method was considered so logical that nobody ever bothered to look back at how well it actually performed. That could have busted the whole ring, a risk none of the participants wanted to take.

The net result after two very frenetic days was to confirm laDoop's initial decision: he, as an extension of the UN Prime Scientific Mission and Executive Director of the Special Committee for Maintaining Earth, representing and incorporating its vast resources, would confront Mary Quintin, carrying the writ of the community's cease and desist order, empowered with the right of instant judgment, armed and versed to perform any sentence.

laDoop made a last, stunning appearance before the twenty-seven Very Senior Staffers in the Secretary General's private conference room. It was meticulous, the only disorder coming from the view out along the East River, smoke stacks and boats and cars moving to their own rhythms. laDoop stood in front of the window, framed by the scene, the light behind him a halo around his dark bulk. Shining, precise, he presented a picture of a man practically transcendent, looking beyond the short-lived ambiguities of matter and personality around him to a deeper realm of self and world. His plan was final.

"I will review the latest data and equations to completely familiarize myself with the phenomenon and its aspects. We will coordinate with DOD to lay down sufficient broad-based interference across the whole telecommunications wave spectrum to jam Mary Quintin's possible modes of reception, while I sneak up under the umbrella of the interference."

"How do you know those are the wavelengths she operates on?" Upshaw interjected. David had not been invited to the meeting. "If you don't cover the right ones, then –"

"We've analyzed the probabilities, Mr. Upshaw, quite thoroughly, I assure you. This is the highest. Now, if I may continue. Thank you. We will keep open one narrow band, selected at random, through which I will communicate with the Team. Through this baby."

He broke into a big smile, and showed a slide of the modified NASA space suit he would wear, outfitted with sensors, with voice and data uploaded to a relay point and then to the central supercomputer bank, for instant review and analysis, which in turn would be interpreted and relayed back to him.

"The entire Team will be plugged into a network of terminals connected through the super bank, organized to present, retrieve, and input data in a logical sequence of filter and review, generating and selecting key and derivative courses of action, incorporating as backup the options graphing and scenarios maps, even including emergency critical path entrance points to accommodate off-chart and chaotic events, to analyze their impact on major actions and assess the sensitivity of critical variables to the new data. Nothing will get past us."

Four hundred forty-seven trained intellects and the most massive computer system the world had ever created would support him. It was a setup that made spaceflight preparation and resources look like cave writing on the walls.

He came back a gibbering idiot, never to speak a sentence that made sense again.

==

Luckily, Shen-ya was not on the mountain the day the scientists tried to restore it, impatient with the progress at the UN and unhappy with feeling excluded from the rest of the world's process. He had long since accepted the strange shimmering space and walked around it. The Chinese had picked up on the particle-to-wave switch, but they did not have access to David's data, only laDoop's, through accessible channels, and laDoop was not about to promulgate any of David's flaky work, especially not now, when he was on his way under his own steam. The Chinese took the data, but they lacked respect for laDoop, and the implicit warnings even his work contained were dismissed as unsubstantiated. Although they had lost several men and pieces of equipment in their earlier investigation of the area, before their first evacuation, they attributed those losses to lack of preparation. Based on this bedrock example of international cooperation and understanding, the Chinese decided that if some local disturbance had caused a discrete set of particles to convert to waves, then perhaps a massive load of particles would overwhelm the topical force and restore to the People's Republic her piece of honored homeland, in the established and successful tradition of using force to overcome disobedience.

The Chinese lugged massive amounts of equipment and generators up the side of the mountain and aimed over thirty particle beams at nothing. The small piece of a knife-edge ridge blinked back into view, but before they could congratulate themselves it disappeared again, then came back but rearranged, and then the people were gone, along with a whole ridge in the LangYaShen mountains that was now completely beyond the vision of those who in any event could no longer see anything. The gap was visible from scores of miles and several villages, and this time the increased area of dissolution did not go away. Shen-ya retired and took to playing with the small children who walked by his cabin, and he and the Comrade Commissar would get very drunk together as often as rations allowed.

⩵

Mary Quintin had at least made one part of their job easier. She had picked for her home an isolated spot south of the White Mountains, built to her specifications, far away from any neighbors, with prize money she'd received for one of her papers. Its remoteness simplified their controlled access – lots of explanations left unnecessary, such as the complete loss of radio and TV reception in the area, intensive amounts of air traffic, or the sight of a man outfitted in a space suit walking down Main Street. She was remote, no doubt for her own reasons, but her need could also be her vulnerability.

laDoop had emerged from, and was a champion of, an era of synthesis. His Big Bang work was not so much driven by a single spectacular breakthrough insight, but rather by compiling, adding up, combining different theories and data into a more unified, explicable whole. He had been brilliant, yes, in selection and rejection, in piercing inconsistencies and establishing a cohesive pattern, complicated enough to be credible and clear enough to gain him broad fame. Few of his colleagues envied laDoop, he was pleased to note, but not for the reasons he thought, his gracious inclusion of their work into his grand scale synthesis. Rather, he represented to them the capitulation of original hopes – to face alone and unafraid a problem of the universe, armed solely with your mind, its instincts as well as its data, its vision as well as its memory, ingenuity that distinguished it from the machines it employed. Altaforce symbolized, in approach, style, and results, all that laDoop was not, and if neither man could fully articulate the depth of the distinction, they both could feel it intensely.

"Harold, you can't let him do this," David vehemently objected when he learned of laDoop's plan, already nearly fully prepared, breaking the armor of emotional neutrality he was so carefully trying to compose. "It would be like pitting an old pinball player against some young video turk. He can't win, but what he could unleash, could make us all lose."

"I can't stop him, David. Maybe you're right, but I'm not even sure I should. I just, well, I just don't know anymore." Even if he wanted to, Upshaw was helpless against the institutional onslaught that the wave of laDoop's credibility, buttressed by his bureaucratic expertise, had created, an elemental modern force, immutable precisely because it was unapproachable, a suborning shield against the spear of logic. David fretted, cast about, resigned himself, and the preparations neared their inevitable conclusion.

Teams of technicians wired laDoop into his suit. Banks of screens faced him, hundreds of scientists parked at terminals, ready to intercept his every encounter, assess it, relay it up a pyramid of synthesizing points, processing until out emerged the best working hypothesis for him to proceed with at any given moment. laDoop was at the center of this intense activity, his every breath memorialized, every move captured, every thought idolized, at the culmination of a career once thought topped by the Nobel Prize. He had never been happier, more excited – or more foolish.

Altaforce was on the outs, but jury-rigged his terminals to hack the input, key synthesis, and output from the UN system. He sat in the apartment feeling as if he was floating unconnected to the floor and walls, as if the apartment was simply a viewing screen, a terminal through which image and data flowed, itself mute and impotent, a relayer not a source, pizza crusts and scientific journals and withered rice in cartons lying on top of texts and treatises all fused together into fuel for a passive machine, David trapped in its circuits, the glow expanding outward but dark and empty and hushed with the sound of passing electrons within, and David, without, David watching in despair and fear. Despair that maybe all that firepower could prevail, that laDoop would solve it, another Prize, and David's brilliant explorations become once again a footnote to the milestones, for a narrow group of colleagues to admire and defend; in despair, too, of not avenging Susan, of having caused the void once occupied by her vibrant self, still and forever, of her faith in him misplaced; but more, and far greater, fear that laDoop was exciting a nerve center exponentially more intensely than his bowling ball at the beach had, fear of earth being pushed over the brink of a new great abyss that this shoddy caricature of thought without reflection was pushing them all towards, while he, David, was powerless to halt it. He spent the morning packing up the clothes Susan had left in the apartment, making arrangements to donate them to Goodwill; he was pretty sure she'd want to do something like that

laDoop had also brushed Antifermo aside. Despite his local strength he was merely a one-phonecall problem, so Antifermo sat with Sebastian and David to watch, still committed to his own form of apprehension of an alleged perp.

laDoop emerged just before dawn from the prep area, prefabbed beige structures with dark brown steel membranes supporting them, abutting the main UN building as if the owner had decided to finally add that extra bedroom in Tudor style on to his ranch house. He waddled in his suit, joyously giving the thumbs-up signal to all he saw, under the glare of spotlights and flashing lightbulbs. The sheer mass of equipment and people created excitement, resources agglomerated on each other, any street a movie set where ten trucks could turn night into day, turn strollers into watchers, residents into extras in their own milieu, actors into focus, the illusion replacing the real *in situ*, so a thrusting microphone and camera crew had become part of the socialized psyche, a button waiting to be pushed, reactions prepared, hell, each person living out their preordained programmed role in the drama, a laDoop at the center.

Yes, he was never happier. He walked with the cumbersome gait of a muscle-bound gladiator as the throngs gave way around him, surrounding him with wires and vans filled with terminals and yesterday's coffee. In the background, rows of trees parsed the view behind of river and industry, dead, dark, old buildings and pale-hued new ones, the lights of the tall East Side buildings alternatingly bouncing back at them or disappearing as the river's waves carried them in other, less affluent directions, as if all they would give of themselves was immaterial reflection, while the lights of passing tugs and barges pierced the leafy veils that in the dark concealed the scum at the tidal concrete edge. His steps went clackaty-clack on the paved walkway, sharp over the squelched insoles surrounding him, then thudly muted as he hit the grass striding. The sun rose over the East River cautiously, as if it knew it belonged but was afraid it had stayed out too late.

On the lawn in the middle of the UN campus a small pneumatic lift picked him up, arms all around him pulling and pushing him inside, as a helicopter – Chopper Charlie, he called it, the expedience of his poetic sense eliminating Able and Baker – swallowed him, vibrated the earth around him, whorled him like a swirling leaf up in a vacuumed eddy of air, leaving behind a sense of emptiness, a bit of the earth waiting to be filled, the crew left to chew gum in the vans while the director gets his angles, and the star moves on to a new location, which was already being readied for him. A stationary satellite had been reprogrammed, a portion of its dish now used to send scrambled signals focused on a remote house in the White Mountains. Jets flew computer-determined courses over the area, further jamming signals, preprogrammed, because once they entered the area they had no means of communicating with their home base, so that they would fly on inertia and installed memory until reaching the other side, like words pushed out in anger and later regretted, too late to pull them back. It was doubtful a bat could navigate in the area, so intense and thorough was the unseen blanket that draped it like summer heat shimmering on an empty midday street.

laDoop was set down about a half-mile from the house, in a valley that allowed an approach that gave no line-of-sight with Quintin's house. The chopper had flown through a light mist into a foggy day. New York had been bright, a cheerful exit through noise and high spirits, the energy of the people and equipment radiated into the whole team until they felt it from within themselves, a vibration resonating like the deep bass of a stadium rock concert, inspiring confidence with its power. This breaking mountain day was muted; a hushed gray infused the area, blotting out contrast, distinctions blurred, the varied natural terrain its own world, distant as a country school girl from a model in full make-up, far away from the concrete in New York that had spawned the strange visitors, greeting them like another bright idea from the head office.

The pilot's breath left traces in front of him, as did that of the technicians in the body of the machine, organs moving in the steel shell, headset wires like nerves connecting the varied parts, compelling silence while instigating activity. laDoop's instruments were on; he sat self-contained, apart, a layer of moisture accumulating on his silvery surface as if the suit itself was sweating in the moment's tension, creating again a blurred line between his surroundings and himself. He was hoisted out of the chopper, the ungainly groans of the technicians lifting echoed in the country silence, no city noises to obscure them, then deposited on the dirt and grass around them, muffled creaks from the suit and the men, and then he was away from the chopper and by himself. The helicopter took off, staying low and to the east as it crept away from the spot like a skulking bully, to keep from being seen by its intended victim. Its downdraft dried out the suit like one last helpful message from home. He began to walk up Annie's Mill Road to Mary Quintin's home.

They tested feedback. All sensors up, voice and data confirmed two ways. So far no irregularities in the field (and in a small room Altaforce squirmed). laDoop was too smart to think it was an easy walk ahead of him. He had, at least, lived by believing in data as it presented, and he knew enough here to sense what lay ahead was not an illusion.

His plan was straightforward, based on the massive resources at his disposal. He was taking a dip in the unknown, exploring while simultaneously seeking to plumb these icy new depths, not for their treasure, dangerous like the corruptions of newfound gold, but to neutralize the threat therein, more like Custer than Columbus. He was both a vehicle for data transmission and a weapon. His gloves and shoulders contained a variety of propellant systems and projectiles, ranging from knockout drops to LSD – unscrew her head, the psyche team had suggested, if you can't talk to it – to bullets and explosives and – he had insisted, such drama, such nobility – he was wired as a living bomb himself, able to destroy one quarter of an acre around anywhere he stood.

"I've never struck a lady before," he had urbanely rhapsodized, "so I'd better get it right the first time." Yes, never happier. He would approach, he would transmit, synthesize, and, one way or another, eliminate.

It was a walk on a country road, up a hill, a smattering of wild flowers, yellow, violet, blue, arranged in a pattern both familiar and esoteric, not random, not orderly, impressionistic, the hues combining at different angles to create the sense of still more colors, as elusive as the images at the side of one's eye. Beyond them, green fields once for hay, now unattended, once flat, now bulging with mounds of earth, as if the dirt belched with the distress of being ignored, yellow-topped long grasses, the green more gray in the mist, only a slight occasional breeze to elicit movement. The sensors heard the song of grasses, the now-and-then cawing or trilling of a bird, sensors designed for millions of data entry points strained to be used, were underloaded, connected to hundreds of personnel ready to interface, a system of people and apparatus awaiting employment.

laDoop turned around the last bend, trudging slightly uphill, his suit lightly coated with the dust he was kicking up, losing its sheen. Ahead on the right where the road curved to the left was a newly built version of an old New England home, clean beige wooden sidewalls, doors and windows outlined in blue, with mottled rust and gray and green roof tiles framed by brown metal gutters, a white front porch promenading along the side of the road, some empty green wicker chairs looking at him, an ordinary house.

Sensors started beeping. Data was interpreted, instructions promulgated, hypotheses tested and confirmed, decisions mapped and relayed. EA2 was on the mic. "Look right and left, scan more, please." To his right, almost obscured by the mist, they could see as he approached the home that the shimmering points of dew on the buds were now shimmering points of nothingness, suspended, it seemed, by the tall grass below them. It was such a pinpoint display of control as to be almost ostentatious.

"The petals have a fractal order," David said to Sal and Sebby.

laDoop stopped, turned around ninety degrees left and ninety right to allow a full scan display, then continued walking, the suit pushing out his arms so that he waddled like nine months pregnant and ready to be delivered. He approached a simple white fence, opened an innocuous gate, stepped across some flat fieldstones and walked up the beginning-to-fade blue wooden steps to the porch. Every step noted, relayed, conveyed up and down the line. He was plugged in, ready to operate, batteries charged, fully tested and licensed, UAL approved, he was on-line, real time, he was *there.*

But the porch was gone. He stepped on to it, and it disappeared. He didn't fall through, he just stood where he was, not exactly standing his ground, looking down to emptiness.

"What is that?" he cried, his head bent, sensors scanning, relaying, tight-beam broadcast unbroken (and Altaforce looked towards the skin of his adversary, seen once before, still pure and clean, no warts, no impurities, as remote as the eyes he remembered, the smooth features of an unborn innocence to cloak the spiritual muddle within, arousing him as before, but fiercely different, so that he clenched his teeth and waited in hope for his turn, the next boy in the class to have a go if the first one was shot down). laDoop tried to forge his steel, looked straight ahead.

"Mary Quintin," he shouted, and the shimmering nothingness was around him, "Mary Quintin, I have come to request you cease your disturbances so that we can resolve any..." and his tight beam broke and snap! he was alone, no more sensors and the team relay ruptured, a billion dollars' worth of machines and at least that much worth of men and women were cut off in the middle of the battle; worse than being beaten, they were simply trivial, reduced by nothing to sitting idle. There was no pandemonium, instead almost complete silence from hundreds of watchers whose screens went blank as if their program was canceled: critical path data transmission points personnel, voice modulation analysts, and online sensor interpretation groups all ready, all waiting, a full-house audience where the early buzz of excitement dies to stunned silence with the announcement that the band isn't going to show up, stuck to their seats because it just couldn't happen.

laDoop looked towards – nothing. He sensed a presence calling out to him. All scanners had, in their last transmissions, picked up waves, mass and function not present the instant before, just glimpsed before the lights went out, now being pored over in the absence of anything else to play with, no more real-time analysis.

"Where are you?" he thought he cried out, but nothing could be heard or felt. He reached out for data interpretation, only to find he was isolated, blind within and without, now a mass alone. He tried to move ahead but, with all contrast gone, was like a skier in a blizzard that joined the sky to the slope, not knowing if it is he who is moving or the wind blowing past his stationary self, an inkling of fear as to whether he would get down the mountain or stay rooted to some spot, as relativity ceased to be an abstraction and its fierce complexities became manifest.

He flexed his legs to move them, felt . . . revulsion, contempt. He was stripped then; looking at his bones, he cried in horror, heard laughter, saw even his sex a mockery, a thin unconnected line, his body a trivial apparition, too late now in respecting that message and its cost, plunged or stood still in the nothingness, heard a deafening whisper he could not decipher fill his ears and mind as if a sea shell surrounded him and echoed all the noise he had ever heard, a lifetime's sounds compressed to an instant at the edge of awareness. He raised his hands in fear and in seeing through them dropped them in terror, lost, no Prize, no game, no epicenter of the known universe, no colleagues or the President on line two, no computers, no data transmissions, no synthesis, no balance and control, no assistants, no hope. He ran, ran, ran, the blizzard of nothingness around him, movement an illusion or not, no matter, no, no, no.

They sent Chopper Charlie back to the checkpoint. He tumbled towards them a few minutes after they landed, like a small cloud of brown dust, ran blind, wordlessly banging into men, machines, support systems all, now restraining him, head down, he kept running, stumbling like a toy that couldn't be turned off. They looped a net around him and hoisted him into the chopper bay, his legs still churning, body rocking.

"Jesus," the technician gestured to the pilot, "look at this." laDoop's suit, his silvery spacewalk protective, weapon-laden, data-transmitting, multi-functional layer, was, from the ankles to the neck, intact, yes, but on backwards, its occupant hovering inside so that he could just fit in, facing the blank wall of the back of his helmet, and they all wondered how they were ever going to get him out.

Chapter Thirty-five

Is anything better than nothing?

laDoop's failure was as stunning as it was sudden. The UN team was demoralized, a bureaucracy without a hierarchy. Staff weren't even generating memos. Upshaw reviewed the analysis over and over again, stymied by the loss of data, by the loss of the man. He had only one place to turn. David knew it, and waited, like taking a seat all night at a party and keeping still until someone came up to him. It might not happen, but if it did he was certain it was genuine, and his chances for success would be that much higher. He waited for Upshaw because they both knew Upshaw needed him, but the question was: on what terms? The longer David waited, despite his impatience, his burning desire to enter the fray, the better his chances of controlling the next confrontation. He told this repeatedly to Antifermo, who was pushing for action, every few hours. While he waited he considered the data, developed his plan, assembled his team.

laDoop had evidently at least found a way to enter the scene without causing an immediate response, either because he was unseen or because she assumed his presence was trivial. The latter was not promising – what if she had chosen to notice earlier? – but did provide a good chance of entrée. David and Sebastian's analysis was that the closer he could get to her before she responded, the better his chances of influencing the outcome, as less time would be required for him to sustain his state of intensity, to keep intact the integrity of his being. Faith abandoned is worse than never having had faith at all, Sebastian said, and far more dangerous, for if faith could raise him to the limitless skies far above the ground of the skeptics, it would also leave him in a position where doubts would plunge him to an eternal fall. As Sebastian described it, if he lost his faith when he most needed it, he would be in "one horrendous shitload of trouble." They could not field test the gun he would bring into battle, so they had to challenge it, break it apart and put it back together as much as they could beforehand. They made the process explicit, but each recognized its limits.

The UN team had used Navy helicopter pilots, trained to participate in a team as part of a coordinated military operation. By the time Upshaw turned to David, David's team and plan were in place, and it was take it or leave it. Upshaw could not call the bluff. He was beyond tired now. Susan's loss, the teams gone, piles of equipment winding though the UN like dead nerves no longer transmitting impulses from moribund limbs, lying like the detritus of a lost civilization that it seemed would take an archaeologist to decipher their ancient purpose, so removed had the system become after its catastrophic failure, no diagnostic in the world could retrieve it. And laDoop gone. Whatever his faults, he had been a likable man for Upshaw, blustery and foolish, but determined, not a coward, undeserving of the blubbering catatonic state he now permanently inhabited, but more depressing, they were all undeserving of the state of dissolution that Mary Quintin would impose on them.

Upshaw's vision was growing shorter as he grew more tired. It was no longer just a huge game played for the glorious stakes of battle. How did they feel in World War II, he wondered, our side, not knowing that they would win? Did they ever contemplate that stomach-wrenching alternative, or did time, courage, and resources, or immersive involvement, see them through before they ever had to contemplate seriously the possibility of failure? Upshaw no longer had the psychic energy to elevate the life of adventure to the positive, the intensity, the sense of being alive, the drama and the stage. Just as years of a regular paycheck can provoke an entrepreneur out of the worker, so can years of uncertainty send him back to the corporation. Upshaw would have settled now for the quiet, for a life of fighting with Marge and being distant from the kids was better than a life in which they didn't exist; that wasn't noble sacrifice, it was the late night realization that it could happen, for real, he could look at their lives and world, his life, and it would be all for nothing.

He crossed a crowded First Avenue to the apartment. As usual, there was construction on the Avenue, a project that had been in progress for as long as he had been in New York, some subtle reiterative reworking of the clay distinguishable only to the sculptors of the Department of Traffic, whose artistry was not comprehensible to mere pedestrians and drivers. Its continuity, like tradition, connected the past to the future – the work would always be there, for its own sake, like the longevity of true art, beyond the irate judgment of those who temporally encountered it.

At least some people have faith in the future, he thought, as he stepped around concrete barriers cramming four lanes of traffic into one and a half for no discernible purpose. And yet, the subtlety of that half lane! What was it for if not to hint with torment what might yet be delineated, each moment forcing drivers to seek the impossible, to collapse their vehicles and themselves to fit that damned space, extend the realm of what they sought, expand the definition of what might be, what was that if not art? Not a worker in sight, the familiarity a comforting reaffirmation of his surroundings. The traffic was unrelenting, endlessly honking and squeezing out of the end of the tube; it reassured him. Nothing had not stopped it yet, this headstrong rush. Using whatever it could, humanity moved: feet, horses, steel, metal, rubber, voraciously grabbing any material to serve its pursuits. People moved. Could there really be something that could turn this mass, this conscious herd of activity, this willful throng, into a whimper of waves that would whisper over the memories of asphalt streets and dear destinations? The traffic was horrendous, but the alternative was worse. He walked up six squeaky flights and opened the door of Apartment 6N.

Altaforce proposed, Upshaw accepted. It was that fast. It was also in place.

To begin with, David had contacted Henry Dawson to fly him in. He had proved strong when it would have been easier and no less rewarding to become weak. He deserved the chance to validate his observations, at long last, and the chance to fight back at them. In David's opinion, he could keep himself together, and constancy was a quality like a thread in the jacket of inviolability which he wanted to wrap around his self. Sebastian was already briefing Dawson as they drove in from the airport. Dawson would fly them to a small landing strip down the valley from where laDoop had landed. The walk to her house was longer, but they agreed that a second use of the same plateau would be too risky, and they would also have more time to acclimatize themselves to whatever anomalies persisted in the area. Since they would be walking up wearing pants, shirts, and sneakers, not massive moon suits, the extra distance would not impose too great a burden on them, even on Antifermo, although he complained about it. He would just as soon have put on the siren and the lights and driven up to the front door, or at least approached in a car with a bullhorn, negotiating for a world held hostage. He had seen the beach, and wanted to go after the thief of the sands.

EA3 fretted.

He too had been at Princeton, not that any of them remembered him. But he remembered her.

She was older than he was, he was pretty sure, but that didn't matter. It was her black hair haloing her pale face that mattered; it was her eyes that looked through him and beyond that mattered; it was her remoteness and indifference to what went on around her that mattered. Wherever she was, it was like she was surrounded by a circle of space; he almost felt he had to shout to get her to hear. When she spoke, icicles of clarity pierced the class, and their melted residue left everyone waiting for the next, however painfully it might pierce their perceptions. At the end of the class she was gone; she arrived just as it began. She looked down from the top row. He was mad about her.

Finally, he ran into her walking across the campus. It was no accident, although it had taken weeks; she walked in the night's whispers and the day's shadows, and he could not get a fix on her.

"Hi," he said, the word sounding false and forced to his ear.

She looked at him, barely slowed. The concrete walk through the lawns was just wide enough for the two of them.

"I'm in the quantum mechanics class with you, Professor Anderson's."

"Uh huh," she spoke. She spoke. To him. Encouraged, he went on.

"Yeah, it can be a bitch, huh." Uh, oh, maybe that wasn't right.

"What can?"

"Oh, you know, I mean, he's not always so clear, right? I guess you always get it, huh?"

"Not always." The path hit a fork. She turned towards him. "Which way are you walking?"

He gambled she would just go her way, not pick the opposite of whatever he chose. She was heading towards a seminar in the Advanced Physics Institute. It was open by invitation only. He wasn't invited.

"The API, some research, you know. Hey, listen, can I call you, have dinner or something?"

She walked faster, on the other fork. Over her shoulder she said all right, and left him standing there. What choice had he had, he wondered, elated and terrified.

"Oh, please, not that." He hadn't touched her, but as he came closer she pushed him away, without touching him.

"God, gee, I'm sorry, look, I didn't mean… it's just you're so…Sorry."

Dinner had been words, mostly his. As in class, she only spoke when it was something that nobody else could say. He would finish: his analysis of a problem in quantum mechanics, talking about a movie, a professor, a fellow student. She would listen, and he wanted to speak into her eyes, get beneath them. But then after he was done, she would take the subject one sentence further, two at most, and turn over and around what he had said. She became cake as well as icing; he barely flour.

He walked her along one of the paths, towards where she lived. The evening was cool, invigorating, inviting. He responded, moving towards her, and with that it was over. She thanked him and walked the rest of the way by herself. For the rest of the term he could barely stand to be in the same class with her; he thought about her, wondered about her, lost weight over her. It was the only time in sixteen semesters he got less than straight A's, but in his heart he knew the true area of his decline, which couldn't be measured. She saw him and through him, and it was as before for her.

And now, now she was back, perched even higher. And they were trying to take her down.

David and Sebby waded through the equipment and papers that now comprised the bulk of the volume in the apartment. Most of it would be left behind, old friends who had served their purpose but were no longer up to the task. The decisions were difficult, but the packing relatively easy. Both men were surprised when laDoop's Executive Assistant number three – they didn't know him by name but David thought he looked familiar – walked into the living room. They were even more surprised when he drew a gun and demanded they stop working. With his blond hair, polo shirt, and light windbreaker he looked totally out of place in the apartment. But he was unkempt, a feverish glaze in his eyes, a look to his skin that was part sweat, part oil, with a low intensity to his voice. He waved them to the back of the room and pushed one of the computer terminals off its stand. The noise of the crash died quickly.

David made a move towards him, asked, "What the hell are you doing?" but retreated as the gun eyed him steadily.

"Stop it, can't you just stop it, let things be?" he said hoarsely.

"Why in God's name should we do that?" asked Sebastian, separating himself from David to another corner of the room. David sensed that, like him, Sebastian's only dealings with the man in front of them were as an extension of the laDoop work machine, and it was as shocking to see the man express a personality as it was to have him facing them with a gun.

"I sat back and watched the old fool drop into it, because I knew he'd never succeed. This is new, too new for him to even see it, but you, you've been catching up to it, and I've got to stop you. She's too important, means too much, we've got to step aside now, you've got to be stopped."

"Too important?" said David. "Too important for what, for whom? She's threatening everything we are, and you don't want me to interfere with her? What the hell are you thinking?" Guns were not a part of David's past, or present. He felt powerless in the face of it, as it followed him around the room, seeming to create a vast, uncrossable distance between him and the man who held it, betraying every opening with its implications. "What can she possibly mean to you?"

"You don't see it, do you? You're so goddamned close to it and you just can't see it. A fool like all the rest, Altaforce, one more fool who thinks he's dancing when it's really the floor that's moving beneath him."

"See what, Sanborn?" Unbidden, the name jumped into his head. Kenneth Sanborn, another in the field of laDoop PhDs, whose waving hand he had ignored at his UN lecture. Maybe that wasn't the best move, thought David, he has a hell of a way of getting attention.

"Christ, don't you see? She's the logical conclusion to the progression of the last century – the eradication of culture and tradition." His words tumbled in gaunt progression, stripped of the high register, spilling uncontrollably. "Fifty million Europeans killed in world wars and genocides, as many again in Asia, first one nation trying to impose on others, external, then turning inwards, Russians and Cambodians, Chinese, Arabs, seeking to eliminate the vestiges of the past. As if a human being could be evolved into a clean slate, *de novo*, empty of past, unconnected to culture or tradition, and still be full, as if such a human being could seek or possess any meaning or values, sense of self or world, any inner guidelines to what is appropriate or moral. They make 'em born dead so that anything that follows is just a bonus. Erasing art and science to serve the truths of government, torn from origin, bereft of education or hope, living not so much in the moment as in a timeless state of disassociated events, a fabric rent of substance. The rise of fundamentalism, the desperate search for any identity, no matter how heinous or disassociated with fellow man, nine-eleven just a step on that road. What is the point of life if art and culture are evicted, if science is not a quest for truth but a slave of policy, if generations of experience are shorn to a bald-pated present devoid of connections? But that's evolution too, isn't it, the invisible hands slicing up our times. Who are you to judge or deny her?"

"Look, Sanborn, Ken, I admit there's been a lot of horror in the world, but there's a lot of good, too, and we've got to try to protect it," said David.

"She is the final step in this evolution," said Sanborn, warmed like a preacher voicing a conclusion beyond his control, just there for anyone with the true believer's understanding to see, "as natural as the toad crawling out of the water, as inevitable as the death of dinosaurs, her ascendance foretold in the backwaters of spiritualism already interpreting the quantum as the antithesis of materialism, and a hundred million dead to voice their support, that if they were not to have died in vain, it was to lead us to join the process; the only way to stop slaughter is to render it impossible. David, you see it more clearly than those moving en masse as before, don't you get it, come to it sooner, what are you so zealously protecting? And how in any event can you fight a future whose growth springs from the seeds of a century?"

"I have to try," yelled David, "don't we all have to try?"

"Let's get it over with, for god's sake, step out of her way. You think she's a new threat, but that's because you've blocked yourself to what goes on around you, insulated, salaried, cloistered with your success from here to there, but if you looked you'd see the world you think you had was already dissolving, gone like yesterday's morality, when men wore hats and tipped them. She's just a continuation of the process, her antecedents well established, we are the origins of her species, and you wanting to deny that is like a lizard trying to bite off an ape's thumbs.

"Give it up, Altaforce, let her be, stop holding on to what isn't there, and acknowledge that what isn't there is what we have." He held the gun out and pointed it.

At that moment Antifermo, who had been waiting for them downstairs on familiar streets, walked in to see what was keeping them. Sebby shouted, Sanborn wheeled around, torn between David Altaforce and Sal Antifermo, frozen. Antifermo stepped forward like a mongoose towards a snake, and that quickly Sanford was down, and they were gone, not even bothering to pick up the pieces.

Chapter Thirty-six

Up close to the initial conditions, they don't look so sensitive.

Upshaw got them a van from UN maintenance, which they pulled up in front of the apartment. Antifermo posted an officer to stay with the van, so it wouldn't get ticketed, towed, or ripped-off – part of the New York planning process. David, Sebby, and Sal carried down the equipment David required from the apartment. They had a powerful portable generator delivered to them. They packed the equipment into the van, along with some low steel carts. No one said it, but each knew they were putting something behind them, forever.

Mrs. Pudanski translated the actions into her most basic recurring concern – they were skipping out of the apartment before the lease was up. She clomped over to them, her ever-dirty pink slippers sounding like the slurps of picking rocks out of mud, and approached despite Sebastian's efforts to head her off.

"Vat's dis, leafing and da lease not haff up? I shoulda known, not to trust."

Sebby reassured her they were returning, and gave her Upshaw's name at the UN as a guarantor of their payments. Upshaw looked at her and smiled politely from a distance, trying to look sincere. She took the name down skeptically; the UN was not in her experience the source of paying customers; it was more like the big house on the end of the block whose family would have nothing to do with the rest of the neighborhood. It was that relationship that led her to believe they would one day tear it down, providing her at least with some morning sun.

"And ver's dat luvly goil, she vas a charmer, he tinks he can do bedda? Lissen, I've loined, ya don go lookin fer otha troubles ven ya know da vone's ya have, dis I've loined," as the ash dangled from her mouth and fell in front of the grey clotted tassels at the ends of her feet. Even Antifermo was powerless to stop her dissertations, and found it fastest not to interrupt.

Her arguments exhausted, she stood against the side of the railing, not leaning on it with all her weight, but muttering, dey shud be careful and ver vas dat Manheim he vould soitinly help if he vas here and sober and if the extra veight dey was pudding on da steps caused a crack she vould have to charge dem for it she had a responsibility to de otha tenants too, ya know. Thus she acquitted the honor of the Pudanskis.

The van fully loaded, Upshaw drove them off, Antifermo in the passenger street, Sebby and David in the back to tend the equipment as it bounced over the streets. Upshaw had obtained permission for them to take off from the Marine Air Terminal, the closest airport, just in from LaGuardia. Its smaller size made it easier to get clearances and handle the logistics. David allowed himself the piquancy of looking at the views, up the East Side and the FDR Drive, crossing the Triborough Bridge, out along the north side of Queens, past factories and cemeteries and brick tenements, generations dead and alive, ignoring any thought as to whether he would see them again. Sebastian sat calmly, as if this were just another ride from here to there, while Antifermo – he sat in the front and yelled at other drivers who tried to cut them off, pointing out less crowded lanes to Upshaw, and gave the finger to any driver who didn't come up to his standards, especially if they were from New Jersey. Telling Upshaw that it was impossible to try to drive in New York and be nice, that holding a steady pace in the middle lane was an invitation to be cut off from cars on either side, a tourist mark. Upshaw finally worked in concert with Antifermo to get out to the airport following Antifermo's two rules of New York driving – keep moving, be mean.

They pulled up to the round main building at the Terminal, unloaded the equipment, and hauled it past the Art Deco appointments and murals. Dawson met them at the field side of the building, having already run his own check on the six-seat Piper Cherokee he had found for them. They used a small golf cart to ferry the generator and the rest of the material on to the field, where they loaded the back of the plane. Behind them the early morning light slanted on the city skyline, the buildings that reflected the light standing out like neon colors on a book jacket, seeming to float on the background. It was a glorious sight.

David turned, looked at Upshaw. "Well, Harold," he said. There was the sound of distant engines. "Thanks, thanks for everything."

Upshaw looked at David, framed against the buildings behind him. "Come back to us, David. I'd miss you if you didn't." David smiled, and followed Sebby and Sal into the plane.

Upshaw waited until they were strapped into their seats. He thought of when he saw the kids off on a train, remembering that moment when they stopped looking out the window at him and started talking to each other, wrapped up in thoughts he couldn't share, their faces no longer turned in his direction as they pulled out of the station and he stood alone as their profiles moved across his vision, watching their lips mouth words he could not hear, a smile or frown a dart at the target of his doubts, afraid that he would be diminished in their lives by these unshared experiences, wondering even if they would remember him.

He looked up into the plane. The men had headsets on, big earmuffs covering the sides of their heads defying the logic of the day's heat, Dawson talking into his mic, the others looking ahead motionless, the engines revving up. He turned and walked back to the stairs leading up to the gate, weary, wondering. From inside he couldn't see them take off. He drove the van back to the UN garage, so slowly the other cars ignored him.

==

"Can't thank you enough for bringing me along, David," Dawson said into his mike.

"After all that fun in the Grand Canyon?" David said. They both laughed. "Never a question."

"Look, you figured out what I saw; the rest just thought I'd gone sky happy. I'd fly through fire for you. Even into that damned cloud."

"Careful what you ask for," David said.

Dawson had worked out a course that extended their time and approach through the mountains. He flew low, hugging the ground, his reflexes trained and pitched so that he could hop around silos and in between the trees, so low over the fields they could pick the corn. The small plane and his solo command felt like a responsive sports car after shuffling power-steered clumps of steel, and he knew that after a lifetime of flying he was on a culminating course, a hundred feet up and at the height of his career, grateful to know the moment as it was happening, trusting its meaning, rather than having to discover significance in retrospect, when multiple interpretations of motive and thought could like mixing vats divest the time of its clarity.

David sat in the second row, feeling as if all his senses were afire, slightly nauseous, gagging on the intense smell of fuel oil that permeated take off, thankful to at least be shielded from the noise. He wondered again – what if he had walked the other way on the beach, gone for a swim, gone home? Susan would still be here, but so would the extensions of Mary. God, how he hated to be linked to her, the irrevocability of his decision gnawing at him, as if faced with an instant choice he had veered into a pack of children to avoid the dog, he and they forever maimed.

The relationship between the observer and the observed, the dry simple revolutionary basis that dwelt at the heart of the quantum, at once its most powerful metaphor and its greatest abstraction. How comforting that intellectual distance left us, he thought. Was that the way they felt upon discovering the pieces of the atom, before the inherent power that was the glue of its structure was revealed, shattering the abstraction? It even left breathing room; at a certain point, uncertainty was a necessity, so it's okay not to know it all, one can't, it's built into the system. If you look you impact. He had looked, peered up her skirts, had his hand slapped . . . but it didn't stop there; the punishment transcended the crime, for the crime had tapped into something deeper, elemental. If he had just left her alone some distance would have remained, Susan would have remained, his world would have remained, maybe for his lifetime, and what more did he want? A lifetime, yes, but of doubt, churning into grim gray concrete the abstraction of uncertainty. Could he have lived with that, could he have sat silently in class while other hands waved furiously and only he had the answer?

Now none of it mattered. In the absence of matter, nothing else would signify. Dawson's hands stayed at the wheel, the plane cut through his choices with the same definition as the passage of time, one way, this way, like the spin of the earth through the solar light, day and night, left or right, no choice.

He felt frail, as if each nerve ending was on his surface, exposed and delicate, all shrouding and cover burnt away. It had to stop, he knew, but couldn't quite bring himself yet to that point. He stared at the instrument panel Dawson seemed a part of, the fluctuating needles and dials reminders of the flux in his life, all their lives. Susan, gone, one last permeating intense world of sorrow, gone, not even time to rebound off, it wasn't there except outside of him, and even that he was preparing to purge. He felt tension around his eyes, and the still air inside the plane evaporated tears, gone. All the others on the beach, disappeared, while in that blinding incomprehensible moment his helicopter had pulled sharply up and to the right, so that he was left facing an open, empty sky, and nothing to return to below, screaming "Susan" while the pilot sought only distance, desperately pulling the stick towards the only wise choice: away.

laDoop, gone too, his mission more than failure, catapulting terror outwards like Mary's advance scouts. Since his attempt, all the wave spaces had gotten larger. He pictured tiny subtle lines weaving in the air, the emanations of an angry goddess, jaded into dissolution, no more caring than other gods before, divorced from the wellspring of humanity. He felt the naugahyde beneath him, could smell it, hear his squeaking movements as his weight shifted as if they were transmitted through his body, the scratches on the window magnified to blanket the view outside, attenuated, and within his chest a feeling that was a source, it was energy, blessed universal energy within him and waiting to be tapped. The plane's motion was lost to him, he sat in his own stillness, Sebastian and Antifermo recognizing the start of the procedure, distancing themselves even as they too sat still, Dawson absorbed in the altimeter, wind gauges, and changing terrain.

Okay, he thought. But then, just one more querying look around him, at all that there was that should be. He closed his eyes and went through the self-hypnosis drills that he had designed to prepare him, the sound and the light and the movement gradually receding in his mind –

He pictured his body filling with golden light, his substance moving – a wave of his hand, the length of his arm – through space moment to moment, through time, a fourth dimension, his unified self held cohesive by . . . yes, that was it, by his spirit, he felt it now as never before, understood it at a level he had never reached. The sense of it filled him body and mind, the fifth dimension casting its glorious golden ephemeral net around the other four, maintaining the message that was his being through the eternal moments that the fastest stroke could not ultimately parse: that if bursts of energy and light were not continuous, but quanta, if time itself was ultimately divided, each second fractionated only to ten to the minus forty-third, beyond which there was no meaning to measurement in the world of discrete quanta, instant to instants, even so there was a force that transcended the limits of the quantum. There was the frontier, his being, the continuousness of his self, preserving the supposedly indivisible world of fundamentals, more power implied by his continuity maintaining its self over time then the fusion of a billion worlds each governed finally by a limit, a measure, a factor that was divisible by the instant. Not him, not the seven billion like him, every abundant life contained within his awareness, surrounding him like the envelope of a dream. He would extend his continuity outward, beyond particle or wave into matter itself, where missiles lost their meaning, missed their mark because he wouldn't play, kiddie games of mass and energy. He felt his self emanating to surround the block, the city, ocean and globe unified, affected, and with a tingling, awake.

The day stayed clear. Occasional thermal updrafts buffeted them as the terrain shifted beneath them, a procession of city and suburb changing into farms, small towns, mysterious divisions of the earth that when sighted from above prompted Sal to ask Dawson what that big circle or strange-shaped patch of dirt or series of tanks could possibly be for. Passing over a college town, students moving in many colors back and forth, patterns random and cohesive. Passing over large brick buildings, once-great factories now defunct or being converted, other uses imposed on them, as if they should take satisfaction in becoming condominiums or outlets or commercial mini-marts and forget the pride of production and employment, as if the law of entropy had applied selectively to drain them of their energy and their builders of their rightful hubris, for who succeeded the first dreamers? Over depleted, mismanaged soil in need of ever greater infusions of chemicals and external artifices to obtain any yield from. Over successions of smokestacks mostly dead, no excretion if no input, and over still fertile hills and green and purple mountains, hugging the smoothed clefts between the mountains, diverting and circling so as to obfuscate the direction from which they came, the direction they were heading, until Dawson brought them down onto the landing strip, a straight patch of brown dirt cut from between the trees rising on both sides of it, punctuated by a wind sock and a small prefab hut, brought them down so smooth they could hardly tell they were out of the air, like the gentlest of a lover's entries.

The strip itself was empty, thanks to Upshaw. A wind rustled out of the trees, its force filtered into a gentle caress by the time it reached them on the field. They unloaded the gear in silence, onto carts and into packs they had brought with them.

They shook hands with Dawson, who carried a Thermos over to the hut.

"Two cups," he told them. "Two cups will be more than enough."

Sebastian worked with David on his final preparation. They had worked out a script with key words to establish certain states within him, first relaxing, then energizing, connecting to his self and defining it from without, becoming totally involved in the moment, all previous studying and experience becoming an already-written prologue to that moment, that time that would encapsulate his total self instant to instant, when he would no longer fear or care, empowered only to give complete expression to his being, until he emerged intact or was gone.

Nobody foresaw the other possibility.

Chapter Thirty-seven

In the end, there is a choice.

Three men walked along a valley road headed to Mary Quintin's house. A warming breeze evaporated the early-day coolness, the dust kicked up on them as they walked in silence along the road, the cart wheels greased into silence like an unctuous bribe to the inspector. They did not know what could betray them – a deep breath, a chance word, the machinery – and fought the desperation and distrust of basic activity bred of that ignorance. They reached a mound that overlooked the house, from which the road dipped down, where laDoop's helicopter had landed, and back up again.

The memory of laDoop turned around in his space suit fought for a place within them, an act of will to keep the nausea down, always almost there. David stared blankly, no reaction to dragging the carts, the dirt kicking into them. Even the sun seemed to bounce off him. A short way in front of them a latticework of dew and flowers, with points twinkling in and out of perception, framed a mushroom-hued epicenter, a vacuum swallowing up soil and plants, pistil and stamen, flower and dew, null memories on the landscape.

It was here, at these first signs of conversion, that Sebastian stopped. It was here that he would set up the equipment, and it was here that he would wait for the others. He needed to be separate from the focus they could create as they entered the house, and they needed space for their diversion.

Also, he would wait here so that he at least could return with more experience should . . . should David and Sal not. David only mentioned the possibility as a consideration of all possibilities, his options matrix, but with a remoteness, the same distance he kept with all the planning. It was as if he was indifferent to the options, to what might happen. Antifermo and Sebastian accepted the outlook; it had driven Upshaw crazy. "It's all right, Harold, it's all right," David would repeat, and repeat.

While David and Sebastian assembled the equipment, started the silent generator, and made all the connections and adjustments, Antifermo paced the perimeter of the hummock, alert, a city kid out on a country walk, blundering into every bush. He nearly knocked over trees if they got in his way, indifferent to a flower or anthill or turd underneath him; he marched around in his own drill, ready to attack, to "nab the perp, what do ya say Doc, do I read her her rights?"

"I'd say she's already chosen her right to remain silent, Sal. How 'bout we extract a confession first, worry later about the constitutionality of the bust?"

"Hey, Doc, we'll have a few beers and talk about it, ok?"

"When we get back, Sal. That would be nice."

David Altaforce, containing bits of New York, California, and points elsewhere, and Sal Antifermo, very much of Brooklyn, took a walk in the country. Up a hill. Their friend Driscol Sebastian, once from Cleveland, walked with them for a while. Their pilot, Hank Dawson, once of Iowa, then a roamer of the world, waited in hope for their return flight. Past the helicopter landing area, the imprint of the machine having vanished in the swirling dust and rebounding grass, Sebastian stopped and sat, overlooking a field of rainbows, seductive, Satanically beautiful, light broken up as if by prisms, intersecting, overlapping, crests and troughs of brightness and dark, the path to Mary Quintin's house. His friends continued up the road to call upon a lady, no point in bringing flowers, while he set to work, and each depended on the other for his existence.

As David explained to Antifermo, Sebastian was, "for a good cause, Sal," going to perpetrate his own crime – a fractal forgery. Sebby placed one set of the holographic array of laser lights at one end of his hill, and the second set at the other end. He aimed the two beams so that they would intersect in the field to the side of her house, a field already partially collapsed into wave functions. Since the laser light was coherent, it would not spread, and would thus maintain the same level of intensity in the distant field as David had demonstrated to Susan in the apartment, in the days when a room could be a universe, before the universe ran out of room. He tested the circuits, kicked on the silent generator, and walked on a ridge from the hill away from the house, barely keeping it in view, while concealing himself from it. In his hand he carried what looked like a television remote control, a simple on/off device. When he reached a spot where he had direct line of sight to the arrays, but could duck down out of view of the house, he crouched, waiting for David and Sal to come into view, the trigger to his fraud.

They walked at a steady pace, not hurried, no extra effort, in silence. Around them the world blinked in alternatives, no more a country walk now, but a trip through a nightmare, threats implied and actual, as if a strobe light were illuminating and darkening their reality, through eyes that did not blink.

After a while they heard an odd kind of noise, jarring and discontinuous. David listened, noticing short bursts and longer ones, realized that the short bursts had the same relation to the slightly longer ones as the next layer had to the next length, and so on, that they were hearing a fractal tempo, the normal country sounds of wind rustling leaves and birds and insects bizarrely distorted as they passed through areas that were flashing in and out of particle/wave existences in a fractal rhythm, her imposition on other orders around her, so that the sound waves were affected by that rhythm. The music of madness, David thought – and people thought Elvis was a threat to their way of life. He reasoned that the hue around the areas of dissolution stemmed from this alternating of states, the observer seeing subliminal remnants of material space. The road itself stayed solid, sanctified or overlooked – or just cheese on the spring of the trap. The two men walked steadily until the house loomed up around the last bend in the road to the right, as they had rehearsed while watching images laDoop had relayed back, before he had been cut off and out. From away and above, Sebastian pushed his button.

In the field to the right of Mary Quintin's house, a mound took shape, first a dull-brown elongated hump, like a large inverted beehive, then lines and edges were etched into its surface, and shadings, and lower peaks, and slanted slabs shading their background, crevices and buttresses in intricate interplay. It was a miniature of a complex mountain sitting in defiance in the field, standing upright while nature herself was bowing around it. It was David's door, no longer innocent. The image was designed to act as a lure for her attention, generated out of fractals and therefore seductive, but shifting continuously, so that if control depended on understanding it would be thwarted, first by the constant changes and then by tossing her weapon back at her – it wasn't even there. It was a fractal tar baby.

As it came into being, Sal and David separated. Sal had said, "Let's make it simple. You go up the front, I'll take the back." David hadn't gotten to those logistics; in truth, much of his planning, such as his visualization of what the encounter might be like, did not include Antifermo.

David walked up the front porch, and Sal walked around the back of the house, past a yard with a stone walkway and some rusted toddler toys amidst an overgrown garden. Once planted, it had never been tended. He stomped through it, indifferently crushing weeds and wildflowers, towards the kitchen door. On the other side, David moved quickly up the porch and towards the front door.

The area around the holographic display blinked out completely, but the image itself stayed intact, a mountain floating in the air. The atmosphere began to buzz, shudder, tremble. David could somehow sense her will seeking to convert it. Her frustration infused the air with its mean anxiety, but her attention was on the immaterial, not the media she was used to manipulating, and was doubly futile. Now he could feel her as she tried harder and harder, reintensifying her efforts, amazed and concerned, sense her beginning to doubt her powers. Around the globe dissolved areas of the earth shifted back into matter: for the first time in seven months a stretch of beach bathed in crystalline sunlight; a mountainside erupted into the sky, turning drunk men sober; a cascading range of clouds became whole; a part of the jungle decreed taboo emerged in splendor; and a glorious red canyon carved out of time returned to space.

For the moment she was distracted. By the time she realized the ruse, David and Sal were in the doors, as two holographic projection systems sizzled into nothingness, Sebastian watching a good distance away from either.

"Hi honey, I'm home," David said, and the world was never the same again.

It was mad, mad, a plunging into a cosmos, looking at the spin of atoms and the boundaries of thought, thought itself as a wave, an electromagnetic interaction, given new resonance and solidity, mad, mad swirling of pieces of the world around him, as walls and rooms and space dissolved, shifting into colors not seen before, mad, mad entering through in around now, before and later, mad, mad at the center, where like the siren's call she lay, the world scattered and oriented around her like iron filings near a magnet. With David Altaforce at the front door, and Sal Antifermo at the rear.

From somewhere they heard her sense: *I have felt you two boys before, gripping, pawing at me, carving out a circle from that touch that was so angry it sped home back to me. I felt it come to me and rebound into my body, as if cutting out a circle of my flesh and showing me my insides. I was amazed at this . . .dissent! But, it gave me for the first time the fully realized idea of what my body was and was to become, yielding, a subliminal seduction. How clever. The contrast enabled me to recognize at last that the dummy spoke with my voice, not his, when you entered you made me realize that space was actually a part of me, I felt it within, here and there as me, and that I could encompass both, and all, yes, I can extend, and it will all be me. I have you to thank for that, boys. So David, you were my first time, again.*

David started, pushed off balance by the memory and the disclosure, as images flashed around and through him, Mary Quintin tangible, full and inviting, a body inhabited with the human condition, a seeming territory for desire and joy. Her white shingled house with front porch and wicker furniture, fields of harvested corn turning yellow under the sun, some patches already plowed, long straight lines of brown earth like the lines that pointed to her in the clouds, once dissolved, parallel lines could meet at infinity or anywhere else they liked. The twinkling of sunlight off choppy waves in a small lake, a faded blue row boat slowly gliding through them in and out of sight, a kaleidoscope of cars in all colors whizzing by, people dodging them, bathers on the beach like punctuation marks moving in the sand, all flashing in and out, whirling around him as if a tornado could be made of thought, a vortex that could pull him in and up and forever away, and just as he felt the tug, the unsettling thrust, she called to him…

Let go, let go, let go.

It echoed in sound and thought, hit him like a barrage, absorbed by his own wave functions to accommodate the energy, himself a shifting pattern letting in letting out.

And yet he stayed solid, a unified golden rod as his core, maintained by his mind. While he adjusted, Antifermo made a move forward, a linebacker's lunge immediately held static, bending in against a barrage as tangible as it was unseen, like leaning against a hurricane. For the first time in his life with a perpetrator in view he halted, but if he was unable to move forward, she was unable to drive him back, banish his very self, and torn now, this no deception but an essence, she cried to David, who had paused by his choice, not hers,

Why resist, why, why? Resonate with me, propagate my reality throughout your illusions.

Matter shattered around her, flowers and trees, floors and ceilings, exploded in colors and disappeared from touch to be felt instead as parts of him as she extended arms the length of all probability, encompassing all possibilities from the rim of matter to the spinning connections of his consciousness, hearkening a link to all that was and all that could be.

– No, he cried out in silence, I act by my choice, not your desire, there is a splendid world not to be thrown out, of the earth, of hearing music and painting colors and touching…

. . . touching touching. She echoed his words with a flow of radiating sensibilities that yes yes did fill him. As he adjusted, the harmonies grew and played, diffracting to new patterns of here and there, her and him, new and exhilarating as great boxes opened up under the tree, some seen in the catalog of human times, others not even dreamt of, not part of the vocabulary, their strangeness beckoning. He had walked in set to conquer fear with neutrality, not wonder, and here were these – god, they were gifts – presents of presence, an extension of senses that themselves were new, tingling his awareness.

"No, David, no!" Sebastian stood up, cried out, looked down upon the house and shouted in a space where sound was not heard, where words were so many colors.

David went back to himself, to that place he had deemed inviolate, and took a step and looked closer at the wrapping, glittering with the embedded jewels of a universe of awareness . . . but

– No, no it's too imbalanced, consciousness needs a core, not the tormented windswept maelstrom of pieces of the world he somehow felt around and through him, no, no, too far, you take it too far.

Then he knew felt her wrath, the acrid emptiness contained within the proffered treasures.

– You move not out of love, not even curiosity, but out of fear, hatred, anger at isolation, unconnected within you and fractionated without. The world has to evolve, guided by the miraculous, not the petty.

And as he moved closer still, he sensed more than felt a stinging, as if the particles emanating from her thrashed him like pitting sands eager to strip him raw, but also a feeling welcome as if for the first time experienced, as he entered within her field of consciousness the fifth-dimensional particles became illuminated for him as well, and, rejoicing in knowing that that feeling itself was a conquest, like pain, an awareness, a messenger of the body that it was alive, a harbinger of treatment. Again he moved closer like a great firestorm towards the northern lights, hues of red and beyond towards curtains of blue and violets extending across the known world, which shuddered. He felt the shudder as a spur, as she fed off its fear, a billion souls each now wondering where was the hand in front of its face or the ground beneath its feet, slipping in and out with fear and wonder, an earth stopped when earth no more it held its breath, the billion moving in and out of their reality, he and she their embodiment, all particles could be anywhere, but they were here

yes yes she cried out to him, open open *yes here I am, all I am, heal me if you dare.*

Antifermo, whose life was service, heard the billion and moved like a hand thought dead against its gravestone, in a silence that screamed, crackling an aura of rainbows. In her amazement she halted him, but the bifurcation of her intensity now weakened her. For the first time she confronted the staring wall within, and Sal stood his ground as the alternatives washed around him but no wave could break through him, her taunt became a plea, and David as David was now able to step forward out of the current.

Particle or wave he went to her, within her, he entered her an explosion, all matter in all time with all possibilities for one infinite moment.

They transcended the intersection of surfaces, the fractal anomalies at the molecular level that produced bumps, holes, and pathways that allowed a bar of gold and a bar of lead to cohabit if left alone long enough, compressing an eternity of a seduction to an instant in which for the first time she moved beyond a fractal understanding into a realm where love could exist, David/Mary she/he forming two completely touching surfaces, beyond the limit of measurement.

They adjusted, he for his world to save and to coax her to let him in and, through that portal them, all of it okay, okay she held him as with her hands, cried out as with her voice, touched his skin as with her skin, and he, he let in the colors through him the sounds felt the sensibilities while thought itself could be held and touched like a vital clay, a new medium for universal artistry, fresh and glorious as the first sun's rise, and they lay together, while Sal stuck in place gathered evidence out of habit, unabashedly looking when others would have turned their heads.

And yes it was like a field of grass, a hard and soft field of matter and yes a field too of waves that swirled by, held, each connected to a point.

David without fear now, he let go of control even as she offered it and a billion souls were touched to touch and yet feel, and understood, and anger itself no longer had a basis, no traffic, no borders, they fed the energy around among them stood on the ground and at will were elsewhere near each other or at the end of space, riding the waves to the dawn of possibilities.

And he, he restored choice but expanded the realm of options, into a place of self-creation, where belief was determinate. Now he alone bridged the two pillars of matter. Now he alone had to pick the laws that guided that span from among all the laws he could conceive and know, all the rules there ever were. He scanned from his training and his heart, what he had learned and what he had taught, what he had lost and what he had kept, all that lay within and was beyond, the revels of surprise and the joys of wonder, the thrill of discovery transcending the rote pleasure of remembrance, the place where fulfillment was glory.

And to govern his new world the mathematician chose . . . magic.

Acknowledgments

My father died when I was eight, and I have a memory of my mother saying it was always his ambition to write. When I visited his gravesite, I would wonder what he was like. One November dusk, with a light snow falling and the Manhattan skyline lighting up in the distance, I realized that the best way I could ever know my father was to give expression to what was in me, for surely that would most contain a part of him. And so, this book.

There are other fathers to be honored, those who have given us the foundations of physics and mathematics so splendid that they cannot be contained by words or pictures. To Einstein, Lorenz, Planck, Bohr, Mandelbrot and all their brethren. And then to one in particular, perhaps not as gigantic, but touchable enough to be inspiring. For I was reading in the bathtub *In Search of Schrodinger's Cat*, by John Gribbin, and in a fugue state with vapors around me began to ponder about the duality of nature as captured by a cat both dead and alive. I thought about matter, its capacity to be both particle and wave, and wondered, *what would that be like, who or what could cause it, how could it be stopped.* And so, this book.

I still have my mother's notes, from early drafts, her keen sense of language coupled with Grace's unflagging support, which propped me up more times than I can count. Family truly matters, with acceptance and care when it's probably otherwise unjustifiable. So for Richard and Barbara, Jeff and Kari, the impossibly varied collection of steps and halves that is another legacy of my father. The dedication of my friends through many years where they were close enough to share my ups and downs, a too-often painful affliction, I suspect, continues to be one of the building blocks of my life. I can't do them all justice, but they have always been there and damn well always better be. As I've finally gotten, at last, this book.

My world gleefully opened with the infusion of Stuart and Stephanie, and how they have let me into my lives, not the easiest of children's tasks. If that weren't enough, they have graced us with Henk, Willem, Nate, Sasha, Jack, James. Let me tell them to persevere and believe, and so, this book.

And then Dan Burstein, who was kind enough to see the possibilities and share them with others, getting me to Lou Aronica, who saw enough sparkles in the crusted manuscript to edit it and publish it, for which my gratitude cannot find words, putting some files on a computer out into the world, this book.

I should acknowledge love. It isn't anything like what you first think it is, although it contains much of that. But only years can yield the full content of love. When thinking of someone brings a smile, a sense of adoring amusement, a shiver thinking of them not being there. There is a depth to love that is commensurate with and a kindly benefit of age, for knowing love in this way you never want to go back. And so to Margot, who has from the beginning taught me to take the best bite first. Who has read through all the drafts, to bring us together, at last, to this book.

About the Author

Robert M. Herzog has had his stories and poems published in *Solstice Literary Magazine, Toasted Cheese, Downstate Story Magazine, Straylight Literary Arts Magazine,* and *South Jersey Underground.* He was a physics major until he read Nietzsche, a political philosopher turned entrepreneur dealing with the major issues of our time, from energy and environment to technology and health care, a Brooklyn boy who's climbed Mt. Kilimanjaro and remembers the taste of the first (and subsequent) great wine he drank.